THE
OLDEST FOE

MARCUS LEE

THE OLDEST FOE

THE CHOSEN BOOK IV

Paperback ISBN: 9798312864823
Hardback ISBN: 9798312865080
ASIN: B0DXDZJRVZ

For more information visit: www.marcusleebooks.com

First print edition March 2025
First eBook edition March 2025

A NOTE FROM THE AUTHOR

Dear friends and fellow fantasy lovers.

This is the book that was never meant to be written.

The Chosen was always supposed to finish on The River of Tears. Malina was to enjoy life with Lotane after being banished to the fey world as she took on Nogoth's mantle, for fear of her power, and darkening soul.

Some heroes, or antiheroes, deserve retirement, a happy ending, and none more so than Malina who had experienced more trauma and heartbreak in her short life than many thrice her age.

So, why are we here, and why are you reading this?

It's because of you!

I've been so overwhelmed (in a lovely way) by the support for this series, and the demands for more. Since writing The River of Tears, I've released two other books whilst contemplating Malina's fate. I didn't want to tarnish her legacy by producing a work that didn't do her or the previous books justice.

The biggest challenge was how to continue when THE END at The River of Tears was intended to be precisely that.

Yet, here we are, The Oldest Foe awaits, and I hope you're happy with what you asked for. Also, thanks to you all, there will be a book five.

Poor Malina.

Happy reading everyone and remember.
Only the strong survive!

Marcus Lee.

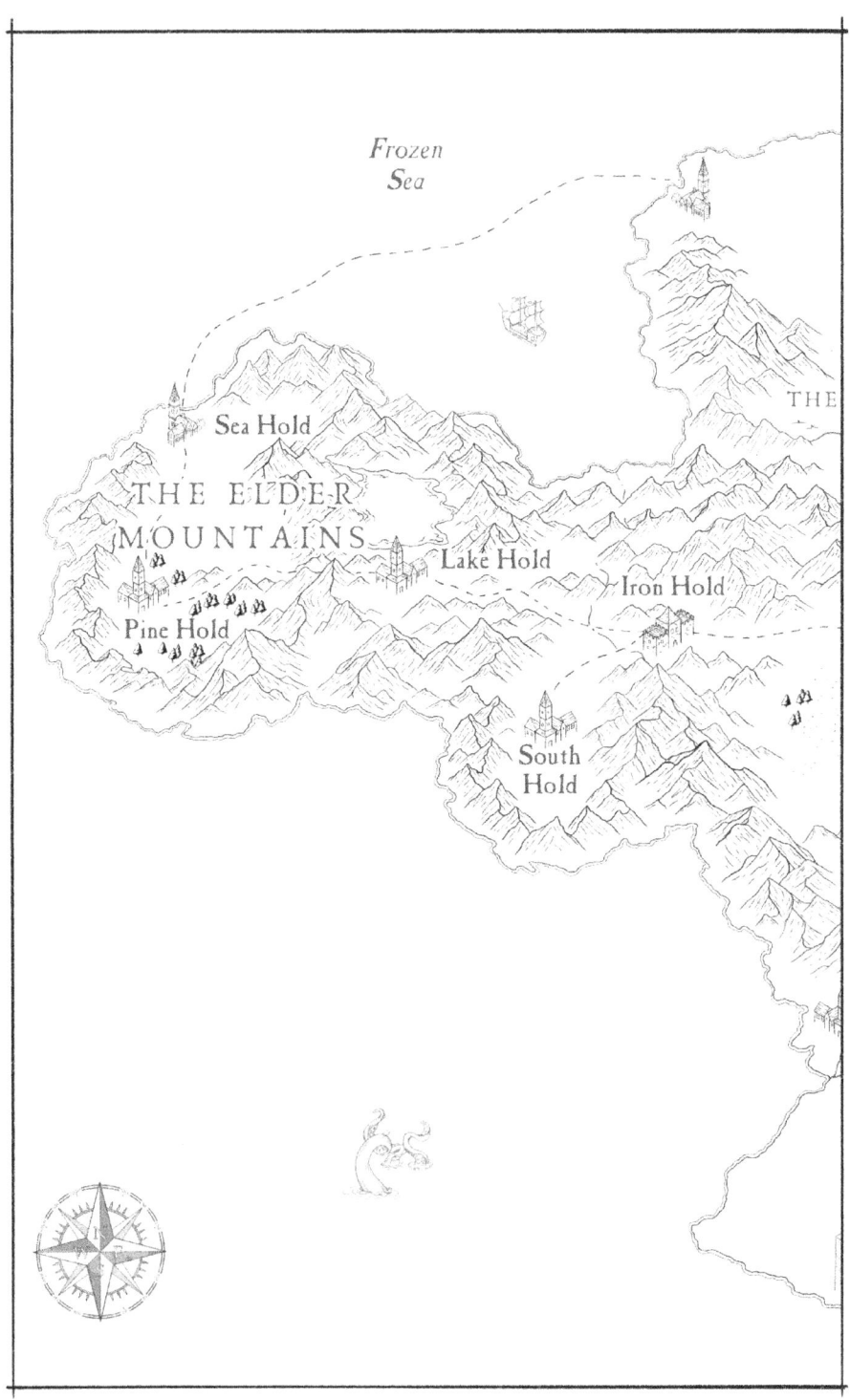

CHAPTER I

Eternal life.

I doubt there's a single adult human or creature of any race, who hasn't at some stage, wished for such a gift. Although, only when eternal life is paired with perpetual youth can such a gift be truly savoured.

Possess both, and you can achieve your dreams one after another, travelling and experiencing the vast tapestry of the world, seeing all it has to offer, visiting new lands, learning languages, immersing yourself in the kaleidoscope of different cultures.

I've traversed this world more times than I can count.

From the deepest caverns where the shades and hags dwell blissfully in utter darkness, to the highest frozen peaks from which the gargoyles circle and soar. From the tropical forest enclaves of the ogres, lush and teeming with exotic fauna, to the vast open prairies favoured by the giants and their colossal herds, and then everything in between.

Over the last four hundred years, my world has given up all of its secrets. I know the customs and histories of every race, the names of all the leaders, their children and their children's children.

There's no ritual nor weapon I haven't mastered, nor a single dish I cannot prepare ... although some of the shades' culinary creations I'd rather not attempt.

A whole planet worships and loves me unreservedly, bound by love and blood magic. As with Nogoth before me, under my reign, peace holds sway, and no race seeks dominion over its neighbour. This world is vast enough for everyone a hundred times over.

Yet despite this harmony, the nature of all beasts remains unchanged. The majority of the fey still thirst for combat and the intoxicating glory of victory. To pit themselves against one another is the ultimate test of supremacy.

Nothing brings the beauty of life into sharper focus than the looming spectre of death, feeling its cold shadow hovering at your shoulder, ready to claim not just you, but everything you hold dear.

Only the Saer Tel eschew the need for such bloody pursuits. Of all the races, they seek glory in what they create. Creating symbiosis between flora and fauna, their daily struggle. To them, all life is sacred. The beauty of nature restored their victory.

So, why if I have their blood in my veins, do I not feel the same?

I, who have lived for centuries, have never been stronger, wiser, never been more powerful. Yet now, despite everything I possess, and all I've learned and experienced, I'm frequently bored, restless, looking for something meaningful that's just beyond my vision and reach.

Except for times like now.

The crowds' roars are deafening, and amplified by the circular arena, buffet me like storm-tossed waves. The tiered seating is packed with creatures of every race. Did I build it for them, or for myself? I should be able to remember, but it hardly matters now.

Sweat stings my eyes, and my palms are damp. The heat is stifling, and I unconsciously summon a breeze, a droplet of power expended from the ocean of magic within me. I twist my feet, taking comfort in the solidity of stone beneath me.

My heart quickens.

The troll's axe glitters as it sweeps in a lightning fast, horizontal arc. I tense, my hands clenching, shoulders tightening, the breath suddenly caught in my lungs.

In combat, it's imperative to stay loose, relaxed, fluid, like water, not immovable like stone. If that axe makes contact …

But it misses, by a hair's breadth, as does the next, and the next sending the crowd's roars spiralling in a frenzy.

'Damn you, Lotane,' I whisper, my voice lost in the din. My eyes narrow, following his every move as he twists and turns, a dancer of extraordinary skill, fluid and precise. The troll barrels after him, an avalanche of raw power and rage.

My hands grip the stone arm rests of my throne as I lean forward, breathless.

At this moment, I'm alive, if only through Lotane. If he dies, part of me will die with him. His love, his loyalty, his mortality are my weaknesses, binding us together tighter than blood magic ever could.

He wanted this, and despite my protestations, a part of me wanted it too. Now, as the troll's axe descends, the threat of losing Lotane ignites something fierce within me, sending my love and passion for him flying to giddy new heights.

I'm alive again.

The axe sends a shower of sand into the air as it crashes into the ground, missing Lotane as he rolls away, rising to his feet with the grace of a predator, to execute a quick bow in my direction.

His jauntiness belies the blood-stained sand at his feet, a grisly testament of what can happen to any overconfident combatant. Despite the preliminary rounds only being fought to first blood, the morgue within the arena foundations tells an entirely different story. Swords, pikes, axes, and clubs, aren't always the most precise weapons in the hands of a raging fey. Even the wolfen champion, victorious in fang and claw, had succumbed to his wounds, raising his bloody paws in triumph only to collapse moments later.

Two weeks of contests, each race segregated, facing its own kind. No ogre can best a troll, and there's no honour to be gained for a troll defeating an ogre. But at the tournament's end, the champions had the choice to enter a final draw, to face each other for the title of champion of champions, a title that would endure for fifty years. Only the giant and troll victors had dared, with the troll decimating his larger, more cumbersome foe with ruthless efficiency, claiming victory without taking a scratch. The giant, meanwhile, had lost his head.

Yet, when the troll had stood before me, the crowd respectfully silent in anticipation of my blessing, Lotane had unexpectedly stepped from my side. The acoustics of the arena had amplified his voice, as he challenged the troll, claiming the right to do so as the human champion despite not having fought a round.

That he's the only human left on this world lent his claim a certain irony, but the fey hold no love for humankind, and after overcoming his initial surprise and seeking my approval, the troll had accepted the challenge, much to the joy of the crowd.

Sunlight flashes from metal blades.

The troll attacks, kicking up a storm of sand, temporarily blinding Lotane. Yet sight is but one of many senses, and Lotane leaps forward over the concealed arc of the axe, having read the drop of the troll's shoulders. The sand cloud obscures what happens next, but the bellow of pain tells me Lotane's sword has found its mark.

The troll favours its right leg, the left staining the ground with black blood from a deep cut just above the knee.

My heart quickens as I watch Lotane. He isn't wearing armour, just a leather kilt and boots. His body glistens in the midday sun, the sweat of his exertion helping to define his superb musculature. I've explored his body more times than I can remember, yet it never ceases to amaze and satisfy me. Supple yet strong, as hard as iron, yet yielding to the touch.

Lotane stalks the troll, just out of range of his towering opponent's longer reach. The crowd bays for Lotane's blood. They might love me, but to them, humans have always been cattle. Only the Saer Tel cares for humankind, pairing with a mate, exchanging love and passion for their mate's blood and the eternal life it bestows.

The troll raises its axe and kisses the blades in salute, a gesture of respect for the first injury it's suffered. Its eyes narrow. Trolls are shrewd, cunning, beyond powerful, and this one is the best of his kind.

The huge axe sweeps out again, this time somewhat hesitant, testing, the troll recognising the danger of his smaller, swifter foe.

Lotane leaps again, but the troll suddenly yanks back on the weapon mid swing, and the double-headed weapon catches one of Lotane's ankles as he descends, spinning him to the ground.

'NO!'

The scream never leaves my lips, but my two Saer Tel attendants must have heard my desperate, silent scream, as their hands grip my shoulders offering silent support. They know my angst having endured the pain of losing countless mates over the centuries.

'We are here. Our love awaits,' they project, their voices a shared echo in my mind.

The axe sends earth showering over Lotane as he frantically rolls first left, then right.

'Yaldul has him,' a voice cries, rising about the baying crowd.

'Yaldul! Yaldul! Yaldul!'

If they love me, why don't they chant for Lotane?

The axe buries itself in the ground no more than a hand span from Lotane's head and Yaldul presses his advantage, his assault relentless, making it impossible for Lotane to regain his feet and attack.

The axe slams down, but this time, Lotane doesn't roll. I'm on my feet, hand pressed to mouth as the crowd erupts, a billowing cloud of sand, dirt, and dust concealing Lotane's fate.

With a bellow of frustration, Yaldul wrenches the axe free from the ground, staggering backwards, and I watch in disbelief as that cruel weapon lifts high above its head to strike again ... with Lotane hanging on to the spike above the butterfly blades.

The crowd gasps as Lotane releases the axe, twists in mid-air, and lands, feet planted on the troll's shoulders, astride that gigantic head.

His sword flashes down ...

Together, they stand frozen, two heroic statues.

Yaldul, the axe aloft, grasped in granite fists.

Lotane framed between Yaldul's massive arms, his sword hovering above the bulbous, incredulous eye of the troll, ready to plunge home.

Slowly, Yaldul lowers the axe and sinks to his knees.

Lotane flips off the heavily muscled shoulders, rolls as he hits the ground, and then turns to face his vanquished foe.

Yaldul presses his forehead to the ground in homage and defeat.

The arena erupts around me. Bellows, roars, howls, and avian cries rise to the heavens as Lotane lifts his sword triumphantly.

He has drawn first blood. His opponent has yielded. He's the champion of champions, and for this moment, the crowd favours him, all historic hatreds forgotten.

He is the one true love, of my long, long, life.

For him, I would do absolutely anything.

So why does he want both of us to die?

***

My fingers trace the golden sweep of Lotane's muscular arms as he lies sprawled fast asleep. Exhausted by our passionate lovemaking, his breathing is strong and rhythmic, the rise and fall of his chest even.

Yes, in this moment of serenity, the perfection of his form, sculpted by centuries of devotion to body and blade, is marred by a tapestry of scratches and bruises, a silent witness to his recent dance with death.

'Damn, I love you!' I whisper, the words barely a breath.

It feels good to say those words again. It feels right, as it should. But it wasn't always so.

I shake my head, the flood of memories from four centuries swirling around me, each moment vying for my attention.

At first, after my banishment, our love was incandescent. We lived a decadent life full of passion, exploring each other as we explored this world, uncovering its secrets one by one. The elixir of life flowed, and we drank to excess. After losing so much, we found in each other more than enough to fill the void of fallen friends and those left behind.

But soon time, familiarity, frustration and boredom took its toll. Over the centuries we fought, raged at one another, spending weeks, months even years apart, each absence a wound carved deeper into our souls.

Those full lips and smiling mouth could also be twisted by rage, the soft look of love within his eyes replaced by barely controlled despise.

The last time our tempers had ignited after an extended period of bitterness, we'd exploded into violence like a volcanic eruption. It mattered not that Lotane's martial skills surpassed mine. Impervious to his blows, my magically enhanced strength and stamina made for an inevitable outcome.

From the beginning, he'd set out to anger me, dominating the fight, laughing, cursing, goading. Time and again his blade landed blows, his mocking smile driving me into a murderous rage, intent on killing him to end his eternal torment.

Lotane had orchestrated the fight perfectly, and as I'd spun away from a dazzling lunge, my blade arched around toward his exposed throat to find him frozen in place, waiting, accepting death.

I'd frantically pulled the blow, turning the blade so it knocked him sideways, instead of severing his neck.

The memory is so powerful, that I whisper the same simple word I'd spoken in that moment.

'Why?'

'My life is empty,' he'd decried, his voice hollow, his arms wide as if to embrace the vast, crushing void between us. 'I've become a monster, drinking the souls of others to prolong a life I no longer care for, and without our love, what is there left for me to live for? Immortality is a curse, not a gift. To truly appreciate life, we must first accept death.'

His words, those brutal, beautiful words, had echoed in my mind for years, and still echo now. That was over a century ago.

Subsequently, we'd fought, cried, laughed, and joined passionately. Lotane, my anchor, my conscience, had brought our love back to life, by convincing me to embrace death.

Having come to such a decision, I'd ordered the cessation of training further Chosen and severed ties with the ssythlans on the Lizard Isles. It had been easy to ignore where the elixir of life had continued to come from since my ascension. It knew it wasn't just those with dark souls who perished to keep it flowing, it was the hundreds of innocents who died during training. How easy to ignore that fact so far removed from the blood, shit, and tears.

As the soul blades stopped reaping souls, the elixir of life slowed to a trickle and stopped. Every existing drop became precious, no longer quaffed like wine.

Lotane drank the last ten years ago, and since then has begun to age. The wheel of time is turning for him, and now for me, as I refuse to drink his blood.

Yet it isn't just he and I who will die.

The Saer Tel will join us,

Their human pairings aged and died long ago, and without the sustenance they provide, I'll soon be responsible for the death of a race, completing a genocide begun thousands of years before.

They've accepted their fate with a grace I envy, their dances and songs more poignant with each passing day.

I rise from bed, careful not to disturb Lotane and quietly pull on loose-fitting trousers, shirt, and boots, before slipping out the door of our room.

The mansion is eerily quiet, save for the whisper of my footsteps. At the end of the landing, a ssythlan waits, silent and watchful.

'Nogotha.' Its soft voice, sibilant, soothing, carries easily.

The ssythlan bows and walks ahead to open the giant doors in the entrance hall whilst I follow down the wide, circular steps.

Outside, the air is as crisp and fresh as a mountain spring, and the valley stretches before me, awash in the golden hues of dawn, the grass a lush carpet beneath me.

Several of my Saer Tel sisters fleetingly acknowledge my presence as they tend the landscape before twirling forever onwards.

Having chosen mortality, not a single dawn or sunset now passes without my appreciating its splendour. I pause, allowing the symphony of morning birdsong and the chaotic dance of a thousand butterflies to wash over me.

One of the Saer Tel twirls over and takes my hand, pulling me into a whirling dance of life. The land here is already as vibrant and healthy as can be. In fact, the Saer Tel have made the entire world a garden of unparalleled beauty.

Within moments, I relinquish control of my body to the music of creation, spinning, twisting, and twirling across the landscape.

By the time we finish, the morning has long passed. I'm at the valley's north end, rejuvenated and excited by what the day holds in store.

Before me, lush grasses of purple, red, and green, wave in the breeze, amongst which a nightmare grazes. From whence these magnificent, horse-like creatures came, no one knows and will forever remain an enduring mystery. Perhaps they're indigenous to this world, or were brought through a world gate like all the other races.

The nightmare raises its head as I approach, red eyes glowing fiercely in contrast to a lightly furred hide which is a black so deep, that it almost absorbs the light. It's also as tough as heavy, leather armour, making these creatures incredibly resistant to external injury.

Despite its foreboding look, the nightmare is a docile, loyal creature, just like the horses of the human world. Yet these are solitary and rarely mate. They were another race that Nogoth had saved from extinction with his power of the quickening, and to this day, I regret not having absorbed that when he died.

He had taken so many secrets with him to his grave, and I often sit and talk to his spirit when I'm unsettled. He was my greatest foe, yet I wish things had been different as I feel closer to him now than ever before.

The nightmare snorts as I approach, then trots to greet me, thrusting its muzzle under my armpit, demanding attention.

'You're like a cat!' I murmur as I scratch its head. 'Will you take me where I need to go?'

That long neck lowers in acquiescence, the heat from its eyes like sunlight against my skin.

Laughing, I vault onto its bare back, grip its flowing mane, and with a gentle nudge of my heels, send us cantering west toward the valley's rim.

Ogres bow as I pass them by.

Humans no longer work the valley. Lotane is the only one left in this world. At his insistence, I'd returned the pitiful descendants of those Nogoth and I had imprisoned back through the world gate to Astoria fifty years ago. I'd felt shamed at their condition. They hadn't deserved to continue paying for their ancestors' foul deeds.

Soon the valley is beyond me.

'YAH!'

I lean forward over my mount's muscled neck, gripping tight with my thighs as I urge him to greater speed.

The valley soon falls behind me and not long after, I spy smoke. I smile, excitement rising within me. Perhaps sensing this, the nightmare surges forward, and I laugh, letting him have his head, daring him to throw me. Yet, my skill is equal to this beautiful creature's speed, and I remain mounted.

Ahead, my destination awaits, majestic and ancient.

A world gate.

There are no temples on either side of its huge ramp, but rather low, stone buildings, built by the ssythlans who live here and study the gate, trying to divine how it's controlled.

The thunder of hooves draws attention to my approach, and a robed ssythlan steps away from a gigantic lens to meet me.

With a gentle tug on the nightmare's mane, I bring it to a halt, and slide off its back.

'Thank you,' I whisper into its ear as I wrap my arms around its long neck. 'Will you wait for me?'

A soft whicker answers my request.

'Nogotha!'

'Ssralan.' I hiss and lisp the word in its native tongue and it bows low in homage.

I sometimes wonder if they'd be so loyal and hold me in such high esteem if they weren't bound by blood magic like every other creature of this world.

'How is your research progressing?' I ask as we walk up the ramp toward where a dozen of his kind are gathered in discussion.

Between the gate's mighty columns, a hazy vista comes and goes as ethereal clouds swirl, offering glimpses of a different world where trees as high as mountains touch the sky while nearby, shaped lenses are focussed on the gate.

Ssralan emits a series of excited clicks as his scaled hands clasp excitedly before him.

'We discovered several runes can be moved!'

'And?'

'Look. See!'

With practiced speed, three ssythlans respond to Ssralan's ushering, interchanging four rune-covered metal plates that have seamlessly blended into the overall structure.

The scene through the world gate fades, then shifts. Ice-capped mountains instead of towering trees reach toward a dark sky dominated by three yellow moons.

'Incredible,' I breathe softly, my heart racing.

'More than you know,' hisses the ssythlan. 'Rotate the plates, change their positions, and it shows different worlds on the other side.'

I reach out, yet the space between the gates is unyielding. We cannot pass the invisible barrier, nor can it be broken or damaged. But I've no doubt we are getting closer to opening it.

'Let's see if today is the day.'

I place my palms against the cool metal of the world gate. It's no longer dead, inanimate, devoid of the magic that infuses all natural things. Despite being crafted by long absent hands, it's becoming something living, with a purpose, albeit barely.

I close my eyes, perceiving the world around me in its magical form, a rainbow of elemental colours, the swirling mists of blue, green, orange and white.

The world gate that had been utterly black, now pulses subtly, muted colours swirling.

Without knowing where this massive construction once drew its energy from … the constellations or some other means, it now has a different power source.

Me.

The magic contained within me, twists and swirls, excited to please, already aware of its destination. It's vast, an ocean, ready to overwhelm and swallow whole cities, or to soothe and hold as commanded. It's a projection of my will and desires.

I desire the world gate to open.

Like water cascading over a waterfall, my power flows into the world gate. It's exhilarating but also frightening as I surrender so much of myself, not withholding anything.

Then, there's nothing left to give.

I'm an empty vessel.

The vista within the gate shines with a clarity I haven't seen before, but then it fades, and I find myself falling into blackness.

***

A dull throb pulses through my head, as if the remnants of some unseen storm linger in my mind. My limbs are like lead, my body weak and sluggish. Even the simple act of opening my eyes feels like an insurmountable challenge.

'Can you hear me?'

The voice is a soothing balm, soft and velvety, but layered with a quiet strength. It cuts through the haze clouding my senses, grounding me. Despite my discomfort, I manage a faint smile.

'I can,' I murmur, my voice hoarse and barely audible. 'Now, let me feel you.'

Lotane chuckles, the sound warm and comforting.

'You'll get a kiss for now,' he teases.

His tone is playful but tinged with a weariness he can't quite hide, and his lips press gently to my forehead.

'You would deny your queen?' I ask, opening my eyes with great effort, scowling in mock disapproval. I'm surprised to be back in my chamber, warm in bed.

Lotane sits on its edge, his usual vigour tempered by exhaustion, lines of worry etched into his face.

'We all thirst for the drink we cannot have,' he says, winking. 'Now, you've been unconscious for two days and exertion is the last thing you need.'

'Two days?' I ask, startled. 'Were you worried for me?'

'I didn't have time.' His grin widens into a full-blown smile. 'I was too busy enjoying the peace and quiet!'

I snort softly, then sit up to be enfolded by his strong arms.

The strength of his embrace is both reassuring and intoxicating, and I find myself marvelling at the depth of my feelings for him. How could I have ever grown tired of this man? And yet, the answer whispers to me like an unwelcome ghost.

Immortality is a curse.

'The world gate?' I ask, gently untangling myself before the growing warmth in my loins overtakes reason and has me drag him into bed.

Lotane's smile fades slightly as he sits back and shrugs.

'Your pet ssythlans advise the gate is still impassable, though they're apparently enamoured with the vistas it reveals.'

'Damn,' I mutter, frustration bubbling to the surface. 'I thought it would be enough. I'm so impatient. How many more years will we have to wait? We're getting older. What if I need another hundred years before I have power enough to succeed?'

I pause, my anger rising as a frown replaces Lotane's smile.

'Don't look at me like that!' I snap.

'Imagine if every dream you ever had came true, how bored you'd be. Oh, wait, we've been there before. Be happy with what we have, Malina!'

He's called me Malina, not Alina, and if that wasn't enough to recognise his disappointment, he pulls a wan smile and stalks from our room.

The silence he leaves behind is oppressive. I sit there for a moment, cursing my impatience and inability to temper my emotions. How can something as vast and eternal as our love still feel so fragile at times?

My legs are weak, but I push myself from bed, reaching for a goblet of elixir, only to curse at its absence. Within minutes, I've dressed and stepped into the corridor, only to find Lotane leaning against the wall just outside.

He pulls a lopsided grin, and before I can speak, sweeps me into his arms, his face pressed into the curve of my neck. His embrace is almost desperate, and I realise with a pang that I'm not the only one afraid of what the future holds.

'Sorry,' he whispers. 'I'm just so afraid to lose you. To lose what we have ... again.'

The raw emotion in his words pulls at something deep inside me, and I run my fingers through his hair, holding him close.

'I want nothing more than to live by your side, my love,' I say, grateful for his apology. 'And even if my musings might indicate otherwise, I want to grow old and die by your side too. Now, how about we go take a look at the world gate together?'

A faint smile returns to his lips, and he steps back, his hands lingering on my arms.

'Breakfast first,' he says and pulls me by the hand, half-running along the corridor. 'We can eat outside by the reflecting pool, and then, once you recover some of your strength, we can go take a look at that gate of yours … unless you drag me back to bed!'

Warmth spreads through me as we hurry down the staircase, Lotane's laughter a melody I could listen to forever. Our ssythlan attendant, ever the epitome of grace, glides ahead, opening the grand doors that lead to the gardens.

Lotane knows I'm impatient to see the world gate again, but he's right to insist I eat, and the thought of a quick joining between the sheets is one I'm happy to consider.

'We'll break fast by the pool,' I say to the ssythlan, half-laughing at Lotane's buoyant behaviour and mischievous suggestion.

It's a somewhat overcast day as we step outside. Yet, the dark clouds do little to dim the garden's colours. Whatever the season, the Saer Tel keep the valley and everywhere they visit beyond it a paradise.

Lotane spins me around in his arms, faster and faster, until we both collapse onto the soft grass, giddy and breathless. The world tilts and swirls around us, but all I can see is his face, lit with a joy that makes my heart ache in the best way.

It's like we're teenagers again. At times like this, I wonder why I have doubts about growing old when the joy of our relationship is manifested tenfold. We lie there for a while, no care in the world, happy in each other's company.

A shadow passes over us, and I open my eyes to see our ssythlan attendant standing a respectful distance away, holding a tray. The gleaming ceramic dome atop it promises breakfast, and my stomach grumbles in anticipation.

'Breakfast is served,' Lotane announces, springing to his feet.

He offers me his hand with a theatrical flourish, and I take it, laughing as he pulls me up.

We follow the ssythlan around to the side of the mansion where a stone table and chairs sit overlooking the reflecting pool. It matters not what the time of day or night, it always shows the three moons clearly. How Nogoth created such a marvel is beyond me, but then I remind myself that I gave Dimitar life. We each had our own unique ways of manipulating magic.

We settle down and the tray is set before us.

The dome is lifted to reveal an array of delicacies: fresh bread slathered with butter and honey, an assortment of cheeses, thinly sliced meats, and goblets filled with cool water. The simple act of taking time to eat without rushing feels luxurious, and Lotane's teasing remarks and exaggerated praise for the meal draw laughter from me despite myself.

'Hold up,' says Lotane, his voice reaching through my merriment. 'It seems we have a surprise guest for breakfast, or perhaps he's coming for a rematch!'

I glance over my shoulder to see the solid form of Yaldul swiftly approaching. Trolls always exude menace with their broad, flat, and vicious faces. However, that grim visage is always strangely at odds with the beautiful musculature of their bodies. He's sweating and breathing heavily, and even more concerning is the massive axe grasped in one of his granite fists.

Lotane spins a small butter knife between his fingers.

'If necessary, I think I can beat him with this,' he jokes, an edge of unease to his voice.

However, I'm not worried. Yaldul's loyalty to me is unbreakable, and with their match in the arena behind them, he'd never hurt Lotane, and nor would any of the fey knowing my love for him.

'Nogotha!'

Yaldul's voice is so deep it can be felt in the stomach. He kneels, placing the axe on the ground, then touches his forehead to the soil. Even prostrated, his form looms over us.

'You know there's no need to observe such formalities,' I chide gently.

It still confounds me that this is the one order I give that seems to be universally ignored. If I told him to cut his own throat he'd do so without hesitation, but not to bow … easier I order the sun not to rise.

'What brings the mighty leader of the trolls to us this morning?' Lotane asks, his voice casual but guarded.

Yaldul lifts his head from the ground and rests back on his heels. It isn't from reverence or respect this time that keeps him on his knees, just practicality to save him looking down to his feet to see us, and we don't need to break our necks looking up.

'Champion.'

That shaggy head dips toward Lotane and there's anger behind those dark eyes.

'Fetch your swords. It's time to fight!'

'Yaldul. What's this about?' I demand, rising to my feet. 'There's no blood to be spilt outside of the arena. You know this!'

'You will need your swords too, Nogotha.'

'Why?' I'm shocked. What's come over this troll to threaten violence?

Yaldul's muscles bunch. The anger he previously exuded remains, but I can now perceive something else … bloodlust.

'Why?' He repeats, his lips pulling back in a snarl. 'Why? Because as of now, we are at war!'

***

CHAPTER II

Lotane lies alongside me, barely breathing, his motionless body covered in grass, dirt, and leaves. For two hours he hasn't moved, nothing more than a piece of the landscape.

I look exactly the same.

'Three thousand troops,' he murmurs, his voice soft, almost blending with the rustle of the wind.

'Another fifty came through the gate just now,' I whisper back, as if there's a chance of being overheard.

I peer through a ssythlan long-glass. Lotane has one too, and the polished lenses bring the faces of the new arrivals far below into startling clarity.

Lotane adjusts his long-glass, his jaw tightening.

'How can the world gate to Astoria be open?' he growls under his breath. 'It shouldn't open for another fifty years. The moons are nowhere near aligned.'

'Does it really matter?' I ask. 'They're here and this is no Astorian scouting party, but an expeditionary force in strength. What the hells are they thinking? The fey are demanding blood and I can't see any reason not to let them have it. Look what they've done to those poor ogres.'

I focus my long-glass on the line of impaled heads. Centuries ago, I had established this ogre settlement to oversee the gate and ensure no fey ever stumbled through. Having dutifully followed my orders, this is their reward.

Despite all fey being bound to me by blood magic, mistakes happen, and under no circumstances did I want the human world to suffer the horror of a fey incursion like it had for millennia. Better the fey remained as fey-tales, mostly forgotten and never believed.

I curse myself silently. Even though the gate was indestructible, I should have raised a mountain over it when I'd had the power, sealing it off forever. But a small part of me had always wanted the choice to return. Now my selfish choice had led to this slaughter. Thankfully, there had been a survivor who had escaped to bring news before succumbing to its wounds.

Lotane sighs.

'Four thousand years have passed in our old world since Nogoth's forces last invaded. They won't remember us. To them, the gate is nothing but an ancient mystery. They've blundered into something they don't understand.'

I close my eyes briefly, considering Lotane's words. Did these Astorians deserve a chance of clemency for their blunder? Hadn't they suffered enough at my hands in times past? Yet the images of the decapitated ogres fill my thoughts. What other atrocities might await if I don't act decisively to protect my kind?

'Unknowing or unaware, blood demands blood,' I hiss, my mind set upon its course of action. 'The ogres living here wouldn't have attacked when the Astorians first came through. Blood magic combined with orders would have ensured they weren't the aggressors, and still they were slaughtered. There will be no negotiation. We drive them back through the gate or destroy them entirely, then, once I've regained some power, I'll bury this gate and the others that lead back to the human world, forever.'

Lotane chuckles grimly.

'Maybe I'm becoming more fey than human, but I agree. I want to see these bastards dead for what they've done. They even killed the ogre infants. What is it with Astorians?'

I glance at him, a faint smile tugging at my lips despite the tension. Lotane was Astorian once, destined to be their king, had Nogoth's plans come to fruition. Perhaps better for Astoria if he had, but not better for me. Without him by my side, my inner daemons would have won, and I'd have become worse than Nogoth and led my fey legions through the gates long ago.

We fall silent for a while as we garner all we can of our enemy.

Even if this force hadn't come through the world gate that leads to Astoria the many black flags and pennants that flutter above the encampment would have identified them. The crossed ball and chain symbol has changed a little over the millennia but is still immediately recognisable.

'So what do we know?' I ask softly, wanting to hear Lotane's further observations to ensure I haven't missed anything.

'Frustratingly, I can't perceive anything through the gate,' he begins. 'So we've no idea how many more await on the other side. However, what's obvious is that they don't have any cavalry, archers, spearmen, or heavy infantry. It's just irregular, light infantry armed with long daggers and unwieldy staffs. The only exceptions are the officers in those long capes carrying sabres.'

There's a moment of silence, but I know Lotane has more to say.

'They're more like a well-armed militia than trained soldiers,' he continues. 'As for their weaponry, it's insufficient to defend against a frontal charge. They've fortified their position, anchoring the end of each line against the temples, but their earthworks are too low and whilst that intermittent wicker shielding they've erected might prove useful against arrows, they won't provide protection from above.'

I study the Astorians carefully as I consider Lotane's words.

Their grey uniforms boast numerous pockets and pouches, yet despite their complexity, appear to be simple cloth and offer little protection. The officers are obvious from not just the way they dress, but how they command those around them, and their curved sabres are likely a nod to their historic cavalry roots.

'I think they're more than militia,' I muse. 'They're moving with too much purpose and the camp is set up too efficiently. Those covered wagons spaced evenly around the perimeter probably hold supplies and could also be used as additional barricades.'

'You might be right,' Lotane says. 'They're just so lightly armed.'

'That they are,' I say. 'They probably won't stand against even the five hundred ogres we have at the ready, but we won't take any risks. We'll wait for Yaldul's reinforcements to gather.'

Lotane shakes his head, the leaves and twigs woven into his hood rustling at his slight movement.

'We shouldn't wait. Every hour gives the Astorians more time to fortify, and for more troops to come through the gate.'

'Our reinforcements are just two days away,' I say. 'Four thousand ogres, five hundred wolfen, and as many gargoyles. With that force, we can crush whatever we face without risk.'

'Overkill,' Lotane mutters. 'Any delay risks them scouting in force, and may I remind you, our home is less than a day's march from here.'

'Noted,' I reply. 'But if the Astorians leave their encampment, they're even more vulnerable than they are now. Let's return to our valley. Our scouts will advise if they make any aggressive move.'

It takes an hour to withdraw from our vantage points, shimmying backwards over the rim of the valley. A dozen heavily armed ogres await, as does Yaldul.

'Nogotha?' he rumbles.

I brush myself down, picking bits of grass from my hair.

'Assuming the Astorians don't scout in force,' I begin, 'we wait two days for our reinforcements before we attack. When the Astorians rout, I want them carrying word that an overwhelming force awaits any foolhardy enough to return seeking vengeance.'

Yaldul nods,

'And if they attack first?'

'We destroy them with what we have,' I say simply. 'But we keep the battle contained to this side of the gate. We defend our world, nothing more.'

Yaldul grunts in agreement, his eyes gleaming with anticipation.

'Your will is mine, Nogotha.'

'When the first gargoyles arrive,' Lotane says. 'Whilst they'll be our eyes on the Astorians, we should send some carrying word far and wide of what's transpired. Just in case this situation escalates.'

I rest my hand on Lotane's shoulder, grateful for his support.

'Make it happen, Yaldul,' I order. 'And know this. On matters of war, you speak with my voice. Act for the good of the fey. Organise the defence of our world, but not beyond its borders. I'll have two of my Saer Tel assist you.'

Yaldul's mighty shoulders slump, his pride clearly wounded.

'You bestow the greatest honour on me,' he whines, 'but then dilute it at the last.'

I almost laugh at the hurt apparent in his voice. Sometimes the biggest fey are like small children and need to be dealt with gently.

'You misunderstand, old friend. They'll handle logistics. Do you really want to be in charge of having livestock provided, slaughtered, and cooked? What about having latrine pits dug?'

Yaldul throws back his head and bellows with laughter. It rings so loud that I wonder if the Astorians might hear it.

'I didn't think I could love you more, Nogotha. You just proved me wrong! I look forward to working alongside your Saer Tel.'

'On another note,' I add, having held this news till the last. 'A handful of shades will join us shortly.'

I can sense Yaldul's confusion as to how I know, but he says nothing. He grimaces, as do the ogres within earshot, yet they daren't object.

Shades are shunned by their fellow fey folk. There's an inherent, undeniable darkness about them that keeps the other races, except the hags, from mingling with them. Whilst the threads of blood magic unknowingly bind every other race of fey to me, passed to them by their parents at birth, shades, like ssythlans, are magical beings and are fully aware of it. Not only that, but their sensitivity to magic allows feelings to be conveyed both ways.

Upon hearing of the invasion, I'd strummed the red veins binding the shades to me with a sense of urgent need, and the nearest group had acknowledged my call to arms immediately.

'We should discuss our assault plan this evening,' Lotane says. 'Yaldul can join us at the mansion.'

'Twice you honour me!' Yaldul beams, his eyes wide with delight.

'You haven't tasted Lotane's cooking or you wouldn't be saying that!'

The three of us laugh.

As Lotane and I begin our return to the valley, I can detect a spring in his stride, and a renewed sense of energy that matches mine.

We might not have been born to war, but we were raised on it.

For all my pretence at virtue, at maintaining peace amongst the fey folk, it shocks me to admit ... I miss the thrill of battle and killing, and I know Lotane does too.

***

Some landscapes are a general's dream ... undulating terrain that swallows armies whole, shadowed copses to hide an ambush, streams to be dammed and diverted, turning the earth into a sucking quagmire. A gradient can give a charge momentum, or blunt an enemy's advance.

But not here.

The world gate sits upon an open plain negating such options. Nonetheless, our enemy has turned this barren stage into a stronger position than last we saw them.

Two days ago, their defences were half-formed, with a crude earthen rampart and scattered wicker screens barely sufficient to deter a raid. Now, the ogres' homes lie in ruins, their stone repurposed into a crescent-shaped wall anchored against the ancient temples. The rampart, once a transient mound of dirt, is now a solid bulwark.

But walls are only as strong as the minds behind them, and the Astorians have made two fatal, strategic errors.

The first are the temples.

My gargoyles have confirmed the Astorians have neither occupied nor sought to fortify these ancient structures, which now provide a blind spot for some of our forces to approach and launch a surprise attack from.

The second is our enemy's woeful weaponry.

Combined, these will give us a decisive victory with minimal losses.

I glance at Lotane beside me, his scaled ceramic armour cuirass, matching kilt, greaves, vambraces, and plumed helm all glisten in the early sunlight. Where the armour doesn't cover his body, his skin glistens as if oiled. He holds a sword and round shield loosely. His eyes shine brightly with excitement, his cheeks are flushed, and I haven't seen him this alive in centuries. He looks like a young god.

I raise my hand.

'SHIELDS!'

Yaldul's command reverberates like a landslide.

A deafening crash follows as four thousand ogres lock their immense shields into an impenetrable wall.

I'm in the middle of the ogre front line, Yaldul on my left, Lotane on my right. The line is two hundred long, twenty deep, and the ogres hold formation perfectly despite wanting to be unleashed in a charging, murderous, vengeful frenzy.

They deserved the pleasure, but I'd refused.

This enemy may lack bows or long spears, but the wagons behind their lines hint that something awaits, and I'll not squander lives needlessly. This will be a slaughter, yes, but one where the cost is borne by the Astorians alone.

'ADVANCE.'

No horns signal the order. There's no need.

I lengthen my stride to match that of the ogres as we steadily close the distance on the Astorians.

The morning air is fresh, the sun low on the horizon to the east where the wolfen stalk, concealed by the temples. Above them, disguised by the sunrise, the gargoyles hover, the Astorians' blind to their approach.

Unlike those around me, I'm not dressed for battle. What need when I'm impervious to weaponry? Other than sturdy, reinforced boots, I'm wearing a short black robe that leaves my arms and legs bare and free of hindrance. However, I am armed with two short swords.

Movement from the Astorian camp draws my eye. Credit to them, they aren't panicked. Troops hurry to position, standing in steady ranks.

'They're definitely not militia,' I say, my voice raised above the stamp of booted feet.

'You're right. You're always right!' Lotane laughs. 'They're going to stand and fight. Credit to them. I thought they'd rout through the gate before we even got close.'

'There's still time for that,' I reply. 'Another minute we'll be in range of any archers, although I can't see any.'

'Their wicker shields are falling!' Yaldul growls, the base rumble easy to hear over the heavy ogre footfalls.

I'd spotted their collapse at the exact moment Yaldul had.

We're still out of bowshot, and it's hard to see precisely, but they hadn't fallen by accident, they'd concealed ...

'Are those bolt throwers?' Lotane yells.

Wheeled machines with a crew are revealed, waiting ominously.

'Whatever they are, we need to close, and fast,' I reply. 'Yaldul ...'

'DOUBLE TIME!' Yaldul bellows.

'URAH. URAH. URAH,' the ogres chant as we break into a jog.

I glance east, seeing nothing but open plain. The wolfen will be closing in through the long grasses, and I'm in no doubt they'll time their attack with ours and the gargoyles perfectly.

Hit from the front, side and above, the Astorians will be decimated, justice delivered, and blood answered with blood.

We're closing the distance quickly, and still the bolt throwers haven't engaged. There are ten of them pointed in our direction, with deep ranks of troops in between, steady, unflinching.

'In their position, I'd been browning my trousers.' Lotane yells.

'CHARGE!' Yaldul bellows.

The Astorians are over two hundred long strides away, but to the ogres, it's nothing. Their roars drown out my battle cry, demanding blood and vengeance.

It's been so long since I felt so alive.

The Astorian crews approach their machines. They've left it too late, they might be able to reload once, but they should have loosed their deadly bolts long ago.

An officer standing tall on a wagon raises his sabre.

When he lowers it, the bolt throwers will open fire and dozens of my poor ogres will die. But at least they'll die knowing they'll be revenged.

I scream, a guttural sound full of ancient, primordial anger as the officer slashes his weapon down ... I know what's coming.

What do I know?

The Astorian line disappears behind flashing fire and thunderous bangs that eclipse any storm I've ever heard. Smoke billows, and suddenly vast swathes of ogres along the line disappear in a bloody spray.

The line falters, a momentary hesitation as the Astorian weaponry ravages the ogre ranks. The mighty shield wall, once unbroken, sags under the sheer brutality of the attack. Still, the ogres press forward, composed, driven by honour and a thirst for blood, and vengeance.

Ahead, the Astorian troops come to life. The first rank lifts their bladed staffs, and a moment later, fire and smoke shoots out. Ceramic shields and armour cracks or shatters, but this time, whatever they're using had less effect. The front ranks kneel, and the second is suddenly hidden by the same fire and billowing smoke.

There are no visible arrows or slingshots, just the whine and crack of projectiles that smack ogres from their feet.

Then, what we'd assumed were bolt throwers roar again.

I've been hit by a troll's axe before in training, smashed by an ogre's shield, I've even been kicked by a giant. Nothing has fazed or scratched me.

Suddenly I'm flung backwards, knocking aside the ogres behind me, only to land amongst the trampled grass and bodies of the fallen behind the front lines.

My heart pounds in my ears as I look in disbelief at the glowing ball smouldering in my lap. It's the size of an ogre's fist, and I heave it to one side before looking for my swords. I've no idea where they are, so I snatch two long daggers from an ogre's corpse, then run after the ragged lines ahead of me.

I can't believe what I'm seeing.

At least half my ogres have fallen. Hundreds crawl on their hands and knees after their brethren, blood gushing from holes in their bodies.

Yaldul, towering and unyielding, roars above the din, leading the remaining ogres onward. His massive shield is splintered, his armour cracked, but he's a mountain unfazed by the storm.

I stumble, dazed for the first time in centuries, my head trying to come to terms with the scale of destruction wrought upon my fey.

The volley of bangs echoes across the landscape again, and Yaldul's back explodes in a spray of blood and ribs, and almost the whole of the front line disappears in a red mist.

'LOTANE!'

My scream goes unheard as the remains of my beloved ogres finally hit the Astorian front line at the same time as the wolfen and gargoyles.

I've never felt such acute loss, nor the need to inflict such pain …

But then I see HIM spinning and twisting between them, his armour blackened by smoke, his sword a blur of death as he carves through the Astorian line.

Lotane is alive … if only to deliver death.

My heart soars and I sprint, running between and leaping over the dead and dying fey, bloodlust and revenge vying for supremacy.

Cries of unbelievable agony and terror rise to new heights as men are literally pulled limb from limb or eaten alive in a frenzy.

Gargoyles swoop low overhead, their javelins sweeping the ramp with a deadly rain as the Astorians rout, and only one out of hundreds makes it through.

It was our plan. He can carry the tale of what befell his comrades.

Maybe four hundred Astorians have gathered to make a final stand. They have their backs to a temple, and are shoulder to shoulder, their strange weapons creating a bristling ring of steel.

Without the fire they belch, it's just delaying the inevitable.

The wolfen are enjoying themselves with the injured, ensuring their demise is infinitely painful. The gargoyles come down to join them, pulling their hapless victims aloft, before dropping them over again like cats playing with a mouse.

My ogres on the other hand, have one purpose. They've surrounded the Astorians with grim intent. My fey are shielded, armoured, and almost immune to the now silent Astorian weapons.

I could just leave the ogres to it, but I don't want to.

By unspoken assent, they wait, containing the Astorians as blood drips from swords, axes, armour, wounds, and tusks.

My footsteps are light as I weave my way between them, coming to stand by Lotane.

'Are you hurt?' I ask softly, worried that some of the blood that covers him from head to toe is his.

A shake of his helm tells me all I need to know.

'The officer is mine,' I shout in guttural ogrish. 'He will die, but not before I learn what I need to know.'

Raising an ogre dagger to my lips, I kiss its blade. Its dead owner's spirit will be grateful it will kill on his behalf.

With a hiss, I charge.

***

There's no need to look or give commands. Lotane and my fey will forever follow me into the hells without question or hesitation.

Instinct and training take over as an Astorian soldier lunges at me with his bladed fire staff. I meet his strike with my dagger, deflecting the weapon to the side in a screech of metal. I slide past, parrying another thrust from my right with my second dagger and ignore a third that glances from my ribs as if they're ceramic plate.

Then I'm amongst them, and they're packed so tightly together that they can barely wield their weapons, let alone defend themselves.

Blood splashes my face, warm and sweet, as I slash limbs and open stomachs. I don't kill instantly. These vermin deserve to die slowly, languishing in agony, holding on to entrails, regretting with every tortured breath what they did to the ogres that called this land home.

Soon there's but one Astorian standing.

The officer.

He stands amongst the carnage, gloved hands shaking, tears running rivers down his shallow cheeks.

An ogre sergeant steps to my side.

'Gather these vermin,' I command in ogrish. 'Do with them as you will, but ensure the world gate is sufficiently guarded at all times. Have the wolfen assist you. The gargoyles are to ferry our wounded back to the valley. The Saer Tel and ssythlans will tend to them there. Now go, and know you speak with my voice!'

The sergeant begins roaring orders. The wounded Astorians are dragged away and I turn a deaf, unsympathetic ear to their cries and pleas for mercy as I circle the officer like a wolf, daggers at the ready. All around, the once vibrant grasses have been flattened and smeared in blood and entrails and my heavy tread only adds to the desecration.

'Drop your sabre.'

He obeys, as though the weapon burns his flesh and it falls with a dull thud to the ground amongst the discarded weapons, torn flesh, and blood.

His appearance doesn't surprise me. Blond hair, cropped short, a cleft chin, typical of the Astorian upper class, tall and thin.

Lotane stands close by, my guardian, not that I need one, but he'll always be there for me.

'What's your name?' I demand.

'Captain Armana!'

His words are clipped, yet a tremor in his voice betrays his fear. He's scared, and rightfully so.

'If you answer me truthfully, I'll let you live,' I lie smoothly. 'What was your mission?'

He stands staring straight ahead, biting his lip, trying to maintain a semblance of composure. Blood runs down his chin.

Despite loathing the thought, it will be easier to bind him with blood magic. He'll answer every question honestly, and without hesitation.

The captain clears his throat.

'Tell me your names first. How is it that two humans live amongst these beasts?' he asks, his voice faint, almost disbelieving.

He stares intently, as if seeing past his fear for the first time, then turns to look closely at Lotane.

'Nogotha. Queen of the Fey,' I answer. 'This is Lotane.'

To my surprise, he shakes his head, laughing while crying at the same time. He smooths down his uniform, runs his fingers through his hair, and whilst remaining fearful, his eyes glare with hatred.

'Then I would rather choose death and glory!'

His hand whips to his waist and snaps up, gripping a small wood and metal club. Lotane is already moving forward, but I'm unconcerned, right until flame blossoms with a bang.

My head is snapped back, the blow spinning me around.

Lotane roars, and as I regain my balance, there he is, standing over Armana, sword raised as the Astorian futilely raises his empty hands.

'NO!' I shout, my voice cracking like a whip.

I stalk forward as Lotane slowly lowers his sword and turns toward me.

He pulls that lopsided grin of his, then suddenly crashes to his knees, the sword dropping from slack fingers.

Ogres rush to drag Armana upright, restraining him as I crouch next to Lotane.

'The bastard got me,' he hisses, looking down at his side.

Laces part under the honed edge of my dagger, and as I pull Lotane's scaled armour over his head, it reveals his blood-soaked linen shirt.

I rip the fabric apart and bend to look at the wound just above his waist.

Blood flows freely from a hole no bigger than the width of my little finger, yet as I look him over for any more wounds, I note a bigger hole in his back directly behind the first.

'It's nasty,' I say softly.

As Lotane rests his head on my shoulder, I wad his torn shirt, pull the laces from his boots, and use them to bind the wound tightly.

Lotane gasps in pain.

'Don't you bloody die on me!' I croak, my throat suddenly constricted by emotion.

The heavy downdraft of beating wings has me look up gratefully at two gargoyles who have come to my aid.

'We promised to die together,' he whispers in my ear. 'I intend to keep my side of the promise. Just make sure your bloody gargoyles don't drop me.'

Clawed hands that can rend and tear lift Lotane as gently as if a newborn, and I watch briefly as he's carried south, the gargoyles staying low to the ground as they race back to the mansion. They are not the only ones. Hundreds are ferrying the wounded ogres back for treatment.

I want to follow, to care for my love, to care for my people, but I can't. Not yet. The burden of leadership is too heavy to be so easily tossed aside.

The need to eviscerate Armana is so overwhelming, that I turn away briefly. The wolfen are still enjoying themselves, feasting on the living flesh of the few Astorians left alive. Around two hundred ogres stand guard halfway up the ramp to the world gate, while others roam the line of our advance, identifying the wounded and gathering the bodies of their dead comrades. The fallen are placed side by side, weapons on their chests to fight with in the next life.

Another unit scours the encampment, gathering the bladed fire staffs and all the other equipment, supplies and spoils, placing it in the temple near where I stand, clearing the field so they can begin dismantling the wall.

I nod in approval.

It has been centuries since the fey have been at war, but excelling in the martial arts is their way of life. Yes, they're farmers, herders, blacksmiths, even wine makers, but never a day passes without them duelling for honour and status. War and all that goes with it is in their blood.

'Armana.' I smile, the way a cat does as it eyes a mouse. 'You'll now tell me everything I want to know, and after that, you'll die the most painful death you can imagine.'

'I won't tell you a thing!'

Armana squeals as I grip his chin in a vice-like grip.

Whilst my elemental magic is nothing but a drop in the vast emptiness inside of me, my blood magic answers the call. It coils and writhes like a nest of red serpents, instantly binding Armana to me in unbreakable chains.

'You'll answer truthfully. You'll do nothing that could possibly cause upset or harm to me, or those who matter to me. You'll remain by my side and tell me everything you feel is of value. All you want is to please me in any way you can.'

Armana's expression shifts almost immediately. His features, once locked in a perpetual scowl, soften into a smile. He nods, his resistance utterly dissolved.

'Are there any more troops yet to come through the gate, and if so, how many and of what kind?' I ask, my voice sharp and commanding.

'Within the next few days, two thousand reserve musketeers, twenty riflemen, and two hundred artillerymen. There will also be cannons, supply wagons, medics, and scouts, Armana responds without hesitation.

'Tell me about your weapons?' I ask, beckoning as I approach what I'd thought was a bolt thrower.

'I tried to kill you with a handgun which fires this ammunition.' He opens a pouch and pulls out a small metal cylinder. 'Only officers and slingers are armed with them. It's accurate to a range of fifteen paces, whereas what you're standing next to is a cannon.'

He runs his hand along its smooth length, his eyes shining.

'This has a range of eight hundred paces and fires solid or canister shot. This,' he says, picking up a bladed fire staff, 'is a musket with a gun-blade for close quarter fighting. It fires a lead ball two hundred paces but is only effective inside of eighty. Rifles are similar, but have a longer barrel and range, but are slower to load.'

Pointing, he leads the way to a wagon within which are crates, metal tins, and solid metal balls.

'The crates contain gunpowder, an explosive that's ignited by fire and used in all of our weapons,' he says, his voice brimming with pride. 'Those canisters are filled with smaller balls for close range anti-infantry cannon fire, and those large balls are the shot for long-range cannon fire.'

Our footsteps draw us closer to the ramp and the world gate.

'How did you open the world gate?'

'Our scientists found a way to power them while also bending and focusing the light of the different moons. But I don't know the precise details.'

I stride up the ramp. The ramp that hadn't felt the tread of the fey in over four hundred years. Four hundred years of peace until now.

What will I see through the gate?

Two thousand Astorian faces staring back at me? Now I know of their weaponry, I must ensure my ogres stand further away.

'What was your mission here?'

'To establish a fortified command post for the coming invasion.'

'Which is planned for when?'

'The full invasion will be six months from now.'

Armana couldn't look happier as he tells me.

'Six months here or back in Astoria?'

Armana looks confused.

'Six months,' he repeats.

They've no idea of the time difference, but it only works in their favour. There are but eighteen days to ready my world to meet this invasion whilst one hundred and eighty pass in his.

'How big is the invasion force?'

'One million troops,' Armana declares.

'One million?' I gasp.

'Yes.'

I stop, utterly shocked. It's impossible for him to lie, and the number given is no exaggeration. An army that size with the weaponry they've developed would be unstoppable.

How had they advanced so far in the art of war?

The answer is sadly obvious. My decision to keep the fey from the land of humans has left them undisturbed for nigh on four thousand years.

A rumbling has me turn, and to my surprise, a large, covered wagon has come through the gate. It's sizeable enough to hold twenty soldiers, and is obviously heavily laden and creaks as it descends ever so slowly toward us.

Six ogres step into its path and strain, bringing it to a halt about twenty paces away. It's covered in a tarpaulin, and one cautiously pulls it back, shield raised at the ready.

'Do you know what that is?' I ask Armana.

The ogre reaches in, then turns to open a clenched fist, dropping a rain of nails to chime merrily on the ramp.

'That's our death!' declares Armana with a bright smile.

As if in slow motion, the wagon disintegrates, first white, then yellow, then black flames billow out and upwards, preceded by a cloud of nails and metal fragments. My ogres are vaporised, and then ...

Then, there is nothing.

***

CHAPTER III

'Wake up, Alina!'

The voice is distant, a whisper barely there, a feather-light caress brushing against the edge of my consciousness. It comes from nowhere and everywhere, pulling me toward it, closer and closer. The familiarity of it tugs at something deep within me, a memory I can't quite touch.

'Wake up!'

I'm intrigued, but ignore the voice. I wallow in a nothingness that's strangely comforting. The absence of sound, light, or even conscious thought is a level of serenity I haven't encountered in forever.

'Alina.'

Again the voice, full of love and concern.

Yet the darkness holds me in an embrace so strong that I'm reluctant to let go, to face the reality of what awaits. Of becoming aware of who I am.

'Alina!'

With a moan, I succumb to the demanding voice. Memories return, a kaleidoscope of images that I'd rather had stayed hidden, buried forever.

The darkness falls away, and I find myself sitting opposite Karson, his smile so bright and beautiful that any regret at being awakened falls away in an instant.

It's been longer than I care to remember since I've dreamt of my little brother. To my shame, I'd almost forgotten him.

A foreboding landscape surrounds me. In the past, Karson has revealed many futures, but none so bleak as this.

Ash, or maybe dirty snow, falls from a sky so thick with noxious clouds that I can barely see the sun's glow behind them. Lightning flashes and thunder rumbles, yet it's subdued, almost powerless, lacking any of nature's usual fury.

Unlike many of my previous dreams, there are no mountains of bodies, just buildings stretching into the distance, rising like broken teeth, black windows hollow and dark. Many belch smoke that rises to poison the sky, but all have a ghostly figure painted on the side, robed, with arms outstretched.

What people I can see are hard-faced and determined. The few trees are twisted, sickly broken things, and as for grass, there's no room for any, as the landscape suffocates under humanity's creations.

The last time I saw a world this grey, so devoid of colour, so leeched of any life, I was absent my soul having travelled through the Soul Gate.

Nonetheless, this foretelling of doom and gloom can't dampen my spirits at seeing my little brother after so long. He has forever been my guiding light, the voice of conscience whenever I've needed to hear it.

With his help, if I listen, I'll somehow avoid this terrible fate.

I try to take him in my arms, so he can feel how happy I am to see him, but I find myself unable to move. I struggle, but to no avail.

He shakes his little head, his initial smile fading to be replaced by his familiar frown.

'You're trapped, Alina. Trapped in a nightmare of your own making.'

'Can we not at least start with a … I missed you.' I say, smiling through tears of happiness. 'It's so good to see you, Karson. Why has it been so long since you came to find me?'

'Perhaps because it's been so long since you thought of anyone but yourself.'

He speaks something of the truth, and I nod sadly.

'I admit my time has been selfishly spent, but I never gave in to my inner daemons. Lotane helped me find my way when I became lost. I know I'm not perfect, but I've ruled over a world of peace and tranquillity.'

Karson comes over to wrap his arms around me and rests his little head on my shoulder. His breath tickles my ear as he stands there, embracing me, whilst I'm unable to respond in kind.

'Yet you turned your back on the world that needed you the most,' he says, his tone reproachful. 'What about that world? What about its peace and tranquillity? Did it mean nothing to you?'

'That's unfair, Karson. I was banished. I promised never to return, to be tempted into becoming that which I'd overcome. Wasn't that what I was supposed to do?'

'Perhaps. But you're a creature of both worlds, and you chose only to embrace one, consciously distancing yourself from the other long after your banishment ended. The child you ignored has grown to become something dark and malevolent without its mother's love and guidance. You were right not to repeat Nogoth's mistakes, but you omitted to learn from his successes!'

I blink frantically as gritty snow drifts into my eyes. A foul wind blows, that leaves an unpleasant taste on my tongue.

'How was I to know?' I demand, trying not to get frustrated. 'I never asked to be Queen of the Fey, I never wanted to rule. I just wanted to be loved, and to find a place called home.'

'And you did whatever it took to achieve that.'

'What is that supposed to mean?'

'Hundreds of thousands died, Alina. But I'm not judging you, simply leading you to one final question. What would you do to keep the one you love, and the world you call home, safe?'

I want to tell him that I'd do absolutely anything, including killing a hundred thousand more. But I don't want to be the subject of his derision and recriminations.

'Why do you always have to choose such grim backdrops for our meetings, Karson?' I ask, trying to distract him. 'You can get your message across without turning my dreams into nightmares!'

I tease, wanting him to become the light-hearted brother I once knew. He can give me his sage advice without the theatrics, doom and gloom.

Karson shakes his head.

'You misunderstand, Alina. This isn't my dream, it's not even our dream, and despite it being a nightmare, it's actually your reality.'

Karson fades from sight, and yet the hideous landscape remains.

'Wake up, Malina,' I tell myself, but the seriousness of my situation becomes clearer as I recognise this is indeed, reality.

Heavy chains secure me head to foot to a bench in the back of a wagon caged by steel bars.

I'm facing backwards and can't see if any guards are in the wagon with me. Snorts and heavy hoofbeats indicate it's being pulled by oxen.

Soldiers armed with what Armana had named muskets, slog tiredly alongside, weapons hanging from a sling over their bent shoulders.

I've been dressed in simple, black linen trousers and shirt, am barefoot, but otherwise in good shape.

My fists clench and anger surges through me. I'll not go quietly.

Straining my muscles, the chains don't give at all, but it was worth the try, so I reach for my magic, only to curse silently as I realise I'd emptied myself trying to activate the world gate, if not, I'd have been out of here in a heartbeat.

Patience, Malina.

Given a little time, I'll absorb enough power to make my escape inevitable. It won't take long.

Although how much time I have, or more precisely, the fey world has, is diminishing with every turn of the wagon's wheels, because from where I sit, things are looking bleak.

The world gate rises majestically into the foreboding sky against a backdrop of grim factories and industrial buildings, above which jagged, snow-topped mountains peek. My way home recedes steadily as the wagon heads along a wide avenue toward whatever fate the Astorians have planned for me. Worryingly, the gate is still close enough for me to see a steady stream of troops and equipment ascend the ramp, to disappear into my realm.

I open my spirit eye, searching for even the faintest glimmer of hope, but what I see steals the breath from my lungs. The world here is steeped in grey desolation, utterly devoid of the vibrant hues that should flow through its air and soil. Elemental magic, the lifeblood of existence, is absent.

There's nothing, not even the faintest wisp to help replenish my power, just thick, black clouds, boiling and angry, instead of the expected streams of colourful magic.

Where has it gone? What has humankind done to this world?

It appears the very fabric of nature and the elemental magic that has coexisted alongside it since the world's creation, has been replaced by industrialisation.

Is this the fate that awaits the fey world?

Shouts and panicked screams have me look up, hope blossoming, as my loyal gargoyles fly through the world gate, around three dozen strong.

Lances rain down, scattering troops on the ramp who throw themselves frantically behind or under whatever cover they can find.

The eyesight of these magnificent creatures is phenomenal, and they head straight for my wagon in a swirling swarm of wings, claws, and talons.

Orders are barked, the voices rising above the screaming wounded and the harsh shrieks of my gargoyles as they come to my rescue.

'FIRE!'

Those harsh bangs that I know only too well sound off to my right where two units of maybe fifty troops apiece line the pavement, a dense smoke cloud around one of them.

'FIRE!'

The sharp command pierces the chaos, and a deafening volley of gunfire erupts. Smoke billows from the second unit, and maybe a third of my beloved gargoyles fall or spiral downwards.

Still, they press on and the survivors split into two groups.

Half continue their race toward me, the rest dive toward the troops who are frantically reloading their weapons, pouring powder down musket barrels from small cylindrical containers.

The Astorians' muskets are powerful, but their flaws are clear: they are slow to reload and cumbersome to wield.

My guards frantically attempt to attach gun-blades to their muskets, preparing for hand-to-hand combat. I study every move, absorbing every detail, how they handle their muskets, how they stand as they aim along the length of the weapon.

Know thy enemy.

Another ragged volley rings out, and four more gargoyles plummet to the earth, but then the remainder are upon the troops. Each gargoyle carries up to six light javelins, and they hover above the scattering Astorians, casting them with practiced, deadly accuracy.

Men and women are impaled, falling screaming to the ground, and then the gargoyles draw swords, and land, lashing out with their weapons, sending blood and bodies flying under their onslaught, ensuring the troops can't reload.

This is not their strength. Their mighty wings carry them aloft with grace, speed, and manoeuvrability, but on the ground it makes them ungainly and they begin to pay the price as the gun-blades attached to muskets draw black blood.

A loose volley from my guards bring my attention back to the group of gargoyles approaching my wagon. Three fall from the sky, and as my escort dives under the wagon for safety, four gargoyles land atop the cage. The remainder, hurl javelins, and send dirt billowing in all directions with the mighty downdraft of their wings.

One clambers to the rear gate, but despite his hugely muscled arms wrenching at the metal, it doesn't give, and then there are the chains securing me even if he succeeds in opening the gate.

'THE KEY!' I shout. 'FIND THE KEY! It will be on one of the officers!'

The gargoyle leaps off and bends, looking under the wagon, then drags a kicking and screaming officer out by his throat.

The man fumbles with a ring at his waist, the keys jangling as he offers it up desperately, tears running down his face.

The gargoyle snatches them, then tears the man's throat out with his talons, before leaping onto the back of the wagon.

'Yes,' I cry, as the gate opens at the first attempt.

The gargoyle smiles. To any human, it would be a sinister, hideous thing, but it warms my heart. He stoops, folding his wings back to fit through the small opening, and kneels before me, grasping the lock.

Something wet splashes into my eyes, and as I blink furiously, I see half of my rescuer's head is missing.

'NO!'

Every death of these noble creatures is one too many. For centuries, none have died except from old age, illness, or fighting in the arena, and now they're falling like leaves in an autumn storm.

More shots ring out, pinging off the cage, but also finding purchase in gargoyle flesh.

To my left, six men walk calmly forward, arms raised. They're wearing long, tanned leather coats, wide-brimmed hats, and wield double-barrelled hand guns. One restrains a slavering dog, a huge beast on a lead.

Flames and smoke billow as they calmly close the distance, firing in a steady rhythm as they do. Two fall to the floor, pierced by javelins, but the rest continue their assault, determined and unfazed.

Each weapon booms twice before being smoothly replaced in a leather holster before another is drawn, ensuring they're always armed and dangerous.

Could these be the slingers Armana had referred to? They're different from the rest, and they twist, turn, sight, and fire, displaying a skill of movement that is utterly new whilst remaining totally familiar. These men have been trained to stand above their peers.

One of my gargoyles flies at them from behind, a sword in each hand. Two slingers die screaming, but two roll away, their weapons booming, and the lone gargoyle tumbles across the ground. As he rises, spreading his wings, one of the slingers releases his dog, and it leaps, tearing at the gargoyle's throat, and they roll across the ground, locked together, tearing each other to shreds.

One by one my rescuers fall beneath the newcomers' onslaught, falling to lie broken and bleeding on the cold ground, trying till their last gasp to reach me, to protect me, to bring me home.

My hopes die and tears blur my vision as the last one falls. Their loss seems even more tragic for its futility.

Rage burns inside me, hot and unyielding, a flame that refuses to be extinguished, fed by the slaughter around me. I clench my fists, straining against my chains, but to no avail.

I have to get back, to rally the fey. No one else knows the scale of what's planned. *One million troops.* The number is staggering. Even if I were at my most powerful, I'm not sure how much I could do.

Doubt flickers like a shadow at the edges of my thoughts, but I shove it away. Every fey, whether adult or child, will need to be ready. No one will be spared this fight.

My only consolation is that whilst the explosion had decimated everything around the ramp, there were enough gargoyles circling high above and ferrying the wounded to have brought the news to Lotane, and despite his injury, he'll not be idle.

The fey will defer to him in my absence and he'll prepare them for the war that will crash through the world gate like a tidal wave.

I push my sorrow aside with effort, forcing my mind to take in the surrounding scene. I can't afford the luxury of grief or despair. Not now. Not ever. Every second, every breath, is an opportunity to learn, to understand this new enemy. I must see what four thousand years of isolation have wrought upon this world.

Of the swamp that used to exist here, there's no sign. Instead, a city sprawls in its place, dark and choking like a cancer on the land. Hundreds of wagons and cannons line the avenue I'm travelling on.

The air thrums with an unfamiliar energy, and my eyes are drawn to the two massive buildings flanking the world gate.

Dozens of enormous lenses are affixed to their roofs, catching the dim light while jagged arcs of energy crackle along thick cables that attach the buildings to the world gate like some twisted umbilical cord. It's unquestionably a violent, artificial power, but irrespective, it makes the runes etched into the ancient artefact pulse rhythmically, like a corrupted heartbeat.

Those buildings are undoubtedly the key to keeping the gate open. I can't help but draw a parallel to the temples on the other side of the gate. Both are responsible for the death of thousands, just in different ways.

Curses and cries for help come from all around.

Troops swarm everywhere, ensuring that every one of my fallen gargoyles is well and truly dead. I can't bear to watch as they stab and hack at the lifeless bodies. Others go to the aid of their injured comrades.

Amidst the chaos, the two remaining slingers who'd prevented my escape, empty, then refill their weapons with small, dull cylinders. Their movements precise, devoid of conscious thought.

An officer shouts and screams at my remaining escort, replacing their shock of the fey attack with the fear of his authority.

A minute later, the gargoyle has been yanked from the back of the wagon, the gate locked, and all chances of my escape lie in bloody tatters all around.

'What about her?' A bitter, female voice demands.

'Send her to sleep!' someone commands.

The remaining guards step away, and a moment later, something metallic is tossed through the bars to roll across the blood-soaked wooden boards. It comes to rest near my feet.

It's the size of an apple and begins to fizz. Sickly yellow bubbles ooze out, followed by dark yellow, billowing cloud of noxious smoke. There's no breeze to take it away and it gathers around me like some evil spirit.

I might be nigh on immortal, but I still need to breathe, and even though I take small breaths, the fumes are like fire in my lungs. My vision blurs, black spots dancing in the corners of my eyes. My head spins, and my limbs grow heavy, unresponsive.

An officer steps forward as the fumes finally begin to dissipate.

'Sleep while you can,' he taunts. 'Because when you awaken, that's when your nightmares will really begin!'

***

An abrasive, artificial wailing pulls me reluctantly back to consciousness. I try to sit, but straps across my chest, hips, legs, and arms, pin me to an unforgiving metal table. My neck, mercifully free, allows me to crane my head and take stock of my surroundings.

The room is a study in sterility. Smooth metal sheets cover the walls, ceiling, and door, their flawless surfaces reflecting the flicker of a buzzing light suspended overhead. The light, glaring and unnatural, reminds me of a sun globe, but it's no creation of elemental magic. The only exception to the order … a heap of heavy cables, coiled like snakes in a corner.

Cries for help, sobbing, and occasional agonised screams filter through to keep me company. It seems I'm not alone in my incarceration.

I strain, pitting my strength against my bindings, groaning with the strain, but the straps are well placed, and absent any leverage I can't break free.

'Bastards!' I yell, my frustration getting the better of me.

A metal hatch slides back in the door, revealing cold, dispassionate eyes. A moment later, the hatch slams shut and footsteps recede, leaving me alone to contemplate my fate.

It's been over four hundred years since I last felt this helpless. I clench my fists involuntarily at the memory of Lotane pulling my fingernails out with metal pincers.

However, I needn't worry. To this day I've no idea what type of power I inherited from Nogoth, but not only is my skin impervious, but I hardly feel pain at all.

True, I can drown, or suffocate, but little else affects me. Poison doesn't, swords, muskets, and explosions, don't even bother. Although, what little hair falls over my face is brittle and crisped.

If they don't realise how to kill me, I'll find a way to get out of here. It's only a matter of time.

The wailing dies away to be replaced by the approaching clack of booted feet and a metallic rattle of keys. It seems that beyond the door, a corridor leads … somewhere. If only my magic was replenished enough to quest out an escape route, to help me prepare.

Four bolts clang in succession.

The door, massive and reinforced, groans on its hinges as it swings open. This room seems built to hold a troll securely, but I'm no troll.

A man steps inside, a slinger, his silhouette stark against the corridor's harsh light. He wears a wide-brimmed hat, and despite it being pulled low, it's easy to discern his typical Astorian high-born trait of a cleft chin. A black leather coat is pulled back, and his gloved right hand hovers over the knurled butt of a polished double-barrelled gun as he briefly surveys the room.

With a tug, he ensures my straps are buckled tight then steps back, assessing me with his intense gaze.

I'm not interested in a staring contest, and seize the opportunity to study this deadly foe. Two more beautifully embossed weapons are visibly sheathed on his right side, attached to leather weapon belts covered in pouches that crisscross his body. From the way he holds himself, and the telltale bulges under his leather coat, he has three more concealed on his left side.

He grunts as if satisfied, then leaves me lying here as he exits the room.

A soft mumble of voices precedes the clack of his heeled boots on the metal flooring as he returns, positioning himself near my head, just out of sight.

Seconds later, a figure enters, a white robe with a hooded cowl concealing their face. The robe hangs loosely, suggesting a weak frame beneath.

A priest perhaps.

Following this figure comes an officer, every inch the embodiment of Astorian arrogance. His polished belt gleams, bearing a dagger and handgun. Four crimson rings encircle each sleeve, denoting a rank of some importance. A thin moustache graces the thin, hatchet face.

Then, two men shuffle in dressed in a one-piece garment that covers them from shoulder to ankle, that's buttoned down the side. Despite being broad and tall, they're gaunt and skinny, yet what shocks me the most is that they're Icelandians. Heads bowed, they manoeuvre a wooden trolley carrying a strange contraption into a corner.

With heads bowed, they attach the cabling on the floor to the contraption, then depart without once raising their eyes. Their body language is defeated, bowed, subservient, and definitely fearful.

'The officer retrieves a small metal and leather-bound tome from within his tunic, and slowly turns half a dozen pages, occasionally looking up at me as he does so.

'Beware she who walks in human form, for she has the beast's soul,' he invokes. 'Beware she, whose skin is the colour of the snake, for she has the beast's body. Beware she who speaks with honeyed words, for she speaks with the beast's tongue. Beware she whose eyes are the colour of putrescence, for she is the Queen of Beasts and death is her companion!'

With shaking hands, he offers the tome to the cowled figure.

A slight shake of that invisible head and the offer is withdrawn.

'I don't need scripture to recognise what lies before me, Commander Asmodial. Her image has haunted me for centuries.'

The voice is male, softly spoken, yet it carries the weight and strength of belief.

'It can't be,' Asmodial mutters, his voice choked, as he studies both the tome and me, the veins in his neck taut. 'It can't be!'

'Do you doubt the Holy Scripture, or perhaps me, Commander?'

The tone is sharp, but not in anger, just in reproach.

To my surprise, Asmodial sinks to his knees, his hands pressed together.

'No, All Father. Forgive me!'

A gloved hand gently rests atop the officer's bowed head

'Rise, my loyal and favoured son. There's nothing to forgive. Faith demands much of us, and doubt is a trial we must all overcome.'

All Father? His title and words suggest the power of position and faith. Yes, definitely a holy man of some religion.

As the commander stands, it's easy to distinguish love and reverence in Asmodial eyes, and I wonder what manner of man is concealed beneath that white hood.

'Why am I chained?' I ask calmly.

I want to scream, hiss, and shout at them. I want to tear them limb from limb to satisfy my need for vengeance. But rage won't help me discover the things I need to know. I'll start with compliant, try a conversation and see where that gets me.

'Evil beasts should be chained, but as for the Queen of Beasts, well ...' the commander begins.

'Queen of Beasts?' I scoff, cutting him off mid sentence.

They don't know my fey. They aren't beasts, at least, not any longer. Unlike the fractured, violent nations that raised me, the fey live in harmony, free from the rot that corrupts human hearts.

The commander's mouth opens, no doubt to spew another insult, but he's silenced. The priest, no, the All Father, steps forward, and Asmodial instantly bows and retreats.

Gloved hands reach up, pushing the cowl back, revealing a mask covering the lower face. Then, as the All Father unties it, this too falls away. I can't help but flinch. I've laid eyes on all manner of creatures in my time, yet even the shades and hags aren't as strangely disturbing as this man before me.

'Don't you like what you see?' The All Father asks with a sad smile.

I'm lost for words. His face, though handsome, is a tortured canvas of pain and devotion. Pale, bleached skin reveals a network of red veins that spider-web beneath the surface. Instead of a nose, two flaps of flesh flutter like twisted butterfly wings over a ragged hole, whilst bright red eyes weep, as though his very existence is a torment.

'Are you not happy with your creation?' The All Father asks, his eyebrows drawn together into a hurt frown. He bends closer, sniffing, blinking away tears. 'Should a mother ever display such cruelty to her child?'

'You're no child of mine,' I gasp.

The All Father shakes his head slowly, sighing as if in regret.

'Your denial hurts. But I am your child. Not of flesh, perhaps, but of purpose. My very existence, my faith, was born because of you.'

'Well, my son,' I say, cautiously, going along with the narrative. 'Will you release your mother?'

The All Father shakes his head slowly, pity evident.

'Only the One God has the power to set you free now. He offers forgiveness to all who repent, and whilst I fear your path of redemption might last an eternity, I'll ensure you're given the chance. I've waited thousands of years to deliver you into HIS arms for judgement and I'll not fail in this task.'

The commander pulls leather gloves from a pocket, and having put them on, comes to stand on my right side.

'Incredible,' he murmurs, his voice trembling with emotion as he leans over to inspect me without getting too close. 'There were times I doubted your existence, yet here you are. Now I believe and will never doubt again!'

The All Father looks on, nodding.

'Commander, your lack of faith saddens me, and yet you were responsible for the capture of our oldest foe. The One God favours you, and now I understand why I always did too.'

Asmodial's eyes gleam, his chest swelling with pride.

The All Father reaches out a gloved hand.

'Your dagger, if you please.'

Asmodial places it hilt first in the All Father's hand.

'Let me show you the dark power of undiluted evil,' the All Father murmurs.

'And if she dies?' Asmodial asks, his eyes searching. 'Does that mean she's nothing but a common fey?'

I can't contain myself anymore.

'Perhaps I'm nothing like what you think I am.'

The All Father looks mildly amused.

'Really? Do you claim to be an innocent, young woman, who was stranded in the fey world, as opposed to the Queen of Beasts, devil spawn made flesh, who sought this world's downfall, relishing in the slaughter and imprisonment of its people?'

He looks at me patiently with an infuriatingly calm demeanour.

'Oh no,' I hiss, suddenly tired of this charade. 'I'm worse, far worse than you can possibly imagine. You've awoken the Queen of Beasts, and believe me when I say, I will tear you limb from limb!' I snarl, revealing my sharp incisors.

For a fleeting moment, they falter, Asmodial and the All Father stepping back as I strain at my straps.

Yet when my bonds hold firm, The All Father approaches and draws the dagger edge across the back of my hand to no effect.

'The scripture says that absent soul, her serpent's skin turneth to rock,' he murmurs, then looks toward his bodyguard. 'When you're ready.'

The All Father and the Commander step away and cover their ears.

There's a gentle sigh of metal against leather, a couple of clicks, and the Astorians' actions give away what's coming. I flinch reflexively as a boom resounds within the small chamber, and whilst I'm aware of being struck in the head, there's no discomfort, let alone pain.

'Our weapons left no mark, and from her own mouth she admits it,' Asmodial declares in a hushed voice. 'It *is* the Queen of Beasts. What should we do with her, All Father? Your wish is my command.'

'Well, she has an eternity of sins to atone for,' the All Father says softly, 'and she must die before she can receive the judgement of the One God. Let us not baulk from such an unpleasant task, and apply ourselves with righteous fervour. Together we'll rid the world of this ancient evil once and for all. After that, nothing can stand in the way of our holy crusade.'

***

What do I know of pain?

I've known the anguish of a broken heart, the guilt of hurting the one I loved, the betrayal of trusted allies, the sting of banishment, and the cold hand of rejection. I've lived through trauma, my parents' death, the loss of close friends, the purges to become a Chosen, the horrors of warfare, and the countless deaths I've visited upon not just the guilty, but also the innocent.

Physical pain has been no stranger either. I've been slashed, stabbed, beaten, and broken. I've endured sickness that sapped my strength and infections that left me teetering on the edge of death. I've been savaged by red wolves, their jaws tearing into my flesh.

What do I know of pain?

I've been there. I've experienced it, far more than most, but time, as with all things, is the greatest healer, erasing the sharpness, dulling the edges, and thankfully so.

Yet there's one exception.

The most painful moment of my life, which stands out far above all others, was being infused with magic.

I don't even need to close my eyes to hear my own desperate, agonised screams. The memory is seared into my mind, as vivid now as it was then. If ever I came close to death by pain alone, absent blade or injury, it was in that moment.

Yet now it stands eclipsed and surpassed.

For days, cables have been attached to my body, and through them, some devilish power flows, but it isn't magic.

At first, the sensation was almost benign: a gentle thrum, a faint vibration beneath my skin. To a body capable of containing the raw forces of the elements, it was an irritation I could easily ignore.

No matter how the commander swore at the Icelandian operatives, it barely bothered me at all.

At night, I slept soundly, unperturbed by the vocal misery of my unseen neighbours. During the day, I remained unfazed, other than by frustration and the gnawing need to escape and return to my people.

But now ... now it's a different story altogether.

I've never borne children, though I've yearned for them for centuries.

Lotane, for all our love, could never give me the child we longed for, however much we'd tried.

Yet I'd always carried life inside of me.

My magic.

The pain I'd endured, had all been worthwhile to gain something that loved me unconditionally, and would do anything I bid, just to seek my approval.

My magic was the child I never had, for I carried it within me like an unborn child. My term wasn't nine months, it was for life.

And now, my baby is being killed inside of me.

I'd been utterly spent when I'd been captured, my magic already drained. Whilst the essence that remained had protected me at the beginning, after days, it's succumbing to the unrelenting fury of the storm.

My back arches, muscles locked in an iron grip as my fingers claw the air.

Steam rises from my body, small colourful clouds disappearing as if swallowed by this magic-less husk of a world.

I try to hold on, to cradle my magic with the fierce, protective love of a mother. But the pain is all-consuming, and I know it's only a matter of time before my child dies inside of me.

For a fleeting moment, the torment subsides. The Icelandians manning their infernal contraption grant me a brief reprieve. Strangely, I both embrace and despise these moments of respite, for when the torture resumes, it always feels worse.

The commander looms over me, pinning me with his gaze.

'How large is the fey army?' Asmodial barks for the fiftieth time.

Absent the All Father, the true nature of this man has revealed itself. He revels in my suffering, gloats at my pain. I've remained silent till now, but perhaps engaging with him might earn me some relief from their terrible machine.

'Larger than you could possibly imagine,' I groan. 'The sooner you close the world gate, the better. Because they'll be coming for me, and for you. If you want a chance at life, you should let me go.'

Asmodial scoffs, the sound dismissive.

'Hah. Close the gate. Really? Our crusade has been centuries in the making. With the One God on our side, we'll destroy whatever denizens of hell oppose us. No rescue is coming. You'll live out your last few days here, Nogotha, Queen of Beasts.'

He leans closer, his voice dropping to a venomous hiss.

'Personally, when your time comes, I think you should be buried alive to rot for an eternity. Poetic justice for you condemning the All Father to the depths of hell alongside our ancestors!'

His words slowly penetrate my pain.

I condemned the All Father to the depths of hell … could he mean …

Nausea churns my stomach as memories resurface. I remember releasing the last wretches of humanity from the temples, emaciated figures, skin bleached absent centuries of sunlight, bodies riddled with sores, deformed and diseased. I'd thought them barely capable of speech as they stumbled through the world gate and had expected them to die in the swamps beyond, their frail forms succumbing to the elements.

But I'd assuaged my guilt by believing they'd at least die free.

Could the All Father have been amongst them? He'd claimed to be thousands of years old, and if he'd truly survived since I, or perhaps Nogoth before me, first incarcerated the Astorians, he would be by this world's measure of time. If the Saer Tel can be gifted with longevity, then why not him?

It would explain how not only had he survived, but had brought the knowledge of the fey world and me with him, reinforcing and twisting the legends and records of old that still existed.

The desire for vengeance can be almost as powerful as love, and had no doubt driven his rise to power, and from there he'd roused a whole nation to seek vengeance on the fey world in which he and previous generations had been incarcerated.

'Perhaps it's true,' I rasp, my voice hollow. 'Perhaps I shouldn't have punished them as I did.'

The commander's thin eyebrows rise. He looks sceptical and somewhat disappointed.

'Are you truly sorry?'

I can't help but laugh as I shake my head.

'The only thing I'm sorry about is that I didn't have the All Father killed along with everyone else. Your ancestors were filthy rapists and murderers. How the Delnorian Empire allows you degenerate filth to exist is beyond me!'

Now it's the commander's turn to laugh.

'Truly, you are the Queen of Beasts,' he sneers. 'Living amongst animals, you know nothing of this world. There's been no Delnorian Empire for nigh on five hundred years. There's only the Astorian Empire now, and it's united under the All Father, behind a single vision … to end the fey threat once and for all. Then, after the world beyond the gate is purified, the All Father will rule over two worlds.'

'Then I'll make sure to kill him after I kill you,' I hiss. 'The last and only Astorian ruler I ever knew I killed. I tore her throat out. I think I'm going to go for two in a row!'

The commander's lips curl into a malicious smile, his eyes glinting with derision.

'You should pay more attention. The All Father is immortal. You can't kill him. Now, this conversation is over. Let me know when you're willing to try and converse like a human.'

I don't believe for a moment he's interested in my repentance, or any scrap of military intelligence. He only desires to savour the sight of me broken, helpless, and at his mercy.

The thrum builds in the corner of the room sending a fresh wave of dread through me.

Accompanied by a snide grin, the commander nods.

The machine's power surges through me again, and my body is no longer mine to control. Muscles spasm violently, my back arches, and every joint strains against its limits. Pain consumes me, yet I refuse to scream. I'll not give him the satisfaction.

Being helpless is not a feeling I'm accustomed to.

Once I could have moved mountains, but my elemental magic has nothing left to give and will soon be a thing of the past. If it's there, I can no longer feel it, and I'm sure it's just a matter of time before my blood magic follows.

If only I could touch Asmodial, the All Father, or even one of the Icelandians. If just one of them would brush against my bare skin, I could bind them instantly. They'd be mine to command, and I'd be free. At least then I could die fighting, not strapped to a table.

But they know, or are simply cautious, and keep enough distance.

Historically, Nogoth had ordered all traces of the fey invasions to be systematically erased, purged from history so humanity would forget what awaited them every thousand years.

I'd done no such thing, and despite the passage of time, humanity has not forgotten about the fey, or me, especially the Astorians.

I thought I'd learned and become a better ruler than Nogoth. Wiser. Kinder. Yet my mistakes are now beginning to eclipse his wrongdoings.

For the first time in my long life, I wish I'd bound Lotane to me by blood magic. So I could feel him close, be connected.

I strum the red threads, letting my people know that I'm alive. They must have hope, and so must Lotane. They'll tell him, reassure him, and ensure he's strong, because without him, the fey world will fall.

One million troops.

It will fall anyway. No matter what he does, no matter what I do, the fey world is doomed. Even if I were there, even if my powers were at their peak, we couldn't stop what's coming. Instead, I'm here, far from where I'm needed.

Or maybe, I'm exactly where I'm supposed to be.

What better way to stop the invasion than to strike at its heart? If I can escape, if I can kill the All Father, Astoria's immortal leader, and his commander, the empire will be leaderless, in utter disarray.

The thought burns in my mind, a flicker of purpose amidst the agony. I focus inward, retreating from the pain and the commander's gloating smirk, and find solace in my blood magic, for therein lies life, for therein lies my only hope of salvation.

I embrace my child along with the million threads linking me to my fey, but even as I do so, along with my elemental magic, my blood magic fades, then disappears completely, and I'm left hollow.

For the first time in centuries, I am truly, utterly, alone.

***

CHAPTER IV

'You may leave us.'

The buzzing stops abruptly, and the invisible force ripping through my body vanishes.

I pray for relief, but there's none to be had.

My limbs continue to spasm, rebelling against the torment they've endured. If not for the restraints binding me, I'd flop uncontrollably like a fish gasping on dry land.

The All Father's gentle order nonetheless sends the two Icelandians scurrying from the room like scolded children, the door creaking closed behind them. Their proud figures are bent, broken by fear of whatever they've witnessed or experienced. How could such a mighty warrior race have been reduced to this? The answer probably lies in the table I'm bound to and the torture I've endured.

I'm left alone with the All Father, his ever-present bodyguard, and the commander. Every day they hover like carrion birds, hour after torturous hour, hungry for the smallest crack in my resolve. The All Father rarely talks, pressing his hands together, whispering silent prayers, whilst the commander gloats, demanding answers, revelling in my pain, yet their frustration mounts.

I have held strong

But now, I teeter at the edge of my endurance, barely sustained by the water splashed on my face to keep me conscious and cleanse the stench of my suffering. Without it, I'd have succumbed long ago.

'Well, what do we have here?'

The All Father leans in close, wetting his lips, his face lit by a genuine smile, and for once, I'm fearful of why.

His gloved finger gently strokes my nose, and as he draws it away, for the first time in four hundred years, I see … my blood, black as night, staining the tanned leather.

He rubs it between his fingers, his face alight with exultation, as if he's witnessed something divine. His eyes close as he prays, looking to the ceiling, his lips moving silently.

'It appears that whatever dark magic once protected you has been defeated by the power of Astorian science and our faith in the One God,' he whispers. 'Your ssythlan followers perished by the hundreds to perfect our methods.'

The All Father's smile broadens. A parody of joy, saved not for love, not for the birth of a child, but for my defeat. For this moment.

'Dagger,' he says, extending his hand.

Asmodial swiftly passes his weapon.

'I believe the time for justice and the beginning of your journey toward redemption has finally arrived,' the All Father murmurs, his voice low and reverent, as if the act he's about to commit is sacred.

He cuts across my arm with deliberate precision, watching through tear-filled eyes as though he's sharing the pain.

For me, the pain is still distant, a dull echo, my body already so broken that the new wound barely registers. The All Father inspects the blade, the blackness of my blood reflected in his eyes.

'Only a creature of pure evil would have blood as black as night,' he murmurs softly, his words spoken with reverence. 'How many brothers and sisters of mine died over the millennia because of you and your kind?'

He pauses, as if hoping for an answer, but I refuse to humour him.

'Hundreds of thousands!' he says sadly, full of regret. 'But soon their spirits will know peace, and maybe one day, yours too.'

'May I?' the commander interjects, then smiles gratefully as the dagger is passed across.

I thought he'd just wanted to see my blood on the weapon, but he's Astorian, and I should have known better.

He leans over me, the dagger hovering above my face.

'I'd take your disgusting eyes out,' he taunts, 'but I believe the All Father wants you to see your death coming.'

With a spiteful flourish, he slashes both my cheeks. The pain is sharper now, fresh and cruel, but I refuse to show it, and hiss, baring my teeth instead. Blood trickles down to the back of my neck, and inside, I weep in pain and frustration.

The All Father sighs, shaking his head slowly as if in disapproval.

'Self-control, Asmodial, is sometimes as testing as faith,' he berates the commander softly. 'Hold still your righteous anger for now until it's the right time to mete out justice.'

He leans in closer, sniffing, as if he can smell my fear, or hopes I'll beg for mercy, but I'll never give him that satisfaction.

'Asmodial, being a vengeful man, thinks I should bury you alive,' he muses. 'But no. Astoria's troops will be uplifted and enamoured to see your corpse before they vanquish your fey beyond the gate.'

'Do you plan to bore me to death?' I sneer. 'Or perhaps you'll get so close that I suffocate on the stench of your deformed flesh!'

My attempt to rile him fails. He merely rocks back, looking vaguely disappointed at my outburst.

'No. Asmodial here will cut the nose from your face first, then your ears, and lips. Then, limb by limb, he'll dismember you, cauterising the wounds as he does so. After, when you're nothing more than a torso, you'll be hung in a gibbet. For a short while, you'll receive the same looks of pity you've aimed at me and finally appreciate the suffering I've endured my whole life, until that is, the crows take your eyes.'

Asmodial claps his hands together, the sound sharp and eager, like a child unable to contain his glee. The twisted delight in his eyes is unmistakable. He's relishing the prospect of carving me apart piece by piece.

'Ashan,' the All Father says softly.

The slinger snaps to attention.

'Organise food and refreshments. The commander and I will dine here tonight ... there's so much to do.'

Ashan hesitates, looking at me meaningfully.

The All Father laughs kindly at his concern.

'The Queen of Beasts is tamed, Ashan. Her claws and fangs have been removed. Now, go.'

Ashan touches the brim of his hat in salute and leaves, the heavy door creaking behind him.

The All Father closes his eyes, his lips moving in silent incantation or prayer, while Asmodial watches with the eager patience of a loyal dog.

'You'll die tomorrow,' the All Father says, his voice measured. 'But how you spend your final hours depends on your cooperation. Repent early. Sharing details of your world and the fey awaiting us there will save Astorian lives, and you, a lot of pain, at least this night.'

I say nothing, and spit instead. My throat is parched, and not much hits the All Father. What little there is, lands on his cheek and his expression flickers briefly before amusement twists his lips into a pained smile.

'How many gargoyles are there?' Asmodial demands, his voice brimming with menace.

I say nothing, just stare stonily back at him.

The All Father sighs, shaking his head.

'Commander, as a warrior of the One God, use whatever means you deem necessary to extract all the information you can.'

Asmodial's gloved hand grabs mine, and he thrusts the tip of his dagger under my thumbnail.

I scream, albeit briefly, before I clamp my mouth shut. But it's too late. The satisfaction on his face is harder to bear than the pain itself.

Hold on, Malina. Don't give them the satisfaction!

'How many gargoyles are there?' he demands again.

I hiss, baring my incisors.

'Can I pull those out?' Asmodial asks, his voice brimming with malice.

The door creaks as a subtle breeze wafts into the room. I inhale deeply, savouring the air, savouring the moment, knowing death is approaching, and with it, freedom … of a kind.

'In a way, it's a shame you won't live to witness the Astorian army kill every last fey,' the All Father says, nodding at the commander, who is staring at my teeth with a malicious grin.

I'm suddenly overcome with emotion and can't stop the tears as they run down my cheeks.

'Don't kill them,' I whisper hoarsely, forcing the words past the lump in my throat. 'Just subdue them!'

'You don't subdue a rabid animal. You put it down!' Asmodial laughs.

The All Father, in a rare show of emotion, laughs along with Asmodial at his comment, but they slowly fall silent as mine lifts above theirs.

I laugh. Despite the fact my body is wracked by cramps, my every nerve burning as if on fire. I laugh, despite the blood running from my wounds, and despite the army waiting to invade and slaughter my fey.

'What's so funny?' Asmodial demands angrily.

'I'm sorry,' I say, struggling to suppress my emotions. 'It's just that, when I said, don't kill them, I wasn't asking you to spare my fey.'

The door clangs shut and the commander spins around with a gasp as the All Father jumps at the unexpected noise. They look back to me, suddenly unsure, and well they might be.

'I was asking my fey to spare you!' I say, holding them with my gaze.

As realisation dawns, they are wrenched to the ground. The All Father and Asmodial choke, clawing at their throats, their faces turning a violent shade of red, panic etched into every line.

Four shades shimmer into view. Two of them have their arms locked around the Astorians' necks, their grip unrelenting. The other two disarm the commander with practiced ease.

Shades are the darkest of the fey. To look at them is to see the face of true evil itself, or so I once thought. The thing with shades, is that I'm sure they don't feel. They don't value life, except their own, they see every creature as a potential food source, and have no qualms about eating flesh of any kind. They don't understand remorse or love, happiness, or sadness. They are devoid of all emotion.

However, they have two qualities that make them invaluable.

One of the qualities they possess that exceeds all others, is loyalty. The other that led them to me, is that being magical creatures themselves, they'd followed the threads that bound us before they were severed, slipping past all the guards at the gate, invisible, untouchable, unstoppable.

'Nogotha.'

No serpent, no ssythlan, no living creature, other than a shade can speak my name as though it's being whispered by death itself. Their voices are ancient, the rustle of long fallen leaves, and the mournful howl of a forgotten wind, muffled by the hollowness of decay.

'Thank you, my children,' I gasp, tears of relief and joy streaking my face.

Fingers with blackened, pointed nails, quickly release me from my restraints, yet, however much I will myself to sit, to move, my body is twisted, bent, not yet mine to control.

But that's why I wanted Asmodial alive. His life force alone won't restore me fully, but it's a start.

I only wish I had days to make him scream.

Instead, I likely have less than half an hour before the slinger, Ashan, returns to discover their corpses and me missing, and once an alarm is raised, there will be blood.

I'm picked up like a child and gently placed on the floor next to Asmodial's quivering form. The shades know what I need. After all, I am Saer Tel.

One shade clamps a hand over Asmodial's mouth, twisting his head to expose the soft, vulnerable flesh of his neck. Two others hold his arms tightly, their silent presence a grim reassurance.

He whimpers, tears spilling down his cheeks, looking out the corner of his eyes as I grab hold of his tunic and pull myself closer to his neck.

'Beware she whose eyes are the colour of putrescence, for she is the Queen of Beasts and death is her companion,' I quote, remembering his words. I snarl, stretching the moment, allowing him to see my pointed incisors, ensuring he feels the cold hand of death before it claims him.

I bite.

My teeth pierce his skin, and I feel the satisfying pop as flesh gives way. His blood surges into my mouth, warm and potent, and his body spasms violently in protest. The shades hold him steady, their unyielding grip preventing any escape.

The frantic rhythm of his heartbeat is intoxicating. I savour each pulse as I draw his life to replenish mine. Strength flows back into my limbs, a glimmer of vitality returning to my broken form.

As I drink, a question long buried rises to the surface of my mind.

I'd often wondered whether or not the fey would love and follow me if they weren't bound by blood magic. If the shades are anything to go by, I now know the answer.

Their loyalty and love are unconditional.

Asmodial's heart thumps a final time, and releasing his limp body, I turn my bloodstained face toward the All Father.

Unlike Asmodial who'd been petrified, his eyes are closed, his lips moving, whispering incantations or prayers, though neither will save him.

'Dagger!'

Izetha, a shade elder, places Asmodial's weapon into my waiting palm, and I drag myself over the floor until I'm kneeling beside the All Father. My body is ripped by cramps, but I refuse to succumb, and hold myself steady.

His eyes snap open and for the first time, he doesn't hide behind a veneer of civility or sadness. His glare is full of hatred, but a surprising absence of fear.

'In a way,' I say, my voice cold and steady, 'it's a shame you won't live to see the victorious fey annihilate every last Astorian.' I offer him a faint smile. 'With you dead, I have a feeling Astoria won't last long.'

I nod at the shade, who relaxes his grip.

Father gasps, his breath rasping like a bellows.

'You cannot kill me,' he whispers, his voice hoarse but defiant. He gestures weakly toward the dagger. 'I'm immortal. Nor can you evade the consequences of your heinous crimes so easily. So, believe me when I say, Astoria will invade, and I'll forever rule your world.'

There's such a steadfast belief in his words that, for a moment, doubt grasps me in its clammy hands.

I've no wish to further converse with this man, nor drink his blood. Instead, I push the dagger into the All Father's chest, and ... it doesn't penetrate.

NO!

Then, to my relief, it grates past his ribs.

Pulling the dagger free, I stab again, the point entering one side of his neck and coming out the other.

Blood froths over his lips as he chokes on his own blood, and I'm satisfied by the sudden look of pain and horror, as he recognises his immortality is nothing but a dream. He dies quicker than he deserved.

Despite feeling half dead, I'm elated.

Astoria's leader and his commander lie dead, and my loss and suffering suddenly seem a small price to pay.

Now, it's time to return home.

There's just one small problem.

I can't even walk, and unlike my shade rescuers, nor can I become invisible. I turn toward the shade elder who'd released me.

'Izetha. Strip him,' I say, nodding at Asmodial.

Dressing up in the commander's uniform might help me pass unnoticed at a distance and assist in my escape. It's the only hope I have.

I just have to hope luck favours me and the fey, because if the invasion still goes ahead, I'm not sure what we can do to defeat such an army armed with weapons of destruction far beyond what we possess.

I half chuckle as I consider eating Asmodial's brains, to see if I can somehow find the answer there. But I'm no savage. I'm a civilised fey after all.

Tearing the dagger free from the All Father's neck, I plunge it through his eye just to make sure, and … because it makes me feel better, then wipe the blade clean on his robes, removing any trace of his foul blood.

Yes. I'm definitely civilised.

***

I'm as weak as a day old kitten, but like the small feline, I can walk, albeit unsteadily, and have the sharpest of claws.

Discarding the soiled rags I'm wearing, I pull on Asmodial's uniform. I'm muscular enough that his clothes fit although they're a bit long on the sleeves. His boots are somewhat large, but manageable. The All Father had smaller feet, but his sandals won't exactly fit the image I'm looking for, even from a distance.

I punch a new hole in the leather belt to accommodate my smaller waist, and secure it tightly. The holstered gun, unfamiliar yet reassuring, sits at my hip, alongside a pouch of ammunition. The dagger slides easily into its sheath. The weight of these weapons steadies me. It's a small blessing to be armed, even if I'm barely fit to stand, let alone fight.

Izetha, ever my silent protector, takes his dagger to my hair, cutting it short, helping to mask my femininity. However, my skin, my eyes, my injuries, will all undermine my disguise the moment someone gets a close look. The illusion is fragile at best.

'I don't have the strength to go far or fast,' I admit, swaying slightly, wondering how long I can stay on my feet. Days could pass before I regain anything resembling real strength, and we need to escape now. 'Lead the way.'

'Return whence we came, we cannot.' Izetha rasps, his words a dry rustle. 'Many Astorians.'

Izetha clicks his tongue, and he and the other shades disappear.

'By your side, I be, Nogotha.' The voice emanates from nothingness.

The door creaks open, and every heartbeat lasts a lifetime until an unseen hand as cold as the grave grips mine, tugging me toward freedom or death. A gentle pressure has me stop, and we stand still, the silence broken by my laboured breath.

Again, the gentle tug, and I try with every fibre of my being to walk straight as I'm guided left out of the door. My captors have always entered from the right, so Izetha is taking me somewhere new. But as behind us there are distant voices, laughter, even shouting, I'm not going to argue.

My cell door closes as if of its own volition, bolts sliding home, and a padlock on each clicked shut.

I must have been deemed an escape risk.

A long corridor stretches ahead, lined with over fifty metal doors a side, each likely leading to a cell like mine. There's a similar number of cells behind us too. So much misery is held within these depths.

At the far end, a metal stairwell beckons under a flickering light.

'Up good,' Izetha whispers.

Yet within a few steps, my body convulses in pain, and only Izetha's invisible grip keeps me from collapsing.

'I carry you!'

It makes sense, speed is crucial. At any moment, someone might return to discover the bodies in my cell, and as there's only one direction we'll have taken to escape, the hunt will be on immediately.

But instead of agreeing, an idea forms, perhaps reckless, but the situation is desperate.

'Have your kin open the cells as we pass,' I murmur. 'Free the prisoners, and if anyone's restrained, release them. But I'll walk, with your support.'

Izetha rattles off a few clicks and doors start creaking open, offering those inside a chance at freedom, albeit a small one.

The shades' language is the only one I've never mastered. The strange clicks that emanate from deep within their throat too alien for me to have untangled. It also communicates far faster than the common tongue that all races learn.

Focusing on each step, I fight to keep moving, Izetha a pillar of strength at my side. Memories of my trials as a Chosen resurface. Life or death. This is no different. I'm vulnerable, a mere mortal again, and if I fail, I die.

No. I'm no mere mortal.

I'm Saer Tel and the blood, the life force I've taken, will help me recover far faster than anyone has a right to do so, if only I live long enough.

With every step, I loosen cramped muscles, force myself to walk taller, take longer strides, and steady my breathing. This façade won't last long, but it has to, at least until I've reached the stairs.

Behind me, murmurs swell into a chorus of shouts and cries. Prisoners stumble into the corridor, many weak and disoriented, but others with strength enough to stand tall. The sound grows louder, a rising tide of chaos.

I don't look back, I just continue my battle of wills. Mind over body, and all the while, the cell doors open as if by magic when I pass.

By the time I reach the end of the corridor, I can barely stand. Turning, I face a filthy, drawn, desperate mob. Some are naked, others have filthy rags, but whatever sex or size, they stare at me with undisguised hatred.

But not because I'm fey. Not because I'm Nogotha. In this gloom, I doubt they can even tell.

It's because I'm wearing an Astorian officer's uniform.

If they release that anger at me, even with my shades, I'll be torn to pieces.

I draw Asmodial's gun and level it at the mob. My hands tremble from weakness, but I force them steady. I don't even know how to use the weapon properly, but that doesn't matter. The sight of it is enough to give them pause. The grumbling stills, replaced by a tense, uneasy quiet.

'All you desire is behind you,' I shout, my voice carrying perfectly along the narrow corridor. 'Your families, freedom … revenge for the pain you've suffered.'

'And who are you?' demands a stocky man who could be either Icelandian or Astorian. His eyes are hollow, he's covered in burns, and looks half broken, but there's no denying the strength of his gaze or limbs. 'You aren't an Astorian commander, that's for sure!' he declares.

'I'm the woman who killed my captors and set you free!'

His demeanour softens.

'Your name. Tell me your name. I owe you a debt of gratitude, one I'll never forget.'

'My name is …' I pause. If they know I'm the Fey Queen, they might still turn on me. 'My name is, Malina.'

'Hah! In Icelandian lore, that name's considered very lucky. It seems fitting you should have it,' the man says. 'My name is Grishen. Thank you, Malina.'

Grishen is Icelandian then, and a short one at that.

Izetha pulls insistently on my hand, but I resist, and knowing Grishen is Icelandian, I slide the gun and pouch along the ground.

He scoops them up, holding them uncertainly, but then grins broadly, as if I've given him the keys to the kingdom instead.

With a final nod, he turns, then pushes his way back through the packed corridor, the mob milling uncertainly in his wake.

Invisible hands hold my arms either side as I'm almost carried up the stairs, my feet barely touching the metal steps.

Everything here has been stripped of nature's magic, beaten and forged into conformity. Whether it's metal or stone, even absent my powers, this place screams out in pain. A pain I know only too well.

After two turns of the metal stairwell, I'm lifted into cold arms, the smell of decay washing over me preferable to the sterility of this cold, lifeless place.

'Outside is up,' Izetha rustles as he carries me. 'Below ground we are!'

I don't want to fall asleep, I need to stay awake, to lead my children.

But it's their turn to look after me, and as those sinewy, bony arms hold me lovingly, my eyes close.

***

Wailing unlike anything I've ever heard rouses me from a fitful slumber.

It's dark, and rain is falling with a vengeance, as if the skies are crying, trying to rid the world beneath of the filth that covers it. Sadly, it's a losing battle.

'Nogotha.'

Izetha's raspy voice draws my attention. I realise I'm lying in his lap, his bony arms cradling me like a child. We're huddled in the shelter of a towering chimney, its cracked bricks slick with rain. He leans close, the gaping wound of his mouth almost touching my ear.

'Slept an hour. Prisoners and guards fight below. No escape, risk too high.'

The wailing from before is clearer now. It's an alarm, shrill and persistent, but it can't drown out the chaos beneath us. Gunshots crack sporadically, punctuated by agonised screams.

Izetha directs clicks at a nearby shade, rattling them off like hailstones on a roof.

'Coast clear. We go!' he says.

The shade he was talking to steps forward, her skeletal hands taking mine. She lifts me from Izetha's embrace, helping me stand, but to my shame, I'm still unsteady on my feet.

Another shade appears, also offering support, and we walk through the downpour across the open roof toward the edge. It reminds me of the first time I visited High Delnor, seeing everything in black and white, the lightning, the disorientation.

Strange how such old memories are coming to the present.

Despite the darkness, old habits die hard, and I kneel at the roof edge, carefully peering over, the shades on either side of me fading from sight. Izetha watches over us a few steps behind.

Four stories below, the courtyard is a grim tableau. Corpses lie scattered across the mud and cobblestones, at least a dozen inmates and two guards, their lifeblood mingling with the rain.

There's a tragic pattern to the deaths, an obvious attempt by these former inmates to reach the spiked metal railings that enclose the compound. Several bodies are impaled on the spikes, others made it a few steps beyond.

Off to the right, a squad of Astorian troops staggers off, their muskets clutched in tired hands as they march toward the sounds of distant fighting.

Suddenly, a crash shatters my calm.

'Stay right there!' The voice bellows above the storm.

I twist around to see an officer raise a gun, as troops bearing muskets swarm onto the roof from behind him to form a line abreast.

Suddenly, his throat opens up, spraying blood everywhere

The officer grasps at the terrible wound, firing blindly, and a shade appears, stumbling away, only to be brought down in a tangle of black robes by a ragged volley of musket fire, another victim of these horrible weapons.

Invisible hands under my armpits lift me urgently to my feet.

'Jump!'

I'm absent my magic, but shades are magical themselves, and I trust them with my life, whereas staying here will be my death.

I leap backwards, as though I'd rather commit suicide than face capture, but instead of plummeting to instant death, I'm held tightly and drift down toward the spiked railings, my rigid arms like broken wings.

'She's still alive!'

The soldier shouts from the rooftop, drawing his friends' attention, but suddenly topples over the edge, screaming as he plummets to his death.

Another appears, his musket pointing toward me, and follows his erstwhile comrade, almost as though he's overbalanced.

A third follows.

The troops must realise they're not alone.

Bangs and flashes light up the low-hanging clouds as they seek to kill Izetha who'd remained to cover our escape.

Our progress is slow, and every heartbeat seems one too many as we drift toward safety. The shades reappear and our ascent quickens as their magical power is drained. Like all magical creatures, their reservoir is limited, and theirs is almost empty.

'The perimeter railings pass a handspan beneath my feet, and then we drop to the ground.

Bright flashes continue to erupt from the rooftop.

Bullets ping and whine from the metal spikes and the cobblestones, sparks flying. Suddenly, the shade on my left tumbles forward.

He struggles to his feet, and I grab his arm, lending what feeble support I can of my own. Ahead, beyond the bodies, a dark alley beckons.

Ten steps.

Another ragged volley from the rooftop.

Nine.

Individual shots whine by.

The wounded shade gets hit again, he lurches, but keeps going.

Eight. Seven. Six.

A zip is followed by a thwack as the shade gets hit a third time. He goes down, crawls forward, then collapses just shy of safety.

Then, we're into the darkness and beyond the reach of those terrible muskets.

Lightning flashes and thunder rumbles, reverberating through my stomach as we push along noisome alleyways sitting between rows of large warehouses. Rats squeak in displeasure as we kick our way through sodden refuse and uplifted cobblestones.

We stumble across occasional bodies of inmates and soldiers but don't stop to check if they're alive.

'I can't go on much longer,' I gasp as I slip and almost fall on the slimy ground.

It's imperative we get as much distance between us and the compound as possible. The bodies show they've already got search parties out, not just for me, but for the other inmates who've escaped.

I wonder what kind of men and women they were. Were they thieves, murderers, or rapists?

Not that it matters, although the prisoner who'd spoken to me, Grishen, had seemed decent. Maybe they were dissenters, political prisoners rather than criminal scum.

The rain is relentless, and we force ourselves on, heads lowered against the stinging onslaught, turning away from the shouts, screams and occasional bangs. We need to find a cellar or an open door into a warehouse. Somewhere to hide, to lay low. A night of rest will do wonders for my recovery. I owe it to all the fey who've died trying to save me to get back alive, or their sacrifices will have been in vain, but it's all I can do to stop myself collapsing.

'HALT!'

The command booms through the alley, and I stagger to a stop more from sheer exhaustion than obedience.

Four soldiers with muskets raised block the narrow alley. I'd blundered right into them, hidden by the rain, caught up in my own exhaustion, and I wasn't the first. At their feet lies the body of a man.

'Kill the fey scum!' screams a heavyset woman, sighting down the barrel of her weapon, seeing through my poor disguise, the shade at my side an unmistakable giveaway.

I squeeze the shade's cold hand, then roll to the side just as the muskets go off. One bangs, but the others fizz in a long shower of sparks and smoke, and then I'm amongst them.

As I come out of my roll at the feet of the big woman, I'm too weak to even stand, but she makes the mistake of throwing her musket aside instead of clubbing me with it. As she grabs for the dagger at her waist, I bury my blade deep in her stomach, and rip down and sideways.

'Gods help me!' she screams, sinking to her knees, holding on to her innards that flop out through her tunic.

Flashing lightning and a long roll of thunder drown out her final words as I twist frantically aside from a musket butt and stab the dagger down through my attacker's boot, then again into the side of his thigh an instant later.

He falls back, slamming onto the slick cobblestones, writhing in agony, and I crawl up over his legs, stabbing into his flesh to help me do so, finally driving my blade into his chest.

I roll off, blinking frantically against the rain as I look left and right, gasping for breath, searching for the next threat.

But there are none.

The shade kneels over the bodies of the two remaining soldiers, her form hunched and shrouded. She turns to me, her hollow eyes locking with mine, kisses her long wavy blade in salute, and then falls to her side.

'No!' I cry.

My fingers find purchase enough to pull myself over the cobblestones, but she's already dead and beginning to decay by the time I reach her.

One of her victims groans, clutching at a chest wound, blood bubbling from his lips as he struggles weakly against death's grasp.

I'm not injured, just broken from the torture, but I sink my teeth into his neck, finishing what the shade had started, ensuring a swift recovery.

I crouch, catching my breath, steadying myself amongst the mud, the blood, and filth. The downpour gets even worse, as if trying to wash away the stains of humanity, but it defeats even this deluge.

A faint groan has me turn, dagger ready to strike, but it's not an enemy. It's the crumpled figure of the man the troops had subdued before we came along. He's bound, but alive, and as I bend over him, I recognise the broad features.

Grishen.

As I cut his bonds, I wince, noting a lump the size of an egg that graces the side of his bloodied forehead. He'd probably been hit with a musket.

'You, again?' he groans, his eyelids fluttering, as he tries to focus.

Shouts from close by have me look around desperately.

'Move or die,' I hiss.

I look up. Once upon a time, the rooftops were my sanctuary.

The old brickwork of the warehouse wall beckons, and I stumble over, uncaring as to Grishen's fate. I've given him a second chance at life, now what he does with it is beyond my control.

Keep going, Malina, I tell myself. *The fey need you, and so does Lotane, never more so than now.*

I smile as a new thought fills my mind.

Perhaps it's me who needs them now, more than ever.

With a determined breath, I grasp the rough edges of the brickwork and begin to climb.

I will do whatever it takes to return to my children … to my love.

Whatever it takes.

***

CHAPTER V

Daylight.

As I open my eyes, smoke belches like an evil spirit from the four looming chimney stacks I'd wedged myself between, joining the ever present filthy black clouds.

I've no idea what burns far beneath me within the factory I'd taken shelter on, but the warmth emanating from the brickwork had kept me warm throughout the storm until it had eventually blown over. That and Grishen, who'd wedged himself in first.

He'd followed me uncertainly the night before, then passed out, unconscious, long before I'd allowed myself the luxury of sleep. Grishen carried no weapons, something I'd made sure of, so I don't consider him a threat, though his physical strength is obvious.

My body is reluctant to move, still aching with the rawness of a fragile, almost human form. The immunity I inherited from Nogoth is gone, leaving me soft, vulnerable, and weak.

Only the strong survive, Malina.

Lystra's words cut through the fog in my mind like a blade as if she were standing beside me. I sit carefully, trying not to wake Grishen, driven by the memory of her scornful gaze.

'Gods!'

I clamp my mouth shut, my heart hammering, but the word has already escaped my lips.

'Nogotha.'

Izetha stands before me.

His presence pulls me from my misery, and for the first time in what feels like centuries, a glimmer of hope pierces the darkness. I'm not the only fey left in this gods-forsaken world. I was lost, but now I am found.

Grishen stirs, groaning and yawning before his eyes snap open. His gaze settles on Izetha, and his reaction is immediate, panic-stricken.

'What the hells is that?'

He flattens himself against the brickwork, patting himself down for a weapon. He has none, I'd made sure of that already.

'My friend,' I say firmly.

Grishen's eyes widen further as he studies me in the daylight for the first time.

I'm not interested in dealing with his concerns, as long as he doesn't do anything stupid, so turn back to Izetha.

'By what magic did you find me?'

'Not magic. Smell. Intuition.'

'We need to return to the world gate immediately. Do you know the way?'

Izetha nods.

'How far?'

'Rooftops. A day.'

'I slept a long time,' I say, noting the faded orb of the sun, its light barely penetrating the murk as I shuffle from my makeshift resting place, stretching muscle sore from both torture and battle.

'You're b-both f-fey?'

I shoot Grishen a warning look over my shoulder, holding him with my gaze. I don't regret saving him, although if he interrupts me again …

'You're real … not just fey tales!' Grishen's voice is thick with disbelief, and he shakes his head as if in denial. 'I knew there was something different when I first saw you.'

'Is there going to be a problem, Grishen?' I ask, my voice sharp, trying to cut through his rising hysteria.

'Beware she whose eyes are the colour of putrescence, for she is the Queen of Beasts and death is her companion!'

Grishen's finger shakes as he points at Izetha.

'I thought everything we were taught was lies. But you're here. You're coming to kill us all,' he continues in a strangled voice.

Despite the weakness clawing at my limbs, I lean over him.

'We're NOT here to kill everyone. But if it makes you feel better or stops you talking, I can make an exception!'

Grishen pales, hands raised in trembling surrender

'It's just that I was taught from birth to fear the return of the fey. You are the death of this world. How do you expect me to react?'

Izetha's wavy dagger appears, gleaming in the dim light, and Grishen closes his mouth with a snap.

'Grateful would be a start,' I snap, irked by his comment.

Grishen flinches but recovers quickly, bowing his head.

'Forgive me,' he whispers. 'Thank you for my life, and freedom. As I said once before. I owe you a debt and won't forget it.'

I nod, softening slightly. It's not his fault. Once upon a time, he'd have been right.

'Look,' I begin. 'Once, those tales were true. In ancient times, the fey did exactly as you were warned. They came through the world gate once every millennium, destroyed kingdoms, killed hundreds of thousands, and enslaved even more. But the last time was over four thousand years ago. It was stopped, never to happen again.'

'That's not what we're led to believe by the Astorians,' Grishen says, his voice tinged with doubt but not disbelief.

I shrug. What's the point in trying to unravel his brainwashing? Then I remember my own indoctrination. Just like I had, he's willing to question what he's been told.

'What stopped it?' Grishen asks, leaning forward.

'Not what. Who.'

Grishen flinches as Izetha addresses him, but ploughs on.

'Who stopped it then?'

Izetha's skeletal finger points at me.

'Nogotha!'

Grishen shakes his head. If he continues to do that, I'm likely to cut it off, but I have a soft spot for Icelandians. Kralgen ensured that.

Kralgen.

I haven't thought of my old friend in so long. It hurts to think his bones are long turned to dust. I wonder if his descendants still live. Could Grishen be part of his bloodline?

No.

I choke back laughter at the thought of Kralgen siring a line of short, stocky Icelandians.

Grishen looks at me expectantly, and I can't fathom any harm in opening up a little more.

'I defeated the King of the Fey, Nogoth. Afterward, I took his mantle, and led the fey from this world never to return.'

Grishen covers his filthy face with blackened hands, perhaps hoping I'll have disappeared when he removes them. Then they drop to his lap as if he hasn't the strength to hold them up anymore.

'In Icelandian lore,' he murmurs. 'Malina is a hero, the woman who saved humanity. She drove the defeated fey from this world, and legend says, one day she'll return in our hour of greatest need. But the Astorians ...' He hesitates. 'They call her Nogotha, Queen of Beasts, spawn of the devil, the death of humanity. '

'I am both Malina and Nogotha,' I say softly. 'But my fey are no beasts.'

'So you're claiming that ...' Grishen shakes his head. 'You're claiming that you're the same figure as in both Icelandian and Astorian legend?'

I incline my head with a gentle smile.

'The same, and I'd like to think different at the same time.'

'That would make you thousands of years old!'

I consider explaining that time works differently on the other side of the world gate, but there's no point. I'm old, whether I'm four thousand or four hundred years.

'Have I aged well?' I ask.

Grishen snorts, and the tension between us eases a little.

He pauses for thought, and so do I. His comments have left me unexpectedly warm. So many times Lotane had tried to assure me of Kralgen's love, and of how deeply my banishment cut him. I'd never truly reconciled myself with what I thought had been his betrayal, until now. His way of making amends, of coming to terms with his own actions, had been to have my name remembered as a saviour.

Damn. I loved you, Kralgen.

'So, are you the saviour of humanity, or its death?' Grishen mutters, trembling.

He's asking that question of himself, not me, which is good, because I'm reluctant to release the memory of my old friend.

'So what now?' Grishen presses.

I shrug.

'I can't think beyond wanting to return home. To be with my people and those I love.'

Grishen nods, his shoulders sagging as he lets out a weary sigh.

'I wish I could return to my family too,' he whispers. 'But I'll never be able to.'

'Why not?'

'Because my parents are both dead,' he says, his voice heavy with regret, 'and I was sentenced to death for sedition, for daring to oppose our enslavement and the All Father's endless quest to destroy you and your people. Hundreds of my kinfolk die every year to fuel his crusade. I believe our people should be free and able to choose their own destiny, but I voiced my dreams in the wrong company.'

'Then, like me, you too must find a way to make your dreams come true,' I reply, holding his gaze. 'Now, which way is the world gate?'

Both a fleshy and a skeletal finger point south and a sense of urgency immediately takes hold. Getting there is the first hurdle, getting through it alive, likely an even bigger one.

'Izetha,' I say softly. 'If something happens to me, you must get word to Lotane. The Astorians plan to send a million strong army through the gate in six months.'

Izetha's head snaps toward me, surprise flaring in his hollow eyes.

'I know. It's hard to believe, but it's the truth.'

Grishen nods beside me, but before he can add anything, I push on.

'To make matters worse, the Astorians burnt every last shred of magic from me. Even if I make it through the gate, I can't bury it under a mountain. The fey will have to fight, steel and claw against muskets and cannon.'

Again, another nod. Izetha would have sensed I'd lost my magic already; however, he'd had no idea of the size of the Astorian army.

'Are you scared for your people, Izetha?' I ask.

'No. Survival we mastered. Hags, shades survive. Others perish.'

I mull over his words and realise the truth in them. They thrive in the darkness, the deeper the cavern, the more isolated, the better. I've embraced the darkness so many times, but the shades, and the hags, *are* the darkness. If they decided not to be found, human eyes would never discover them.

'You came for me, Izetha. Your fellow shades died for me when this war would have passed them by unnoticed. I'll never forget the deed and will strive to be worthy of such loyalty.'

That cowled head inclines.

Does he feel pain at the loss of his own kind? Does he feel remorse for coming?

No.

Shades don't feel as every other race does, of that I'm sure. Perhaps they're the lucky ones.

The clouds above flicker with occasional flashes of light, but I don't think it will rain. Still, traversing the rooftops won't be easy. I look down at my ill-fitting boots and uniform, knowing they won't serve me well.

Before I can voice my concerns, Izetha gestures toward a sack tucked between the chimneys. I tug it free, and laugh softly as I pull out black clothes and boots, serviceable and sturdy.

'You'd make a good husband, Izetha,' I say with a chuckle. 'Have you ever considered getting married?'

The unusual silence and shift in atmosphere has me look up to see him bowed, rocking slowly backwards and forwards.

'Married yesterday. Not today.'

The weight of his words hit me like an Astorian cannonball.

'Your wife came with you?'

'Wife. Offspring. Both.'

'Gods, no!'

My throat tightens. I've always believed shades don't feel, that they exist beyond such emotions. But seeing Izetha's tremble, I know how wrong I was.

'I'm so sorry, Izetha.'

'Why?'

'Because my life wasn't worth theirs, nor the dozens of gargoyles who came to save me either.'

'They believed so. I believe. All believe.'

I shake my head, utterly at a loss, the sudden guilt a heavier burden than I'd ever felt before.

Even with his head raised, it's hard to see Izetha's face.

'You Nogotha. You care all fey. Protect all. Yes?'

'Yes,' I whisper, my voice breaking under the weight of emotion.

'Then wife, offspring, at peace.'

Izetha offers nothing more, and Grishen wisely remains silent while I dress myself in the clothes and boots Izetha had sourced for me.

With a deep breath, I consider my position.

Whilst I have a dagger, I have no armour nor my magical powers. I'm in the midst of a hostile kingdom facing an enemy with deadly weapons to which I'm now utterly vulnerable. There's also the slight problem of a million strong army.

Enough, Malina. Think of the positives.

I have the love of my children, and Lotane, and a fey world who will unite behind me, and there's one more thing.

My training.

Before I was Nogotha, I was Malina, one of The Chosen.

Izetha looks south. He says nothing, but the meaning is obvious.

Grishen stands and clears his throat.

'For the life you gave me, and for the torture I endured, I want to assist in your escape. It's the least I can do.'

Will he be useful, or a hindrance? He likely knows this city, and might have information on the Astorian war machine. However, he could slow us down. He won't be trained for this.

Izetha's hissing sigh reminds me that the time for thinking is over. It's now time for action.

It's time to return to the world gate.

***

The checkpoint looms below, its presence stark and unyielding. Six soldiers stand at the ready, muskets gripped firmly, eyes scanning every approach, a guard dog tethered to a lamp post beside them.

'Papers!'

The demand reaches me easily, sharp and commanding

An arm thrusts outward, clad in the grim uniform of the Astorian military. From my perch above, I survey the road junction, now a bottleneck of tension.

Is this standard procedure, or the result of the prisoners' breakout from the compound? Irrespective, it's proving a problem.

'Security is always tight in the military sector,' Grishen mutters beside me, answering my unspoken question. 'Random checkpoints, patrols, and guards ...'

His words trail off as two men present a small book from their trouser pockets, and hold out their left arm. After a scrutinising glance, the soldiers lower their muskets and wave them through. Ahead, another checkpoint awaits the two men like a predator anticipating its prey.

'Those little books carry a stamp that matches a tattoo on the soldier's arm,' Grishen mutters. 'Soldiers get tattoos, but we get these.'

He rolls up a ragged sleeve to display ugly weals on his forearm where he's been branded like livestock.

'This is my identification number, and it also tells them where I work. Or used to, anyway.'

I sigh in sympathy, but also in frustration at our slow progress.

My mind drifts to a simpler time in my youth, a time before I understood the true scope of the war I'd stumbled into. Back then, I was just a righteous collector of souls, moving throughout the seven kingdoms with ease, leaping from rooftop to rooftop with the help of my magic. I'd felt invincible. But not now. Now, I'm a hunted fugitive and my mortality is painfully obvious.

Yet it's not my fear of falling, nor lack of power that hinders me.

It's Izetha.

Surprisingly, Grishen is mostly up to the task, but my loyal shade …

My ignorance of these magical beings led to me so many assumptions, and I know my disappointment is founded in that, but it still frustrates me.

My rescuer, a creature that can become invisible, and slay with near impunity, is nearing the limits of his endurance. His strength, once formidable, is waning, his abilities taxed from his role in rescuing me. Though his powers are not completely spent, Izetha dares not use them. We need him to pass through the world gate unseen, and if he exhausts himself now, all will be lost.

'We'll backtrack, move along a block or two, and try again.' I keep my voice low, steady, encouraging. Without him, I'd be dead. We'll take as long as necessary.

Izetha's bony shoulders slump almost imperceptibly beneath robes that catch and absorb the light, but he doesn't complain, that isn't the shades' way.

He turns around, Grishen and I following him back over the rooftops, reversing our progress. Up here we're untouchable, unseen, whereas down below, despite the time, the streets are full of yellowish light that flickers and fades one moment only to return to incandescence the next.

Beneath our feet, the populace sleeps, but even without Grishen's ongoing narrative as we travel, it's become obvious that this city is not a hub of trade or learning. So many buildings exude the acrid stench of industry, absent comfort or beauty and they all serve one purpose ...

Building or feeding the machines of war.

Everyone is either uniformed or wears strange garments that Grishen calls coveralls. It's an attempt to instil unity that to me, only serves to display oppression.

'Look there,' Grishen hisses, as we head north again.

Off to our right, what might once have been a park contains row upon row of cannons and wagons alongside similar weapons of war ... squat ugly creations, with mouth-shaped barrels pointing skyward like toads awaiting prey.

'Who are those young children?' I ask, surprised to see a small group out this late. They carry sacks and are escorted by two women wearing heavy robes.

'Orphans,' Grishen says followed by a soft sigh. 'Everyone is put to use, irrespective of age. They keep the streets clean or are used as servants when they're young and join everyone else in the factories when they're older.'

'And the women?'

'Sisters of the All Father's Church Eternal,' he growls. 'They preach love and forgiveness, and if you're Astorian, they're kind and nurturing. But if your heritage is from somewhere else ...'

I nod. Some things have changed so much, others are sadly familiar.

'Here,' I whisper, spotting a broken lamppost. It rises from the street below, offering a quick way down. Its light is long extinguished, and the road below is mercifully empty.

I glance at Izetha and a skeletal hand gestures for me to go first.

We've done this enough times now that I'm no longer bothered.

I approach the edge of the rooftop, gauge the distance, and then gently step off, flinging my arms and legs tightly around the wooden post as I fall. Squeezing tight, I slow my descent, then step away from the bottom of the post.

A few seconds later, Izetha joins me in a billowing mass of robes followed by Grishen with a heavy thump.

Ugly, red weals mar my forearms as I pull up my torn sleeves. This is about the tenth time we've done this tonight, and my skin is raw, a feeling long since forgotten.

Despite the numerous street lights, they're well spread out and the pools of darkness offer us plenty of opportunity to cross the road where we glide through the shadows, invisible, unnoticed, until we reach the next corner.

'Patrol behind us,' Grishen warns, his voice tense.

Ahead, another patrol is barely visible through a veil of steam rising from a sewer vent.

We're caught in the middle.

With a silent prayer, I glance quickly around the corner to discover the adjacent street is empty, and we cross swiftly, ducking into the shadows of yet another row of nondescript warehouses.

I grimace.

There's nothing redeeming about this city. The warehouse before me is built with the same ugly conformity as most everything else, a grotesque repetition of brick and iron with no individual design or flair. Sickly, yellow lights are evenly spaced about fifty paces apart. Windows are filthy, square panes. Doors are bland, with no embellishment. It's as if only one person, someone born devoid of hope or joy, designed the city.

Half a dozen chimneys rise up, evenly spaced, adjacent to one another, creating an ideal opportunity to access the roof.

'Go!'

Grishen climbs first. The mortar between the brickwork is corroded, giving him plenty of purchase to place one foot on the chimney to his right, the other in a crevice on the left, and up he goes, slowly, but surely.

'You next, my friend,' I whisper softly to Izetha. 'Take your time.'

Of course, every instinct shouts at me to hurry them up, but it would be foolhardy to do so. No one is in good shape, least of all Izetha.

He doesn't have Grishen's innate strength, nor has he been trained like me. He's also expended so much of his power coming to my rescue.

Izetha has only ascended to just above my head height when the sound of booted feet approach.

'I tell ya. I swear I saw summat,' someone grumbles.

'You're fantasising about me sister again, I reckon,' another chuckles.

I sink into the shadows between the two chimney stacks, my dagger behind my back. Izetha and Grishen freeze above me.

Six soldiers slog past, heads down, muskets in hand. One lingers, hesitating.

'I need a piss.'

He turns around, reaching out to lean his musket against the brickwork and I step from the shadows before he realises he's not alone.

His mouth opens to shout, but I drive the dagger up under his chin, a vicious blow that penetrates his brain, killing him instantly.

With a strength born of desperation, I hold him upright while I grab the falling musket.

'Just hurry up!' someone calls.

I pull the dead man into my arms, then push him into the corner. I quickly unbuckle his leather pouch belt, then sling his musket over my shoulder, and begin to climb.

Thankfully, the others, driven by a strength born of desperation, make the roof quickly, and I pull myself over the edge just as a shout of alarm pierces the silence.

We set off at a ragged jog across the rooftops, putting as much distance between ourselves and the commotion as possible.

When we get to the end of the street, and peer over the edge, two dozen soldiers are below, but they turn the corner, running toward the faint shouts and cries for help.

Once again, a lamp post beckons.

As I slide down, a curtain draws back from a window on the other side of the street and a burly man in night robes looks out. I can tell from his face we've been spotted as I run across the road into the alleyway adjacent to his building.

I turn back, and am surprised to see Grishen support Izetha as he reaches the ground. It appears he's getting over his fear of the shade. A common enemy or goal can help create allies of the unlikeliest people.

The others follow me into the shadows a few seconds later.

It's dark enough to forgo climbing to the rooftops again.

'Off you go. I'll catch up in a moment,' I say, urging them on with a gentle push.

As they head off, I look back along the street, it's empty apart from the form of the All Father that graces the face of most every wall.

Swiftly, I sidle along the front of the building and wait beside the door, counting silently in my head.

Ten. Nine, eight, seven … three, two …

There it is, the sound of crashing footfall.

The front door to the building is flung open, and I plunge my dagger straight into the burly man's heart.

He staggers back, a gun dropping from his hand, and I give him a shove, helping him on his way as he falls onto the hallway floor.

I wipe my dagger clean on his uniformed trousers, quietly close the door, and then head silently after the others, grinning darkly.

Two Astorian soldiers down. Nine hundred and ninety-nine thousand, nine hundred and ninety-eight to go.

***

The world gate.

To my eyes, these ancient constructs are as majestic as they are enigmatic. Scattered across the fey world, more than fifty stand as silent sentinels to a forgotten past. I've spent days at each one, marvelling at their towering forms, their elegant simplicity of design, and the aura of mysticism they exude. Smaller gates and strange structures accompany some, metal monoliths, stone circles, and other formations, some adorned with runes, others eerily bare.

How I've yearned to unlock their secrets, to find out where the gates lead, to discover new worlds, perhaps even new peoples. The opportunities, if I had ever managed to unlock them, could have been endless.

Yet, as I look at the one before me that leads home, I realise how foolish I've been. I sought adventure, something new and fascinating to end my tedium, but I could have just as easily stumbled across a species a hundred times worse than the Astorians, a thousand times more advanced.

What then for my fey?

Lotane had never supported my quest, and I'd teased him for being old and boring. Upon reflection, he was right all along.

What happens when two worlds are joined has been enacted out countless times. The fey were once dominant, and they conquered this world. Now, it's the Astorians who are the dominant power, and they are moving swiftly to exert it.

And once they conquer my world?

The thought chills me. The Astorians have the power, and, as Asmodial boasted, the science, to take everything. And knowing them, one conquest will never be enough. Why stop with one world when countless others will then lie within their reach?

'Look over there!'

The venom contained within Grishen's voice is palpable, and I follow his gaze.

I gasp, unable to believe what I'm seeing. It can't be. It just can't be.

The All Father.

I'd stabbed him in the chest, torn his throat out, and seen the life fade from his red eyes before I'd driven a dagger into his brain.

This can't be him ... it has to be someone else.

Yet who else would be dressed in white robes, with pale, translucent skin, and a mask covering the wound where a nose should be?

Whoever it is, stands out, glowing in the harsh glare of the many lights that now surround the world gate. He's the focal point of a huge amount of activity, the calm amidst the storm as he directs others to do his bidding.

Around him, ten slingers with a guard dog form a protective circle, their long coats and wide-brimmed hats marking them as his elite guards. They vet everyone who approaches, taking security seriously, yet the All Father greets all who do with a caring smile, or with hands clasped as if in joyful prayer.

Around them, masses of troops, cannons and wagons, are gathered, some passing through the gate even as I watch.

This isn't the million-strong invasion force, but perhaps the further two thousand reinforcements Captain Armana had said would be joining him.

Despite just over a week having passed since I was captured, not even a day has gone by in the fey world. There will be no one organised to oppose them. From the amount of cannons visible, I'm sure they're planning on reinforcing the already heavily fortified position around the gate, ensuring further troops can push through in safety.

'I think your escape has caused quite a stir,' Grishen murmurs. 'It's extremely rare to see the All Father outside of a nighttime. Did you know he's ruled for nigh on five hundred years and is supposedly immortal?'

I can barely tear my eyes away.

'He tortured me with his commander, Asmodial, before I escaped,' I whisper, still unable to believe my eyes.

'Really? *He* tortured you?'

'Every day. For someone who tries to appear fatherly and kind, I'm quite sure his soul is as dark as night.'

Grishen clenches his fists, his knuckles whitening.

'Gods. To the Astorians he's a benevolent ruler, a protector, a saviour. To us slaves, he's far worse than y ...'

'Worse than me?' I laugh softly.

'Worse than you're *supposed* to be,' Grishen says, looking sheepish. 'What he's done to my people and the others. We're starved, worked to death, and our women are often taken off the street, never to be seen again. Amway, I'd do anything to cut his throat.'

'I wouldn't bother,' I reply. 'It seems he really is immortal. I already stabbed him in the chest, cut his throat out, and stabbed a dagger through his eye, and yet there he stands!'

Grishen looks back and forth, from me to the All Father, his mouth opening and closing.

'When you said you'd killed your captors to escape. I had no idea!'

I shake my head.

'It doesn't matter now. What does is Izetha and me getting through that world gate. All I need is a diversion.'

'All you need is a miracle,' Grishen replies grimly.

Gods! I want to scream in frustration. To be so close but to be so far.

From where we hide on the rooftop of a large building, I could shoot an arrow through the world gate. But Grishen is right. It will take a miracle to get past so many troops and their damned muskets.

If only I hadn't drained my magic trying to open another world gate. *Stop it, Malina!*

Looking backwards doesn't help me move forwards.

'I need ideas. However improbable, speak your mind,' I urge, looking around for a weakness in the security.

Grishen doesn't hesitate.

'You kill a soldier and wear his uniform. I take a couple of shots at the All Father with the musket. You slip through the gate in the chaos, and I run.'

I nod appreciatively.

'Izetha?'

'Grishen idea good. But I kill All Father. In chaos, you escape.'

'Anything else?'

Silence is the only answer I get, but I can see they're thinking.

'Both your ideas have merit,' I say, a hollow feeling in my stomach. 'But only have the smallest chance of success. One lone gunman or a deadly shade trying to kill the All Father won't have thousands of troops leave a path to the gate. In fact, they're more likely to be alert, and I'd be challenged at some stage.'

We crouch in silence, searching for an alternative.

The monstrous factories belching smoke either side of the gate draw my eye. Interestingly, parts of the building are inside the perimeter.

Another plan takes shape in my mind.

'I could shimmy along that,' I say, pointing to the thick cabling that connects the factories to the world gate, 'drop down by the gate and pass through before anyone realises what's happening!'

Grishen frowns.

'What about the soldiers on the ramp, the wagon drivers and everyone on the other side?'

I'm silent for a while as I watch teams of oxen pulling cannons and powder wagons through the gate under the watchful eyes of an officer and a squad of soldiers who check the drivers and contents before waving them on. At least a hundred more wait their turn and more are joining the line every few minutes.

'I should be able to get through before they react. It's also night time on the other side of the gate. Izetha will cross first and create a distraction to draw people's attention away, and I'll just vanish into the darkness.'

'Plan good!' Izetha's hood rustles as he nods.

Grishen looks sceptical.

'So, I can see how you'll get into the factory,' he says, rubbing his bristled chin. 'The wagons going there aren't checked. However, crossing those cables ...' he shrugs.

'Crossing them won't be a problem.'

'I'm not doubting your abilities, but do you see that?' he says meaningfully as lightning arcs between the cables. 'If that happens while you're on them, it will be your undoing! Not forgetting you'll probably be seen and shot, or fall, and break your neck.'

Silence follows his statement.

'When go, Nogotha?' Izetha asks. 'Follow plan!'

A cold wind blows, heavy with the promise of rain. In the far distance lightning flashes and the rumble of thunder follows.

'When the storm hits,' I reply. 'It will mask our approach.'

'The soldiers' muskets will be useless too,' Grishen says thoughtfully.

'The gods are smiling on us then!' I say.

'But it will also make the cables slippery,' Grishen mutters.

I nod solemnly, he's right.

'The gods are truly capricious.'

'What about if I had a better plan?' Grishen asks.

Izetha hisses softly in warning, his wavy dagger appearing as if from nowhere.

'Nogotha's plan good. We go!'

Grishen looks affronted.

'With my one, we kill lots of Astorians.'

The wavy dagger disappears.

'Maybe yours better.' Izetha laughs.

Grishen winces at the sound but can't help but smile.

'It is, but it relies so much on you ...'

***

'Karson! I'm so glad you came.'

My little brother smiles as he lowers himself between the unmoving forms of Izetha and Grishen who are sharing first watch in the deep shadows of a chimney while I get some sleep.

They couldn't sleep, whereas I have no problem, but my slumber won't last long. The storm is approaching fast, and soon it will arrive, and that is when our plan will be put into action.

Karson's smile is warm, familiar, and for a moment, I can almost pretend everything is fine. I smile back, even as I brace for the inevitable. How long before his smile fades and he begins to scold me? Yet, I enjoy the moment for what it is.

'What no harsh words for me, little brother? Come now, don't keep me waiting.'

Karson shakes his head.

'If my words ever sounded harsh,' he says, with his sweet voice that warbles like a bird, 'be assured they were only ever spoken with love. You always looked after me, Alina, and you were often stern when you did. Can you blame me if I have only learned from you?'

I reach for him, wrapping my arms around his small waist, pulling him in close.

'I don't blame you!' I say, burying my head in his neck, enjoying the comfort of his little arms around me.

'The question is, have you ever learned from me?' he asks, his tone shifting, sternness creeping in. He slips from my grasp and steps out of my reach. 'The answer appears to be no!'

I raise my hands in defeat. I've learnt by now, I can never win with my little brother.

'Will you go on to make the same mistakes I warned you about just days ago?'

'No!' I say firmly. 'I listened to what you said. Soon I'll be home and do whatever it takes to protect the one I love and the world I call home.'

Karson sighs, his expression somewhere between sorrow and exasperation.

'You only heard what you wanted to hear, but you didn't listen and you didn't learn. These are now your futures, Alina. Look and see.'

The world shifts suddenly, the dark, smoke-filled night giving way to a brilliant day, and the stench of industry is replaced by the scent of a million blooms with fresh rivers running through lush meadows.

'Is this so bad?' I ask. 'To return home?'

But even as I speak, the idyllic scene twists. The corpses of thousands of fey appear around me, twisted, broken, scorched, and mutilated. The rivers run black with fey blood, while smoke chokes the sun, plunging the world into shadow. Lotane lies dead, half his face missing, and not far away I recognise my own corpse too.

Crunching boots has me look up from the horrific scene.

Ahead, an Astorian army stretches to the horizon. A million strong, ruthless, unstoppable. Absolute victors.

'It doesn't have to be like this,' I storm. 'We might win!'

The sun sets, darkness falls, then rises again.

Trolls and giants in their thousands charge, enough gargoyles to blacken the sky swoop, wolfen packs swarm like angry bees, and ogre hordes roar. The whole of the fey world has come together, and they are mighty.

This time, the piles of dead fey tower above and beyond anything Karson has previously shown me. Lotane's corpse is twisted and broken, riven by shrapnel. Of me, there's little left below the waist, just entrails and a shattered spine, white against the black.

A dozen more times the sun rises and sets, and each time the scenes are different, but the outcome remains the same.

'Is there a future where Lotane and I aren't killed?' I ask from my knees, having fallen under the weight of so much darkness.

'Only ones where you and Lotane take your own lives,' Karson whispers sadly. 'I only wish I knew what you should do, Alina, but I can only see what you've done, and what you shouldn't do.'

'But you're so wise, little brother.'

Karson laughs sadly.

'The words I speak are not always mine, Alina. I'm but a vessel, a conduit, but for what or whom, I'm not sure. But I feel the gravity of what I speak. Pay heed to my previous words, Malina, for therein lies the path you must take.'

I frown, confusion clouding my mind.

Karson shakes his head sadly.

'You said you'd listened. Must you always forget Alina? Just stop making the same mistakes. Remember. The child you ignored has grown to become something dark and malevolent without its mother's love and guidance. So, what would you do to keep the one you love, and the world you call home, safe?'

'Riddles. Always riddles!' I say, my frustration building. It helps to know it isn't Karson's fault, but I'm still tempted to shake the answer from him.

'Just remember my words, Alina, and think of me kindly. After all, family shouldn't argue.'

He begins to fade, and I know my time with him is over.

'Come here,' I say, opening my arms and he steps into my embrace gratefully.

We hold each other tight until he disappears, and I'm left with empty arms and an empty heart.

***

CHAPTER VI

I watch Izetha and Grishen, silently, not letting on I'm awake, impatient for the storm to hit, but dreading the moment it does.

My dream of Karson lingers. Is there a path that doesn't lead to death, for me, Lotane, and all the fey? The question is at the forefront of my thoughts, refusing to be dismissed.

The child I ignored had turned into the Astorian Empire, the All Father, or indeed both, dark and malevolent like Karson had said, and if I go through the gate and fight, death awaits.

So perhaps the answer is not to fight.

The fey world is vast. Perhaps it's large enough to hide in. Izetha has already said as much. His shades and the hags will survive for the simple reason they'll never be found.

Maybe survival lies in retreat, in disappearing into the wilderness, becoming something the Astorians cannot conquer because they cannot find us.

Rain starts to fall, heavy drops and my companions look over. We're safe on the rooftops, but exposed to the elements and they come over, and we huddle together against the brickwork of a large chimney that keeps us both a little warm and sheltered.

'The gods weep at mankind's folly,' I say, looking at Grishen.

'I have a feeling they're tears of laughter,' he replies with a chuckle, pulling the musket tight against his chest.

His thick fingers pull back the S-shaped hammer, cocking the weapon. I have to admit, he's been a font of knowledge about the different types of ordinance the Astorians use, the types of ammunition and how they work.

Without him, we wouldn't have our new plan.

He pulls out the cord that's coiled around the hammer.

'Dagger, please?'

I hand him my blade, and he uses it to cut the cord into two uneven lengths.

'As I said last night. This is match cord. It will burn even when damp.'

He opens a pouch and pulls out a small metal rectangle, flips its lid, then flicks his thumb across a small wheel. Sparks blossom until a small flame appears.

'Judging by the looks on your faces, you've never seen a lighter before,' he says, grinning. 'I guess you backward fey folk are still using flint and steel …'

Izetha's hiss matches mine and Grishen stops mid-sentence, letting the flame die away.

'I'm sorry. I joke when I'm nervous,' he says. 'Or when I like someone. I swore I'd do something like this ever since my parents died, but never thought the opportunity would arise. If only I could tell them …'

I rest my hand on Grishen's shoulder, a pang of guilt twisting in my chest. I hadn't really bothered to get to know him. There hadn't been the time, and I hadn't deemed it necessary to try, but now I'm glad he's shared a piece of himself.

'Actions speak louder than words, my friend,' I say gently.

Grishen wipes his eyes and gives me a grateful smile.

He lights the two lengths of match cord, and they smoulder brightly despite the train. Izetha takes the longer piece while Grishen carefully puts the other in a pouch.

'Izetha,' I say. 'You know what to do?'

His head dips in a solemn nod.

'Then we'd better go.'

Grishen discards the useless musket, and together we move swiftly in a crouch along the rooftops, away from the square surrounding the gate. The rain pummels us in sheets, and yet the roads below are still busy. Every minute wagons pass by on their way to the gate and patrols are everywhere, but people are wearing oiled skins, hoods pulled low to shield their faces from the rain.

'Izetha,' I say, resting my hand briefly on his shoulder. As he turns toward me, I wrap my arms around him, the sweet scent of decay filling my nostrils as I pull him close.

'I will never forget what you did for me, my friend. I owe you my life. Now it's in your hands again. If all goes well with our plan, I'll see you on the other side, but if not. You know what to tell Lotane, yes?'

'I not fail!'

Arms devoid of warmth envelop me, then Izetha gently pulls away. A heartbeat later, he disappears.

'Damn!' Grishen whispers. 'Not good at goodbyes is he.'

There's a gentle thud, and the lamppost adjacent to us sways slightly as Izetha slides down to the road below. The rain is relentless, and the drains are struggling with the deluge. As I peer over the roof edge, I can briefly see Izetha's progress as the water swirls around his invisible feet.

A jagged fork of lightning splits the sky, and the following thunder shakes the small stones on the rooftop.

'Let's go!' Grishen says impatiently.

'No. We wait a little longer, the street is too busy.'

I shiver with the cold. It's been so long since I've had to worry about such things. Once, my elemental magic would have kept me warm without having to ask. Now, I'm mortal again, stripped of everything, suffering like everyone.

Grishen lies next to me, and I wonder if he feels as bad as he looks. Izetha had got me new clothes, but Grishen is still dressed in not much more than rags and a pair of old boots. He looks like a vagrant, but then again, I suppose he is.

I look over the edge, knowing I can't delay things much longer, but in my mind I'm visualising Izetha's progress. About now, he'll be nearing the main square.

Grishen taps my arm, but I shake my head.

Izetha will be taking his time, ensuring he doesn't bump into people lest he be accidentally discovered. Assuming all is well, he'll be making his way to the ramp, probably walking directly behind a wagon. Another few minutes and he'll be through ...

I look up and down the street below us. A squad of ten soldiers have just slogged by, and a wagon is approaching, the oxen pulling it plodding along the cobbled road.

In a minute's time, another wagon will pass.

'Get ready,' I hiss.

Grishen positions himself at the edge of the roof.

'Go!'

Two seconds after he steps off, I follow.

The lamp post is so slippery, that for a moment, I'm shocked by my rate of descent, but I manage to squeeze hard enough to avoid slamming into Grishen as he lands heavily below me.

I point left, confirming which side he'll take although we'd gone over it just hours before.

He splashes up alongside the left side of the wagon, as I do the right.

'Excuse me!' Grishen calls out, his voice carrying just enough to attract the driver's and guard's attention.

I don't hesitate, leap up next to the driver, slitting his throat before I lean over to clamp my hand across the guard's mouth, muffling his panicked scream as I pull his head hard toward me, stabbing the dagger backwards, deep into his heart.

I seize the reins, snapping them to keep the oxen moving forward.

This is our most vulnerable moment. Thankfully, the weather is so foul that apart from ensuring doors are locked as they pass, the squad of soldiers don't bother looking behind.

Grishen leaps up. He works frantically beside me, unbuckling the strap from the guard's musket to tie its erstwhile owner firmly in place. He then wedges the musket against the footrest and tries to balance the guard's head on the end of the barrel to stop it flopping around.

It's no good.

'Hold his head steady,' I whisper, leaning in.

Reaching across, I stab my dagger up under the corpse's chin, driving it through the roof of the mouth. Grishen winces, but the barrel fits perfectly into the wound.

Satisfied, he scrambles to shove a wooden pole and whip through the seat's slats to prop up the driver. The man's lifeless form is precariously balanced, his head listing slightly to one side, but it holds. Barely.

Staying low, Grishen leaps over the backrest, and disappears under the tarpaulin while I crouch, trying not to make it obvious that there are three people on the front of the wagon where there should be only two.

The oxen continue to plod along, requiring next to no direction. They must be used to dragging this wagon around for hours, and the rain doesn't seem to bother them.

The driver topples over to his right, and the wooden pole snaps.

Damnit.

The main square is slowly approaching. If anything, there appears to be more soldiers there now than before it started raining. I can even see the All Father being sheltered by an umbrella held above him by one of his slingers.

I look around for something to secure the driver, but there's nothing, and if I lean him against the guard, they'll both end up in a heap.

'Done,' hisses Grishen as he leaps from the back, to run along beside me. 'Let's go.'

'I'll catch you up,' I reply. 'This bloody driver needs to stay upright.'

'You've got just under two minutes,' Grishen snaps over his shoulder as he darts off into the shadows of a doorway. A flash of lightning, a rumble of thunder, and he puts his shoulder against the door, forcing it open, and slips inside.

I turn to the driver next to me, and struggle, frantically trying to wrestle his oilskins off over his limp arms. I expect to hear shouts of alarm, or gunshots, but fortune is finally with me, and it comes free.

Thankfully, it's easy enough to push the driver down to my feet and cram him under the seat, then I quickly shrug on his oilskins, settling down, the cowl pulled low over my face just in time.

The square approaches, all bright white lights, and I'm waved through the first cordon of troops. An officer points to the right where a long row of wagons like mine are lined up side by side, their guards and drivers hunched miserably against nature's onslaught.

Grishen had said just under two minutes. What, almost a minute ago?

I slowly guide the wagon, pulling on the reins. Nerves make me feel like I'm the centre of attention, but despite the number of soldiers, everyone has somewhere to be or something to do.

Off to my left, the All Father and his slingers oversee the organised chaos, ensuring everything goes smoothly.

I guide my wagon toward the end of the line, and only realise too late that I should have swung wide as its turning circle is awful. I frantically pull on the reins, trying to adjust sharply, but instead, my oxen lumber into the team of the wagon I should have been alongside, and their distressed bellows rise angrily above the storm.

'You idiot!' shouts the driver of the stricken oxen as soldiers stop and ridicule my useless attempt at getting my wagon into position.

Suddenly, so many eyes are on me.

I raise my hands in apology, then lightly leap off the seat and begin walking away.

One minute.

'Where do you think you're going?' an officer demands.

I walk past, adroitly swaying away from his grasping hand.

Fifty seconds.

He runs to stand in front of me, his hand resting on the butt of his gun.

'How dare you ignore me, you little piece of ...'

There's no way out of this confrontation.

Forty seconds.

I stab him in the heart as I walk up to him, and don't even pause my stride, carrying on walking as though there's nothing to see.

'He's been stabbed!'

'Stop that woman!'

Thirty seconds.

'It's her, the Queen of Beasts. Kill her!'

Somehow the All Father's voice carries above the others, and I risk a glance over my shoulder to see him pointing in my direction.

I run.

The square explodes into chaos. Soldiers shout, a dog barks, and muskets fizzle uselessly in the rain as I dodge and weave, slashing at fingers and ducking under rifle butts, the slick cobblestones treacherous underfoot.

A hand grabs my oilskins, and I twist free, the fabric tearing as I stumble forward, off-balance.

Someone crashes into me from behind, and I'm sent skidding across the wet cobblestones. I roll under a cannon, and frantically grab a dog's collar to stop it ripping my throat out as my dagger slices his. I scramble out from my shelter, away from the boots thundering toward me, but a soldier rams into me from the side.

We go down in a heap.

I lash out, my dagger scoring a deep cut across his brow, and as he reels away with a scream, I'm up and off again, dodging left and right, ducking and rolling, gasping for breath.

Suddenly my legs are struck from the side, and I stumble, a thrown musket rattling on the stones behind me.

Twenty seconds.

The edge of the square draws close, but I'll never escape. The road I'm aiming for teems with soldiers, and even as the thought registers, I'm tackled solidly from behind.

My legs have nothing left, but as I fall, I claw my way into an overflowing gutter, only for my assailant to jump on top of me and push my head down.

I resist, momentarily keeping my face out of the water, but more weight bears down and I collapse under the surface. I can't twist or turn, I can't stab with my dagger. I can't take a breath or I'll drown.

Fists drive into the back of my head, my ribs, but I accept the blows, the crush of people on me hinders their delivery.

Ten seconds.

My chest heaves in protest, my heartbeat thundering as the world narrows to this single moment. The shouts and yells of my assailants are muffled, distant. My lungs heave, demanding ...

Three seconds.

Just hang on, Malina.

Two.

One.

Zero.

***

Nothing.

I hold on as long as I can, but instinct wins. My body convulses, forcing a ragged breath, and water floods my lungs. I begin to convulse, the bodies above me relentless in their pressure.

Then, through my closed eyes, I see it. Through the stones beneath me, I feel it. Through the water filling my ears, I hear it.

A thunderclap as if thrown by the gods themselves has the earth move, and the weight of the countless bodies bearing me down just disappears from one second to the next. A rapid series of further booms, and the ground heaves and shakes, throwing me from my watery grave, choking, into the fires of hell.

I cough violently, bringing up a lungful of water, then snatch a breath of scorched air while cannon balls and canister hiss and bounce across the cobblestones, sending sparks showering everywhere. I swiftly roll back into the gutter as gunpowder wagons situated further from the initial blast explode one after another, wreaking further destruction.

Long buried memories surface of the attack on High Delnor's port, the firestorm that followed, and my part in saving the stricken marines, but this time, I'll render no aid.

I'm still clutching my dagger as I lever my bruised and aching body from its watery tomb.

I've been in battles before and witnessed the morass of twisted, disfigured bodies, and there's little to no difference in the scene around me. Death is everywhere, with corpses strewn like a flower's petals radiating from the initial blast.

Screams and moans fill the air, mingling with the crash of collapsing masonry. The front of every building surrounding the square has been blasted in. A large warehouse collapses in a rumbling cloud of dust. Fires burn everywhere, and even the torrential rain is unable to douse them.

There's only one thing in sight that stands undamaged, my destination, the world gate. That towering monument stands unscathed, its surface unmarred by the explosion.

The cobblestones are slick with blood and entrails as I force myself forward, slipping and sliding with each step. Soldiers, some blind, others dazed, but all bleeding profusely, stagger or crawl, their hands outstretched, desperate for help, yet they give me no pause, and my heart is hardened to their plight.

Lotane and my beloved fey are almost within reach, and they're all that matter.

Flashes light up the world gate, and I smile grimly. Izetha has dealt the same devastating blow to the Astorian forces on the other side of the gate. Grishen's plan, to bore a hole in a gunpowder crate and have the match cord burn through to the other side had been reckless, but utter genius. When I pass through, there will be only chaos, death, and destruction, and my escape will be all the easier for it.

Then something gives me pause.

Amidst the blackened charred corpses, something pale moves, like a maggot on rotting meat …

The All Father's arm.

The leader of Astoria stirs weakly underneath the corpse of a slinger whose clothes and flesh have been almost completely stripped away by the blast. Only the gun belts help identify him as one of the All Father's elite bodyguards.

Despite my urgent need to escape, I'm safe for the moment. Any Astorian in the vicinity is dead or dying, and the collapsing buildings and fires discourage any soldiers from outside the blast radius from coming any closer ... at least for now.

I drag the body of the slinger aside, revealing the All Father's ruined form beneath.

His face, never pleasant, is now a nightmare. The skin has been torn away, and his eyes are just blackened pits of jelly. One arm is gone, severed at the shoulder, and blood pumps feebly, driven by a cold heart soon to give up the fight.

He draws several deep rattling breaths, then sniffs loudly and his blistered lips lift in a weak smile.

'It's you, isn't it? The Queen of Beasts. Come to gloat.'

Ignoring his question, I reach down, drawing one of the slinger's guns from his belt. It's double barrelled and has a heavy, comforting weight.

The All Father wheezes, the sound wet and broken.

'It doesn't matter how far or fast you run,' he rattles, 'I'll find you again. Maybe tomorrow. Maybe next week. When I do, I'll kill you and soon after, your fey will cease to exist.'

Raising the gun, I sight along its barrel to the small pointed triangle set on the end, and position it in the middle of that bloodied forehead.

'I'm ... immortal,' he croaks. 'Kill me as many times as you want, but I'll never stop until ...'

I squeeze the trigger twice, the gun fire lost amongst the background noise. It bucks in my hand, surprising me, but even more so is the way the All Father's head just disintegrates.

Casting the horrible weapon aside, I run.

A mighty crash comes from my left, and one of the factories powering the gate collapses in on itself. Seconds later, the pile of rubble erupts in a mighty explosion, and I throw myself flat as a billowing cloud of dust and broken brickwork flies outwards.

I'm up on my feet an instant later.

The runes on the gate flicker, then steady, and to my relief, it remains open. The flashes on the other side have ceased, and despite the carnage, I've never been happier.

Everything I love, everything I live for, is on the other side. Yet as I approach the world gate up the blood splashed and scorched ramp, I slow, then pause, looking through to the fey world beyond.

My dream of Karson comes to mind and how every battle I fight will end in defeat or death. If I pass through, my happiness will be fleeting at best. I consider the Astorian army, a million strong, soon to flood through the gate, and if the All Father is immortal as he seems to be, he'll lead them and make good on his promise. Even if we run, one day we'll be caught.

Karson's question rings clear in my mind.

'What would you do to keep the one you love, and the world you call home, safe?'

'I would do anything,' I whisper, tears coursing down my cheeks as I finally realise what I must do.

'GO!'

Grishen's urgent bellow reaches me across the square.

'I can't,' I yell, leaping from the ramp, and head toward the remaining factory.

It's damaged, part of its front wall has collapsed, and a heavy cannon rests amongst the rubble having been thrown through the brickwork by the explosion. I pause, grabbing another dagger from a soldier's corpse.

'Damn it!'

I turn to see Grishen picking himself up off the ground, having slipped in someone's guts, but despite the tumble, he runs toward me, arms outstretched to help maintain his balance.

I pause, watching my unlikely ally slip and slide until he reaches my side. He looks almost as bad as the corpses at my feet. Torn clothing does little to conceal the wounds he suffered at the hands of his torturers. He's covered in blood and guts, and soaked through to boot.

Yet a smile as bright as a summer's dawn splits his craggy features.

'Even if I die now, I'll be bloody happy!' he whoops. 'My ancestors will have heard that blast in the afterworld. Now get yourself through the damned gate.'

'I'm not going back, my friend.'

Using the word surprises me, but what else can I call this man? He might have owed me a debt of life, but he's gone over and above to repay it, and he's still here.

Grishen's laughter fades.

'What?'

I gesture toward the factory.

'Follow me if you want to make even more noise!'

He doesn't hesitate. As we push toward the collapsed wall. I catch movement inside through the smoke and dust. It seems the fight isn't over yet. Despite the number of fallen muskets, Grishen grabs a dagger too. The Astorian muskets are soaked and useless in the rain.

'Why?' Grishen huffs as he keeps pace.

I look about the square before answering. Fresh troops are beginning to emerge, scrambling over the heaps of rubble, their officer's screams galvanising them into action.

The visibility is so poor with the rain that I doubt we'll be recognised for anything but survivors, but we mustn't hang around and need to get out of the open.

'If I go back, there's nothing to stop the invasion,' I say. 'I'll lead my people, but only to their deaths. But if I can stop the Astorian army going through the world gate, I've already won half the battle. I've got to destroy this factory to close it!'

'Half the battle?' Grishen prompts.

I grab his elbow to keep him upright as he slips.

'I've got to find a way to kill the All Father, for good. I just blew his head off, but he vowed to be back.'

'That's something worth fighting for, and this will help!' Grishen exclaims, bending down to loot a dead officer of his gun belt. He resembles a child with a sugared treat as he quickly buckles it around his waist, but his smile suddenly fades.

'But, how can you return home if both factories are destroyed?' he asks as we start climbing the rubble as opposed to finding a door.

'I can't!'

The weight of my decision suddenly hits me like a physical blow. I will never see Lotane again, feel his touch, hear his laughter, or see the love in his eyes.

But to keep him and my world safe, I will do anything.

It's hard going, the debris moving dangerously under our feet.

'You will work through the night!'

The barked order cuts through the din, and I raise a finger to my lips as we clamber over the rubble.

'You'll be split into two teams,' the sharp voice continues. 'One to shore up the building, two to keep the furnaces burning. When the next shift arrives, you'll still work. You work for the glory of the Astorian Empire and the All Father's love!'

The rubble shifts and bricks tumble as we reach the top of the mound.

I skitter down the other side of the pile, taking in the strange new world before me. Metal pipes and cables run everywhere. Steam billows from vents and grates, fires burn within giant ovens, spreading an evil red, orange glow. The air is thick with dust and ash, the floor strewn with debris.

It's like I've entered hell.

'Get in line, quickly and help!'

That authoritative voice unsurprisingly comes from an Astorian officer, who barely glances over his shoulder as he hears us descend into the factory. He has about forty bloodied men and women of both Icelandian and Tarsian heritage lined up in front of him, all bowed and ready to do his will. They hold shovels, pickaxes and various other heavy tools.

I walk right up to the Astorian, and he turns around, just in time for me to stab him in the heart.

'You're beyond help!' I snarl, ripping the blade clear.

As he falls to his knees, I kick him onto his back, my eyes roving over the gang of workers, who are backing away into the gloom, petrified.

Grishen comes up alongside me and pulls the officer's gun free of its holster, looking even happier now he has two.

'How do we destroy this place?' I ask him.

'I don't know. I worked in a foundry,' Grishen responds, then repeats my question.

'How do we destroy this place?' he demands of the workers.

Yet none of them say a word.

***

'What happened to Icelandian and Tarsian bravery?' I demand quickly, using both their native tongues, enjoying the rough texture of words that I haven't used in centuries as I try to establish a connection.

'To speak in our old, native languages is punishable by death!' a scarred Icelandian woman cries in the common tongue. 'Look at what you've done,' she continues, dropping a shovel and looking around as if worried she'll be overheard. 'If you leave now, we'll wait till you're gone before we call for help.'

I take a step toward her.

'You'd call for help, from who?' I demand, my voice cold and sharp. 'The Astorians who enslave you? By the gods, to be a coward was once a fate worse than death for an Icelandian!'

I turn to Grishen.

'Are you the only real Icelandian left in this world?'

'He's no Icelandian,' a gangly Tarsian man declares. 'He's a half-blood Astorian spy, pretending to be Icelandian!'

I'm shocked by this accusation, but even as the news sinks in, Grishen lifts his recently looted gun, and fires twice in quick succession.

The tall man who'd spoken staggers back, dropping a metal bar, clasping hands to his stomach. His eyes are wide and disbelieving as Grishen stalks toward him.

I could stop Grishen, but this moment is his. If he can cow the workers into compliance with his violence ...

Grishen walks up to the Tarsian, draws his second gun, and fires.

Yet this time the Tarsian just turns and stares, as do the others, at the body of another Astorian officer who'd come upon us from behind some pipework.

'I'm no bloody Astorian spy, and whilst I might only be a half-blood and half your height, it appears my balls are twice the size of yours!' Grishen says, going to the downed officer. He casts aside one of his guns, draws the officer's unused one and holsters it at his waist.

'Easy for you to act tough holding a gun,' the Tarsian says shakily, trying to cover his fright with bravado.

Grishen nods thoughtfully, then hands one over.

I appreciate the deviousness of this trusting gesture. It's the one he's already fired.

'Then see how it feels, brother. I might be half Astorian, it's true, but I've only ever wanted to be accepted as Icelandian. Once I spoke of independence, now I fight for it, and it's time you did the same.'

'Were you two responsible for all this destruction?' demands the scarred woman in disbelief.

'Yes,' I say. 'So, if two of us can kill nearly two thousand Astorians, tell me, what exactly is it that stops you from rising up and throwing off the invisible shackles that bind you?'

I stare hard at the workers, willing them to join us, but suddenly they all turn and run, weaving through the labyrinth of pipework as if Grishen will shoot them in the back.

All but one.

The tall Tarsian remains, the gun cradled in his shaking hands. He turns it over as if it's something disgusting. It's a feeling I share.

'I don't know whether to run or help,' he mutters, his eyes downcast.

'You've nothing to fear from us,' I reassure him.

'Where are you f-from?' he asks shakily.

I suddenly realise he has no idea who I am. The smoke, steam, dust, and gloom have all combined to help conceal my identity.

I'm half Hastian, half something else. I've two bloods running through my veins, a bit like Grishen here. You can trust him, and you can trust me.'

'H-Hastian, eh? I've n-nothing against Hastians, but I h-hate Astorians!'

With a final sideways glance, he passes the gun awkwardly to Grishen as if it's burning his hands.

'I can't abide violence,' he explains.

'Will you help us?' I ask softly, wary that this man might turn tail after his co-workers if I'm too aggressive.

His eyes close and he bites his lip. I look across at Grishen for help, but he's struggling to reload the spent gun, and just shrugs.

'It's alright to be afraid,' I soothe, my voice firm but gentle. 'But you'll feel better if you take your fear and hatred, and give it an outlet. Help us destroy this place, and you might feel better for it.'

His eyes open and he nods hesitantly.

'As long as I don't have to hurt someone.'

'Then show us a way where we don't have to. What's your name?' I ask.

'Hargna.'

With shaking hands, he picks up a metal bar on his second attempt, then looks around, drawing a deep breath.

'I'll help you. Turn every red wheel to the right as far as it goes!'

I don't hesitate, and run from one to another, swiftly doing as instructed as Grishen does the same.

'Those red wheels are safety valves,' Hargna shouts.

Having conquered his fear, he goes round smashing glass-covered dials with a nervous energy.

'They help maintain the correct pressure for the generators a floor above us.'

I've no idea what Hargna is talking about, but pipes start groaning and shuddering as we work our way further into the building. In the background, a siren begins its mournful wail, creating a greater sense of urgency.

Hargna leads us down a level where we stumble upon a group of Tarsians frantically spinning valves in an effort to fend off the impending disaster.

An Astorian officer stands amongst them, barking orders, his back turned to us. Hargna freezes at the sight of the uniformed figure, and I run past to cut the Astorian's throat before the man knows death is even upon him.

'Run for your lives,' Hargna shouts, his voice breaking with panic.

Grishen laughs manically and follows up with a shot from his gun that pings musically off the metal pipes as if they're some crazed instrument and the Tarsians scatter.

Again, we run amongst the hideous machinery, under flickering lights, sweating from open furnaces, flinching as almighty bangs and shudders reverberate through the building.

Footsteps clang on a metal stairwell, and Grishen draws his other gun as two soldiers armed with muskets descend in front of us, the sounds of more following close behind.

Grishen fires wildly, emptying his weapons. The soldiers fall and those following turn and flee back up the stairs.

The men aren't mortally wounded, but I finish them off quickly, ignoring their cries for mercy.

Looking a little nauseous, Grishen opens his belt pouches, one after another, to reload.

'They're bloody empty,' he complains.

'Probably so there's never enough ammunition to do much harm if an officer's weapon is stolen,' I say.

He tosses the guns aside and snatches up the two fallen muskets.

'Let's go,' Hargna pleads desperately. 'We've done enough. We don't have long!'

Angry shouts spur us on as Hargna leads us to a closed door, yanks it open, and starts up a narrow stairwell, dimly lit with the occasional flickering light. Round and round we go, the groans of tortured metal and the wailing alarm driving us on.

A huge bang, the walls shake, and I squint as dust and mortar cascade down from the walls.

'One more flight,' Hargna yells, his panic obvious.

Another dozen stairs, and he kicks open a door into the closed end of a narrow alley. The ever-present rain greets us, cold and cleansing after the furnace-like heat of the factory.

'Damnit,' Grishen complains, tucking the muskets into his body.

'Quickly!' Hargna urges.

I don't need any encouragement, and lead the others down the dark alleyway. There's a single, hanging light right at the end luring us on.

Grishen stumbles, cursing as he drops one of the muskets in a puddle.

'How far do you think is safe?' he asks.

Suddenly I'm flung from my feet, the others landing alongside me, as an explosion tears through the factory. A huge dust cloud rolls over us, full of small stones that fortunately don't do more than sting.

'Round about here,' I mutter, picking myself up, looking back to see the factory has collapsed in on itself, leaving the world gate visible, the runes dulled.

I feel dazed, not just from the fall, but from the realisation that the world gate is now closed, and that I'm on another world to Lotane, millions of leagues from the one I love.

'We have to get as far away as possible,' Hargna says, his words tumbling in a panicked torrent. 'I know somewhere safe to hide!'

The heavy thud of boots has us crouch behind a pile of rubble as a squad of about twenty troops run by. As soon as they pass, we're up and moving, but only for a minute before we shelter in a doorway as more approach.

'Look there!' An unknown voice shouts.

Figures move quickly toward us through the rain, indistinct but unmistakably hostile.

'Run!' I yell.

We take off again, splashing through puddles, slipping and sliding as we run without direction, turning left and right at random, frantically trying to lose our pursuers.

I'm frustrated by my companions' lack of speed. I could escape easily and just disappear into the darkness, but I can't just leave them to an unknown fate. But if I'm honest, it's more because I don't want to be on my own in this strangely unfamiliar world.

Grishen has accepted me for what I am and has proved his loyalty, although Hargna is still very much an unknown entity and seems frightened of his own shadow.

I'm likely better off with them than without them, apart from when we're trying to escape.

Luck keeps us from running headlong into another patrol, but it abandons us as we reach the end of an alley, only to discover it's a dead end. Sheer walls loom on either side, slick with rain, without so much as a window or door to offer hope.

A bullet whines from the ground at our feet.

'Slingers!' Grishen calls, scrambling for the cover of a chimney breast, pulling a frozen Hargna along with him.

I crouch behind a mound of debris, and peer over as eight of Astoria's finest approach cautiously down the alley, firing as they come, keeping us pinned down. They have the numbers, the training, and the weapons. There's nowhere for us to run or hide, and they know it.

My two daggers feel insignificant against such weaponry. Grishen holds his one shot musket as if it's a lucky charm. Hargna is frustratingly unarmed and looks too petrified to be of any use.

I look up, because only divine intervention will get us out of here. For the briefest moment, as bullets zip and whine overhead, I take in nature's beauty, the raindrops falling, almost like shooting stars as they briefly catch the light.

The light.

'Grishen. Shoot the light!'

He doesn't hesitate. He kneels, aiming the long weapon. Bullets bite chunks out of the chimney breast as the slingers get sight of the barrel. They might even know what's coming. But I doubt it.

Snap.

'Gods!' Grishen yells, frantically pulling back on the hammer and aiming again. There's a fizzle as Grishen squeezes the trigger, just before the weapon is knocked sideways.

Yet the slingers' attention is on Grishen.

I heft one of my daggers, turn, then spin on my heel, launching my weapon.

The hilt was wet and slippery, the rain is falling, blurring my vision, the distance is hard to gauge, and I can't even stand up to throw.

Lystra would have been proud.

The single lamp shatters, plunging the alley into utter darkness.

Except for me.

With my fey sight, everything is clear and nothing more so than the blood pumping through the veins of the men and women before me.

When did the dark become my friend, my lover? Perhaps in the tunnels beneath High Delnor, perhaps not. Irrespective, I feel warm and safe in its velvety embrace.

I cross the alley, entranced by the beating hearts of our hunters, who have now become my prey.

'Stay there!' I breathe softly, my voice a ghost in the dark. Grishen's wide eyes turn toward me, having been unaware of my approach.

The rain, and occasional rumble of thunder, conceals the sound of my wet footfalls as I approach the slingers. They're milling around, unsure what to do, keeping their guns raised.

I ghost through their oblivious ranks, saying nothing, reclaim my thrown dagger and sheathe it, keeping my other to hand.

It's time to show them who owns the night, and it's not them.

Reaching around, with one swift slice, I open the throat of a female slinger. She drops to her knees, her fingers clamping uselessly over the gaping wound, and I catch her gun before it can clatter to the ground.

Her wet gurgles have the others spin frantically toward her and I slide between them, knife in one hand, the double-barrelled gun in the other.

I wait, but not for long.

The dark can play with a mind, feeding fear, and one of the slingers fires blindly into the dark toward the hideous sound, and immediately the others follow suit, riddling the dying slinger with bullets.

As the guns roar, mine adds to the symphony, and two more slingers join their dead friend.

Three down, five to go.

'Circle. Circle!' a man hisses, and with searching hands they manage to form a loose ring, facing outwards.

But I'm already inside.

I heft my now useless gun, and lob it over the head of the man in front of me so it clatters on the ground a dozen paces away, and in that split second, I stab in a frenzy, both blades plunging deep, four times.

Two were killing strokes, but the other two strikes glance off bone, and my victims scream as I spin away, putting a safe distance between us.

Five down, three to go. Two are badly injured, each holding on to a shoulder of the uninjured man in the middle.

Lightning forks through the sky, illuminating the alley in a flash of brilliance that feels like it lasts forever.

'THERE!' screams a woman as I'm suddenly highlighted.

Guns roar, and I'm spun around, a searing pain tears through my left shoulder.

Bullets whine and ricochet from the ground as the slingers continue firing long after the lightning fades. Each time they fire twice, they holster a gun and draw another, their rhythm practiced and relentless.

Their hearts beat manically in their chests, and I'm a little dizzy with hunger at the sight of the blood in their veins, but then, as I advance, my left leg almost gives way, and I realise that's not the reason.

Damnit.

I throw my remaining dagger spinning through the air. I've practiced throws like this a hundred thousand times, and it doesn't miss, hitting the central slinger square in the chest.

As he collapses, the other two fall to the ground with him.

'No. Please no!' One of the slingers begs, eyes wide.

I hobble over unseen, praying no more lightning gives me away.

The slinger points his gun blindly left and right and I snatch it away before he can react.

'She's here. She's here!' he cries, his voice breaking with panic.

I throw myself flat just as the other slinger's gun roars, staying silent, letting the two injured slingers believe I've been hit or run away.

Slowly, as if a shadow, I rise. I'm not proficient with these guns although they're easy to use, and I can't afford to miss.

They make it easy for me as they shuffle together and sit back to back.

The metal of the gun barrel almost touches their heads before I quickly pull the trigger twice in quick succession.

Then, as if by magic, the rain stops.

I stagger back to Grishen and Hargna.

'It's over,' I say.

It's strange, looking at their feet as they stand over me. I don't recall falling, but the wet ground is cool and soothing against my face, a stark contrast to the excruciating pain radiating from my wounds.

It's rather inconvenient being mortal again.

***

CHAPTER VII

'Drink this, it will help.'

Grishen's voice is gentle yet firm as he offers me a mug of cold soup, but my hands are shaking too much to take it. I'm frozen to the bone, and it's impossible to get warm despite the three blankets weighing me down. The cold food isn't helping. Yet only half an hour ago I'd been sweating profusely ... and so it goes, around and around.

'Here, let me. Just lean back, drink and relax,' he soothes, holding the mug to my lips. But he's far from calm. His elevated heartbeat gives him away.

Not that it's easy to be calm when we're below an Astorian detention centre full of screaming, shouting soldiers, sitting in a damp cell with only a tiny, filthy square of pavement glass letting in a sliver of yellow light from the outside.

The lone wooden bed I'm on has just mouldy straw for a mattress, and a stained pillow, but nonetheless, I'm grateful. The others have nothing but their ragged clothes and a cold stone floor.

Across the cell Hargna sits looking thoughtful, no doubt wondering what the hells possessed him to help us. He could have stayed out of this, returned to whatever life he'd left, but not now, not after what he's done.

Now it's a cramped cell with one bed, foul water, and disgusting food.

This is not where I'd thought to find myself when I awoke. In truth, I'd almost broken down, wondering when the torture would start again, the victorious face of the All Father the last thing I'd ever see.

Bizarrely, it transpires we're in the safest place in the city.

Hargna's safe place ... although the question has yet to be asked, why he ever needed one, is without doubt the last place an Astorian search party would ever look ... within one of its own festering gaols.

Our cell is at the far end of a dark corridor removed from both entrances. One leads up into the heart of the detention centre, and the other opens onto the street, through which I was first carried, limp and unconscious.

Grishen crouches beside me, his face lined with worry.

'Your wounds are infected, but eating will help you beat it,' he mutters.

He forgets to add ... *if you live long enough*.

'But why save her?' Hargna grumbles. 'I recognise who she is now. The Queen of Beasts. She'll be the death of us!'

'Forget that Astorian bullcrap. You might not be Icelandian, Hargna, but I'm sure you know some of our lore. Malina is a saviour, destined to return in our hour of greatest need. She could change everything!'

'Saviour? All I've seen is her killing,' Hargna argues.

'Rubbish,' Grishen declares hotly. 'She saved us when those slingers had us dead to rights.'

'And how did she save us? By killing.' Hargna retorts. 'And only because her actions put us in peril!'

'Our actions, Hargna,' Grishen chuckles. 'You helped.'

'I did, didn't I?' Hargna whispers half to himself.

Is there pride or regret in his tone? It's hard to tell.

There's a calculating side to this tall Tarsian. He isn't all as he seems. I want to tell him of his ancestors' strength and honour and what it once meant to be a Tarsian, but in truth, I can't focus enough. I manage to swallow a little cold food, but it won't save me. My wounds are infected, and I'm delirious.

In fact, the bed suddenly feels warmer, and my teeth stop chattering.

'Malina,' Grishen whispers. 'Stay awake. Stay awake and fight!'

I try to obey, but I'm drifting, my eyelids feel heavier, and the world blurs at the edges. Darkness beckons, but it doesn't claim me. Instead, light blooms behind my closed eyes, soft and warm, wrapping around me like a comforting embrace.

.

'I've won!'

I laugh and spin, arms outstretched, surrounded by a sea of vibrant flowers. The sky above is endless and blue, and birdsong weaves a melody so sweet it feels like the universe itself is celebrating.

Karson is here, and I pull him along with me, and I can't stop smiling.

'To see you again,' I whisper, tears streaking my cheeks. 'To see you three times in such quick succession ... is such a gift.'

Karson's expression shifts, growing sombre, and our dance slows.

'You're dying, Alina.'

'I know,' I reply softly, though the admission doesn't sting as it should. 'But it doesn't matter now. Lotane won't forgive me for not dying with him, but he'll live. My fey will live. After all the dark things I've done... this feels like redemption.'

Karson studies me, his gaze tender but searching

'Have my sins been erased? Is this my afterlife?' I ask, hoping Karson knows the answer.

He gently pulls away and sits down, beckoning me to join him.

'You're so shortsighted, Alina,' he says, shaking his head. 'Your childish innocence has never left you. I love you for it, but it also frustrates me!'

I sit beside him, taking his hands in mine.

'Perhaps we should embrace that childish innocence. Neither you, nor I got to enjoy it for very long. Our childhoods were stolen from us both.'

He nods, his eyes downcast.

'I sometimes wonder,' he murmurs, 'what my life would have been like had it not been snatched away when I was young.'

'Exactly, little brother,' I say, squeezing his hands. 'You died way before your time. That orphanage was a death sentence for so many.'

Karson's eyes suddenly harden.

'What about the thousands of young men and women you just killed? Many of them were barely adults. Did they die before their time?'

'They were evil!' I say, somewhat shocked.

'They weren't evil, Alina. Just misled, manipulated, and coerced. Does that sound familiar?'

Suddenly the field of flowers vanish, to be replaced by the cold, harsh expanse of the training circle on the Mountain of Souls.

'You were once led to believe your deeds were righteous. You thought bringing about the return of The Once and Future King was worth any cost.'

'What else could I have done?' I demand. 'I did whatever it took.'

Karson shakes his head, his expression confused.

'In truth, I'm not sure. But what I know is this. You've changed nothing.'

His words hit like a blow.

'How could I have changed nothing? Look at what I achieved. The gate between the fey and human worlds is closed!'

'Forever?'

'For another five hundred years here. Surely that's enough!'

Karson's eyes narrow.

'The Astorians haven't forgotten in four thousand years and they now have an immortal leader. What do you think now? Is it enough?'

The Mountain of Souls fades to be replaced by the fey landscape, and there's my valley, the mansion in flames. Around it the Saer Tel nourish the land a final time, their blood seeping into the soil. At the entrance to the mansion, hair singed by the heat, lies Lotane in bullet-riddled armour.

'You haven't changed the future, Alina,' Karson says, his voice steady, unyielding. 'In truth, you've made it worse if you die.'

'They'll rebuild the factories and reopen the gate?' I sigh, already knowing the answer.

Karson nods sagely.

'And if I don't die?'

I'm so tired, I almost hope he'll say it makes no difference so I can just stay here forever until whatever awaits beyond claims me.

'Who knows, Alina? Is there another to take up your mantle? I don't believe so. But you've yet to do everything you can to protect Lotane and the fey. Nor have you done anything to protect your other child ... this world. A mother cannot abandon her children when she's tired, that isn't the nature of things, nor is it your nature.'

'It's a Saer Tel's nature to grow,' I say in a last gasp attempt to deflect my responsibility. 'It's to replenish life, to restore health and balance to the world in which they exist. I am Saer Tel.'

Karson smiles, but it's tinged with sadness.

'You are of two worlds, Malina, but in this one, it's not your heritage of being a Saer Tel that will aid you, it's your training as a Chosen. Once, I believed and hoped that there was no such thing as fate, but now I know better. You were always fated to carry this burden, to shoulder the guilt of worlds. In doing so, you've lost your soul, but I can only hope, in the same breath, that your actions bring about your redemption too. Now, do whatever it takes to keep your children safe.'

...

..

.

'Malina.'

I open my eyes to the darkness of life. Strange how being so near death had been so full of light.

Grishen's face hovers above me, pale and lined with exhaustion.

'I thought we'd lost you.'

'Grishen,' I croak. 'What would you be willing to do, to set your fellow Icelandians free, and everyone else too?'

His eyes harden.

'I'd do anything. Absolutely anything!'

'What about you, Hargna?'

He looks at me shrewdly, measuring my words as if tasting them for any sign of deception, then shakes his head nervously.

'Bah. What use are dreams?'

I consider my dreams with Karson. If I survive, I might share them with him, but I don't have the strength or time left now.

'Grishen,' I say, forcing my words out through cracked lips. 'I need something from you or I'll die, and our dreams will die with me.'

Grishen's face pales further.

'What is it, Malina? Just name it, I'll go find it.'

I shake my head weakly, managing a grim smile.

'Everything I need from you is right here. I'm the Queen of Beasts, and what do beasts hunger for ... blood.'

Grishen stiffens, his brows drawing together.

Hargna shies away, his face pale.

'She's mad. You're mad if you do this!'

Grishen doesn't respond, just looks at me, resolve burning in his eyes.

'If it means keeping that dream alive, Malina, do whatever is needed.'

I gently take his hand, and pull him down next to me on the bed, drawing his wrist to my mouth. The world narrows as his pulse thrums against my lips. It's life in its rawest form, and for the first time in what feels like an eternity, I taste hope.

***

I stretch, testing my limbs and muscles under Grishen's somewhat worried gaze and Hargna's calculating and nervous one. These last days have drawn us inevitably closer and we're no longer strangers.

Drinking Grishen's blood has created a bond akin to blood magic between us in addition to something akin to hero worship. His seeing me as a saviour is so misplaced, and yet it's incredibly useful to have such a steadfast ally, and after all, am I not supposed to save two worlds?

As for Hargna, he might not have given me his blood, but familiarity has broken down his fears over who I am, especially as there are no secrets in this bedroom. Talking had been our only solace to stave off the insanity of close confinement whilst I'd recovered and we'd waited for the madness on the streets above to quieten down.

Grishen, it turns out, had always been shunned. His father had been found to have a consensual relationship with an Astorian woman, of which he was the product. His father and mother had subsequently been ostracised by both Icelandians and Astorians, as had Grishen from birth.

As punishment for joining with a low-born, his mother had been worked to death in a factory, and with her passing, his father's hatred of the Astorian people had become incandescent ... a hatred that had eventually led to his death for striking an Astorian officer in a fit of rage.

Grishen's dreams of an independent Icelandian people had been born from this loss, and he began speaking of freedom, of an independent Icelandian people proud and strong like in the legends. But, being a half-blood, he was considered untrustworthy and viewed with disdain by his giant kinsfolk, but had never given up such was his tenacity.

The Astorians didn't view his sedition favourably either, and when one day, soldiers had turned up at his sleeping quarters, he'd been arrested, tortured, and sentenced to death.

Hargna's story, which he'd reluctantly shared, hadn't been happy either.

I'd initially viewed him a coward, unworthy of being a Tarsian, but a man can only take so much before he breaks. I'd been on the verge of that myself. I shouldn't have judged him so harshly, not forgetting he'd overcome his fear to help destroy the factory.

His brother had died of malnutrition during a winter famine when the Astorians had taken almost all the food for themselves. His sister had vanished from the streets one day on the way home from work. As for his father, he'd disappeared, presumed arrested, for subsequently daring to demand justice at the Palace of the Ancients after which his mother had been forced to sell herself to make ends meet and had died of the pox. Lastly, he'd tried to tell us of his wife, but had broken down and been inconsolable for hours without being able to share her grisly tale.

He himself had been the victim of torture, but not for wrongdoing. It was employed simply to ensure compliance, and this was a common method of control employed by the Astorians on all peoples other than their own.

All fight, all resistance was tortured and beaten from them when young. Their heritage was fading into the mists of time as was their language, the use of which was punishable by death.

But perhaps what had bound them most to me, beyond the shared pain of our youth, were my old tales that challenged the Astorian narrative. Hargna's eyes shone as I told of the Tarsians' fight for independence against the old Delnorian Empire, and Grishen was mesmerised by my tales of the Icelandians' part in Nogoth's defeat.

Such things had been erased from history, and the only thing they'd been taught was of Nogoth's last invasion, and how Astoria had stood alone, driving back the dark forces of the fey at great loss, while the other kingdoms stood by, too fearful to help.

If it hadn't been for whispered legends and lore being passed down through the generations, then all sense of heritage and pride would have long ceased to exist for Grishen and Hargna's people, but even so, it was on the brink of extinction.

Having finished stretching, I'm satisfied I'm back to near full strength and hunker down on the cold cell floor beside my two companions.

'It's nearly time to leave,' I say softly. 'The provisions here are nigh on exhausted and the furore over what we did at the world gate has died away. Either the Astorians think I'm dead or back in the fey world.'

'Or,' Grishen adds with a wry smile, 'they know you're in their gaol and have simply locked us all in without our knowing.'

'Don't even imagine such a thing,' Hargna hisses, his face pale.

Grishen chuckles, leaning back against the wall.

'So, what next, oh wise one?'

I can't help but smile.

'We have to ensure that the world gate is never reopened and the Astorian army never invades the fey world,' I say, wishing it was as simple as I made it sound.

Grishen rubs his bandaged wrist, looking thoughtful.

Feeding from his neck would have seemed too intimate, too unfaithful to Lotane and his wrist had been the next best option.

'And how will that help free my fellow Icelandians and Hargna's Tarsians? You're supposed to save us,' he says thoughtfully.

'I think your legends have been a little too kind on me,' I laugh, somewhat uncomfortable. 'But to stop the invasion, we have to kill the All Father. With him and his dreams dead, there'll be no need for your people to be worked to death to support his crusade.'

Even as I speak, my words sound hollow.

'But he's immortal,' Hargna says.

'I'll find a way to ensure he stays dead this time.'

'This time?' Hargna asks, leaning forward, interested.

'She's killed him twice,' Grishen explains. 'Once during our prison break, and again at the world gate.'

'His death at the world gate is as much down to you as me, Grishen,' I say, only to receive a smile that lights up the cell.

Hargna raises his hands.

'You were also part of the prison break?'

Hargna's stare is intense. He's hiding something, and yet I don't perceive a threat, only an acute interest that cuts deeper than mere curiosity.

'I escaped and let the others out when I did,' I explain.

'Wait a moment,' Grishen says. 'Assuming the All Father stays dead, what happens if whoever replaces him still wishes to invade your world? They'll just rebuild the power stations.'

'Then I'll keep on killing whoever takes his place for as long as it takes. If anarchy reigns, then so much the better,' I reply.

'You've no idea,' says Hargna. 'This dream is imprinted on every Astorian child from birth. You won't be able to kill an entire people, and nor should you.'

I'm not yet ready to admit defeat. There must be another way.

'Then we need to dismantle the Astorian Empire. Overthrow it. Have all the enslaved kingdoms rise up. I know you yearn for freedom.'

'Of course we do! But you can't fight muskets and cannons with fists, iron bars, and the occasional dagger!' Hargna says. 'The Astorians hold the weapons and thus the power. Their armies occupy every kingdom bar Ssythla. No one dares rise up, and even peaceful protests are ruthlessly put down. There's as much chance as you moving a mountain as there is a successful rebellion!'

My beloved ssythlans. Had I not severed contact with them, perhaps I'd have known this storm was coming. Yet another mistake to rue.

'If you challenged me to move a mountain, I would,' I state boldly.

Grishen chuckles and it softens the tension.

'I'm in awe of anyone who can take down eight slingers single-handed. But no offense, Hargna could probably lift you above his head, and he couldn't do it!'

'That's because he lacks vision,' I counter, my tone sharp but carrying a flicker of amusement. 'And self-belief.'

'Then how would you do it?' Hargna demands, leaning forward.

There's no threat, his posture is more inquisitive than aggressive.

'The same way I'd dismantle the Astorian Empire. Piece, by small piece.'

Even as I say the words, I know they've struck a chord.

'So, what's the first piece of the mountain we have to move?' Grishen asks. 'This is a cause I've always dreamed of fighting for!'

Hargna shoots him a measuring glance, then turns to me expectantly.

'It starts with me finding a way to kill the All Father, for good, and to have any chance of doing that, I need weapons.'

'We should have looted those slingers when we had the chance,' Grishen mutters regretfully.

'Whilst I'm not proud of suggesting it, surely you can kill some soldiers and take their muskets.' Hargna adds.

I shake my head, reassessing Hargna. He's obviously extremely uncomfortable with violence, and yet in this broken world, violence is the only method to effect change. He's struggling with the concept, but it seems he's coming to reluctantly accept it.

'You've got it all wrong. I'm not after guns. I want different weapons entirely. The type of weapons I've fought with my whole life. The type of weapons your people once fought with. I want swords, knives, a bow, arrows and armour.'

Hargna snorts, struggling to stifle a laugh.

'I'm not a man of war, but even I know you don't choose a sword over a gun. Those kind of things are obsolete!'

'Tell that to those slingers,' Grishen mutters, looking thoughtful.

'You must have blacksmiths who can make them?' I say, somewhat horrified. 'I'm no slinger, and have no desire to be. Guns aren't weapons of stealth, and whilst they dominate a battlefield, that's not how I intend to fight.'

'Blacksmiths?' Hargna echoes, incredulous. 'There are no blacksmiths nowadays. Everything is made in factories and foundries.'

My heart sinks.

'The Great Hall of Victory,' Grishen declares, snapping his fingers.

'The what?' I ask.

'It's in the east district of the city within the Astorian sector,' he replies, excited.

'You'll never get there undetected.' Hargna declares. 'Patrols walk the streets day and night. There's no way you'll go unseen.'

Grishen smiles at me and winks.

'Stop talking yourself out of this expedition, Hargna. Like it or not, you're part of our nefarious gang now, and who says we'd walk the streets. Malina has shown me other ways to navigate this city, and they afford the best views.'

'Will someone tell me what the Great Hall of Victory is?' I ask, as Grishen gets up and pulls a reluctant Hargna after.

'It's better we show you,' Grishen laughs, his excitement infectious. 'In every major city, there's a Great Hall, and it's law that every child under twelve years, of whatever nation, visits it once a year.'

'Then lead on,' I say. 'It seems my education is somewhat lacking.'

I take a final look around our filthy sanctuary. I might almost have died here, but now, if I'm lucky, the seeds of rebellion might well have been born here.

***

I could well be mistaken for the mother of two oversized, bumbling children as I lead Grishen and Hargna across the cold rooftops of Astgate. The night sky offers no help, no flash of lightning, no gleam of moonlight, not even a single star. Up here, above the reach of flickering streetlamps, darkness reigns supreme, thick as ink.

This is my place, my world.

'Come,' I say softly, guiding them. 'It's flat for the next thirty paces.'

So emboldened, they tread with more confidence. Their larger hands holding mine as we navigate toward our final destination. How many lamp posts we've slid down, roads we've darted across, and walls we've climbed, I don't know, but what I do know, is that we've been blessed by good fortune and no little luck.

Without a curfew like the military sector, the Astorian civilian sector's roads are busy. Despite the chill air, families enjoying an evening out, walking and eating, have complicated our journey tenfold.

Staying hidden while maintaining a good pace has been our biggest challenge. Grishen has done remarkably well, and together, we've helped Hargna get over his initial fear and clumsiness.

Two nights we've travelled together, barely avoiding discovery, where alone I'd have taken less than one with no risk whatsoever. But solitude, I've realised, is a burden I no longer wish to carry. Of all my fears, living, or dying alone, cuts the sharpest.

'Lotane. I miss you!' I whisper, my voice barely more than a breath.

'What did you say?' Grishen asks.

I consider deflecting his curiosity, hiding behind a quick *nothing*, but what's the point of having companions if I can't share the weight of my feelings?

'I miss my soul mate,' I admit, the words hanging in the air.

'The Queen of Beasts has a soul mate?' Hargna chuckles, his voice tinged with disbelief. 'Pray tell, is it an ogre, or a troll?'

There's no malice in his tone, only a tentative jest, and I find myself smiling despite the ache in my chest. Hargna is becoming bolder, finding the confidence to speak his mind. Also, talking about Lotane, even in jest, brings him closer, as if he's walking beside me.

'No, not a troll or ogre,' I reply, 'Although he can be as stubborn as both. Lotane is human.'

'Human?' Grishen asks. 'From where?'

'He is, would you believe, Astorian.'

There's a moment of silence.

'Why the hells would you choose an Astorian?'

Hargna's incredulity cuts through the stillness, his voice laden with judgment.

Anger flares within me, quick and hot. No one, but no one, can speak ill of my love, not even a new ally. But before I give my scathing response, Grishen interjects.

'Were you asleep in the back of the history class?' he hisses. 'Malina called him *Lotane!*'

'Lotane. Lotane,' Hargna mumbles. 'Lotane, the Great Betrayer?'

'The Great Betrayer?' I echo, my irritation giving way to intrigue.

'In Astorian lore,' Grishen says softly, recounting what is obviously an oft-told tale, 'Lotane is a hated figure said to have been cursed with one green and one blue eye. He killed the legendary Queen Asterz, the first Astorian martyr, saviour of the world. After committing this heinous act, he fled with his fey lover, Nogotha. Ever since, any child born with mismatched eyes is put to death.'

I'm astounded. It's unbelievable that the legend and punishment Astoria had in my youth has continued, but instead of Ardenthal as the betrayer, it's now Lotane. I think he'd be rather happy knowing he's infamous.

'That would make him thousands of years old,' Hargna scoffs. 'Don't be ridiculous.'

'And how old do you think our new ally is then?' Grishen retorts.

He's quite my stalwart defender, and whilst I can easily fight and win my own battles, he's demonstrating just how loyal he is.

'She looks quite good for her age, don't you think?'

I smile at Grishen using similar words to those I'd spoken to him.

Hargna laughs.

'That she does. Alright, Nogotha, Queen of Beasts. Is he the very same Lotane as Astorian lore speaks of?'

'He is,' I say proudly. 'The legend of him slaying Queen Asterz and coming to the fey world with me is close to the truth, but I can assure you, that Asterz was no martyr. She instigated slavery and rape, and fled the final battle against Nogoth when she believed it lost. Not long after I'd killed him, she subsequently tried to kill me, but as legend says, that didn't end well for her.'

Hargna sighs, and despite the darkness, I can perceive genuine regret.

'Forgive me, Malina. My ignorance clouded my judgement. You chose very well indeed. I've come to learn that not all fey are monsters, nor all Astorians ... and ...' he clears his throat, 'not all half-Astorians are traitors either. Forgive me, Grishen. I misjudged you too.'

It's a rare and vulnerable admission, one that has a rare smile tug at my lips. I bring my allies together in the darkness, and they embrace awkwardly, Grishen's face pressed against Hargna's chest. It takes everything in me not to burst out laughing.

'If you two need some privacy to really make up, just let me know,' I snort, unable to resist.

They step awkwardly apart and we laugh softly.

It's the first moment where Hargna has relaxed his defences and truly feels part of our small group, and I say nothing more, unwilling to risk spoiling the moment.

'Come,' I say, taking their hands again. 'I'll tell you two some more bedtime stories when I tuck you in tonight.'

Whether they understand my humour or not, the joke lightens my heart as we traverse the final rooftops toward our destination, the sight of which has me walk near the edge to better appreciate the view.

The Great Hall of Victory rises before us, majestic even in the darkness. Huge ornamental columns support an overhanging roof crowned with a burnished metal dome. Even at night, it reflects the light from the streetlamps below, a beacon of Astorian grandeur.

At street level, twenty steps lead up to three separate giant sets of doors. Bronzed statues of heroic, muscular warriors are set intermittently into the walls, standing triumphant over the twisted metal bodies of gargoyles and ogres.

But it's not the Great Hall itself that suddenly captures my attention, it's the scene unfolding below. For there, in a beautiful plaza lined by eateries, stalls and galleries, moving with the ease of a benevolent ruler, is the All Father.

I freeze. My breath catching in my throat, my fists clenched, as I watch him, impossibly alive once more, mingling with the people as though I hadn't killed him twice already.

'Gods. He truly is immortal,' Grishen whispers.

I say nothing ... just watch in disbelief as the crowd converges as word spreads of his presence.

Children run up to him, and he rests his hand upon their heads, murmuring blessings. Mothers hold out food, and he breaks pieces off, sharing their meal as though he's part of the family. He embraces the elderly, laughs with the men, and clasps hands with the merchants. The people flock to him with reverence, basking in his presence.

Amongst such an adoring crowd, his slingers hang back, discreetly shadowing him at a distance, ever watchful but giving him the moment.

'Their love is bought with our blood,' Hargna murmurs, 'and their gilded homes are built with our bones. It makes me sick.'

Grishen leans in close, keeping his voice low.

'Generations ago, it was our kinsfolk who died in their thousands building this. Astorians don't dirty their hands with such things. Hastians are the architects, Icelandians and Tarsians work the factories and foundries, Delnorians farm the fields, and the Rolantrians and Surians fish and mine. Astoria takes, and everyone else gives.'

I absorb this new information while following the All Father's every move. Whilst I want him dead, I can't help but admire him a little. Despite his physical weakness, he's a survivor. He's channelled his hate, which, along with his immortality and manipulating people's fear, has enabled him to take full control of Astoria, conquer the seven kingdoms, and pursue a path of vengeance against me and my world.

As a Chosen or Queen of the Fey, I've never had a worthier target. But, with a different mission tonight, I resist temptation, especially as what's needed to carry out an assassination is within the Great Hall.

We pull away from the roof's edge and settle against a chimney, waiting silently for the All Father to move on and for the crowd below to settle.

Eventually, the noise dies away, and a quick glance over the edge reveals the All Father and his slingers turning a corner back from whence we'd come.

'Let's go,' I say, returning to my friends and pulling them to their feet.

The Great Hall of Victory might stand alone, but its expansive roof stretches out close to the avenue of buildings on either side. These are also exquisitely crafted with balconies and trellises covered in plants and sculpture, indicating the wealth and status of those who live here.

Curtained windows emit a gentle glow, and if it weren't for the knowledge that this place was built on slavery and persecution, I'd have wondered at the warmth, kindness, and culture of those residents who lived within. Being an Astorian certainly has its privileges.

Staying low, ensuring we don't alert the residents beneath us, we tread softly across the rooftop until we're adjacent to the Great Hall. From a distance, the gap between the buildings appeared no more than a single step, but up close, it's much wider.

'Damn,' Hargna moans. 'How are we going to get in now?'

'With a little bravery.' I say, squeezing his shoulder. 'Have faith. You're almost tall enough to step across. It's Grishen who should be worried!'

Grishen snorts, his good nature easing the tension. 'Careful, Malina. I'm starting to think you care.'

'Don't flatter yourself,' I shoot back. 'I just don't want to drag your broken body the rest of the way.'

I take a few steps back, measuring the distance, and subconsciously ask my non-existent magic for help. A rueful smile tugs at my lips. Nowadays, I have to rely on my muscles and skills alone. With a steadying breath, I run, the reassuring stickiness of the rooftop underfoot giving me confidence. My leap carries me effortlessly over the yawning gap, and I roll smoothly on landing, my back scraping painfully against the rough stone roof.

'Not a bad landing,' I mutter.

As I turn back, Hargna is shaking his head, as Grishen urges him on.

'Come on, Hargna,' I whisper, adding my voice to Grishen's, willing him to find the inner strength to start conquering his fears.

Grishen moves closer to the roof's edge, his silhouette briefly illuminated by the lights below. I'm about to hiss a warning when Hargna begins his run. His hesitation is palpable, his movements unsure, and as he nears the edge, I can see he hasn't fully committed to the jump.

Grishen recognises this too and grabs Hargna at the last instant, heaving with all his strength.

I leap at the same time, landing on my stomach, grabbing Hargna's arms as he lands short, his waist smacking into the edge of the roof. He's badly winded, and I desperately hang on as his weight starts to drag me toward the edge.

Hargna is dazed, and I daren't let go, but if I don't, we'll both fall to our deaths.

With a thud, Grishen lands beside me, reaches down, and, despite Hargna being the bigger man, yanks him up and deposits him on his back, wide-eyed and gasping for air.

'Long legs and a big heart,' Grishen says kindly, patting Hargna on the shoulder as he sits beside us, catching his breath.

'Please tell me we'll never do that again,' Hargna wheezes.

'Only after we've done it once more,' I chuckle. 'How else are we going to get out again?'

'Just show me the front door,' he groans, his head falling back against the roof with a dull thud.

I stretch, easing the tension in my limbs.

'Come. Enough lying around,' I say, getting to my feet. 'My tour of the Great Hall is somewhat overdue. Let's find a way in.'

'And another way out for Hargna,' Grishen chuckles.

I smile, the gentle banter a fleeting reminder of happier times when I was with my fellow Chosen. Life had been simpler then … before I discovered the truth.

The truth.

Would this world be a better place if I hadn't discovered it and had simply followed the expected path laid out for me as a Chosen?

The answer saddens me, for I fear that it would.

I've made many mistakes in my life, and for the first time, I wonder if killing Nogoth was the biggest one of them all.

**

A circular metal stairwell leads down from the roof, and I wince with every heavy step my two companions make.

I glare, though in truth, they're trying their best to move stealthily. Kralgen would have been so disappointed in them.

The loss of my old friend hurts despite the centuries that have passed. There was no closure, no goodbye to someone who was a brother to me. He was the best of the Chosen, a simple, loyal soul, kind, gentle, and deadly as hell.

If only he were here, or Lotane, I'd feel supremely confident.

The stairwell clangs under a heavy footfall, and I sigh, the memory of my friend pushed rudely aside by the reality of the situation.

Hargna looks abashed, and we continue our descent, the ever-present flickering lights and their tainted glow guiding us through the gloom.

As we reach the bottom, we find ourselves in a cramped storeroom. Shelves line the walls filled with numerous hand tools, but nothing useful for our mission, unless the small door at the end of a narrow corridor is locked.

It isn't

'Even if this place is closed, we stay alert!' I say, inching the door open carefully.

I stand still, rooted to the spot, unbelieving.

'It takes your breath away a little,' Hargna whispers at my shoulder.

The service door has opened onto the grand entrance chamber and I can't help but shake my head in admiration and amazement.

Row upon row of life-size and incredibly detailed statues of Astorian cavalry stand forever tall and proud. The horses are all mid-gallop, their riders leaning low, sabres or lances extended, their cold eyes staring into the distance.

Despite this not being a sightseeing mission, I go and stand with my back to one of the gigantic entrance doors, and note that the riders are subtly angled inward, so that as you enter, it's as though you're the focal point of their charge.

Above, the ceiling is a masterpiece, painted to depict a raging storm, but even more eye-catching are the stone or plaster gargoyles that jut from the painted tempest, lances ready to cast at any visitor below foolish enough not to show the proper respect. Further stone reliefs, depicting more of the winged fey, grasp every column as though ready to descend on the unwary.

Only half the lights are on, and whether by design or otherwise, they swing ever so slightly, and the shadows sway, giving the impression that the horses, riders, and gargoyles are actually alive.

At the rear of the entrance hall the wall has again been painted by a true artist, lines of Astorian warriors stand shoulder to shoulder, stern and unyielding, their eyes fixed on an unseen, distant horizon. Behind them, the city of Ast looms, a symbol of defiance and strength.

'This depicts the last battle where Nogoth was defeated by the Astorian army,' Grishen says, breaking the silence. 'Hence this is called the Great Hall of Victory.'

There's so much detail and skill, that it's hard for me to look away.

'It's a fitting name, but whilst the art is incredible, it's very misleading,' I reply. 'I led the cavalry charge alongside Kralgen and Lotane. Queen Asterz was with us. But, the main battle line ...' I gesture toward the mural, '...was Icelandian. Astorian civilians were conscripted to bolster our lines, but it was your ancestors who should be celebrated here.'

We pass under a towering arch into the next chamber, a faceless, hooded statue with hands clasped overseeing our passage.

'The All Father looks over us every step we take,' Hargna mutters.

I barely hear him as another incredible, but this time, sad sight greets me as we enter something akin to a giant morgue, no doubt designed to terrify the observer. Enormous frames and glass cabinets display the skeletons of giants, trolls, ogres, and gargoyles, their forms frozen for eternity.

The walls are painted in dark, violent hues, with terrible splashes of red, showing what these mighty creatures once looked like as they feasted on the flesh and blood of their human victims. Black stone benches are scattered everywhere for visitors to sit and contemplate the horror.

'This is the Hell of Remembrance,' Grishen murmurs.

'You mean hall.'

'No. It's Hell. On my first visit here I remember begging my mother to get me out,' Grishen says, his face downcast. 'But by law, I wasn't allowed. One hour we had to stay here before being moved on.'

Hargna nods in agreement, his expression glum.

I sigh, shaking my head. With such horrific imagery imprinted into young hearts and minds, it's no wonder the fey remain the stuff of nightmares, an ever-present threat to Astoria, and the wider-world's existence.

'Is this a lie too, like the entrance hall?' Hargna asks.

He looks at me expectantly, then at Grishen's bandaged wrist. He knows I drink blood. There's no use in lying.

'Once, it was true. But under my guidance, the fey have, for the most part, been farmers for four thousand years. Their diet is now like yours and mine.'

Hargna mutters something under his breath.

'Let's go,' he says. 'I hate this bit, and what we want is deeper inside.'

Another arch, the robed figure of the All Father seeming to watch over us as we pass underneath into a vast space full of benches surrounding low glassed cases that contain open books, aged tomes, and yellowed pieces of parchment.

'The Hell of Truth. Written records of what transpired the last time the fey invaded,' Grishen offers, as we walk straight through the middle and beneath the next arch.

The next gigantic chamber has lines of lifelike models of Astorian soldiers spanning numerous eras. Heavily armoured knights with swords and maces mixed in with light cavalry greet us, but I'm disappointed to discover their weapons are lacquered wood. As we move further, the old gives way to the new. Uniforms, muskets, handguns, and cannon highlight the military might of Astoria.

Hargna notes my obvious disappointment.

'You'll find what you seek in the rooms off this one, but also the shame that all other nations wish to forget.'

I'm intrigued by his words, and head toward the room signed Icelandia. Hargna and Grishen drag their feet, but voice no complaint.

When I open the door and enter, I understand Hargna's comment.

This room, like the others, is full of lifelike models. Icelandians in furs kneel, chained in manacles, an Astorian soldier standing above them, musket at the ready. Two walls are painted as a frozen wasteland, ice huts the primitive abodes from which these barbarians came. The other two depict a battle, Astorian cannons and muskets firing, the Icelandians fleeing, leaving behind the dying, drowning in rivers of blood.

'Now you know my shame,' Grishen whispers.

'What, because the Astorians painted your ancestors running from battle?' I say, shaking my head in disbelief. 'History is written by the victors, but it doesn't make it true. I've fought alongside tens of thousands of your countrymen, and not one, not one, ever ran! Yes, you were defeated, but not through skill in combat, just by what the Astorians label science.'

Around the walls and pillars, glass cases display jewellery, furs, and weapons. It takes but a quick glance to recognise these as genuine artefacts. The giant axes, bastard swords, and maces all gleam dully but look strangely distorted.

'Take your pick, but be quick,' I say.

'What?' Grishen asks, startled.

'None of these are good for me,' I explain. 'I'm not tall or strong enough to wield them properly. They were made for Icelandians. They were made for you and will suit Hargna too.'

'I can't,' whispers Hargna, his hands running over the glass as if caressing the long-sword underneath. 'My father tried to convince me to fight, but I've always abhorred violence. I couldn't even…' His voice trails off, his expression pained.

'Allow me.' With a crash, the glass shatters under my elbow, and I reach in to find the sword embedded in a transparent jelly-like substance.

Whatever it is, it has preserved the weapon perfectly, and it parts easily under my touch. I pull out the sword, offering it hilt-first to Hargna.

'I don't know if I could use it,' he whispers.

His voice trails away, and he looks sorrowful.

'The pointy end goes in the enemy,' I say. 'With this is your hand, you needn't be frightened anymore. The Astorians will be frightened of you!'

Hargna reaches out slowly, taking the weapon, a look of trepidation on his face as he hefts the sword, testing its weight.

Another tinkle of shattered glass and I turn to see Grishen holding two axes, their honed edges glinting faintly in the dim light.

'You two stay here while I find something more suitable for me in another room,' I say. 'When you come find me, look like warriors and not slaves.'

I peer cautiously around the door before stepping out and heading toward the room labelled Delnor. Inside it's much the same, the painted walls depicting Delnor's defeat by the glorious armies of Astoria. Life-size, manacled models of Delnorian soldiers, downcast and defeated, huddled on the ground lorded over by their Astorian captors.

I'm like a child in a cake shop.

The Delnorians favoured short swords, and soon I've chosen two that are perfectly balanced with lacquered wooden scabbards. Turning to inspect the daggers. I soon have six put aside.

Pulling a blue cloak from one of the models, I spread it on the floor and add my new weapons, along with a dozen leather straps and cords. Frustratingly, the Delnorian models lack armour, likely another Astorian attempt to belittle their legacy.

I bundle up the cloak, carefully heave it over my shoulder, and then leave Delnor's defeat behind, wondering where to head to continue my outfitting as I consider the other signs.

Rolantria, Suria, Tars, my birthplace of Hastia, and then my attention is drawn to a final sign. The Chamber of Beasts.

Apparently, I'm worthy of my own room and I'm drawn toward it.

Grishen and Hargna step out into the main hall, and I can't help but laugh softly as they blush at my attention. Grishen is dressed in a fur jerkin, and has even found some paint to daub his cheeks with. Hargna has donned a leather cuirass, and both have their weapons strapped to their belted waists.

'I feel like a fraud,' Hargna says, looking downcast.

'Rubbish. You look like a warrior,' I say. 'Strong, wild, and most of all, proud. Without a sense of self-worth, others will never find you worthy. Without a purpose in life, you will forever wander lost.'

I reach out, gripping their forearms in turn, solidifying the bond between us.

'You might want to consider another room,' Grishen says as he recognises my destination. 'It's not pleasant in there.'

'I still need armour, a bow, and arrows,' I reply, undeterred.

'The Tarsian room has bows and arrows,' Hargna offers.

'Please get me some,' I ask, 'and join me here after.'

As I open the door to the Chamber of Beasts, I immediately understand Grishen's hesitation. Unlike the other rooms, this one isn't a tribute to Astorian victory ... like the Hell of Remembrance, this room is designed to put the fear of the fey into whoever enters.

It's larger than the others, but then that's because the story it tells is not just of me. The paintings on the walls are somewhat perverse.

One depicts Nogoth with me as both his consort, and Lotane's seducer. It's quite the piece of erotic art, and the imagination of the artist is rather commendable.

Another wall shows us overlooking a bloody battlefield, violet flames in our eyes as the fey armies slaughter, rape, and pillage, before dragging any survivors through a world gate.

The third wall is shrouded in shadow, its details obscured, but as intrigue draws me toward it, I appreciate this is intentional. Standing closer reveals families cowering in caves, holding one another, crying in the darkness as monsters loom behind them. No doubt a reference to the temples adjoining the world gate.

The final wall shows Lotane stabbing Queen Asterz in the back as she stands over me, sword raised to strike a killing blow.

The Great Betrayer.

There's little likeness to me, Lotane, or Nogoth, but it doesn't matter. The message is clear; we are evil personified.

The lifelike models are equally horrific and detailed.

One shows me naked, joining with ogres and wolfen in a carnal feast. The next has me standing robed alongside Nogoth and Lotane, bloodied swords raised to snakelike tongues, our coloured eyes glowing like gems.

The one closest has me dressed in black, scaled armour, my hair a nest of snakes, leaning over a screaming baby in a crib, my teeth bared, ready to feast.

I drop my bundle of weapons to the ground, and strip the armour and clothing. Within minutes, I'm dressed in black trousers and shirt. Over the top are leather greaves, vambraces, kilt and the scaled cuirass.

It won't stop a musket ball, but will provide some protection, and just as importantly, I feel prepared.

Grishen and Hargna return carrying three bows and a quiver stuffed with arrows.

Other than a nod of thanks, I ignore them to fashion a harness for my swords, so both hilts jut comfortably over my left shoulder. Two daggers go in my boots, belt, and under the vambraces.

'Damn,' Grishen breathes, looking me up and down as I stand ready before them. He says nothing more, but the admiration in his tone is unmistakable.

I take the bows, testing each carefully, and discard two that have lost their flexibility, then raise an eyebrow.

Grishen looks apologetic.

'No bowstrings that weren't brittle,' he says. 'We searched!'

A rope hanging between two posts acts as a barrier to prevent people getting too close to the painted walls, and one of my swords makes short work of cutting a suitable length.

'I'll make my own later,' I explain, coiling the rope and tucking it under my belt.

'Now what?' Grishen asks.

'We find a safe place to sleep. We certainly need the rest.'

'I have another safe place in mind,' Hargna offers cautiously.

'Hopefully with three beds, decent food, drink, and a better view,' Grishen jokes.

'Perhaps,' Hargna concedes, giving nothing away.

I nod thoughtfully. Hargna remains a mystery, a man whose secrets are tucked away behind a fragile and guarded exterior. Nonetheless, he is also an ally, and we all have our secrets.

'Perhaps you'll tell me later how you know of these places,' I say, heading toward the door with a faint smile. But just as I reach out to open it, voices are raised outside.

'They just went in there, I swear,' a trembling voice declares shakily.

'Don't worry, whoever committed this sacrilege won't live to enjoy it!' growls another.

I press my face to the sliver of light showing between the door and its frame. Through the gap I spy an old man, likely a museum caretaker with four slingers, weapons in hand.

We're trapped!

***

CHAPTER VIII

There's no exit to this room, only the one doorway. The ceiling has no panels, the wall no air grates.

Five flickering lights hang from the ceiling. If I smash them, the darkness will give me an advantage, but only while the door remains closed.

'Come out. We know you're in there,' demands a steady, almost bored voice.

'What do we do?' Hargna whispers, shaking like a leaf.

Grishen, on the other hand, already has his axes in hand and looks at me expectantly.

Come-on, Malina. Think. What do I know?

I know if we step outside the door, the light will identify me, and the slingers will gun me down immediately. Could I kill all four before they react? No.

Yet I'm missing something obvious.

All four ... yes, that's it.

If they knew it was me in here, there would be more than four, and nor would they be so casual. Which means the old man only saw my friends enter.

'We have one chance,' I whisper. 'Go to the back there.' I point to the far wall. 'Get on your knees, weapons on the floor, and hold your hands up empty in surrender, but be ready to strike when the moment comes!'

Hargna is about to argue, but thinks better of it and rushes to the far wall, Grishen at his side, and kneels under a lurid picture of me locked in an obscene act with Nogoth.

I draw my sword, then stand by the crib right in front of the entrance.

A moment later, the door is edged open as the slingers tire of waiting. I daren't move as their guns sweep across me, and I brace myself for the blast, the brief searing pain. Instead, they hold their fire and train their guns on my two friends at the back.

'Bloody cowards,' the bearded lead slinger mutters. 'We hoped you'd come out swinging so we could put you down. But no matter, you'll all swing tomorrow at the end of a rope, unless you want it clean and quick in the head now?'

'No!' cries the old man, his voice trembling. 'They certainly deserve it, but there's so much mess to clean already.'

'Tie 'em up!' orders the lead slinger.

Two of his comrades holster their guns, pull cord from their belts, and walk right past me as if I'm invisible.

I don't move a muscle as the lead slinger and his partner edge forward to keep a clear line of fire on Grishen and Hargna.

'Something's not right,' mutters the old man. 'Something's not right.'

'Shut up you old fool,' the bearded slinger snaps.

'One, two, three,' the old man begins to count, ticking off his fingers. 'Four, five, six, seven. But there's only supposed to be six models!'

Quiet as the grave, I step behind the bearded slinger. The old man freezes, clutching his chest, his mouth opening and closing soundlessly as I cut my sword through the back of the slinger's neck in a vicious blow. The blade slices clean through, and I spin, keeping my momentum, batting aside the other slinger's raised gun, plunging my sword into his chest.

I step behind him, holding him upright as the other two slingers turn and fire in a long-practiced fluid motion, and his body jerks from the impact.

Grishen and Hargna leap up. Grishen cleaves his axe into the back of the slinger in front of him, whereas Hargna wraps his arms around the other, stopping him from drawing his other guns.

The Astorian struggles futilely against Hargna's desperate grip, and I pull my blade free, wipe it clean on my victim's leather coat, before sheathing it on my back.

The slinger's eyes widen as I approach, but I walk past, bend down, and pick up Hargna's sword.

Returning to stand in front of the slinger, I raise Hargna's blade, tilting it so it catches the dim light. I lower the point until it touches the slinger's chest, then exert my weight.

It slides in easily, and the slinger gasps before going limp.

'Next time, remember … stick the pointed end in the bloody enemy,' I say coldly.

Hargna releases the body with a horrified whimper as I drop the sword at his feet.

Turning to Grishen and the slinger he'd killed, I nod in grim approval.

'There will be no prisoners, and no mercy,' I say. 'I know you don't like violence, Hargna, but if you hesitate again, we're likely to die.'

'It better not happen again,' Grishen snaps, glaring at Hargna.

Hargna looks miserable, but he nods, tears in his eyes.

'Now, quickly gather your weapons, and then let's loot these slingers. It's important we understand these guns, even if they repulse me.'

We strip the closest two slingers of their weapon harnesses, and the ammunition from the others, bundling them up in one of their long leather coats, and then head toward the door. Grishen stays close by my side, whereas Hargna stumbles in our wake.

The old man is still there, leaning against the frame panting, panting heavily and clutching his chest. I scoop up my discarded bow, and pause before him, meeting his panicked gaze.

'Do you know who I am?' I ask, my voice low and steady.

He says nothing, just gasps for breath.

'Look at me,' I hiss.

He jerks as if branded by a hot poker and raises his head.

'Do you know me?'

The old man nods. 'I, I, p-promise to say n-nothing,' he stammers.

I press my hands together in thanks, smiling warmly.

'Thank you,' I say. 'Don't worry, you'll be safe. Stay in this room until you're found tomorrow, and when you're asked who did this, you say they had cleft chins and looked Astorian. Astorian. Do you understand?'

The man nods gratefully.

I usher Grishen and Hargna past as the old man mutters to himself.

'Go to that corner,' I say, pointing away from the bodies.

As he shuffles off, I draw my blade and decapitate him in one swift motion. His body crumples silently, and I let out a slow breath.

Hopefully, the Astorians will think I'm gone from this world a while longer.

Then I consider where I'm standing, the Chamber of Beasts, now soaked in blood, and the irony doesn't escape me.

They'll know. They'll know.

***

It's early evening as we rest high above the crowded streets, hidden amongst the noisome but essential warmth of four smoke-belching chimney stacks. For the last four days and nights, we've moved silently west, away from the scene of our crime. Our journey has been painfully slow, as the city swarms with Astorian patrols that make even crossing a street hazardous.

The Queen of Beasts is at large, and Astgate is on full alert.

As with every other time we've paused for a break, I occupy myself with crafting a bowstring from the rope I'd appropriated, and this time is no different.

'Not long now,' I say, as the sun's fading glow dips toward Astgate's western skyline.

Opposite me, his legs stretched out, Grishen looks up.

'I'm so hungry,' he moans, 'that I'm actually tempted to eat you!'

I roll my eyes as he tears a strip off a reward poster bearing my likeness, before stuffing it in his mouth and chewing thoughtfully.

'I'm disappointed. I thought you'd taste better,' he chuckles, then tears off another strip, going for seconds.

'Can you believe this?' Hargna mutters, looking at me as he holds up another poster to the dimming light. 'It claims Astorian forces bravely held back a fey incursion led by you at the world gate. Apparently, they shut down the power stations to trap you on this side, but a malfunction caused both to explode, leading to massive casualties.'

Grishen snorts with laughter.

'Lies and more lies. Anything else?'

Hargna scans the text, his face dour.

'Only that she's alone and on the run, hence the reward posters.'

'I feel insulted,' Grishen says, screwing up the remains of his poster and tossing it at Hargna. 'Not even a mention of her two heroic companions.'

Hargna flinches. Grishen is a ball of positive energy, whereas Hargna … he's conflicted over something.

'Hargna, this might mean it's safe for you to return home,' I say. 'What do you think?'

He holds his head in his hands, sighing deeply before looking up again. 'Home?' he mutters. 'Just because I had somewhere to sleep doesn't make it home. I've also been absent for too long. I'd be severely punished for not reporting for reassignment. Better I stay with you.'

'You know what Grishen and I are intending to do?' I press, wanting to make sure he's committed, but also half-hoping he isn't. He slows us down, and he's still hiding something. But without him, the gate would likely still be open, and we wouldn't have survived during my recovery. Both are debts not easily repaid.

'Yes. Though I fear the three of us alone won't be enough,' he says, rubbing his chin.

Hargna murmurs something to Grishen, who scowls in return.

He's right. Three of us don't make an army, and whilst I've spent these last days trying to keep the three of us together, perhaps he wants to part ways and is afraid of telling me.

'Come on. Out with it, Hargna,' I say, my voice low, commanding.

He remains silent, but the discomfort lingers.

'Voicing your concerns is the only way to ease them,' I say, not letting it go. 'Being strong isn't just about the strength in your limbs, it's the strength of your mind. If you want to part ways, don't be afraid of saying so. I won't judge you.'

Again, silence.

Grishen rolls his eyes at me, but I shake my head.

'We won't leave you here,' I continue. 'Even if we're close to the residential sector, we'll ensure you get safely to wherever you want to go.'

Hargna stares at his hands, then exhales deeply.

'It's not that,' he says softly. 'Although I've considered it more than once. It's the way you butchered that last slinger. It sickened me. The others were necessary, it was them or us, but the fight was already won, and yet you slaughtered the last man.'

Hargna's hands are shaking, and I'm sad he's afraid of me. Yet, I also feel he's skirting his biggest concern.

'What else?' I prompt.

Hargna shifts uncomfortably, hesitant, but I suddenly guess what's truly troubling him.

'It was me killing the old man, wasn't it?'

'Yes,' Hargna mutters, barely audible. 'I'm worried you're as demonic as we've been taught, and I can't help but wonder what the hells I've done.'

'So now we reach the heart of it,' I say, nodding slowly. 'It wasn't my finest deed. I could have rendered him unconscious, bound him. But consider this: he wasn't some innocent old man. He brought the slingers. He wanted you dead. Had I let him live, do you know what the Astorians would've done if they learned two slaves had aided me?'

Hargna looks away, as if trying to avoid the answer.

'They'd execute a dozen of our people a day trying to discover our identity,' he mutters.

'Or worse,' Grishen adds.

I pause, thinking how best to continue. Any of the Chosen would have never lost a moment's sleep over what was done, but these are different times and Hargna is grappling with his conscience ... something I once had, long ago.

'I'm not claiming my actions were right, Hargna. But for every decision made, there are consequences,' I say, watching his reaction. 'The old man made a choice, and it cost him. Had he said nothing, or waited until morning, he and the slingers would still be alive.'

'What you did still feels wrong,' Hargna says, his voice strained.

'It should,' I reply. 'Killing should never feel good. The fact you question it means your moral compass is still intact. But when the guilt creeps in, remind yourself, he'd have celebrated our deaths and taken pride in his part.'

Hargna looks pained, but he's stopped shaking.

'Not forgetting,' Grishen adds, 'he and his ancestors have oppressed our peoples for generations.'

Hargna nods slowly.

'And what about you, Malina?' he asks. 'How did you feel killing him?'

Hargna is studying me closely, and I hesitate. It's not that I don't have the answer; it's just that I'm worried if the truth will jeopardise our alliance when I've yet to decide whether it's worth saving or not.

'I didn't feel a thing,' I admit, grimacing. 'It's not that I've no feelings, far from it. But in my youth, I was … indelibly changed, making me far more than I used to be, but also far less at the same time.'

Memories resurface, the purges, the sense of righteousness when I stopped fearing the act of killing and began to embrace it instead, all in the name of the Once and Future King.

'Without honesty, there can be no trust,' Hargna says, pulling a wan smile. 'I'd like to stay with you, if you'll have me.'

Grishen pats him on the back, and I nod in agreement despite relief and concern vying for supremacy. Hargna is still holding something back, of that I'm sure.

I turn my gaze south in the direction of the moon gate. How many years before the Astorians rebuild new factories to open it? Even if it takes five, that's just six months in the fey world.

What could Lotane achieve by then? How ready will he and the fey be to withstand the onslaught that awaits?

My tiny army and I must ensure he never has to find out.

Are letting my thoughts wander, a help or a hindrance?

Not that I've been idle during our discussion or whilst contemplating what lies ahead.

Turning back to the bowstring I'm fashioning, I unwind two long threads from the rope, and use them to further reinforce the loop at the end. I study my handwork carefully. About four hours of labour, and I now have a usable bow.

Picking up the bow, I stand, slip the string loop over the limb tip, and wedge it firmly against the inside of my foot. With a grunt of exertion, I bend the bow, slipping the other string loop over the opposite end.

Smiling to myself, I draw the bow, testing its pull. I'd need to loose a dozen arrows to truly understand its potential, but it feels powerful. I lay it carefully to one side. Leaving it strung will diminish its power over time, but I can't afford not to have it ready.

Setting the bow aside, I check the quiver of arrows my friends had gathered for me. They'd crammed about forty arrows into a quiver meant for no more than thirty. I kneel, carefully extracting them one by one, inspecting the flights and shafts.

By the time I've finished, the sun has set, and I have twenty arrows true enough to hit whatever I aim at and feel a lot better for this addition to my arsenal. I replace them carefully in the quiver, pushing the points deep into the cork at the bottom to prevent rattling or loss while running.

Putting the rope to further use, I fashion a sling for the quiver so it can hang across my back, the arrows easily reachable above my right shoulder, just as my sword hilts are over my left.

The crunch of marching feet rises up from the street below, in itself, nothing unusual, however, the marching suddenly stops with a stamp of feet.

Intrigued, I cautiously approach the roof's edge and peer down. Twenty soldiers have split into groups of ten. One enters the block opposite and on the warehouse we're sheltering on.

I've seen many searches before, but this is different. As I glance up and down the street, squads are simultaneously entering other buildings.

Retreating back to Grishen and Hargna, I place my hands hard on their shoulders.

'We have to move,' I whisper.

'What's wrong?' Grishen asks.

'Maybe nothing,' I reply. 'But this building is being searched, as is every other on this street. Let's move away from the access hatch.'

They groan softly as they rise, their movements slow and stiff in the near darkness.

'Don't forget the guns,' Grishen whispers to Hargna, who stoops to grab the bundle.

'Quickly,' I urge, impatient to get moving.

I take their hands, guiding them across the flat rooftop. The faint glow from the streetlights below casts the parapet in sharp relief, but the sky above is a mass of dark clouds, refusing to lend any natural light.

We settle in the northwest corner of the building as far from the roof access as possible. Peering over the edge, I see more units waiting in the streets below, alert in case they're called to action.

Our usual escape route of sliding down a lamppost will only see us delivered into their arms if we need to leave that way.

'Look!' Grishen hisses.

Lights appear on rooftops as far as I can see across the city to our south and east, and two blocks to the north and west. We're at the fringe of the Astorian search net, and with a squeal of rusty hinges, the access hatch on our roof clangs open, and a dozen musket-armed soldiers emerge.

'They've worked out how we're getting around,' Grishen murmurs.

'What are we going to do?' Hargna asks, his usual desperation apparent.

'Let me think. Just stay calm!' I say, my mind racing.

A lantern flares within the group on our roof, then more, lighting up the far corner where they begin their search. Four guards remain at the hatch, muskets ready.

I glance over the parapet again. Soldiers still patrol below. Descending now would mean certain death.

'We should attack,' Grishen suggests, his hands clenched into fists. 'We might be able to kill them all, especially with surprise, the guns, and Malina on our side.'

'And what happens after that?' Hargna counters. 'One scream, one musket or gunshot, and this building will be swarming with soldiers before we can escape. Even if we kill them silently, there are soldiers in the street and we can't leave without being seen. We need to move around and hope they don't spot us.'

It's not a bad plan, but as I look at the nearest buildings, individual soldiers are already standing with lanterns in each corner. They've already considered Hargna's idea, and are keeping every area lit, and our rooftop companions are following the same thorough routine.

'Death or glory,' Grishen mutters, realising as I have that hiding is now impossible. 'Just say when, Malina. There's no way we can escape this fight.'

Yet something Hargna previously said comes to mind.

'You're a genius, Hargna,' I whisper, rising to my feet. 'Stay low and get ready to run.'

Reaching over my shoulder, I pluck an arrow from the quiver and choose my target. It's a long shot, the soldier I'm aiming at stands two streets away holding a torch, I draw the bow effortlessly, then slowly release my breath and the string a moment later. The thrum of the bowstring is strangely comforting, but I'd overestimated its power. I reach for a second arrow while the first is still mid-flight, nocking and drawing, adjusting my aim, anticipating my victim's reaction as the first arrow splinters on the parapet just before him.

As the soldier goes to investigate the noise, my second shot hits him in the upper thigh. I'd aimed for his chest, but am rewarded nonetheless. He drops his lantern, and his screams pierce the night air as he's engulfed by oil-fed flames.

Even without the other soldiers highlighted by the human torch, I could still see them, and three more of my arrows find their mark, all within the space of a dozen heartbeats.

Lystra would have been scathing in her judgement of my first shot with an untried bow, but proud of the others.

As Hargna predicted, the noise draws every soldier within earshot like moths to a flame.

Our rooftop is cleared within seconds. Peering over the parapet, I see the unit below is gone, replaced by another squad sprinting along the road toward the commotion.

'Let's go,' I say, slinging the bow over my shoulder then leaping off to slide down the nearest lamppost.

I crouch at the bottom waiting for the others, and when Hargna comes down last, desperately clutching the bundle of guns, I turn north, only for him to grab my arm.

'This way,' he says, pointing west. 'My hiding place isn't far.'

'Nor are the slave quarters,' Grishen warns as we break into a run, darting along the street. 'There's no curfew there, and someone might give Malina up if they've seen the posters. At the very least, we'll draw unwanted attention. Look at how we're dressed!'

I grab Hargna's shoulder.

'Hargna, we can't afford to be seen.'

'We won't. Not where we're going to hide.'

'Then we walk from hereon, so we don't draw attention,' I say, annoyed with Hargna for being so secretive.

A group of people appear at the end of the street, milling outside a food hall, so we turn into a quieter street, staying in the shadows, passing a couple of Tarsians and an Icelandian on the other side, but they pay us no heed.

After a few minutes of lucky progress, I take Hargna's arm.

'It's getting busier. Let's return to the rooftops.'

'No need, we're here,' he huffs, leading us to an open doorway nestled between two closed shops. One is a cobbler, the other a baker, and both look like the owners take little pride in their establishments or have little money to spend on their upkeep.

As we step inside, I gag.

'Gods!' I gasp, as we navigate the foulness of what is easily the worst public latrine I've ever encountered. Faeces smear the floor and walls and the air is barely breathable. 'No one will look for us in here. But we might die from the smell!'

Grishen retches, spits, then nods unhappily in agreement.

'I'd rather be shot than die from whatever we'll catch in here.'

'Not much further,' Hargna says, beckoning us onward.

I step over a pile of something hideous as Hargna turns into a small cubicle. An open hole in the ground leads directly into the city sewer, and Grishen turns away and vomits, adding to the already horrendous stench.

Unperturbed, Hargna grabs a black and pitted, rusted metal ring and twists. Silently, a concealed door swings inward to reveal an empty cell. Metal bars run floor to ceiling, their regularity only broken by a gate. Wooden panelling behind the bars conceals whatever lies beyond.

Hargna steps inside, wiping his boots carefully on a thick mat.

I follow cautiously, with Grishen just behind.

'Close the door,' Hargna says.

Grishen doesn't need asking twice, and the door clicks shut as he pushes it to. I finish wiping my boots and he follows suit.

The air here is marginally better, but still far from pleasant. I approach the gate and try to open it, but it's locked.

Glancing around the cell, I note it's empty, nothing to hold food or water, both of which we sorely need and there's no handle on the inside of the door we entered through.

'What's going on, Hargna? Where's the food?' Grishen asks, as if reading my mind.

Hargna shakes his head, and paces up and down, the bundle of guns over one shoulder, as if angry, or nervous. Nervous, yes, something isn't quite right …

'We'll be safe here. We can rest up,' he says. 'We won't stay long.'

'Grishen,' I say, my intuition screaming in warning. 'Time to go our own way. Let's get that door open.'

Suddenly, the wooden panelling on two sides falls away.

My bow is drawn, an arrow nocked, before they even hit the floor.

'Release that arrow and it will be the last thing you ever do,' says a stern looking Icelandian woman.

My arrow is aimed at her chest, and the bars won't stop me from hitting her. But she's not bluffing, the fifteen odd muskets aimed in our direction are unlikely to miss either.

Hargna has betrayed us.

***

'It's her, the Queen of Beasts!'

'By the gods, the end of days are upon us!'

'Do we kill her?'

'Arelen!' shouts the woman who'd first addressed me, turning to a man by her side. 'Go tell Tooran who's fallen into our lap, and get two sets of manacles while you're at it. Hargna has bought us the Queen of Beasts!'

The man darts off down a rough, stone corridor.

I keep my arrow trained on the woman. While obviously the leader of this bunch, from the way she's biting her lip she's uncertain, and definitely not in overall charge. Perhaps Tooran is.

'Hargna. What the hell is going on here?' I demand, resisting the temptation to put an arrow through him.

Before he can answer, the woman speaks again.

'Hargna. Step away from those two and come here, now!'

With an apologetic shrug, he approaches the gate.

'Nogotha. Grishen!'

The woman half spits the names.

'Put your weapons by the back wall, move away, and kneel with your hands behind your heads. If you don't, I swear we'll cut you down!'

'Do as she says, please,' Hargna says, frowning. 'Trust me. This will work out. You'll be safe if you do as Valeria asks. These are members of the underground.'

An underground resistance? My irritation gives way to intrigue. This could be useful ... potentially very useful. My shoulders relax slightly. Hargna hasn't betrayed us before, and no one has shot us yet.

'Ten, nine, eight, seven ...'

'Damnit. Alright. Stop the bloody countdown!'

I hate being mortal again, and lower my bow, placing it in the corner by the entrance door. With a sigh, I unstrap my harnessed swords and quiver, and drop them alongside before unhooking the two sheathed daggers from my belt, then make a show of putting them down.

Grishen does the same with his two axes.

'She also has a dagger up each sleeve and one in either boot,' Hargna says to Valeria.

'DAMN YOU, HARGNA!' I roar, pulling them out and casting them onto the pile. 'Are you going to have my teeth pulled out next?' I snarl, baring my incisors.

A murmur of disquiet ripples around the group as they witness my anger, but they're safe, behind bars.

Under the constant threat of the muskets, I kneel, interlacing my fingers behind my head, glaring at Hargna. He could have forewarned Grishen and me if he really trusted us and felt we'd be safe.

Grishen's scowl matches mine as he sinks to his knees beside me.

'Out of the storm and into a fire,' he grumbles bitterly.

'We'll find common ground in our common enemy. Don't worry,' I say, half to convince him, half to convince myself.

The looks of hatred, fear and distrust haven't diminished despite giving up our weapons, and Grishen is almost as much the target of their loaded stares as I am.

Valeria's messenger returns holding two sets of manacles.

'Just be aware,' Valeria warns as she unlocks the gate, 'that if you make any move to take Arelen hostage, both of you will be shot instantly.'

I snarl at the man, making him jump. It's childish, but it makes me feel a little better at my predicament.

The manacles fit snugly around my wrists as they're secured behind my back, and Grishen receives the same treatment. Arelen quickly exits, returning the key to Valeria, who tucks it into her breast pocket.

'My whole bloody life they've treated me like shit,' Grishen moans as he stands. 'Half-blood. Traitor. Arse face.'

'Arse face?' I snort, more out of shock than amusement.

'It's my mother's gift of an Astorian chin. Not that they'd say it to the face of any true Astorian. They don't have the balls for that!' he says, raising his voice as we're ushered out of the cage.

I know what it's like not to fit in, to be shunned. It's the sort of trauma that never leaves you. Happy moments are so quick to fade and hard to remember, but those that scar you, last forever. However, considering what Grishen has done these last days, I hope he's finally accepted.

The corridor leading away from the cage is narrow, and while Hargna walks on ahead alongside Valeria, Grishen and I are kept between four pairs of fidgety musket-bearing underground fighters.

However, as I inspect them more closely, despite their fierce glances, I think a soft wind might bowl them over. Angular cheekbones, hollow eyes, all give away that our guardians are malnourished.

I also note on closer inspection that their muskets are battered, pitted with rust, and from their lack of pouches, probably lacking spare ammunition. I can't help but laugh softly as I notice a final detail ... if I'd been more aware, I might have chosen to break the entrance door down and leave without the fear of being shot.

Nonetheless, as we're led deeper underground, descending roughly hewn steps slick with moisture, I can only hope that this underground movement will be an unexpected ally in this otherwise hostile land.

We've descended maybe twenty steps, the fetid air unusually warm, when a huge chamber opens before us, stretching into the distance. Massive stone columns support the ceiling and restrict my view, but what I can see doesn't fill me with any great hope.

Basic workstations are dotted around, although only one is in use, with a whip-lean woman crafting a pair of boots. A large group of malnourished Icelandians and Tarsians sift through a soaking mound of refuse, setting aside items that might be salvageable. As a whole, they move listlessly, devoid of energy.

'So many have a hand missing. Are these from accidents in the factories?' I ask Grishen softly.

'Maybe one or two, but most will be from stealing food, not working hard enough, or in the case of the women, resisting ...'

He doesn't even need to say the abhorrent word, and we continue in relative silence.

Massive pipes, some releasing unpleasant yellow steam, line the walls, radiating heat, but it's damp and unpleasant. They shudder and clang, while overhead the sound of industry rings unpleasantly loud. The turbulent noise of rushing water carries up a nearby corridor and I see several men carrying armfuls of dripping waste to be sifted.

Beneath my feet, the hard packed earth and stone ground is covered in an oily film. Pale white mushrooms grow prolifically everywhere, and nearby, several women with baskets collect the larger ones. Further off to the side, others are pulling up roots from a vast fenced area of ground.

'To think I always wondered about joining the underground,' Grishen mutters beside me. 'In hindsight, I'm glad they distrusted me. This place is like a prison.'

'Except I've seen better fed and more hopeful prisoners,' I reply.

As we pass between scattered groups of people, they're stirred by our passing, and follow us, their whispered mutterings strangely disquieting.

Patches of darkness where lights have failed add to the gloom of this underground hideout as we're escorted toward the far end of the chamber. I glance around, trying to estimate how many people are down here. Including the crowd behind us, maybe five hundred are visible, but numerous doors and passageways lead off, so there could be many more.

I'm cheered a little as I snatch a glimpse through an archway to see a smiling group of men and women working on looms, and in another sub-chamber, a kitchen busy with people cooking.

Ahead, a thin, robed Icelandian with a silvered circlet and scraggly beard stands atop a dais awaiting our arrival. A dozen chairs are arranged in a semi-circle behind him, but only one is occupied.

It seems introductions are going to happen sooner rather than later as we're heading straight for them. We stop just short of the dais while Hargna continues forward with Valeria.

A Tarsian man with a wrinkled, yet proud face rises from his chair and staggers forward, opening his arms. Hargna tosses the bundle of guns to the ground and they embrace warmly as tears of joy run down the old man's cheeks.

'My son!'

'So much for his father going missing,' Grishen whispers, grinding the toe of his boot into the cold ground.

His words mirror my own thoughts. Hargna has proven adept at lying. Then again, revealing his father's involvement in the underground to the wrong person would have led to an untimely death.

'I thought you'd died in the generator explosions,' Hargna's father sobs, choked with emotion. 'The Astorians announced something went terribly wrong during a shutdown to prevent a huge fey invasion!'

Hargna laughs softly.

'That couldn't be further from the truth, Father,' he says, stepping away. 'There's so much to tell.'

'There certainly is!' snaps the robed Icelandian, interrupting the reunion, stepping past them both to stare down at me with eyes as cold as winter snow. 'So, tell me, Hargna, son of Harkonen, why the hells have you brought the Queen of Beasts and this half-blood traitor here?'

Hargna shifts uncomfortably but steadies himself, and I find myself smiling at his small display of inner strength.

'They're both hunted by the Astorians, and unlike what our masters' announced, it was these two who destroyed the generators at the gate … with my help!'

'You were responsible for the carnage at the world gate?' Harkonen gasps, his face shining with pride. 'I didn't think you had it in you, Son!'

'ENOUGH!

Hargna and Harkonen flinch and fall silent.

'I'm Tooran, leader of the underground,' the Icelandian declares.

He looks down haughtily upon me. Had he been a king on a throne, it might have worked, but he's king of a shit hole, and it fails to impress.

'So, you're Nogotha, Queen of Beasts,' he says, hands on hips. 'How does it feel, your invasion army stranded on one side of the gate, you on the other, your dreams of conquest in tatters?'

I nod respectfully, although I'm already beginning to dislike him.

'That's just Astorian lies,' I state. 'There's no fey army waiting to invade. Everyone knows the Astorians were just months away from invading my world. The only way I could stop them was by destroying the factories that powered the world gate. Grishen and Hargna helped me. Trust me, I'm only interested in preventing a war, not starting one.'

Tooran's dark laughter echoes through the chamber as he crosses his arms.

'Prevent a war? Convenient words for someone who has been the villain of every tale ever told to us. The fey have invaded this world before, haven't they? Took men and women, as cattle. Do you deny it?'

I sigh. This meeting isn't going as I'd hoped, and the line of questioning isn't helping either. Yet not answering truthfully will only lead to disbelief and, even worse, mistrust. I've already told Hargna what happened in the past, so he could easily challenge any lie if he has the mind to do so.

'In ancient times, the fey did invade under their king, Nogoth, partly for that reason. However, it was me who opposed and defeated him. Only then was I named Nogotha, Queen of the Fey, and my first order was the immediate release of everyone taken captive, with one exception … the Astorian men. Since that time, not a single fey has crossed to this world.'

'And that makes you good?' Tooran scoffs.

'No. I don't claim to be good. Who in this world is, unless still a babe in arms? But I've never directly killed a child as depicted, nor sought to enslave a people like the Astorians have. Perhaps your mistake is giving credence to Astorian history over your own. My name, Malina, means saviour amongst your people, and it was my friend, Kralgen, an old King of the Icelandians who honoured me in such a fashion.'

'You knew Kralgen, *the* Kralgen,' Valeria says beside me. 'He's a legend amongst us Icelandians, although nowadays he's considered more a myth,'

Her dark grey eyes study me intently, perhaps trying to establish whether I'm lying or tell the truth.

'I did. I grew up with him, trained with him, and he was my finest friend. I know he'd want you to help in my quest, not chain me.'

'And what's that quest, if not to invade this world?' Tooran interrupts.

'I intend to kill the All Father,' I say loudly, ensuring my voice carries. 'But together, we could aim higher and bring down the Astorian Empire!'

Murmurs swirl, tinged with disbelief, and as I look around, those gathered stare at me with distrust and no little hatred.

'Beware she who speaks with honeyed words, for she speaks with the beast's tongue,' Tooran invokes, pointing at me. 'She seeks to seduce, mislead, and lure us to our doom. The All Father is immortal and can't be killed, and if we rise up against the Astorians, how many thousands will they kill in reprisals when we fail?'

I roll my eyes.

'How many Icelandians and Tarsians will perish if you don't? Look at you. You're already half-buried and starving to death with the boot-heel of Astoria on your necks and their guns to your heads.'

Tooran's eyes narrow and he shakes his head.

'And yet, they share their homeland and give our people food to eat. You, on the other hand are promising only death. Hargna made a grave mistake bringing you here. We should just cast you out and be done with you!'

'Tooran,' Harkonen shouts. 'That's against our code. How can you even consider it?'

'I can, because I'm the leader of the underground and the voice of reason,' Tooran snaps. 'Just look at your son and the sword at his waist, and have no doubt he was complicit in the killings at the Great Hall of

Victory. How long has he known her, and he's already a murderer? His life above ground is over thanks to her!'

'Bullcrap!' I snap. 'His life above ground, and yours, is over thanks to the Astorians, not me.'

Tooran raises a hand and points a finger at me.

'Enough! It's time for you to leave, unless you want us to deliver the Astorian's justice for them!' Tooran hisses, nodding at my escort.

Muskets are raised, and silence falls. The crowd swiftly retreats, afraid of being caught in any violence. Grishen sidles away from me with an apologetic smile. However, my blood is boiling and violence doesn't seem such a bad idea.

'Once, a threat from an Icelandian carried the weight of mountains.' I sneer. 'But you're a weak leader, Tooran, and you couldn't even stop me from killing you in your own hideout if I had a mind!'

Tooran's face pales.

'Lies, and more lies from the Queen of Beasts. Valeria, teach our *guest* some respect, then throw her out onto the streets!'

Valeria steps hesitantly toward me.

'I'm sorry,' she mutters, her expression conflicted.

Everyone in the room can see the punch coming as she draws her arm back almost as far as yesterday. My hands are manacled behind my back, and I just stare her down.

'Do it!'

As her fist flashes toward my face, I duck under the punch, step forward, and drive my knee savagely into her stomach. She collapses with a thud, heaving for breath.

'Valeria!' Hargna shouts, moving forward.

I leap, bring my manacled hands under my feet to my front, then kneel and find the key in her breast pocket.

'Don't just stand there watching,' Tooran cries. 'Shoot her.'

My manacles drop to the ground as guards squeeze their triggers in vain. Hargna, to his credit, has his sword drawn, although he just levels it hesitantly at me as he advances. He'd have done better to pick up a gun from the bundle on the ground, but I'm not complaining.

Stepping inside the point, I grab his wrist, sweep his legs from under him, and twist the sword from his grip as he crashes onto his back.

I leap onto the dais, and the sword blade whines through the air, only to stop a hairsbreadth short of Tooran's neck. The underground leader's eyes are wide as I lift his chin with the point.

'I speak the truth,' I say, raising my voice so that everyone can hear. The chamber is silent, even the guards have given up trying to shoot me, so with everyone hanging on my every word, I continue. 'I'm not your enemy unless you make it so. I intend to kill the All Father and destroy his Astorian Empire. I can do one on my own, but not the other. I can train you to do that.'

'We don't need your help to learn how to fight,' Tooran blusters, but falls silent under my withering gaze.

'Valeria couldn't hit a restrained woman, Hargna lies disarmed, and your guards didn't even have their muskets' match cords lit. You need me more than you realise!'

Lowering the sword, I toss it to land at Hargna's feet.

'Tooran,' Harkonen says, lifting his voice. 'It's the council's place to decide her fate, not yours alone. You acted rashly!'

'It's not for you to lecture me!' Tooran hisses, his face flushed. 'And lest you forget, we need food to survive, not lessons in fighting!' He takes a deep breath, calming himself. 'But you're right, the council will convene. Nogotha is our guest for the night.'

Hargna goes to help Valeria up, but she angrily shrugs him off, and as I look over the gaunt, hostile crowd, Tooran's words weigh on me, and I fear he's right after all.

How can these people fight when they're borderline starving?

One step at a time, Malina. One step at a time.

***

CHAPTER IX

'Harkonen's son decided to help and bring you here,' Tooran begins, his face dour. 'Maybe his motives were pure, but I fear his judgement was clouded.'

The private chamber we're now in is far removed from the crowd, but like everywhere else I've witnessed, it's dark, musty, and more a prison than a refuge. It also feels claustrophobic with Tooran, Harkonen and the rest of the hastily gathered council sitting in a cramped semi-circle. I stand before them, Hargna and Valeria flanking me. Grishen is absent, having been deemed too untrustworthy to attend, a fact neither he, nor I, am happy about.

'Perhaps I can see more clearly than you think,' Hargna says defensively, his voice quavering but resolute. 'Malina and Grishen struck a bigger blow against the Astorians in just a few days than any we've witnessed in our lifetimes!'

'The fact you call her Malina, and not Nogotha, demonstrates that the Queen of Beasts already has you under her influence,' Tooran retorts. 'Are we not warned to beware her honeyed words for exactly that reason?'

I laugh softly, and draw everyone's attention.

'To the contrary,' I say. 'It was Hargna's influence that led me and Grishen here. He's not under mine at all, far from it.'

Harkonen's lips twitch with the faintest hint of a smile, and his silent encouragement spurs me on.

'I understand you've been taught to fear me since you could walk, and overcoming a lifetime of conditioning isn't easy,' I continue, my tone steady. 'But, put aside the fey tales a moment and ask yourselves this: If there's been no fey invasion for over four thousand years, who enslaved and persecuted you if not the fey?'

I challenge Tooran with my stare as I ask the question. He's been hostile since the beginning, and his support will be pivotal.

'The Astorians,' he says finally.

The words sound as if they're wrenched unwillingly from his throat, but it matters not.

'Yes. The Astorians,' I say thoughtfully. 'The Icelandians and Tarsians of old were independent, towering warriors, muscled and proud. But now, your people are hiding in the dark, their strength sapped by endless oppression. You say you need food, and you're right. But tell me, when was the last time you saw a hungry Astorian?'

The room grows quieter still, several of the council shifting uncomfortably.

'Let me help you,' I press on, my voice steady but forceful. 'Does not Icelandian lore tell of my return in your hour of need? Well, here I am, willing to help.'

'Malina has it right,' Hargna declares, his words carrying the weight of a newfound conviction. 'We should believe Icelandian lore, not Astorian lies. It's time to become those warriors we once were, not the slaves or criminals we've become.'

'Son,' Harkonen huffs. 'Is this really you? Forgive me, but you're no fighter. Bravery isn't one of your virtues. Just because you carry a sword like a warrior, doesn't mean you are one.'

Hargna looks embarrassed.

'What your father is trying to say,' Valeria sneers. 'Is once a coward, always a coward!'

'Valeria!' Tooran snaps. 'Let me remind you, you're here as a guard, albeit not a very good one. Keep such comments to yourself, however justified they are.'

Hargna's lips tremble, his face a mask of shame, while Valeria's cheeks flush an angry red. There's history here, a story waiting to be uncovered, but now is not the time.

'Do you have anything else to add, Hargna?' Tooran demands.

Hargna lifts his chin, a flicker of defiance breaking through his shame.

'Only that Malina killed eight slingers with two knives,' he says. 'She's also killed well over a thousand Astorian soldiers with Grishen's help … Grishen, who we ostracise and ridicule. If two people can slay that many Astorians with nothing but courage and knives, imagine what we could achieve if we decided to fight under Malina's guidance!'

Tooran shakes his head slowly.

'You're forgetting it was Astorians with muskets and cannons that decimated our warrior ancestors wielding swords and spears. Do you honestly think knives will win a gunfight and courage overthrow trained Astorian troops?'

'You're right to voice such concerns!' I say softly into the silence that follows his statement.

'Excuse me?' A greying Icelandian woman leans forward. 'I lost two sons to Astorian *justice*, and a daughter who just disappeared. The desire for revenge has burned in my heart for decades, but Tooran has always championed peaceful resistance. Now, just when I think you might be the one to help me get revenge, you're saying he's right?'

Her words draw murmurs from the council, and for the first time, their distrustful stares seem tempered with a flicker of curiosity.

'I understand your frustration,' I say, meeting her gaze directly. 'He's only right when he says knives won't win a gunfight. Your history has proven this, and would do so again. I've honed my skills over hundreds of years, yet to kill with a gun hardly needs much practice. So, for you to fight the devil, you must use the devil's own weapons, and courage must be allied with strategy beyond a berserker charge.'

'No!' Tooran shouts, springing to his feet, shaking his head. 'There's no need to fight with any weapons. The All Father has long promised an end to the hunger and conditions we endure. We just need to continue working toward our common goal a little while longer.'

'And what's the common goal?' I ask, sure I already know the answer.

'To defeat the fey, and live in … your world,' Harkonen says with an apologetic shrug. 'You've seen the weather, and it's barely autumn. Icelandia has been uninhabitable for generations, and everything west of Lakehold too. The All Father warns a cataclysm is coming, but promises once the fey are defeated, we can safely create a new home in a land of plenty.'

I silently assimilate this latest news. The All Father is very shrewd to dangle salvation before a desperate people. Why would anyone risk rebellion when paradise always seems so tantalisingly close?

'Has the All Father ever kept promises before?' I ask, turning to the elderly woman who'd spoken earlier.

'Never,' she says, shaking with suppressed rage. 'I don't trust a word that man says.'

Murmurs fill the room, but as Tooran glares at the council, they fade away.

'Did he specifically promise that the Icelandians will be free to pursue their own destiny?' I press. 'Or any of the other enslaved peoples?'

Silence answers my question, and I nod thoughtfully, my gaze sweeping across the council.

'Has he even offered clemency and a new start for you, or those like yourselves who are criminals and outcasts by Astorian law?'

Tooran avoids my eyes, his rigid posture betraying his discomfort.

'The leaders of Astoria have always been cruel,' I press, 'and the All Father is no exception. His promises are certainly calculated lies to keep all the enslaved kingdom from rising up. You must be able to see that.'

An old Tarsian rises unsteadily to his feet.

'The only certainty is that you're the Queens of Beasts and will do anything to protect your fey, including lying. Who are we to trust? We've all seen the weather worsen in our lifetimes. Are you telling me a cataclysm isn't coming, and that your world won't offer us everything we need to thrive?'

As he falls back into his chair, anger vies with frustration over how to phrase my response, but I bite it back. He's behaving like a maltreated dog, that no matter how hard it's kicked, returns dutifully to lick its owner's feet.

'Actually, I know this world has turned against you,' I say, choosing my words carefully. 'I can perceive the magic of creation, and it's fighting against the industrial cancer Astoria has unleashed. Rid this world of factories and furnaces, and given time, you'll reclaim your ancestors' homeland and honour their memory, and I have the magic to help that happen.'

Tooran snorts, shaking his head dismissively.

'You can perceive the magic of creation. How convenient is that? Let me tell you, there's no such thing as magic, only science. How can we trust you when you lie so blatantly?'

My anger soars, and it's a good thing my elemental magic has gone, or he'd find himself burned alive. I also bite back on an angry explanation.

Revealing that the Astorians tortured my magic away will only have them appear more powerful than they already are.

'For the sake of the gods!' Hargna shouts, shocking Tooran and the council to silence with his uncharacteristic outburst. 'We have Astoria's oldest foe willing to not only kill the All Father, but to help us fight for independence ... as foretold by Icelandian lore. This hostility must stop. Must we behave like Astorians?'

Harkonen looks long and hard at his son, then a rare smile creases his lips and he nods in agreement.

'My son has it right.'

Tooran sighs in frustration and rolls his eyes.

'Please, continue, Nogotha,' he says, without enthusiasm. 'Convince me you can save us!'

I draw a deep breath, ordering my thoughts, and the room quietens.

'How many Astorians live in this city?'

'Around three hundred thousand,' Tooran offers reluctantly.

'How many of those are trained soldiers?'

Hargna shrugs. 'Around ten thousand.'

'Where's the rest of the army? I've heard it's a million strong.'

The old woman rises unsteadily.

'It's true, their army is vast. They train and camp out on the Delnorian plains, where food is more plentiful. Only the gate defence force is based here at the city barracks.'

'How many Icelandians and Tarsians are part of the underground?'

'Just shy of a thousand.' Harkonen offers. 'Not nearly enough.'

'Then how many Icelandians and Tarsians live above ground?' I ask.

'Around thirty thousand,' Hargna replies.

Tooran sits, drumming his fingers on the arm of his chair.

'Even if every one of our kinsmen rose up, we couldn't defeat three hundred thousand in battle!' he says, receiving nods of confirmation from most of the council. 'And even if we somehow did, the million-strong army would descend upon us in a month or two. Fighting only guarantees our deaths.'

'But we're already dead,' Hargna says, his voice rising. 'This is a living death. Every day, dozens of our kin die from hunger, exhaustion, or a bullet, while others suffer the indignity of assaults and worse. We have to fight!'

Valeria scoffs, but says nothing.

Her disdain for Hargna is as evident as it is unexplained.

'It's just a beautiful dream, Son,' Harkonen says, smiling sadly. 'The numbers don't lie. It's impossible to win.'

I shake my head.

'No, the odds are far from insurmountable,' I say. 'We only need to defeat the soldiers. The civilians won't fight.'

'We. We,' Tooran mocks, rising to his feet. 'You use that word so easily. But it's us and our children who will die unnecessarily, whereas you're obviously immortal!'

The temptation to snap Tooran's neck is almost irresistible.

'I am as mortal as you, Tooran. True, I've lived thousands of your years, but I can die. Now, perhaps you can share a truth of your own with me...' I rub my chin as if in deep thought, although I already know the question I'm going to ask.

'If the fey invaded tomorrow, a million strong, intending to enslave or kill you and yours ... what would you do? Would you kneel and bare your neck to the sword or order those under your command to fight?'

'Of course we'd all bloody fight!' Tooran growls.

'Then why would you fight the fey but not the Astorians?'

'Don't try and coerce me with your honeyed words!' he rages.

'Then forget the honeyed words and consider this,' I growl, looking around the room, letting everyone feel the weight of my gaze. 'I've already killed the All Father twice, and will keep doing so until he stays dead. So, if I'm not just willing, but honoured to die trying to save my people, then why the hell aren't you?'

Tooran stands again, his demeanour still hostile.

'Do you have anything else to add?'

Words like, *you're a damned coward if you don't fight for freedom*, come to mind, but diplomacy wins.

'Just let me show you how to fight and win,' I continue. 'This city could be yours. Its weapons of war, its supplies, all of it. Fight with me, and together, we can regain your honour.'

It's impossible to determine whether I've captured the council's imagination, but there's an edge of excitement to the atmosphere.

Tooran extends his arms.

'The council have heard you, Nogotha. Take your rest in the quarters Valeria will show you. We'll meet to discuss further on the morrow. We have much to consider. Hargna, you stay here.'

Valeria gestures toward the door and bows her head respectfully. She's still angry, definitely at Hargna, perhaps with me for so easily putting her down. I wonder if she'll be trouble.

With a final nod to Hargna, I take my leave, following Valeria as she leads the way through the labyrinthine catacombs. The air is damp and heavy, the corridors dimly lit by flickering lanterns. Doors and passageways branch in every direction, a maze of secrecy and refuge. People huddle in small groups everywhere, their faces etched with suspicion, fear, and occasional intrigue.

Will there ever be a time when people look upon me with kindness, admiration, and love? Or will I only ever receive that from my fey?

'How far does this hideout stretch?' I ask, breaking the silence.

'Far enough,' Valeria replies curtly.

'Who built it?' I ask, ignoring her attitude.

'It's part of Astgate's old foundations,' she answers reluctantly. 'They stretch across the city so the subterranean pipes can be accessed and serviced. Over the years, much has collapsed or been sealed off.'

'How many entry and exit points are there?'

Valeria shakes her head, refusing to elaborate.

I try another train of conversation.

'How many of your kin above ground know you exist?'

'The council and their immediate families,' she sighs. 'They give us access to some of the food stores, and in return, we take in those who need shelter. Now, enough questions, here are your quarters.' She gestures to an open, but sturdy wooden door. 'Most of us don't have our own rooms and sleep together on the ground, so consider yourself lucky. The lights are off at night and back on at dawn.'

Before I can respond, she turns and strides away.

'Welcome to our beautiful new home,' Grishen calls from a rickety bed in the corner. 'It's insulated, no chance of rain or snow, but on the downside, there's no view or fresh air, and more spiders for company than seems natural. On the table, there's a jug of water and a bowl of soup, but be warned, it tastes vaguely of mushrooms, is cold, slimy, and even the roaches would turn their noses up at it.'

'Ah, so we have roaches to keep us company too,' I reply with a smile. 'Perhaps we could add them to the soup for a little texture and extra nutrition!'

'Blah.' Grishen pulls a face as I approach the old table. It's splintered, and soft from damp, the initials of countless people scored into the wood. I pick up the bowl, bring it to my lips, and gulp it down despite Grishen's accurate assessment of its taste and texture. It's been too long since I've eaten, and I'm surprised to find myself wanting more.

'If this is what counts for rations, then we'll soon be looking like our hosts,' I say, staring wistfully into the empty bowl before placing it back on the table.

'How did your meeting go?' Grishen asks.

'It finished better than it started,' I reply, glancing around the room. 'Unsurprisingly, the council found it hard to overcome a lifetime of Astorian lies about who I am and whether they can trust me. But even the Astorian's darkest fey tales don't compare to the evil you've all experienced first-hand. I'm hopeful they'll support my cause, but even if not, my mission remains unchanged.'

'Whatever their decision. I'll do what I can to help,' Grishen says, sitting up. 'What I lack in skill, I make up for in enthusiasm.'

'Don't forget heart. You have a big heart, Grishen.'

He flushes at the compliment as I take a look at my bed.

'I pulled it slightly away from the wall so you don't get too many eight-legged visitors at night,' Grishen says. 'The sheet and blanket are clean enough even if they do smell damp. Hmmm, what else? Ah yes. Turn left when you leave our room, and there's a small chamber with a pot. Otherwise, it's a dead end.'

'Only one way in and out?' I muse, a sense of unease taking hold.

My instincts are rarely wrong, and I curse loudly, causing Grishen to leap out of bed and follow. Sure enough, back the way Valeria brought me, a door has been closed across the passageway.

'Don't tell me it's locked,' I say as Grishen rushes to open it.

His face is grim as he turns back, and he tries to crack a smile.

'Then I'll just say I can't open it,' he replies.

The door is sturdy, there's no keyhole, and it refuses to give at all when I throw my shoulder hard at the wood.

'What do we know?' Grishen asks.

I shrug, my mind whirring with possibilities as to why we've been locked in. None are particularly good, but not all are awful either.

'We don't have the tools to break ourselves out, so let's get some sleep,' I say with a shrug, turning back toward the bedchamber. 'After all, a bed is better than a cold rooftop, and it's been a long day.'

As we head back, the lights flicker, then dim, and as I lie down, they go off altogether. I sit for a while, watching the spiders come out of cracks in the walls and ceilings to hunt. Like me, they're predators of the night and are ruthless assassins.

I rather like spiders.

***

Even asleep, I'm attuned to the unusual.

The rustle of insects scuttling across the wall doesn't bother me, nor does Grishen's gentle snoring. The occasional clanging of the pipework barely registers, but the soft scuff of a boot heel ...

I'm awake, and across the room in a heartbeat, my back pressed against the wall beside the doorframe as a flickering light carries down the corridor. As far as I can tell, there's only one person approaching, so if they're coming with evil intent, they'll regret coming alone.

'Malina.'

My name is spoken softly, barely a whisper. It's Hargna. Nonetheless, as he steps into the room, I snatch the lighter from his hand and extinguish its flame.

Darkness descends ... for him at least. He's unarmed, and the blood pumping furiously around his body betrays his nervousness.

'Stay there. Don't move,' I growl as I cross the room silently.

'Grishen,' I murmur, leaning close to his ear. 'We have a visitor.'

'Wha ... who?' he mumbles groggily, blinking into the darkness.

I keep an eye on Hargna standing blind and uncertain in the doorway as I shake Grishen's shoulder a little more firmly.

'Hargna, the son of Harkonen, the one who tricked us into coming here, has decided to pay us a visit.'

'Hargna?' Grishen yawns. 'Well, I hope he's brought more food. I'm starving!'

Despite myself, I snort softly. If Grishen can be so forgiving, perhaps I can be too.

'P-please can I have my lighter back?' Hargna whispers. 'I have a candle if you'll let me light it.'

After a moment's pause, I hand it back. A stubby candle flares to life, casting its warm, flickering glow across the damp chamber.

'Look. We don't have much time,' Hargna begins. 'Tooran convinced all but my father that the risks of an uprising are too great …'

'The bloody coward,' Grishen interrupts.

Hargna bristles at the interruption but carries on.

'What's worse is that he deems it too dangerous to cast you out, now you know the location of this hideout.'

'So we get to stay after all?' Grishen says. 'What's the worry?'

'He's pushing for you to be poisoned,' Hargna says, looking grim. 'My father and the other council members are opposing him on this, but Tooran often gets his way in the end.'

I meet Grishen's gaze, and it's clear we're thinking the same thing.

'Then we kill him,' I say, giving voice to those thoughts.

'N-no! You can't just do that!' Hargna exclaims.

'Why not?' Grishen asks, his brow furrowing. 'He's willing to kill us.'

'Because killing someone shouldn't always be the answer,' Hargna sighs. 'Also, it would prove Tooran right. He believes the Astorian lies that Malina is evil, and killing him would confirm that to everyone else. You'll never be welcome here after that.'

'I've rarely been welcome anywhere,' I sigh.

'Nor me,' Grishen echoes. 'Maybe it's best we leave, Malina.'

Hargna nods eagerly.

'Look. I've got your armour and weapons bagged up. We'll collect them at the exit. The night guards are fast asleep. I gave them some extra soup with the wrong type of mushrooms. They won't wake for hours.'

'That was brave,' says Grishen, slapping Hargna on the back.

'You should come with us,' I say, surprised by Hargna's loyalty and initiative. 'The guards will know you drugged them once they wake up.'

Hargna shakes his head firmly.

'Tooran will be furious, and the council and guards won't be happy, but my father will ensure my punishment isn't too severe. Overall, the council aren't bad, they just believe your way will get too many killed.'

'I know they're not bad,' I reply. 'But, their weakness is part of the bigger problem. Grishen, are you ready?'

'I've finished packing,' he says with a grin. 'I'm ready when you are!'

Hargna reaches for the candle and extinguishes it. In its place, he ignites the lighter once more, casting a smaller circle of light.

'The main chambers are in darkness,' he says. 'Only a few lights are on in case people need the latrines. The shadows are deep enough for us to go unrecognised even if we're seen. We just walk out without looking as if we're up to something, and everything will be fine.'

Hargna stares at me, seeking approval.

'Sometimes the best plan is the simplest,' I reassure him. 'You two head off. I won't be far behind. I don't need the light. Now, lead the way.'

With a nervous nod, Hargna sets off down the passageway, Grishen by his side. I wait for the circle of light to fade before slipping into the shadows behind them.

Hargna pauses at an intersection.

'Trust your instincts,' I whisper, and reassured, he continues.

He's chosen the right passage, I could have told him which, but even now, I want him to put more faith in himself.

A few minutes later, Hargna extinguishes the lighter and I understand why. Ahead, a bulb sheds a dim circle of light.

'Look exhausted,' I whisper, when he begins to hurry.

He slows to a shamble, Grishen mirroring his every step like a large, eager child.

Whilst they walk just within the light's reach, I stay entirely in the darkness, stepping over the refugees who sleep on, blissfully unaware of my passing. I pause and watch a couple, their arms holding each other close. They're terribly underfed, live underground, and yet still obviously find love and solace in the other. Tears sting my eyes unbidden, while jealousy and loss twist in my chest. I'd give anything to hold Lotane one more time. Anything.

'Watch where you're going, you oaf!'

Ahead, Hargna presses his hands together in apology, backing away from a man he'd accidentally stepped on in the gloom. The man grumbles but settles back down, twisting into his threadbare blanket. A few nearby figures stir, but it's clear this sort of disturbance is common.

We weave through the sleeping masses, twisting in and out of the giant columns. Finally a corridor beckons, next to which a man with a musket across his lap slumps against the wall, mouth wide open, fast asleep.

We creep past, and hurry along the corridor, pushing ourselves up the incline without slowing, reaching another door without incident.

Hargna opens it, and we follow after.

It's a room similar to the one we entered via the latrines. Bars line the walls, and in the middle of the bare floor, partially concealed by a worn blanket, are our weapons and armour. The slingers' guns and harnesses are conspicuously absent, but the sight of our gear still brings a sense of relief.

Grishen strides forward, snatching up his axes and slips them through his belt, rubbing their metalled heads lovingly.

'Missed you,' he mutters, just loud enough to catch my attention. He's looking at me, and the corners of his mouth lift into a grin.

I quickly harness my weapons, conceal my daggers, and turn to Hargna.

'Are you sure you don't want to come with us?' I ask.

Grishen steps forward, seizing Hargna's wrist with an almost brotherly affection.

'Yes. Come with us, Brother.'

Hargna shakes his head, his expression torn. Despite his size, he's so gaunt under the flickering light, and I fear he'll waste away even further consuming such meagre fare as the underground eats.

'I wish I could,' he says, his voice thick. 'But I've been separated from my father and ...' He coughs, clearing his throat awkwardly. 'And from Valeria for too long and can't leave them now.'

'Valeria?' I repeat, utterly perplexed.

'She's ... she's my wife,' Hargna explains, his eyes glistening.

Grishen and I exchange a swift glance, but say nothing. I think about Hargna's upset and the barbed comments she'd previously directed his way. Something is terribly broken between them, and I sigh. Love is rarely simple.

'Hopefully, you can work your differences out.' I say gently.

Hargna nods gratefully, but his sad eyes display little hope.

'We'll come back and visit once we've killed the All Father,' Grishen says brightly, attempting to lighten the moment.

Hargna forces a smile.

'Kill the All Father and your welcome will be different next time,' he says, happy to change the subject. 'Though I'm sure Tooran will still find a way to blame you for any hardships.'

Crossing the room, Hargna pulls out a loose brick from the far wall, revealing a small handle. He hesitates, his shoulders sagging.

'Parting like this doesn't feel right,' he says. 'You gave me hope, and for a moment, I truly believed this was the beginning of something great.'

He looks so miserable and broken, that it stirs something fierce in me.

'Weakness can be as contagious as the plague,' I mutter, 'and I almost caught it too. I'll not run from this fight, any more than I'd run from the Astorians. Grishen we're staying! Hargna, in your heart you know now is the time to act. Trust in me, and believe in yourself, it's time the underground had a new leader.'

'But I'm not ready!' Hargna gasps.

'I'm glad you realise that,' I say. 'I meant your father.'

'But what about Tooran?' Hargna asks. 'He doesn't deserve to die.'

'That decision is his,' I reply firmly. 'But you and Grishen must bring him and the other council members to the central dais. Bind him if you must. And make sure your father knows what's expected of him.'

'And what will you be doing while we drag everyone out of bed?' Grishen asks, his grin returning.

'Me?' I smile darkly. 'I'm going to show Tooran and the council something they can't deny and will never forget!'

***

I survey the giant chamber, the people asleep, clustered together in the darkness, glowing red with life, their bodies and mind fragile, weakened by centuries of oppression.

It isn't their fault, instead, I'm coming to recognise it as mine.

The Icelandian legend about me has been convenient, it had helped secure Grishen's loyalty, and might still play a part. With our goals aligned, I can still be their saviour, because, unlike them, I'm strong, and in this world, only the strong survive.

Had any of the people I've encountered entered the Mountain of Souls, even as adults, they would have died. For the strong to rise, the weak must perish.

I draw my swords. Enjoying their perfect balance. These blades have yet to taste true combat, their edges are pristine. Their time will come, but not yet. Carefully, I place them against the wall beside the unconscious, bound guard, ensuring they won't hinder me. My daggers follow, and then my weapon harness and armour.

As I remove my boots, feeling the cool earth beneath my feet. I grimace. The Saer Tel in me recognises and recoils at the sickness infusing it. What noxious fluids have soaked into the soil over the years remain, continuing their poisonous work long after they've visibly disappeared.

This hideout is killing all who shelter here even as they hide from Astorian justice.

Tooran had argued they needed food and scoffed at the idea of magic.

It's time to address his concerns and misconceptions.

I close my eyes, allowing my spirit eye to open, and take a long sweeping step, my foot brushing, almost caressing the dank soil. The song of creation back on the fey home world would have swept me up in an instant, a symphony of life and renewal, but here it's silent. But the gold must be here, behind the boiling blackness, just waiting for a worthy conduit to be revealed.

Me.

I begin to dance, bringing to mind the song, twirling and swaying even in its absence. The sleeping bodies at my feet only add to my creativity. I leap and spin over them, landing as light as a feather, leaving them asleep and unaware of my passing.

My hands grasp, finding emptiness, knowing that soon, my call will be answered. I am Saer Tel, and the song of creation is as much a part of me as the air I breathe. The black clouds churn, gold flickers, and my heart leaps, my undulations noticed.

The gold will cleanse this place and will bring it to life.

Tooran wanted more food. The gold will cause the mushrooms to grow, the root vegetables to thrive, and who knows what else. It will show the council and the people magic. Not the raw forces of nature, but the nurturing power of creation, the gold, the bringer of life.

I'm aware of the lights coming on, illuminating the dais where the council now gather, their faces etched with confusion, betrayal, and fear as they follow my dance.

But I will show them life. I will lure them to my side with beauty. I will earn their loyalty with hope. They will become strong, and Kralgen's spirit will be at peace.

I dance with wild abandon, knowing I can't be ignored, and suddenly, in response to my efforts, I hear the song. In that instant, I allow it to take hold of me, and my dance takes on an inescapable life of its own.

It's horrendous.

There's no sweet symphony, just the howl of emptiness, of death, and destruction. It's the agonised gasp of a world in such pain, that it wants to lash out at those who inflict it, whatever the cost.

My movements falter, lose their sensuality, becoming vicious and broken, and whilst I invoke life with every step, it's ugly and malformed.

Swarms of insects scurry from the ground and drop from the ceiling. Rats appear, their harsh squeaks waking anyone still asleep, driving them in a crying, shouting frenzy of fear toward the dais, and I dance after them, the creatures and insects of the night following me in a black wave, ready to be unleashed.

Hargna and Grishen stand frozen, disbelieving at the betrayal of my actions, and the fear and hurt in their eyes is what saves me ... and them.

They are good people, and the tragedy that has befallen this world is not their fault, and to punish them would be as unjust. To bring a plague upon them had never been my intent.

I shut my mind to the terrible song, dancing again to my own tune, the familiar one that saw me dance across the prairies of the fey world. I picture swaying grasses, the heady scent of freshly opened blooms, the songs of a thousand birds, and I dance with a beautiful desperation, pleading and imploring with every step, every twirl, and every leap.

Gradually, the blackness recedes. It watches, intrigued but unsure, and as I persevere, as I beg and cajole with every move, a strand of gold emerges.

I pause, balanced perfectly on one leg, and reach out slowly, tentatively, as if to take a lover's hand after a fight, brushing it with my fingertips, featherlite, and it swirls around my hand as if experiencing my touch for the first time.

Then we join as if for the first time.

Now as I dance, it's with the magic of creation, of life, and springtime. The darkness falls away as if the mist before the sun, and the gold shines with a passion as if it's been waiting an eternity for its release.

Now, as the conduit of such magic, I shine from within, a warm, ethereal glow as if translucent.

The night creatures flee, vanishing into the shadows from which they came, and as I continue my dance, the effect is immediate and transformational.

Never before have I witnessed such regrowth.

The ground turns green with soft mosses, the sickly mushrooms swell and ripen, the tangled roots which hang from the ceiling, sprout green leaves, thickening and flourishing, creating verdant living curtains.

I begin to slow, reluctantly relinquishing the bond I've established, confident it will answer me again when I call, but knowing now is the time to address the council and the people here.

Despite the exertion, I feel revitalised in a way no food or sleep could provide. Only one thing has ever come close, making love with Lotane. The memory brings a fleeting ache, but I push it aside.

The people crowded around the dais murmur in wonder, looking at their prison, now become a paradise. Behind them, the council stand, open-mouthed, all except for Tooran in the centre, whose face is mottled by anger.

'Who do you …' Tooran begins.

The crowd parts instinctively as I stride forward, and as I leap onto the dais, Tooran shuffles back, his confidence and voice fading.

In days gone by, I'd have killed him without remorse, to cow the mob, to establish my control through fear and terror. But Hargna is right. I will try another way first, although perhaps not that different.

I wrap my arms around Tooran, and kiss both his cheeks. He stiffens, but I hold him tightly.

'Harkonen is now the leader of the underground,' I whisper in his ear. 'The destiny of these people will rest in his hands. This can be a bloodless handover if you accept it. But if you resist, I promise the alternative for you won't be pleasant. Pass him the circlet when I release you. Nod if you understand.'

Tooran nods, his defiance extinguished, and I somewhat reluctantly release him.

He walks over to Harkonen, and lifting the silver circlet from his head, passes it over. The symbolic transfer of power leaves the crowd stunned and Tooran steps down from the dais, retreating into the anonymity of the masses, his shoulders slumped.

The chamber is silent, the air heavy with the weight of change, and everyone gazes upon me, full of expectation.

'Long ago,' I say, my voice carrying in the silence, 'I too was a slave. They were dark times for me, full of death and despair, and honestly, I wouldn't have survived … but for one thing.'

I pause briefly, allowing the anticipation to build while contemplating my next words.

'That one thing,' I continue, 'was a dream. Something worth fighting for, and dying for. It was the dream of a golden era, an end to inequality, injustice, and war. As I look around, I know you have the same dream, and that's why I returned ... to make it come true with the help of my friends and yours.

I beckon Harkonen, Hargna and Grishen to stand beside me.

'In this life, we must be willing to fight for what we need, not pray for it. You dream of freedom, and the price of that will be steep, make no mistake. To achieve this seemingly impossible task, you must first overcome your fears, and then there's one other thing.'

As I look around, I have the crowd completely, even Tooran watches.

'An old friend I held so dear said something long ago that now comes to mind. I'll adapt it to suit the circumstances, but the heart of it remains the same. It was shortly after our first battle against Nogoth. We were defeated, captured, and while incarcerated, people turned on one another. It was a very dark time.'

Everyone listens, hanging on my every word.

'People were afraid, afraid of the dark and the victorious fey, who back then, were everything you feared they'd be. My friend, Kralgen, saved our lives when we were attacked by a large gang. As the battle hung in the balance, he actually tore the head off one of the gang leaders, and said something to his effect ... *You're afraid of the dark, afraid of hunger, afraid of the fey, but come here like this and you should add one more thing to that list. ME!*'

I pause, letting them digest my words.

'Kral believed in himself, and self-belief was part of what made him the greatest warrior I've ever known. He won that battle single-handedly with his actions and just those words. I know he'd want me to use them to remind you, that inside you're strong, and that self-belief, combined with overcoming your fears, will allow you to achieve anything. So let me start ...

'It's not the Astorians you should be afraid of. It's me!'

My roar echoes through the chamber, and the people tremble, unsure.

'Harkonen.' I dip my head toward him, willing him to understand.

'It's not the Astorians you should be afraid of. It's ME!' Harkonen yells, taking my lead, and then looks for guidance.

I nod toward Hargna and Grishen.

'Don't you two have something to say?' Harkonen demands.

'It's not the Astorians you should be afraid of. It's ME!' Hargna and Grishen bellow in unison, laughing as they lift their weapons aloft.

'YOU!' Grishen calls, taking the initiative to point his axe at a man. 'And you, you, and you. In fact, all of you, tell me as one. Shout so our ancestors can hear us. Tell them what they want to hear!'

As the roars of those assembled shake the very foundations of the factory above us, I smile.

The seeds of rebellion have now taken root, and it's only a matter of time before the Astorians feel our wrath.

***

CHAPTER X

Despite the comfort of newfound friendships, there's a liberating relief in being out and about on my own. Hargna and Grishen, loyal and enthusiastic as they are, slow me down in ways I can't afford. Initially, they'd both insisted on joining me for this reconnaissance mission, but swaying their minds took little effort.

A casual remark to Hargna about Harkonen needing to solidify his leadership of the underground, paired with a concerned word within earshot of Grishen about Tooran's trustworthiness, was all it took. By the time I was ready to leave, they were both reluctantly suggesting it was better they stay behind. Now, they're content, unknowingly doing exactly what I intended without their feathers being ruffled.

Now, I have the silence of the city and my thoughts to myself, both a blessing and a curse. Beneath my solitude lies the ever-present weight of what comes next. I need a plan to take the city.

Harkonen and the council are optimistic that the workers above ground will rise up, but only if they believe a rebellion is guaranteed to succeed. But war offers no guarantees.

Still, thirty thousand workers, or even twenty thousand if not all are willing to fight, will put the odds heavily in our favour, but only if surprise remains on our side.

Grey snowflakes cling to me as I perch on a rooftop in the heart of the military sector, the faint glow of the world gate just visible to the south. Here, under the open sky, I'm ... elated. What does it say about me that with the fate of worlds resting on my shoulders, I've begun to enjoy myself more than I have in centuries?

Lotane's absence cuts deeper than I'd ever admit, yet the thought of returning to him no longer calls to me. No, it's not home I now long for. It's the hunt. I want him here, at my side, reaping souls together in the shadows.

Is this thirst for the hunt just a lingering echo of the conditioning I endured all those years ago? Was I so profoundly changed that the need to hunt, fight, and kill will always remain a part of me?

Then again, when I consider the Astorians, or humanity as a whole, it's clear we've never truly embraced peace. Humans create life with one hand and destroy it with the other.

I'm certain it's the will of the gods, to ensure humanity never rises high enough to challenge them. Before we get too close, we destroy ourselves. Perhaps that's why I'm no longer burdened by guilt about what I do, and guilt is certainly a weight I can ill afford.

The rooftop beneath me is slick with moisture from the light snowfall that's fallen during the night, carrying the acrid scent of industry. A few steps away, an Astorian soldier sprawls asleep under a heavy, furred oilskin in the corner of the rooftop. His musket lies wet and neglected by his side, a testament to his overconfidence.

I resist the urge to kill him. He's the fifteenth potential victim I've encountered since reaching the military sector. Yet so far, they all remain alive. It doesn't speak to a softening of my nature, just to strategy. I don't want to poke the hornet's nest before I'm ready to destroy it.

I'm about to retrace my steps when my stomach betrays me, grumbling softly in complaint. The soldier stirs, a moan escaping his lips, and I freeze, my dagger hovering above his throat. If he awakens, he'll die. That much is certain.

Kneeling beside my unsuspecting victim, I carefully pull back the oilskin and shake my head in disgust at his soft snores. Falling asleep on guard duty is a cardinal sin, a mistake he's now going to pay for.

After three nights scouting the city, my food pouches are empty. I could make just the one exception … drain his blood and replenish my strength.

Instead, with a swift slice of my dagger, I sever a bulging pouch at his waist. Lifting it to my nose, I'm rewarded with the smell of cheese. I allow myself a small, satisfied smile before replacing the oilskin and lightly retracing my steps.

The soldier might bemoan the unexplained disappearance of his food, but he won't dare report its loss and admit to his lapse in vigilance.

Withdrawing to the far side of the roof, and settling into the shadows, I waste no time enjoying my ill-gotten gains. Once I finish my scout of the military sector, it will be time to return underground with my newfound knowledge.

Harkonen has some old maps that will undoubtedly prove useful in planning our assaults, but seeing Astgate fully with my own eyes has been invaluable ... and sobering.

A soft sigh of frustration escapes my lips for the hundredth time. Shelving my plan to kill the All Father and shatter the Astorian command in a single stroke will have to be put on hold till after the city falls.

I believed I could do it, after all, am I not the King Slayer? But I'd been overconfident, buoyed by the victories of my past. Hubris had me make promises I now know I can't keep, at least not on my own.

The bloody Palace is impregnable.

But that doesn't stop me from visualising it over and again to try and discover something I might have overlooked.

There were no wooded glades, flowering gardens, or vine-covered trellises, offering multiple points of approach and entry. In fact, it's less a palace, more a grim fortress capable of housing five hundred soldiers.

I'd spent hours circling it from a distance, trying to find a weakness that I could exploit, but I'd come up empty-handed. Its Astorian simplicity of design, its greatest strength.

A single iron-bound entrance gate, high walls with only a few, barred windows, firing slits and crenulations at the top through which cannons point outward. At a distance of two hundred paces all around, a tall, spiked, iron-railed perimeter fence creates an almost insurmountable obstacle. Beyond that, covering three sides, is a moat, ensuring the only feasible approach is from the south where a heavily guarded iron gate is the only genuine access point.

Yet there's no cover there at all, just a vast open area where citizens gather to listen to the All Father's speeches.

Absent my powers, I can't breach the palace on my own unless the All Father himself invited me in.

I chuckle softly as I run and leap to another rooftop on the other side of an alleyway. My eyes rove, the darkness hiding nothing from my fey sight.

During my scouting, I've recognised a symmetry about Astgate, and having realised this, I move with more certainty. There's a large north-south avenue, bisected by an equally large east-west avenue, roughly quartering the city. The world gate lies near the southernmost fringe of the city, and like spokes on a wagon wheel, streets and avenues radiate outwards. The street I'm on is industrial, and I'm atop a factory. In the middle of each rooftop is a large glass skylight, offering some degree of natural illumination through the filthy panes to the floor below.

Peering into the darkness, I make out timber being fashioned into shoulder stocks for the muskets, and grips for handguns. As I progress further along the line of factories, I discern weapon barrels and mechanisms being crafted, and a final factory displays all the different parts being assembled.

The next building I approach has me pause briefly. Even from a distance, the four guards stationed on the roof are visible, the red halo of their lifeblood betraying their positions. I peer over the roof's edge, and in the street below, stationed at the front gates, are a dozen guards behind a semi-circular wall of swollen bags, along with what Grishen had called a hand-cranked siren.

Silent as the grave, I work my way stealthily amongst the oblivious Astorians. Without light they're blind, yet their presence serves as a warning that whatever my plan, it will not go unopposed.

A quick glance through the glass panes into the depths of this building reveals guards patrolling towering aisles of crates that crisscross the warehouse floor. Hundreds of newly finished firearms piled on tables await packing into even more straw-filled crates.

This will be one of the rebellion's main objectives.

It takes me another hour to discover that two rows of buildings distant there's a similar avenue, but this time the final heavily guarded warehouse contains ammunition for light infantry and heavy weapons.

Predictably, a further two rows later finds me peering down into a warehouse stacked with large crates. I know their look only too well ... gunpowder.

Unsurprisingly, the guards here aren't armed with muskets, but daggers and spiked clubs, and there are twice as many both inside and out. Taking these three warehouses will be paramount for the success of the rebellion. I commit every detail to memory, knowing that each needs to fall into the rebellion's hands. A musket cannot be fired without gunpowder, and is ineffective without a bullet. It's no coincidence the Astorians have kept them separate from one another.

Finally, I make my way toward the main Astorian barracks.

Hargna had advised me they stood south of the gate and would be easily found, and he was right. Frustratingly, just like the Palace of the Ancients, this building is built to withstand an assault.

As I work my way around, I discover a closed gate to each side. There are no smaller side entrances, no lower windows, just the familiar firing slits and cannon barrels poking through the walltop crenulations.

Woe, betide any foe who tried to storm this monstrous building.

The pre-dawn siren wails across the city and a short time later, two gates visible from my position open outwards disgorging troops. Some are in formation and begin drill practice, whereas others head into the city. Staying low, I follow a group that passes below, but they only go as far as a nearby eatery before they split. The majority file inside, whereas several dozen begin patrol duty, their sullen voices carrying easily.

I've seen all I need to, and it's time to return to my new allies.

My mind is awash with what I've seen.

The Astorian military is formidable. Thirty thousand rebels would get slaughtered storming the barracks even if there was siege equipment to hand. Likewise, on an open battlefield, the Astorians would dominate. They've been trained in the use of firearms, whereas the Icelandians and Tarsians have only been trained to obey.

But the art of war is far more subtle than meeting an enemy face on.

Raiding the warehouses during a storm will render the Astorian's muskets useless while turning the odds in the rebels' favour. Numbers, size, and a thirst for revenge will count for more than Astorian discipline in holding a firing line.

However, thousands will die on both sides, and who knows if the rebels that remain will be sufficient to evict the Astorian civilians, let alone hold the city once they're gone.

Instead, I need to utterly defeat the Astorians with a minimal loss of life to the rebel forces, and I have the beginnings of an idea on how to do just that.

I can't help but chuckle. I must be getting soft in my old age.

***

'Karson,'

'Hello, Alina.'

I smile, we're off to a good start, he's using my affectionate name.

'Tell me, has my future changed?' I ask, somewhat scared of the answer, but encouraged by the fact I'm still in my creaky bed, and not surrounded by piles of corpses, thunderous skies, or winged demons.

Those little shoulders shrug, and Karson pulls a silly face.

'Surely you already know?' he asks, his voice lilting like morning birdsong.

'I'm not sure I do.' I laugh nervously. 'Is it looking better?'

'When does your future hold anything but death and despair, Alina?' Karson sighs. 'If you succeed, thousands die. Mothers and fathers will lose their sons and daughters. Children will lose fathers and mothers. Then, if you fail, exactly the same will happen. Sometimes I wonder if you're being punished for the devilry of a previous life, however, I'd prefer to think that perhaps this is your destiny, because you're the only one with a chance of saving two worlds.'

'Oh, so I have a chance!' I joke, even though I don't feel like it. 'I won over the underground, and have a plan to take the barracks. Now all I need is to unite and coordinate with those above ground, and this city will be ours.'

'A city. What an accomplishment that will be.'

'Don't tease, Karson. It's a start. From small seeds, mighty trees grow!'

'But you're the mother of worlds, a mighty forest beyond measure, Alina, not a seed or a tree. Ask yourself, even if you somehow take this city, what then? What will happen next?'

'I haven't thought that far. When have I had the time?'

'You've lived for over four hundred years in the fey world, how much time does it take for your imagination to grow?'

'That's not fair,' I complain. 'My world has been turned upside down over the last few weeks, and since then I've done nothing but fight to ensure the fey world will be safe. Even now, my plan to take the city will stop the factories from being rebuilt. The gate at Ironhold is frozen under snow, and the one in Ssythla has always been too hot for humans to operate there. Where's the flaw in my plan?'

'The flaw is you are still thinking of seeds, not forests. You're thinking only of the fey world, not both. You're thinking of the now, not the future or even the past. You have no vision beyond what's in front of you.'

'How about you just tell me what I need to hear, instead of these silly riddles and games?' I say, reaching out to take Karson in my arms. There's no way I'm going to get upset with him again. I've missed him so much.

His little arms go around my neck, and he squeezes me tight.

'I am but a messenger, Alina. I say what comes into my mind. Who or what places it there, I don't know. In truth, what I say means little or nothing to me. You seem to forget, I'm your little brother. What do I know of grand strategies, or the will of the gods?'

'I'll consider your words, oh wise one. Now, do you know anything else that will help me?' I ask, somehow strangely relieved that he's just my little brother after all.

Karson smiles, and he leans close to my ear.

'I know I love you, Sister, as you do me, and that love binds us through life and death.'

'That helps more than you know,' I say, suddenly tearful.

A final squeeze and he disappears, and I continue my sleep, absent dreams.

***

Hargna, Grishen, Harkonen, and Valeria, wait impatiently for me to start our meeting, their expressions a mix of anticipation and tension. They've become my closest advisors over these crucial days, their insights invaluable. Though once my knowledge rivalled any kings, the world has moved on, and their grasp of Astorian science and its uses in war far surpasses mine.

However, despite our shared goal, the atmosphere remains strained. Valeria, whose disdain for Hargna is second only to her hatred of the Astorians, barely tolerates his presence. She stays away from him as if even his touch might taint her.

Together we gather around a battered, yellowed map of Astgate, spread across a massive wooden table scarred by age and use. The original markings, avenues, residences, and landmarks like the Palace of the Ancients, have been overlaid with charcoal lines tracing hidden tunnels, underground chambers, and secret exits.

The northwest sector under which we currently hide, is the Icelandian and Tarsian area. It's a stark place with factories, food halls instead of cafes, while the few shops that exist offer little beyond repairs and working clothes.

To the east and northeast is the Astorian sector, with sprawling educational, correctional, and scientific complexes, interspersed with housing and public establishments. The Palace looms in the north, an unyielding fortress, while to the south, the military sector clusters ominously around the world gate and barracks.

'The underground passages and your knowledge of them will be pivotal to our success,' I say, addressing Valeria directly as the others lean forward. 'Let's begin with our primary objective … defeating the Astorian military and taking control of Astgate.'

Grishen smiles, his fists clenching in anticipation.

'Yes!'

Even Hargna, who is so often opposed to violence, can't hide his excitement. His Tarsian blood stirred at the prospect of battle.

Harkonen, however, shakes his head, his expression heavy.

'A father should never have to bury his son,' he murmurs. 'Don't get too excited about a battle.'

'I'll be fine, Father,' Hargna assures him, clasping his arm.

'So tell us,' Grishen demands. 'We're going for a big street battle, yes?'

'No,' I say sharply, cutting through his excitement. 'We're not going to fight the Astorian army. We're going to make them surrender.'

Valeria chokes on her water, sputtering in surprise.

Grishen slaps her back, laughing.

'One look at Nogotha in her black armour,' he says, 'and they'll fall to their knees and beg for mercy!'

'Nogotha doesn't strike me as the joking type,' Harkonen chuckles, a smile threatening to disrupt his grim demeanour.

'Not in this instance,' I reply dryly. 'Make no mistake, there will be fighting at the weapons, ammunition, and gunpowder stores, to arm your people and force the Astorian civilians to leave. Patrol units and prison guards will also need to be dealt with. But the main Astorian forces? They'll surrender.'

Hargna frowns, his grimy finger tracing a line from the barracks to the warehouses.

'I've learned enough to know we'll raid the warehouses during a storm when the Astorians' muskets are useless. But once the alarms go off, the Astorian barracks will erupt like a kicked bee hive. They'll come pouring out, armed with daggers and gods knows what else, and there's no way they'll surrender, not without losing a bloody battle first.'

'But they won't get out,' I say simply.

Valeria tilts her head, her scepticism clear.

'Why not?'

'Because their gates won't open,' I reply.

They wait, silent, expecting me to elaborate.

'Look, the Astorians wanted their fortresses to be impregnable, so the gates are designed to open outward, set deep into reinforced frames. It makes it extremely difficult to force them from the outside.'

'Go on,' Grishen urges as I look at them in turn, gauging their reaction.

'We'll exploit that. Three teams of volunteers carrying timbers fitted with iron stakes will each approach a different barrack's gate. The first timber will be placed across the base of the gates, and the stakes will be driven into the ground and gate, locking it in place. Additional timbers will ensure they remain sealed tight. The walls only have firing slits, so unless they have very long ropes to scale the walls, they'll be trapped inside.'

Grishen lets out a low whistle. 'So we turn their barracks into a prison. I like it.'

Harkonen rubs his chin.

'What about the sentries at the perimeter? They'll raise the alarm as we approach.'

'I'll deal with them, and any on the approach and the surrounding rooftops,' I say with confidence. 'They'll die without being aware of it.'

'I don't doubt it,' Valeria mutters. 'But surely, just sealing the gates won't be enough.'

'You forget. Once we have control of the city, we'll have cannons to play with!' Grishen laughs, his enthusiasm infectious. 'We'll turn their own weapons against them.'

'There'll be no need,' I say firmly. 'Have you any idea how much food and water ten thousand troops consume daily? The sector around the barracks is full of eating halls, and whilst I'm sure the barracks have supplies, they won't last long. Especially if we cut off their underground water supply.' I nod to the pipes running across the roof.

'That will work,' Grishen whispers in disbelief. 'As long as we can get those doors sealed and stop anyone from removing the timbers.'

'Whoever seals the gates will probably die,' Hargna mutters, looking pensive.

'Better not risk yourself then,' Valeria snaps. 'Just like when you stood by and did nothing while I was raped!'

Her words hang in the air as she turns and storms out of the chamber, tears streaming down her face, leaving a shocked silence in her wake.

'She's telling the truth,' Hargna whispers, his cheeks burning. 'I'm a coward. I lost my wife that day, and my unborn child. She's right. You can't count on me.'

I'm aghast at the revelation, as is Grishen, although Harkonen clearly knew. He takes Hargna into his arms as his son sobs uncontrollably.

'The Astorians had guns, Son. You couldn't have done a thing,' Harkonen murmurs, his voice heavy with both sorrow and regret.

'We all carry shame for past deeds, Hargna,' I say softly, unsure if my words will reach him. 'But while you can't change who you were, who you choose to be now is in your hands. You didn't run when I needed help and here you are, helping to plan an uprising. You're already changing.'

'Malina's right,' Grishen says. 'I'd trust you at my back in a fight and Valeria will be sure to feel that way too … in time.'

Hargna wipes his eyes clear, his hands trembling.

'I always detested violence,' he says, 'and to this day, I still struggle with it. But what happened to Valeria changed me. I see the need to fight now, but I'll understand you wanting nothing more to do with me.'

'Stay,' Harkonen says, his voice firm. 'Help make the Astorians pay for what they've done to you both.' He glances at me, seeking my approval.

I nod.

'As your father says. Stay.'

'So what happens when the gates are sealed?' Grishen asks, eager to put the uncomfortable moment behind us.

'We storm the warehouses,' I continue, keeping an eye on Hargna. 'That's where casualties will be highest. We also need to secure the city food stores, and ensure the Astorians don't lower troops down to remove the beams.'

'And the Astorians inside the barracks?' Harkonen asks. 'What happens when they surrender?'

'We give them safe passage out of the city in groups of a hundred,' Grishen suggests. 'Any more, and they might try something stupid.'

'Safe passage out of the city,' I repeat. 'However, once out of sight of the city limits, they're to be killed.'

'What?' Hargna recoils, horrified. 'We can't just slaughter them after they've surrendered!'

'You must,' I insist. 'Otherwise, they'll regroup and return, armed and merciless.'

'This is too cold, Malina!' Hargna whispers.

'Is that what Valeria would want to hear, that you'd rather let her rapists walk away free? This is war, damnit!' I growl. 'Kill or be killed. The only time for mercy, is when you've won. Not a skirmish, not a battle, but the whole bloody war! Do I make myself clear?'

Grishen obviously has no problem, but Harkonen and Hargna gaze at me warily. However, I'm not overly bothered. Better they resent me for this than falter under the weight of such decisions themselves.

'So, if this is just one battle, how the hells do we win the war when the Astorians have an army a million strong?' Harkonen demands.

'Let's just focus on Astgate,' Grishen interjects. 'One thing at a time!'

'No,' I say. 'It's a good question. We mustn't just think of seeds, but forests, and a kingdom, not just a city.'

The others look at me as though I'm talking gibberish, and I laugh.

'Let's just say I've already been giving it some thought thanks to my br ... thanks to a dream. But I need a map of the seven kingdoms to help show you. Do you have one?'

'Hah. I don't think it's been called that in years. Nowadays it's just the Astorian Empire, but it's one and the same,' Harkonen says, opening a drawer and pulling out a large, worn scroll. Unrolling it reveals a faded map, showing a familiar landscape, but with far more cities marked than in my time.

'So, we have five other main cities in Astoria?' I ask, poring over the map.

'Yes. What of it?' Harkonen mutters.

'Do all the cities have Icelandian and Tarsian slaves?'

'Yes. With some other nationalities too.'

'Roughly the same population in each?'

Harkonen rubs his chin.

'I've lived here most of my life, so I can't say for sure. But I grew up in Ast, and it was similar in size, so I'd say yes.'

'Then we have a hundred and fifty thousand potential allies to join our uprising,' I say.

Grishen laughs, somewhat incredulous.

'I'll support you whatever, Malina. But we struggled to get the underground here on board, and they know what we've done. So, how in the hells are we going to convince the slaves in other cities to join us?'

Everyone is expectant, but also sceptical, as I look around the room.

'We lie,' I say flatly, and before anyone can object, I press on. 'We send runners to each of the other cities with a message for whoever leads the slaves.'

'What message?' Grishen demands impatiently. 'What lie?'

'The message is that Astgate is fully liberated and there's enough weapons, ammunition, and supplies to sustain everyone for years. Furthermore, the messengers will state that the slaves from the other cities have already joined us, and that they've only one week to do the same or they'll be forever excluded from this safe haven!'

Harkonen shakes his head in disbelief.

'That's the most outrageous lie I've ever heard,' he murmurs. 'But it would work. They'd come running, no question.'

'But what's your plan to stop the Astorian army from crushing us next spring?' Hargna asks.

I point to the River of Tears on the map.

'Four thousand years ago I planned to stop Nogoth's invasion of Astoria. We built a huge wall just there.'

'That wall is still there,' Grishen declares. 'A marvel of Astorian ingenuity, or so we're taught. It's sheathed in iron nowadays, with dozens of cannons facing west.'

I can't help but laugh in relief.

'Then immediately after Astgate falls, we send ten thousand, well-supplied troops to take and hold that wall indefinitely. After that, make no mistake, Astoria can be yours.'

Grishen runs his fingers over the map as if it's something precious, his expression awestruck.

'The Astorians have their army on the Delnorian plains, leaving Astoria near defenceless. We'll still have to overcome local city garrisons, but Astgate's is by far the largest. There's sure to be resistance, but if we rule fairly, maybe the Astorians won't rebel against a change of leadership.'

'Does everyone agree?' I ask, looking around the room.

One by one my co-conspirators nod, and whilst I didn't need their unanimous approval, their agreement will make things far easier.

'Right, Harkonen,' I begin. 'Choose and outfit ten of your fittest to begin their journey to the other cities at nightfall. They must be utterly trustworthy and able to go along with this subterfuge without qualm.'

'Leave it to me!' he growls with grim certainty.

'So, when do we attack?' Grishen demands.

'When we're fully ready,' I reply. 'There are a hundred other things to consider and plan besides the barracks and warehouse assaults. The Palace must be surrounded to prevent the All Father escaping. Patrols will need to be put in place to maintain order until the Astorian civilians are evicted. Rationing must be enforced until we know the extent of the city's food stores. Then there's the distribution of weapons and supplies. The list goes on.'

'Gods,' Hargna mutters. 'I had no idea.'

'That's why we take our time,' I say. 'We ensure every detail is covered before presenting the plan to your over-ground kin. As for the bigger lie about the other cities' slaves, we keep that between us.'

'Why not tell them everything?' Harkonen asks.

I smile wryly.

'If it's known we're lying to solicit help elsewhere, it will undermine our cause here. Now, is there an overall leader?'

'Bardala,' Harkonen says. 'He and his council have been waiting for a moment like this for decades. Hargna should meet them, it will be safer. They know he's my son, and once he tells them I'm the new underground leader, they'll listen to what he has to say.'

I bite my lip, my head spinning with the sheer amount of information and the delicate timing everything will require.

'There's something else, isn't there?' Grishen asks, studying me.

'You're very intuitive,' I say. 'We need to find the barracks' water supply.'

'Along with water, their oil pipes and power cables are underground too,' Grishen adds with a sly grin. 'If we cut those off, they'll have no light or heat either.'

'Valeria should accompany you,' Harkonen says. 'She's explored these tunnels more than anyone.'

Hargna's expression darkens, but I slap him on the back.

'You can show her the man she wants you to be,' I say encouragingly.

He nods, resolute. Harkonen, typically dour, looks excited, while Grishen just laughs.

'We have a great plan,' he says. 'And it's going to work!'

***

'Gods, this gun harness is uncomfortable. No wonder the slingers are so miserable,' Grishen grumbles, striding around the chamber.

His legs are wide apart, his hands hovering over the gun handles as he swivels his head dramatically, snarling.

'Hah,' I laugh, enjoying the light-hearted moment.

'What you smirking at!' he growls, grabbing a gun from its holster.

'You're dead,' Hargna crows as my dagger thunks into the upended wooden table beside Grishen's head before his gun clears leather. 'You're dead!'

'Damn. The evil Nogotha claims another poor innocent's life. Will you feast on me now?' Grishen says with a lopsided grin and wink.

Is he flirting? It's hard to say, but he's already turned away to help Hargna with his harness.

'Get serious!' I say, my smile still lingering.

'Seriously then, how are you so damned fast already?' Hargna asks, struggling with the buckles on his harness.

'Drawing and throwing knives isn't much different than drawing and aiming a gun,' I say with a shrug. 'And you forget, I've had a few centuries of practice.'

'It's a shame you're so old,' Grishen mutters, practicing his draw over and again. 'I normally look for someone more my own age.'

I shake my head in mock disapproval as I cross the chamber to help Hargna adjust his harness.

Most evenings, after a full day exploring the underground passages and planning sessions over a hasty dinner, we spend time here practicing weapon skills. Grishen with his axes, Hargna with his sword, and all of us with guns.

Despite my initial disdain for firearms, I can't deny the satisfaction that comes with mastering a new martial skill. Perhaps it's a remnant of my conditioning, but becoming proficient in drawing and reloading the weapons gives me a thrill.

I know the slingers will be faster, but I'm already quick. Grishen is proving rather adept, but as for Hargna ...

'I feel like a total fool,' he says, pacing the dimly lit chamber.

'Draw,' Grishen commands, facing him.

Grishen's gun clears his holster and levels at Hargna's stomach in an instant whereas Hargna fumbles his, and the weapon clatters on the ground.

'Now, who's dead?' Grishen laughs, smoothly holstering one gun while drawing another in true slinger style.

'When do we get to shoot?' Hargna mutters, clearly embarrassed. 'I'm probably better at that.'

Grishen's eyes light up as he looks at me.

'Come on, Malina. After four days of pulling an empty gun from a holster, planning, getting lost in tunnels, and listening to Hargna argue everything, we deserve some fun.'

'I don't argue everything!' Hargna protests.

'See what I mean?' Grishen chuckles, pointing.

We all laugh, and it's a welcome moment.

'I've already cleared it with Harkonen,' I say. 'Hence the new additions to this chamber. As Grishen says, let's have some fun.'

'Yes!' Grishen punches the air, his enthusiasm infectious.

'We have just over a hundred cartridges. So let's not go too wild,' I laugh. 'Now, help me move these tables and old mattresses.'

Together we lean the rotten mattresses and tables against the far wall. Someone has left some chalk, and after a moment's thought, I sketch an outline of a hooded figure on three of the tables.

'Do we have to shoot at you?' Grishen jokes, laughing at my crude drawings.

'It's the All Father,' I reply, shoving him playfully. I glance at him sideways, unable to help the faint smile tugging at my lips. I have to admit he's not only confident, proficient, and constantly optimistic, but also fun to have around.

Hargna, on the other hand is still struggling to find his inner strength, but I have hopes he'll get there.

The chamber is large, about fifteen paces long, and reeking of damp. We stand side by side, facing the targets. Hargna is in the middle, Grishen on the right, and I take the left.

'Aim for the chest. Two shots when you're ready,' I murmur, sighting down the barrel of my raised gun. Strange how a sword feels made to fit my hand, whereas this just feels … wrong.

I breathe out slowly, using the same technique I'd apply when shooting a bow, and squeeze the trigger twice. Grishen and Hargna follow suit.

'Gods, my ears!' Hargna moans.

'Add complaining to arguing!' Grishen laughs, holstering his gun.

'I don't arg …' Hargna begins, then wags his finger. 'Hah. You won't get me again!'

We go to inspect the targets, smoke curling lazily in the still air.

Grishen looks smug as we stand before them.

'Two to the chest, as requested. Anyone else?'

'I think my gun is faulty,' Hargna moans, looking perplexed. 'I haven't hit anything.

'I win then,' I say lightly. 'I got two to the chest, and one to the groin. I think Hargna helped me out.'

We return to our positions and swap guns.

'Eight shots. Four more to the chest, four to the head,' I order, reloading my gun with practiced precision.

The chamber echoes with sharp cracks as we fire in unison. My ears ache from the noise, but after Hargna fires his last round, we step forward, eager to see the results.

Lystra would be proud of me. Every one of my shots has hit the target, and while two of the headshots have just clipped the chalk, I'm satisfied. I've also got three more holes in the wood that have nothing to do with me.

'One,' Hargna mutters.

'Six out of eight,' Grishen declares happily, patting his target, 'and a whole lot of collateral damage to the table. Maybe if you aim at my target, Hargna, you'll hit yours next time.'

'I've had enough,' Hargna moans, shrugging off the gun harness as if it's burning him. 'I'm better with my sword anyway.'

My meaningful glare silences Grishen from saying anything that would further inflame the sudden tension.

'You're right, Hargna,' I say, resting my hand on his shoulder. 'You're far better with your sword.' It's not a lie, and the words fall from my lips smoothly, but in truth he's not got much further than knowing which end to stick the enemy with.

'Grishen. Take Hargna's gear and fetch us something to eat. I'll meet you back at our room.'

He scoops up the harness with a nod and leaves without a word.

Hargna stands uncomfortably before me, shifting from foot to foot.

'Stand still,' I bark. 'Stand straight!'

He stiffens to attention like a new recruit.

'Relax, Hargna,' I say, smiling. 'Now, tell me, why did Grishen do as I bid, and why did you?'

'Because you told us!'

'But why?' I press. 'You're a man, with your own will. You could have said no.'

'It's because you're a queen,' he says, his voice shaking.

'No,' I say gently. 'Or at least not mostly. It's because I'm a leader. Now, tell me, was I born into leadership? Was I born into nobility?'

'I don't know,' he admits, his brow furrowing.

I sit on the cold stone floor and gesture for him to sit opposite me.

'My family ruled Hastia once,' I begin quietly, 'and I was a princess. By the time I was nine, I'd mastered the bow, and could kill a bird in flight from two hundred paces. By the time I was ten, I'd mastered the sword and shield and was an expert in the polearm. When I was eleven, my parents were assassinated, and I found sanctuary in a monastery that believed in the prophecy foretelling the return of the fey. Because of my skills, I was chosen to train alongside others from many nations to prepare for that event, and to oppose it when it came.'

'Incredible,' Hargna breathes. 'I just knew it!'

'No,' I say with a soft smile. 'You didn't.'

'But it all makes sense,' he insists. 'This is why you are, who you are.'

'Only because you believe the lie I just told,' I say earnestly. 'I was indeed orphaned, but my father was a fisherman who died at sea trying to support my family. So why did you believe the lie? It's because I spoke it full of confidence.'

'I don't understand. Is this a lesson of some kind?' Hargna asks, looking confused.

'It is, Hargna. Training doesn't have to be limited to shooting guns or wielding swords. This short lesson is about confidence, and that's the key to most things, be it leadership, life, or love.'

'But I'm not confident,' Hargna says, picking at his nails.

'That's where the lies come in. Just imagine, a man walks through that door and says he's trained his whole life to fight and kill. Would you fight him for five hundred gold pieces?'

'No!'

'But what if he's lying? What if he has a bad heart and back, and will surrender if you just look at him confidently and accept his offer?'

'If I knew, I'd accept!'

'Therein lies the power of a bluff. Bluffing is just another word for lying. Lies are used every day to manipulate people. Grishen teases you, not because he's mean, but because he's confident. Or maybe it's a lie, and he jokes to cover up his inner fears.'

'This is all very confusing,' Hargna says.

'It's simple. Just say things with conviction,' I smile encouragingly. Hargna says nothing. By now, Lystra would have snapped his neck, but rather than get frustrated, I continue.

'Those who appear confident also appear strong, whether they are or not. People follow and respect others who display such qualities. Show confidence, even if you don't feel it, and you'll be a leader like me. Now, stand up!'

Hargna gets to his feet, as do I, and I can't help but laugh softly.

'You just followed an order because you perceive me as the leader. Do you understand?'

Hargna nods, and I see the realisation finally taking root.

'Try it for yourself,' I say encouragingly.

'Sit down.' Hargna says.

'Again, with more conviction. Believe that I'll obey you.'

'Sit down!'

I shake my head.

'I don't feel it, Hargna. Louder, with anger. Imagine your voice is the force that pushes me to the ground.

Hargna nods and leans forward.

'SIT DOWN!' he roars.

I nod, looking him in the eye.

'That was much better. Much better indeed.' I lean in close. 'But if you speak to me like that again, even in private, I'll cut your throat. Do you understand?'

Hargna stumbles back, trembling, his eyes wide.

'Y-you're bluffing, r-right? This is a t-test?'

'Are you willing to bet your life on it?' I growl, pulling my dagger clear.

Hargna gulps and shakes his head frantically.

'Our next lesson will be about deciding whether someone is bluffing,' I say, sheathing the blade. 'I never bluff. Just remember that.'

Hargna looks so confused that I can't help but laugh to myself all the way back to my room.

**

CHAPTER XI

'We're through!' Grishen shouts, looking back over his shoulder, his white eyes contrasting against his filthy face. His voice echoes through the flooded tunnel, distorted by the steady drip-drip of water and the low groans of the ancient pipes overhead.

The tunnel is half-flooded, water up to our knees, its icy grip gnawing at our legs. The stench of damp and decay fills the heavy air, choking us with every breath. After nine gruelling days of grubbing under the earth like worms, I should be used to it, but I'm not. Each breath feels like swallowing rot, each step a battle against exhaustion and the cold sludge sucking at my boots.

I hand Grishen the lantern and take the iron bar in exchange. The weight of the tool in my hand feels oddly comforting, a solid reminder that even here, beneath the earth, we can carve out our path. Edging past him, I peer through the small hole he's made in the wall. My heart pounds as I lean closer, peering into the darkness beyond. I'm not sure what I expected, but it's just another flooded chamber, dark water lapping at the crumbled jagged little islands formed below where the ceiling has partially collapsed.

'Good job!' I shout over the roaring water, though my voice feels hollow in the oppressive air.

Now Grishen has created a hole, the integrity of the wall disintegrates and the bar makes short work of bricks and mortar already weakened by years of damp and immersion. Within half an hour, the gap is large enough for my small party to clamber through into the new chamber.

The air inside is no better although the water starts shallower, but the slight gradient soon brings it back up to our knees. The source of the flooding is immediately apparent, a deep channel cuts through the chamber, carrying a roaring torrent of water toward a dark hole in the far wall. Rusted pipes crisscross overhead, disgorging effluent and rainwater into the flow below.

'Another bloody drain!' Hargna yells as the lantern's glow cuts through the darkness. A loud bang makes us all jump, but it's just one of the pipes above shaking violently before settling back into an uneasy silence.

'Watch yourselves!' Valeria shouts, as a chunk of debris splashes into the water beside us, but fortunately no more follow.

The noise draws us to the chamber's centre, where the torrent flows beneath a narrow stone bridge. Beyond it, a rusted metal ladder rises, leading to a narrow hole in the ceiling. My heart leaps at the sight, as it's another chance to get our bearings.

After crossing the bridge, I approach the ladder.

'Careful, Grishen says, his voice low but firm. 'That ladder's probably older than you are. One bad rung and you're going to get hurt!'

'Careful indeed,' I mutter to myself as I test the first rungs gingerly. Rust flakes away and the ladder creaks ominously with each step. Grishen waits below, ready to catch me if I fall.

At the top, a corroded metal cover awaits, set in a crumbling frame. Rotting debris clogs the drainage holes, and the smell makes me gag as I pull it away, letting the mess drop below. Grishen's curses rise from beneath, and despite the situation, I suppress a laugh. He should know better by now; it's not like this is the first ladder I've climbed.

As I clear more of the cover, the gaps I create reveal a sliver of the surrounding area above ground and I can't help but gasp. After days of disappointment, losing our bearings, getting lost, and retracing our footsteps, we've finally made it.

There it is, the monstrous barracks.

I almost let go of the ladder in my haste, forgetting momentarily that I've no magic to catch my fall.

'Slow down, Malina,' I mutter as I descend.

Grishen greets me with a handful of gunk as I reach the bottom, but I duck his clumsy throw and laugh at his snarls as I pass him by unscathed.

'Grow up,' Valeria snaps, rolling her eyes. 'We've got work to do.'

Grishen pulls a face behind her back. Valeria remains cold, but at least she's stopped with her barbed comments at Hargna.

I beckon everyone closer.

'It's close,' I say. 'The barracks are just a hundred paces that way. If the next passage is clear ... we've reached our destination.'

'Then let's not waste any more time,' Valeria says. 'The sooner we're done here, the sooner we can get back, and I can stop smelling like a latrine.'

Hargna leads the way, lantern held high as he picks his path carefully over a mound of rubble. The air is tense; every sound, every drip and groan amplified. A small cascade of stones bounces off my head as I pass beneath a low arch, and my stomach clenches in anticipation of a heavier fall, but none comes.

The passage narrows until we reach a corroded iron gate. Its hinges are rusted to the point of disintegration, and look like they'll give. Flakes of rusty metal crumble under my touch as I grip it tightly and give a sharp tug. The gate groans, resisting, and the ceiling above releases a shower of dust and small stones.

'Please don't do that again,' Hargna groans, clutching his head.

I reluctantly let go, disappointed not to explore further, but nor do we really need to and it's certainly not worth the risk of getting buried alive.

'These are definitely the barracks water and oil pipes,' Grishen says, rapping his knuckles against the unyielding metal overhead. 'And behind them are power cables.'

I look at the pipes, seeing the rubble perched precariously above.

'Let's go back.'

A few minutes later, we're standing in the drainage chamber.

'We can break the pipes here,' I say. 'That passage isn't safe and we're close enough to be sure. But not until the Astorians are sealed in. We can't have them investigating or getting suspicious if their water and oil get cut off too early.'

'Will they be able to escape this way once their gates are sealed?' Valeria muses.

'Good point!' I say, cursing myself for not having thought of it. 'The roof in the passage is close to collapse. We'll give it a little help when the pipes are broken.'

'Is it time to return, I'm famished?' Grishen asks.

'Nine days to find this place, but thankfully it will only take us about two hours to get back,' Hargna says, arching his back and groaning as he stretches. 'I wonder what culinary delights await?'

'Fried mushroom and rat for breakfast, roasted mushroom and rat for lunch and dinner. No daylight ever again, but no work for that matter either. Life couldn't be any better,' Grishen laughs.

'So, why do we want to go mess up such a good thing by getting rid of the Astorians?' Valeria says, joining in, surprising us all.

'Maybe because I'm willing to kill someone for a simple piece of cheese already,' Hargna chuckles.

Valeria's face turns to stone.

'How wonderful. You'd kill for a piece of cheese, but not to save your wife.'

Our smiles fade as she storms off.

'Give it time, Hargna,' Grishen says.

We begin to retrace our journey, eager to return, wash, change, and eat. Ahead, Valeria uses a big piece of chalk to draw an unmissable arrow on the walls. Without her, this would have taken twice as long. Having spent the last two years of her life underground, her knowledge and sense of direction have helped us find routes around collapsed and flooded tunnels.

I just wish she'd forgive Hargna, but who am I to judge how long it should take. Hargna hadn't followed her into her self-imposed exile, and that had likely made things fester like a cancer between them.

'Everything is now ready,' Hargna says as we trudge through the tunnels. 'As soon as we return, I'll go meet Bardala.'

'How long will it take for you to see him?' I ask.

'A long time,' Hargna says sadly.

'Damnit,' Grishen growls. 'How long is a long time?'

'All of half an hour.' Hargna laughs. 'Whose factory do you think we've been hiding under?

'Am I tempting fate by saying our luck seems to be improving?' Grishen says, thumping Hargna on the back.

The mood between us grows lighter, and even Valeria manages a small smile as we catch up with her, and it doesn't feel long before the welcoming glow of the underground beckons ahead around a final corner.

Even more welcoming are the people who meet us as we enter. It isn't something I'm used to, and even if their smiles and greetings are mostly for Hargna and Valeria, Grishen and I aren't entirely left out.

Valeria eases herself away from the pressing crowd as Hargna turns to me and Grishen.

'You two can clean up while I spend some time with these people,' he says, his face flushed. 'Then I'll be gone a little while!' He lifts his eyes upward, and we know exactly what he means.

Grishen and I head off, leaving Hargna behind.

'It's good to see these people living with hope for the future, not just living out their days waiting to die,' Grishen says softly as we head toward our room. 'It's thanks to you they'll soon stand proud and fight under the sky, and if they die, they will die free. Harkonen is being lauded as their leader, but I'll always know the truth of the matter.'

I smile gratefully.

'It's because of you too, Grishen. Without you, we'd never have got this far.'

Grishen blushes, somewhat abashed, and we walk in companionable silence to gather our clothes and boots before heading to the nearby washroom.

'After you,' Grishen says, going to sit on a rickety wooden bench.

'There's room enough for two, Grishen. Don't worry about my modesty, I lost that long ago!'

He blushes again, but follows me in.

The washroom isn't pleasant, but after wading through effluent, and getting covered in general filth, it's a welcome luxury. The room is dim, lit only by the flickering light from the corridor, thus offering a modicum of privacy to any within who don't have fey sight like mine.

It's damp, the flagstones underfoot are somewhat slimy, but it's warm, and more importantly, has hot water. I toss my work boots and coveralls onto a bench, to join a growing pile of other discarded clothes.

There's a large pipe punctured with tiny holes running the width of the room, and as I step beneath it, the hot water it continually sprays washes over me. There's no soap, but it doesn't matter, and I scrub hard, doing my best to rid my hair and body of the day's accumulated dirt.

The underground might be devoid of almost all pleasures, but this is one luxury they enjoy. However, I make sure to keep my eyes closed, as they'd been terribly sore after the first time I'd come here. I hum softly as

I wash, fragments of the song of creation finding its way into meaningless verse.

When I finish and step from under the deluge, I open my eyes to find Grishen staring at me.

'Gods,' he chokes, turning away, embarrassed.

'Grishen. Have you not seen a woman naked before?' I laugh. 'Or are you checking to see whether the Queen of Beasts has six nipples for her brood to suckle upon?'

'I-I've never seen anyone so beautiful,' he mumbles shyly, unable to meet my eye. 'I can understand why Lotane became the Great Betrayer, and killed Queen Asterz for you.'

There are some old pieces of fabric piled in the corner, and I toss one to Grishen as I dry myself off with another.

'The legends have it all wrong,' I say, a swift pang of jealousy, something I haven't experienced in centuries ripping through me. 'He actually left me for the queen. It wasn't his fault, he had no choice, or so I console myself. But in the end, after I left her bleeding to death, he killed her quickly. In some ways, he betrayed us both, just at different times. But I betrayed him too, so who am I to judge? Yet ultimately, he was there for me when I needed him most, and he has been my eternal love ever since.'

'He's a very lucky man,' Grishen says gruffly. 'He chose wisely at the end, even if not before.'

I'm quiet as I pull my clothes on, mulling over Grishen's words. He's forming an attachment to me and having made the mistake of betraying Lotane once, I'll never do it again, even if we are worlds apart.

Grishen is clothed in his trousers and fur jerkin by the time I pull my boots back on.

'You look like a true hero of old,' I say lightly, then see him blush again. I'll have to be careful from hereon lest he get hurt.

I quickly run my fingers through my hair, although there isn't much point. It's more habit than anything else, and Grishen's eyes follow my every move. How hadn't I seen his interest growing?

'Let's get something to eat, and wait for Hargna's return,' I suggest, not wanting the atmosphere to become awkward should Grishen say any more.

We set off at a brisk pace, familiar after these many days with the underground's layout. A few minutes later, we have bowls of soup in hand and lean over the map.

Valeria is already there with a thin stick of charcoal, filling in the final stages of the tunnels we'd passed through. Everything else is already clearly marked. She's earned the honour of smashing the pipes and will take a small group with her when the time comes.

Every second feels like a minute as we await Hargna's return. Harkonen eventually joins us and tells stories about Hargna in his youth, and even Valeria stays to listen. The look of warmth and pride on Harkonen's face and the passion he speaks with makes the childhood tales engrossing, and before we know it, two hours have passed, and Hargna enters the chamber.

His smile is the broadest I've ever seen.

'Bardala is coming tomorrow two hours before sunrise,' he declares, clenching his fists in excitement. 'He's said he's waited his whole life for this moment and it cannot come soon enough.'

By unspoken assent, we all embrace. It's a pivotal moment. Our independence day just drew closer.

***

'How do I look?'

Grishen's pupils are dilated as he assesses me.

'You're a vision to die for,' he mumbles.

'You look quite imposing too,' I say, and I'm rewarded with a broad smile.

Despite only having had a few hours' sleep, we're putting the best version of ourselves forward for our Bardala's arrival.

'Come here,' I say, turning Grishen around, straightening a twist in his belt before taking the knife from his hand he'd been attempting to shave with. Grabbing his chin, I turn his head, tightening the skin on his neck and shave him, sharpening his look before doing the same to his cheeks.

I stand away and nod.

In his furs, with red cords tied around his arms and his beloved hand axes tucked in his belt, he looks every bit the old Icelandian warrior, albeit a short one.

I'm once again clad in full armour, with swords and quiver strapped to my back, six daggers sheathed, and my bow in hand.

'Come. It's almost time. Hargna will be a bag of nerves if we're late. Let's get to the planning room.'

'How can this early in the morning be late?' Grishen moans.

I can't help but laugh, no truer word has he said.

As we enter the main chamber, everyone is awake, excited, and rightfully so. Couples stand, holding on to each other, not just with love, but with hope. It's packed, almost everyone who lives underground has come, and like us, they're putting on their best show.

They might still wear filthy coveralls, but hair has been braided, coloured cords are wrapped around arms, beaded necklaces adorn necks. Many clutch weapons, knives, iron bars ... whatever they can find. A show of strength, commitment and unity.

The transformation is incredible, from a defeated rabble waiting to die in the darkness, to the beginnings of an army, hungry for action and a chance at freedom.

Harkonen stands rigid and proud on the dais, the old council huddle together nearby, and even my detractor, Tooran is smiling amongst them. Valeria and her guards stand behind, their old weapons polished. I snort as I note the gentle wisps of match smoke curling around them. She's making sure they look ready in case they're inspected.

'I'm not one for welcome speeches,' I say, leaning close to Grishen. 'Hargna's waiting, so let's go. I'm sure watching old friends like Harkonen and Bardala reunite will be touching, but that's not for me.'

A ripple moves through the crowd as we pass behind it, but when Grishen spots an old empty crate that's normally used as a seat, he steps up and reaches out a hand.

'Come on, don't be such a grouch,' he laughs. 'Hargna can wait a moment. This is a historic event.'

With a grimace, I allow him to pull me up so we can see over the crowd.

'That can only be Bardala,' Grishen says. 'Big fellow, isn't he!'

'Taller even than Hargna.'

He approaches down the corridor Hargna had taken us along as an escape route all those nights ago. His massive frame has his head almost brush the ceiling, and his shoulders touch the walls. He truly looks like an Icelandian of old, tall, proud and ruggedly healthy.

Barely visible behind his bulk are his counsellors, robed like their leader, but lacking his presence.

As they reach the chamber, the crowd respectfully holds back as Harkonen steps down from the dais and embraces his old friend.

'Touching can be good!' Grishen says with a wink.

I shake my head in exasperation, but can't help but smile.

The murmur of the crowd smothers what passes between the two leaders, but Harkonen bows his head, and steps away, sweeping his hand to encompass the room.

Bardala holds up both hands.

'Quiet, my friends. QUIET!'

The chamber settles into near silence.

'He has quite the commanding voice,' Grishen whispers.

'My whole life I've waited for a moment such as this,' Bardala calls, his face alight with enthusiasm. 'For too long you've lived below ground, denied daylight, separated from your families. Today, we will bring an end to this travesty!'

Grishen covers his ears, laughing as the chamber erupts in a chorus of whoops and applause.

I can't help but laugh too, glad I haven't missed this moment. The faces around me glow with a rare fervour, and the crowd settles again as Bardala raises his giant hands.

'To achieve our dreams, we must come together,' he calls. 'We have to support the one man who can unite us and make us whole again.'

'Harkonen! Harkonen! Harkonen!'

As the room erupts, Bardala lifts his hands, and after a minute, silence again descends.

'No,' he says, his tone sharp, cutting through the excitement like a blade. 'Not Harkonen. Not the man who'd have you die for a lost cause.'

A ripple of confusion spreads through the chamber, and as Grishen turns to me in disbelief, I notice more people coming down the passageway behind Bardala.

'Get Hargna, now. We've been betrayed!' I shove Grishen off the crate as angry murmurs fill the chamber.

'I'm talking about the All Father!' Bardala shouts over the growing unrest. 'He has promised to forgive you. You can return to your families today, if you just hand over the Queen of Beasts, Harkonen, and Hargna, who have fallen under her influence!'

Slingers flood into the chamber behind Bardala, spreading out, guns levelled at the crowd. More slingers push in from side tunnels, corralling the crowd, cutting off the exits. Valeria and her guard are swiftly disarmed and pushed along with the old council to join everyone else.

Even I can appreciate how perfectly the trap has been sprung.

I draw an arrow, nock it to the string, but I'm uncertain what to do. If I shoot, mayhem will ensue and the crowd will be slaughtered.

Then I see him.

His approach has been concealed by Bardala's frame, but a deathly silence settles a final time as the All Father himself stands before the crowd. He pushes back his white hood, revealing that sad, ruined face, but before he can speak, Harkonen stumbles forward.

'Bardala. Why? Why would you betray us after all these years?'

A slinger raises his gun. A shot shatters the silence, and Harkonen crumples to the ground, lifeless.

'Life is such a fragile thing.'

Strangely, the All Father's voice carries around the room and caresses my ears like a serpent's hiss.

'When you have but one life, mistakes can be final.'

The All Father extends his hand, and the slinger who'd shot Harkonen places the gun in that frail palm.

'Why would you betray us after all these years?' he says, repeating Harkonen's comment slowly. 'It would seem, Bardala, that despite swearing loyalty to me, you knew about the underground all along!'

Another shot rings out, and Bardala crashes to the ground.

The All Father looks slowly around the room.

The slingers shift, and I recognise their intent. They're going to open fire shortly whether I surrender or not.

I wait a few more heartbeats until …

The All Father catches sight of me and our eyes lock. I want him to know it was me and will always be me.

The arrow flashes across the room, taking him in the throat, sending him stumbling back, clutching at the wound.

'KILL THEM ALL!' Tooran yells, suddenly charging at the line of slingers. At least half a dozen bullets hit him, twisting him around, but he still manages to plunge a dagger into a slinger's chest.

The crowd surges forward, screaming with bloodlust and hatred as all hell breaks loose.

The storm of gunfire is deafening, and so are the screams. The Icelandians and Tarsians at the front of the charge never stand a chance. The slingers fire with practiced efficiency, discharging one weapon, then drawing another to continue firing with the other hand.

My bow sings, a slinger drops, and I snarl with pleasure. More follow, their dying screams lost amongst the battle. Yet, however accurate I am, I can't make enough of a difference. The battle isn't going to last long, the hail of bullets is devastating, and a red mist hangs in the air above the faltering charge.

Then the Astorian flank to the right suddenly disintegrates into a twisted brawl as Hargna, Grishen, and a dozen others attack from behind. I see Grishen laying grimly about him with his axes, Hargna flailing wildly with his sword.

The rolling roar of guns suddenly disappears as the slingers run out of loaded weapons, and in the next moment the battle hangs in the balance as the remnant of the crowd finally closes in on them. Casting my bow aside, I draw my swords and sprint across the chamber, leaping over the dead and dying to reach the Astorian front line.

Some slingers struggle to reload while their comrades frantically try to fend off their Icelandian and Tarsian attackers, but they now have nothing but their hands against daggers, iron bars, teeth and nails.

I thrust, taking an Astorian in the throat, swing, cutting another's forearm in two as he vainly lifts it to block my blow, my blade continuing through to splinter his skull. I land a heavy kick to a slinger's knee, gut stab him as he stumbles, then duck as another lifts a reloaded gun and fires. His look of horror as he realises he's missed doesn't last long as I punch my left sword through his teeth, and out the back of his neck, and he goes down in a heap.

I lay about in a frenzy, stabbing and slashing anyone in a long slinger's coat or wide-brimmed hat, whether they're standing, crawling, or crying in agony on the ground.

And then, there's no one left to kill.

The red mist lifts, and I look around to discover no more than a dozen of the underground left standing. Everywhere is covered in blood and strangely the Great Hall of Victory comes to mind. This scene should be immortalised there on the walls of my chamber, a testament to the death I bring wherever I go.

I wipe my swords clean on a leather coat, relief washing over me as I see Grishen, Hargna and Valeria still standing, but I bite back on my elation, because this is no victory.

Hargna drops to his knees, and I rush to his side, but despite being doused in blood, it's apparent he isn't injured. Tears carve tracks down his cheeks as he kneels beside his dead father.

'Let's give him a moment,' Grishen says beside me.

I turn away, and my attention is drawn to the All Father's body. I walk over, and am surprised to see his eyes open, flickering left and right, his lips covered in frothy blood, moving, forming unheard words.

The bastard actually smiles when he sees me standing over him.

'I'm already coming for you again,' he gurgles. 'I won't be long!'

Before I can say anything, Grishen steps forward and the All Father's face shatters under the edge of his axe.

'What now?' Grishen asks.

I look around at the devastation. The underground is no more. Their hideout has been betrayed, and the All Father will forever know of its location. What comes next is beyond me, we all need time to recover from this, but then I look to my right as I hear the distant sound of pounding feet.

Down the end of a long corridor, another wave of slingers appears, and there's only one thing to do.

'We run!'

***

Grishen grabs Hargna under one armpit, and together with Valeria, yanks him to his feet as I sprint ahead, snatching up my bow.

The remaining people scatter, heading for whatever sanctuary they can find, death breathing down their necks.

'That way!' Valeria shouts, pointing.

Taking her lead, I turn into a corridor, straight into a slinger. I knock his gun away as he fires, butt him in the face and keep hold of his forearm as I drop my bow and grab a dagger from my belt.

I stab him furiously three times in the stomach, catch his falling gun, then pull the trigger, taking off the top of his head with its final shot.

Staggering backwards, I grab my bow, then throw myself sideways around the corner as another three slingers come into view twenty steps away.

Bullets smack into the walls and doorframe as I draw an arrow, then lean around the corner to release. I duck back just in time, but now there are only two slingers left, and they won't be pushing forward in a hurry.

'This way,' Valeria shouts, beckoning, aiming for another corridor.

Before we even get close, dozens of slingers stream into the chamber, leaping over the piles of the fallen. Gunfire explodes, and stone fragments erupt from the walls around our destination, cutting off our escape.

'The tunnels,' Grishen shouts, leading the way as we charge down the all too familiar passageway.

I turn and draw, releasing out of instinct, and a slinger steps into view, his gun raised, and is thrown from his feet before he can even pull the trigger.

Ten more steps, I turn and loose again, this time spinning another slinger around with an arrow to the arm. He fires as he falls, and two bullets whine past.

The others haven't waited, and I turn the corner and sprint across the room then duck through the broken wall opening, following my friends ahead who are outlined by the glow of a lantern.

At the first corner, I pause and turn back, kneeling in the darkness, my last arrow nocked and ready, the illuminated entrance chamber twenty paces distant.

'Please. Give up,' I mutter. 'Let us go.'

Just as I'm about to relax, dozens of slingers pour into the chamber. The first one dies with my final arrow in his forehead, and as gunfire echoes down the tunnel, I turn and run after my friends.

My now useless bow ends up in a side tunnel, and I run unhindered by the darkness, leaping over puddles, ducking under low overhangs, turning left and right, aware of my pursuers falling behind.

It's not long before I catch Valeria, who is lagging behind the others.

'No need to wait for me,' I urge. 'Let's put some distance between us and those bloody slingers.'

'Sorry,' Valeria grimaces. 'I can't go much faster.'

'Hah. You're like a rabbit in a warren down here. It's Grishen who slows us down, not you.'

She exhales sharply, half a chuckle, half a groan, then lifts her shirt.

'A shot rabbit maybe,' she sighs.

'Damn, Valeria,' I gasp, seeing blood leaking out of a hole in her side. I turn her around and sigh with relief on discovering an exit wound. I rip one of my sleeves off, cut it in half, wad up the pieces, and stuff them in the holes.

'What's wrong?' Hargna cries out, running back. 'Oh gods! Tell me she's going to be alright?' He moans pitifully as he sees she's wounded.

'If you don't whine, I will be!' Valeria snaps.

Pulling my empty quiver over my head, I cut the cords that had held it in place, then tie them tight around Valeria's waist.

'You'll be fine for now,' I say, despite my worry. She needs proper treatment and who knows where we'll get that.

Loud voices and splashing carry to us.

'How the hells are they following us?' Grishen demands.

'Your bloody great footprints,' she mutters, 'and my chalk marks on the walls.'

'Let's go,' I urge, and we head off.

I keep glancing behind, worried by the ever-present glow of the slingers' lanterns. If only I had my bow and more arrows, but I have nothing but swords and daggers. However, if their lanterns go out, they'll not die to the dark, they'll die to me.

'So how exactly are we going to get out of this mess?' Grishen asks as we climb through a narrow opening. 'Because those bastards aren't giving up.'

'We could leave an easy trail, double back, and hide in a side tunnel until they pass us by,' Hargna suggests hopefully.

'They'll recognise the ruse too quickly,' Valeria hisses. 'Then we'll be trapped between them and an unknown number of slingers back at the entrance.'

'There's a lot less of them now than ever before,' Grishen says. 'How many did we kill? A hundred, maybe more?'

'Maybe more,' Valeria agrees. 'But there are still too many for us to handle.'

A few minutes later, having splashed through knee deep water, we burst into a large drainage chamber, and beyond the bridge spy salvation rising before us.

Hargna is distraught. Shocked by his father's death and Valeria's wound. He's withdrawing into himself, and I need him to snap out of it.

'Get up there, Hargna,' I order. 'Open the drain cover!'

'Go!' Grishen urges him. 'Save Valeria and save us all.'

Encouraged by Grishen's words, Hargna sets his lantern down and scrambles up the rusted ladder, while I support Valeria with an arm around her shoulders.

Grishen gives me an amused grin.

'I'd have got myself shot ages ago if I thought you'd hug me,' he chuckles.

I shake my head, but am glad for his levity. I look up at Hargna, then back at the tunnel we'd come through.

'No sign of our pursuers,' Grishen says, reading my mind. 'But we can't have long.'

Suddenly, there's a succession of clangs, and Hargna curses loudly as a series of rungs give way, throwing him in a shower of rusted metal to the ground.

'Next one. Let's go!' he groans, rising unsteadily to his feet, grabbing the lantern.

He goes to take my place, but Valeria's raised hand stops him short.

I take Valeria's weight and we press on, heading for the next passage. A volley of gunshots ring out and Hargna curses as rock fragments cut his cheek, but then we're safely into the cover of the next passage, pushing the pace for all we're worth.

The slingers' shouts are too close, and I curse every lengthy passage, my shoulders tight, anticipating a bullet, but we just manage to keep out of sight.

'Damnit,' Valeria hisses, her face screwed up in pain as she presses a hand to her side. 'Leave me behind!'

'Help me,' I order Grishen, ignoring her.

'What if we jump into the next drainage channel?' Hargna suggests.

'We'll die,' I say with certainty. 'The current is too powerful, and who knows how far underground it goes and where it empties out.'

We struggle on. Valeria gritting her teeth, determined, Grishen and I supporting her when the space allows.

Three more times we pass through drainage chambers, but the slingers' bullets drive us from the ladders before Hargna is up even a few rungs.

Then we enter the last chamber.

'Hargna. Get that rusted gate open. We'll be right behind.'

Hargna sprints ahead, disappearing into the passage beyond the bridge.

'I can't open it!' Hargna's faint voice reaches us as we make our way over the raging waters.

'Go help the oaf. I'll make it. I promise,' Valeria says, pushing us away.

I don't hesitate. We're all dead if that gate doesn't open. Grishen and I run into the tunnel to find Hargna covered in debris, new piles of rubble around him. Blood flows down his head as he pulls and pushes at the rusted iron.

'Together,' I shout, throwing my weight against the gate.

Grishen follows suit and we find a rhythm, slamming our shoulders into the resisting metal. Gunshots echo down the passage and Valeria stumbles into sight, bouncing from the walls as we continue our frantic attempts to batter the gate down.

Debris rains down as Valeria staggers forward, throwing herself at our backs, adding her weight to ours.

With a final, tortured squeal, the frame breaks away from the wall, and we tumble through in a heap, the lantern spinning away. With a deafening roar, the passageway collapses, showering us in dust and stone, separating us from our pursuers.

We lie there, stunned for a moment, the rock fall settling, silence descending, until faint voices and the grating of rubble being cleared away filter through.

'Damnit. Why can't they just give up,' Grishen moans, crawling to get the lantern.

Hargna stands and offers his hand to Valeria, who ignores it, turning to me instead.

With an apologetic smile to Hargna, I help her to her feet.

'How are you, my lo ...' Hargna begins to ask.

'Don't you dare call me that,' Valeria hisses, and shrugs me away.

We're in a small chamber, the air thick with dust. We head over to a passage entrance. Unlike the crumbling tunnels behind us, the brickwork here is solid, the mortar in place. We follow it along and enter another chamber, which is reinforced with thick pillars supporting a vaulted ceiling across which runs a network of pipes.

A large arch beckons and as we step through, we come to a complete standstill.

'Gods,' Hargna croaks.

There's no doubt we're immediately beneath the barracks. The vaulted chamber stretches off as far as I can see. Giant columns support the ceiling above, and there's a ramp nearby leading up to a set of wooden doors in the stone overhead. However, it's not the scale of the space that has Hargna rooted in place, it's the thousands of gunpowder crates and piles of cannon balls spread out before us.

'Let's go,' I say, heading for the ramp.

'I think I'll stay here.'

We stop in our tracks, turning to Valeria who winces as she lowers herself painfully with her back against one of the stone columns.

'What are you talking about?' Hargna demands. 'Get up!' He leans down and takes her arm, but she wrenches it free.

'Keep your damned hands off me!' she hisses, and Hargna backs away, shocked. She turns to Grishen and holds out her hand. 'Give me an axe.'

Grishen looks for my approval.

'Now!' Valeria demands.

I nod, and he passes one over.

With a grunt of pain, she chops at a crate beside her, splintering the wood, and a cascade of black powder spills out onto the ground.

'How long do you need?' she asks me, her gaze determined.

I consider the huge size of the barracks, that we'll have no idea where to go, and the unlikelihood of us escaping anyway.

'Count backwards from four hundred the moment we get going,' I say, pulling the lantern from Hargna's hands and passing it to Valeria.

She smashes the tough glass with the axe, then tosses the weapon back to Grishen.

Hargna looks back and forth from me to Valeria as what she's proposing to do finally registers.

'NO!' he cries, tears flowing. 'You're not badly injured.'

Valeria's laugh is bitter and dark.

'Not badly injured? I've been mortally wounded for years, Hargna. Years!'

'Listen,' he begs. 'We'll fight our way out together.'

Valeria shakes her head vehemently

'You had a chance to fight for me once. You lost that privilege forever.'

'I'll stay here with you then.' Hargna says desperately, shaking with emotion. 'We'll die together!'

Grishen and I stand back, silent, giving them space.

'Don't do this.' Hargna begs. 'Come with me. I'll make everything better. I swear it!'

Valeria's anger dissipates a little. She smiles sadly and ruffles Hargna's hair.

'Do you love me?' she asks, tilting her head shyly to one side.

'With all my heart.' Hargna sobs. 'More than you'll ever know!'

'Then prove it,' she says, fierceness returning to her eyes. 'Don't give up. Don't lie down, and don't die here with me. I utterly despise that version of you. Instead, become the man I always dreamed you could be. Die fighting the Astorians. Die fighting for our people. Die fighting for me. If I see you do this, then I swear you, me, and our child, will be together for eternity!'

Valeria kisses him gently, a lingering kiss, and I realise I'm crying.

She pushes Hargna roughly away, then looks up at me and smiles.

'Take this big idiot with you, and teach him how to fight.'

'Grishen, Hargna,' I say, my throat tight. 'It's time to go.'

Valeria nods and hefts the lamp, turning up the wick so her face lights as if with an otherworldly glow.

Hargna takes a long last look at her.

'I'll see and our child in the afterlife. I'll never let you down again,' he says.

We run for the ramp, her voice soft behind us.

'Three hundred and ninety-nine.'

***

CHAPTER XII

The wooden doors resist for a heart stopping moment, and then groan and slam back with a crash as we scramble up into a small chamber filled with coiled ropes.

A door beckons. I yank it open, and sprint out into an empty hallway.

There's no time for stealth, and I draw one of my swords as I pound down an empty flagstoned corridor bedecked with faded banners and dusty paintings.

Another heavy wooden door awaits, but the others aren't with me.

I turn to find Grishen pulling Hargna along.

'Damn,' I growl. I'm tempted to order Grishen to leave him behind.

Every second stretches as I wait for them to catch up.

My hand whips out, smacking Hargna hard across the cheek. It's a ringing blow that has him stagger backwards. I follow it up with another.

'You promised Valeria,' I hiss. 'Don't you dare let her down.'

I follow it up with two other lashing blows, and a spark of anger flashes in his eyes.

Another smack and his lips draw back in a snarl.

'Let's go, and you'd better be ready to fight,' I say to Hargna. 'You fall behind now, and you stay behind!'

Having received a determined nod, I yank the door back and run through into yet another corridor lined with dozens of closed doors.

The first one crashes inward under my kick to reveal a bedroom. Inside, a lamp flickers and a man is half-dressed, pulling on a jacket.

He turns with a shocked yelp that quickly changes to a whimper as I press the edge of my sword to his neck.

'The exit?' I hiss. 'Tell me quickly and I won't kill you.'

'Th-that way,' he stammers, pointing. 'Down the passage, turn right at the end, th-through the hall, down another passage, another right, and it's there!'

I slit his throat, then re-join the others outside.

'What the hell?' bellows a man as he comes out of a room a few steps ahead. Grishen leaps forward, his axe swinging, splitting the man's skull, showering blood and brains everywhere.

Doors start to open and people look out, only to slam them shut in terror as we bear down on them.

Grishen flings the door open at the end, and we turn right. I drop back, letting Hargna take the lead as the shouts of dismay diminish behind us. The corridor is empty and thankfully isn't long, but as we near the heavy door at the other end, it opens, a woman walking through with a tray of food in her hand.

Hargna hasn't even drawn his sword and simply shoulder barges her out of the way. I wince as her head slams into the edge of the door, her tray spinning its contents over the ground.

The hall opens up before us.

'Keep going,' I shout, running past Hargna. I drag my other sword free, then sprint as fast as I can.

Shouts of alarm rise around us as we cross a hall filled with several hundred Astorian officers breaking fast.

Chairs screech, and a couple of brave ones leap to intercept us, but as their blood sprays and their screams add to the noise, the rest throw themselves out of the way. But then, as we reach the other side, they find their courage and give chase with a mighty roar.

The wail of the morning sirens adds to the clamour of shouts and pounding feet as we run along the next corridor, slamming the door shut behind us as we turn right to find the entrance chamber immediately ahead.

Daylight beckons as the gate guards open it up for the day, and with their backs toward us, in rigid formation, are squads of soldiers ready for their morning drill.

Behind us, the officers flood screaming into the corridor, and as we run between the formations, I swing my sword to take a man's throat out as he turns in shock.

Then we're through the doors, empty ground before us, and a charging mass of soldiers behind us. A pair of metal perimeter gates are already open, the guards in their sentry boxes as we pound across the empty ground.

Sporadic musket fire forces us to zigzag, the bullets zipping past or kicking up sparks near our feet, but most of the guards just chase us, not taking the time to light their match cords.

Seeing our approach, the perimeter gate guards scramble to shut us in. With a desperate grunt, I launch one of my swords spinning end over end to catapult one off his feet and his fallen body gets in the way of his comrade.

Hargna finally draws his sword, and with a wild, desperate blow, cleaves the remaining guard's leg half off. The man crumples, screaming, and I snatch up my thrown sword as we pass through, our pursuers mere steps behind and closing fast.

They're fresh, and however much the blood rush is pushing us on, it's not going to be enough. An eating hall looms ahead, its doors open, and by common assent we veer toward it.

Hargna and Grishen dart in first, sprinting past a counter covered in piles of bread and cauldrons of steaming broth toward another door at the back with me on their heels. The laboured breathing of a guard is just a few steps behind me as I reach out, snatching at a metal handle.

As I run on, there's a clang, cries of pain, and I allow myself a smile just as I'm hit in the legs and brought crashing to the ground.

I twist and kick backwards, smashing the man's nose who'd tackled me, watching a dozen others behind him floundering in a chaotic heap, slipping and sliding in the soup as they claw their way over one another to reach me.

A final kick for good measure and I'm back on my feet, still holding both swords, following the others out the back.

They're off to the right and I run after them, a dozen soldiers erupting through the doorway behind me.

As I catch up, we turn left back onto the main avenue straight in front of hundreds of soldiers milling around, who immediately give chase with a roar.

'M-maybe, we should s-stop and f-fight,' Grishen pants, his breathing laboured.

A factory beckons, its large double doors wide open.

'T-there,' I gasp, barely able to get the word out.

Hargna is a few steps ahead thanks to his long legs when the ground jolts, and I fall, the ground rushing up to hit me viciously in the chest as Grishen also tumbles.

I get to my knees, and suddenly Hargna is there, grabbing my arms, dragging me into the shelter of the factory entrance, Grishen crawling after as Valeria says her final farewell.

It's suddenly impossible to breathe, and I gasp for breath, the air sucked from my lungs as with a roar the world seems to end. A howling wind sends the bodies of countless Astorian soldiers cartwheeling and tumbling past the entrance, followed by a scorching wave of fire, as we huddle in utter shock.

I sheathe my battered swords just as bricks start to fall around us, and look up to see the wall bowing inward.

'Go! Go!' I shout, making myself heard above the storm.

Like drunkards, we stumble through the factory weaving between giant furnaces. A few shocked workers are yelling, their faces contorted with fear. Then the wall collapses behind us with a crash, revealing a raging inferno, the scorching heat licking at our backs. Everything starts to disintegrate around us. The ceiling starts to sag and collapse, bricks falling like rain as we run toward a set of back doors.

'We'll never make it!' I shout.

'Here!' Hargna shouts, leading us toward a furnace. It hasn't yet been lit, and he runs up a ramp and clambers in through the opening. Grishen and I push through after him.

The factory collapses a few seconds later, and we look at the top of the furnace, praying that it holds firm as it shakes under the impact of roof beams, tiles, bricks and whatever else rains from above.

The clamour goes on for a few more seconds, then begins to die down.

Grishen begins to laugh.

It's half a laugh and half a sob, and as he continues, tears of relief and joy running down his face, I can't help but laugh too. Hargna suddenly joins in, and the furnace echoes with our relief while the world outside burns.

Confined to our refuge, and with our nervous energy spent, I manage to relax. We can't leave just yet, and whilst my body screams for rest, there's too much to do.

'Hargna, Grishen, are you with me?'

Hargna turns toward me, his eyes bloodshot from the dust and tears, but he manages a determined nod. Grishen just grins as if he can't wait for more chaos.

'This is a pivotal moment,' I continue. 'The Astorian military in Astgate is nigh on destroyed, and we must take advantage of the mayhem. We need to get your Icelandian and Tarsian kin to rise up, and it has to be done now.'

Hargna exhales sharply.

'How are you going to do that?' he asks. 'Bardala and his council are dead ... they're leaderless.'

'No, not me,' I say earnestly. 'You. Just you!'

'Me?' Hargna gasps. 'I can't do this on my own!'

'You can do this,' I insist. 'If I go, it'll only bring distrust, fear, and maybe outright resistance. The same goes for Grishen. You know the plan and you have to see it through. Tell them how you destroyed the barracks, of how their kin from the other cities are coming, and you'll raise a strong enough force to take the warehouses. Once those are in your hands, the doubters will quickly fall into line. Just remember the lesson I gave you on leadership and bluffing, and you'll be fine.'

Hargna clenches his fists, trying to stop his hands shaking.

'And what about you and Grishen?'

'We have our own mission that can't wait.'

'The All Father,' Grishen says with a flourish.

'Absolutely. We just can't risk him escaping while you mobilise enough rebels to siege the palace.'

'So when do we leave?' Hargna asks.

'Look out through the furnace entrance,' I say. 'Tell me what you see.'

Hargna looks out and shrugs.

'I can't see a damn thing, there's too much smoke. It's ... it's the perfect time to leave,' he groans.

'I'll make an assassin of you yet,' I chuckle. 'Now let's go.'

***.

'When you're ready, lead on,' I instruct Hargna. 'We'll stay with you a short while, but then we'll go our own way.'

Hargna needs to assume the role of leader, and even if he only gets an hour to feel comfortable doing so, every little helps. Grishen flashes a knowing smile. He's becoming rather good at reading my thoughts.

A minute later, we finish tying torn sleeves around our mouths and noses and step outside of our shelter.

Following Hargna, we pick our way slowly through the rubble and broken beams, barely able to see five paces due to the thick smoke, trying not to cough although our eyes are streaming.

Tooran had warned of a coming cataclysm, but it feels like it's already here. Twice before I'd experienced the power of a gunpowder explosion, one on either side of the gate, but this was something else entirely.

There's no point in talking. Outside of the furnace, the never-ending crash of falling rubble, the roar of flames, wailing sirens, and the distant screams of the wounded make it pointless. For a moment I wonder why their screams are so faint, then realise that anyone nearby probably wouldn't have survived.

Our progress is painfully slow. Visibility is minimal, every step, the mounds of debris shift beneath our feet, threatening to send us tumbling, or the thatch-work of beams over our heads, crashing down upon us.

Finally, we make it out of the factory, the jagged remains of a wall, the only indication we're now in a street.

Hargna turns around, disorientated.

'I don't know which way to go,' he admits, his makeshift face mask and the billowing smoke lending an eerie, hollow quality to his voice.

'Think, Hargna,' I encourage him, taking his shoulder. 'Look around. What can you see?'

'Nothing. Just smoke and the glow of flames.'

'Which direction is the brightest?' Grishen prompts, immediately picking up on my hint. He's a fast learner, and if only he were trusted by his peers, I'd send him instead of Hargna in a heartbeat.

'There,' says Hargna, pointing.

'That means if we ran through an eating hall which is north of the barracks, then that glow is …' Grishen prompts.

Hargna nods, turning his back to the fire.

'To the south. This way.'

As we stumble slowly through the rubble, a wind occasionally grants us a glimpse of our immediate surroundings. Jagged walls rise up like broken teeth, localised fires smoulder, but nothing living moves.

This might not have been a residential sector, but enough people had still lived here. They would have begun opening up the factories ready for people to start their morning shifts ... until their world came crashing down upon them.

Another ten minutes of scrabbling and slowly the streets clear, the buildings mostly undamaged except for broken windows everywhere.

Four musket bearing soldiers appear briefly ahead as the smoke thins, their backs toward us, facing a small crowd.

Hargna stumbles to a halt, but I push him forward, pulling a sword free over my shoulder and glance to my right. Grishen already has his axes in hand. Hargna nods and pulls his longsword free, and we spread out.

Crackling flames, the murmur of the crowd, and the crash of falling masonry disguise our approach but as we get closer, several people point and we break into a run, closing the distance.

The soldiers have daggers affixed to their muskets, but they don't turn with any urgency, expecting perhaps, some walking wounded.

I don't worry about Grishen, but focus on the two soldiers nearest me and Hargna on my left.

My first target's neck opens up under a downward diagonal right to left cut and then, putting my left hand behind the pommel, I stamp forward, thrusting, and plunge my sword's bloody tip into the second Astorian's heart.

Yanking my sword free, I raise the blade and parry Hargna's bloody longsword an inch from my face.

He stares at me horrified, whether at disembowelling his opponent who lies screaming at his feet, or by almost killing me with his uncontrolled swing, it matters not.

His sword drops from shaking fingers, but I step in and catch it before it hits the ground, thrust it into his still screaming victim's throat, then bend to wipe both our weapons clean on the soldier's tunic before handing it back to him.

'You did just fine,' I say quietly. 'When in a close fight, don't swing, just use the point ... and don't drop it again.'

'What now?' Hargna whispers, as we half-turn our backs to the shocked and whimpering crowd.

'This is where it starts, Hargna,' I say, gripping his shoulder. 'That's a crowd of Tarsian and Icelandian workers, and they've just witnessed you stride from the ashes of the barracks, and slay an Astorian soldier with a bloody great longsword. You're a hero of old, now lead them before you lose them.'

'You can do it, Hargna,' Grishen adds, leaning in close. 'You have the look of eagles, proud and dangerous. Now sheath your sword before you talk to them, or they'll run screaming.'

Hargna laughs shakily, nods, and takes a deep breath before sheathing his blade. Grishen and I stand back as he opens his arms and walks to the crowd, which edges away before his approach.

'Brothers and sisters,' he begins, raising his voice. 'I am Hargna, son of Harkonen, leader of the underground. Today, alongside my wife and two comrades, I destroyed the Astorian barracks, killing every soldier inside.'

'He has a good voice,' Grishen whispers.

I nod. Every second is precious, but I want to see this, to know that when Grishen and I leave, it's with the assurance that Hargna won't let us down.

Worried murmurs ripple through the crowd, but Hargna draws his sword ringing from its sheath and holds it aloft, and they quieten immediately.

Hargna points his sword at a woman, broad of shoulder, although gaunt, like everyone else.

'What are you?' he demands.

She blinks, somewhat startled at having been picked out.

'A factory worker.'

Hargna shakes his head sadly.

'And you?' he asks, pointing to the man beside her.

'A factory worker, of course!'

Hargna shakes his head again and steps forward.

'Wrong! You're warriors like your ancestors, and today, you are FREE. If four of us can kill ten thousand, then imagine what we can do together! This city is ours for the taking, and I swear to you,' Hargna bellows, 'that if you follow me, by the end of today, every one of you will be armed, every one of you will have regained your honour, and every one of you will be a hero!'

A moment of silence follows Hargna's speech, then the energy shifts, the crowd pushes forward, drawn in by his words, gathering around him full of hope, voices raised.

I turn to Grishen.

'It's time for us to go our own way.'

'Anywhere with you, Malina,' Grishen says.

He's covered in dust, cuts and bruises, his clothing torn, but I've rarely seen him happier. Then, suddenly, with a sinking realisation, I finally understand why he's been making flirtatious comments like this since we destroyed the factory. Having drunk his blood for days on end has bonded him to me beyond the bounds of friendship.

We've paired.

Gods.

'Are you alright?' Grishen asks, perceptive to my emotional turmoil.

'Never been better,' I lie. 'Let's go.'

We ease quickly past the crowd and slip through the streets. It's still early, and thankfully both the cloudy sky and the smoke maintain a perpetual gloom. Thunder rumbles in the distance, and I grin. Hargna needed a storm to help minimise casualties when he attacks the warehouses, and he's going to get one.

'Look!' Grishen hisses, grabbing my arm.

Ahead, four soldiers limp along the road, their muskets absent, uniforms hanging off their bloody bodies in ribbons. Grishen reaches for his axes, but I shake my head.

'Why not?' he whispers.

'Every injured soldier helps our cause,' I say. 'The more soldiers looking after the wounded, the fewer there are to fight … and they'll sap morale.'

Grishen nods.

'I learn something new every day.'

We turn down a side road and even here, further from the blast, chunks of masonry litter the street, thrown by the explosion, walls have gaping holes, and some have collapsed. We walk swiftly, our heads down as the wind begins to pick up, but we're not entirely inconspicuous and our progress slows as people in the streets look toward the pulsating glow dominating the morning gloom. They're Tarsian and Icelandian workers, unsure what to do now the factories they work in have been turned to rubble.

'Bloody Astorian,' someone mutters as we hurry past a small group of men and women huddled around a doorway. 'Get lost!' a woman calls after, her voice bitter.

'Don't worry, it doesn't bother me much,' Grishen says.

'They think you're Astorian despite what you're wearing,' I say, amazed.

'Everyone just immediately notices the cleft chin. It's been my lifetime's curse.'

It feels strange walking in the open. But speed is of the essence, and the rooftops around here will not only slow us down, but are probably dangerously unstable in places. However, before long we'll have to leave the streets behind. The Queen of Beasts won't go unnoticed for long, and everyone beyond Grishen and Hargna is a potential enemy.

'Damn,' Grishen hisses as we reach another main avenue.

A dozen soldiers are struggling along, supporting one another, paying no attention to anything but their own misery. Another lies in the road where they've left him. He's still moving, trying to crawl after them, blood running from his ears and nose, but they're deaf to his pitiful cries for help.

'Where do you think they're going?' Grishen asks.

'Probably the same place we are,' I reply.

Grishen snorts.

'Hah. I doubt those poor bastards have any more chance than us getting in. Only the All Father's bloody pet slingers can enter.'

'Let's take another route then.'

'So how exactly are we going to kill the All Father?' Grishen asks as we hurry along an empty side street, crunching through broken glass and rubble. 'Wait for him, either make a run for Ast or come into the city, and kill him then.'

'Killing him isn't the problem,' I remind Grishen. 'Ensuring he stays dead is. I'm sure the answer to our problem lies inside his damned Palace.'

Grishen laughs darkly.

'Then maybe we should just walk up to the front gate, and say … Excuse me. We're here to kill the All Father, can you show us the way?'

'Always the jester, but never the fool,' I say, smiling warmly.

I come to a halt, my mind whirring as I try to gather my bearings. Everything looks far different from street level as opposed to from the rooftops.

'Where was the underground hideout from here?' I muse.

'Thinking of joining back up with Hargna?' Grishen asks, trying to read my intentions. He indicates a sharp left. 'The residential sector is this way.'

'No. I want the actual hideout.'

Grishen shakes his head.

'Hargna won't go there, it will be too dangerous. The slingers will never leave their dead and injured behind, or their weapons for someone to loot. He'll know that.'

'It's nothing to do with Hargna. We're going there.'

'Then it's obviously a fantastic idea, whatever the reason.' Grishen smiles as he turns down the next alleyway.

I motion for silence, not because I can sense danger, but because talking is a sure way to be unaware of it. Grishen loves to talk, although admittedly he's quite entertaining and good company. He also reminds me a little of Lotane with his cleft chin, and strong frame …

Lotane. An overwhelming wave of guilt washes over me. He'd be distraught if he knew another man had paired with me, even if by accident.

Never again, Malina, I promise myself, and push the pace, leaving Grishen struggling to stay alongside, punishing him for something that isn't his fault. I need his help to kill the All Father, nothing more, and if he dies in the process, it won't matter at all.

But as my chest suddenly tightens at the thought, I know it will.

***

'That's a lot of dead slingers,' Grishen whispers as we watch another body carried awkwardly out of the underground's latrine entrance by two slingers and dumped onto the back of a wagon. It sits fourth in a line and the others are already full. 'It's a shame we didn't get them all.'

'Normally I'd agree, but in this instance, I'm glad some are alive.' I whisper, peering over the roof's edge. 'It makes your plan even better.'

I nod downward at the two slingers who are standing sentry below at the street corner, their long coats flapping in the rising wind. Their presence, along with another pair standing at the far end of the street, keeps prying eyes well away from the massacre. A junction beyond the latrine entrance likely has more of their kind guarding that approach too.

'When exactly are you going to tell me what *my* plan is?' Grishen snarls, the skin around his eyes wrinkled, giving away his amusement.

'You're getting old and senile.' I tease as I pull back from the edge.

Grishen smiles broadly.

'So, let me guess. We hide amongst the dead in the back of a wagon and hope they cart us straight into the Palace?'

'Hah. We only just escaped a cremation, but you aren't far off.'

Grishen stares at me blankly as we crouch. The storm is almost upon us, the wind clawing at our clothes, forcing me to raise my voice.

'We steal their clothes, then we're going to walk right up to the gates, exactly as you suggested. We've seen what, maybe two dozen wounded slingers making their way back? They'll be let in, and so will we, thanks to you, and your chin!'

'I never thought I'd be happy to have it,' Grishen says, scratching his bristled jaw, accepting my plan without batting an eyelid. 'So, what do we do about them below?'

'I slide down the lamppost next to them, and do what I do best.'

'Now who is getting old and senile?' Grishen laughs. 'That way might get you dead. Now follow me.'

We scurry like rats along the rooftop until we are almost opposite the latrine entrance. Even here, chunks of debris from the explosion litter the roof. Some pieces of rock are as big as my fist.

'It's too risky,' I say as Grishen eyes the lamppost just below. 'Those two nearby will probably see us. Let me do it my way.'

Grishen picks up a chunk of rock, hefts it, and then hurls it high into the air around the far corner of the building near to where the two slingers are standing.

'My way,' he grunts, then leaps off to grab the lamppost as the slingers dart around the corner to investigate.

I'm after Grishen in a heartbeat, watching the other pair at the far end of the street. I roll on hitting the ground, then head after Grishen, who is limping toward the latrine entrance.

No shots, and no shouts follow us as we step inside its foul interior.

Nothing has changed other than the tracks of a hundred feet through the foulness as I ease past Grishen and take the lead, swords in hand. He's hurt his ankle, the idiot, but I can't deny his plan worked.

I push ahead, absent even a whisper of instruction to Grishen that might carry down the corridor. Meeting a slinger in a long corridor won't go well for me, but there's no place for us to hide in wait, so I move ahead quickly, swords in hand.

As I reach the main chamber, I look upon the slaughter, finding it hard to believe that only hours earlier, this place had been full of hopes and dreams instead of corpses.

Two slingers, stripped down to trousers and boots for the bloody work, drag a dead comrade by the arms backwards toward me, unaware of my presence. I wait at the tunnel mouth, allowing them a few more heartbeats of life. It's not mercy that delays my hand; it's just tiredness.

'Your turn to take the legs,' one mutters.

His comrade sighs, drops the arms, walks around, bends over and grabs the corpse by the ankles, then looks up to see me.

The one closest, drops the hands, and shuffles around, as if by moving slowly, whatever has caused his friend to go as white as a ghost, will have disappeared. He's young, a thin moustache barely shadowing his upper lip, and his eyes slowly fill with tears as he brings his hands together beseechingly.

'Please,' he begs, dropping to his knees. 'Don't kill us. We're just workers!'

Despite its age, the Delnorian steel I wield cleaves through his skull, not even shattering it, just cutting it in two like a piece of fruit. A straight diagonal cut that sees the top half slowly slide away before it drops to the ground. The body stays kneeling for a couple of heartbeats as I stare at the other man, then falls backwards.

With a whimper, the man turns and runs, dashing for his guns, that along with his shirt and leather jacket are piled neatly against a wall.

My first dagger takes him in the back of the left leg, and he manages two more steps before he collapses. My second dagger takes him in the right thigh as he rolls to his back, trying to push himself backwards with his hands.

He lifts his head, sobbing, and then it slams back against the bloodied ground as my third takes him in the right eye.

I pause by his body to retrieve and clean my weapons, then take stock. A pile of discarded bandages marks where the wounded had been tended, and several dozen more dead slingers still await removal. But the bodies of those I had come to know well lie where they fell, destined never to receive a burial.

I glance over my shoulder as Grishen hobbles into the chamber.

'Get changed,' I say, pulling off one of my recent victim's boots, measuring it against my foot. 'Make sure the clothes fit well and strap that ankle.'

'Yes, Mother,' Grishen chuckles.

Despite all the dark deeds I've done, looting the dead still unsettles me, especially as thousands of glazed eyes follow my every move. Yet a sharper chill ripples down my spine when I realise one specific pair of red eyes is missing. I look around and swear softly.

'The All Father's body has gone,' I say.

Has his corpse been taken, or did he rise again and walk out of here on his own? I push the thought aside. I'll find out soon enough if the gods are with me.

Spurred on by the fear of getting caught and the desire to get out of this morgue as swiftly as possible, I'm quickly dressed in bloody trousers, well-fitting boots, and a shirt covering my vambraces. I refashion my sword harness so they hang at my waist. A long slinger's coat conceals them nicely, but I shrug it off as I've yet to complete my look.

Taking a roll of bandages, I kneel next to the half-naked body of the slinger who'd donated her clothes. Taking one of my daggers, I cut her stomach open and pull out some intestines, cutting a length free.

'What the hells?' Grishen gasps, recoiling.

Ignoring him, I wrap the bandages around my midsection, stuff the intestines inside, making sure to leave a little hanging free, bloodying the once white linen. Having completed my disguise, I pull on the slinger's gun harness and coat.

Grishen is almost ready, but being stockier, he's found it harder to find clothes that fit, so I inspect the guns I'm wearing. Slipping a metal clasp on the grip forward, the double barrels drop down, revealing two unfired cartridges nestled inside. I check each weapon, ensuring they're all loaded.

Opening the pouches, I find ten cartridges in each. Four cartridges and those in the barrels. Each slinger has the ability to kill fifty-two people at a distance.

I smile wryly.

I've killed far more with a bow, but in the hands of a novice, a bow is next to useless, whereas these guns would be deadly in the hands of a child.

'Ready,' Grishen calls.

He looks an utter mess. His leather coat is ripped and smeared in gore, his face barely distinguishable beneath soot, dust, and congealed blood. I know I look just as bad, if not worse. Our disguise is perfect. Almost.

Searching through my jacket pockets, I find a pair of supple leather gloves and pull them on, hiding my green skin.

Grishen, ever attentive, follows suit.

Leaning down, I pick up two wide-brimmed hats and toss one over, then settle the other low over my face.

'How's the ankle?'

'Better already. Just a small sprain, I'll manage.'

'Let's go then.'

We head back to the entrance, and I'm pleased to see Grishen walking with only a slight limp.

'Let's hope we don't run into Hargna and a band of bloodthirsty rebels,' he jokes.

I can't help but laugh.

'Don't be such an angel of doom,' I reply. 'Now, heads down. We're injured slingers, heading home.'

Together, we exit the latrine straight into the full fury of the storm. Rain lashes down with a rare force and I'm grateful for the long leather coat and wide-brimmed hat.

Guiding Grishen past the wagons, we turn right toward the Palace. Up ahead, as expected, two more slingers stand sentry at the next junction.

One of my hands rests on Grishen's back as if I need his support, allowing me to hold a drawn dagger out of sight. The other is tucked inside my leather coat, as if clutching my wounded stomach as I bend over, feigning agony, my head well down as we make our way toward them.

'Feels like a date. All dressed up, going for a walk,' Grishen murmurs.

'Shut up, you oaf!' I hiss.

'They've seen us,' Grishen continues. 'But at least they haven't drawn their guns yet.'

'Keep talking,' I say.

'You look lovely in a hat.'

'Not that, damnit. How far are they? Are they coming to meet us?'

'Twenty paces, and not yet.'

'The wagon with the injured left about half an hour ago. Why weren't you on it?' One of the slingers yells.

'This one was buried under the dead,' Grishen shouts back as we continue forward. 'Took a while to find her.'

'Just keep walking,' I hiss. 'Don't stop.'

But as we continue, I see the slingers' polished boots covered in rain as they come to stand before us.

'Bloody slaughterhouse in there,' one says. 'Rebel scum, they blew up the barracks too.'

'Never thought they had the balls for that,' Grishen says, stopping.

I moan loudly, hoping Grishen takes the hint and put pressure on his back, a gentle nudge to get him moving.

'We'll get some payback though, that's for sure,' the same slinger says.

'The only good Icelandian, is a dead one,' Grishen says, laughing.

'That's what I always say,' laughs the other.

'Hey, what's your name?' the same voice asks. 'I don't recognise you!'

'Arasta.'

'Arasta. Arasta,' the slinger mutters. 'Who is your captain?'

'Erm ...'

The slinger's boots shift ever so slightly as he adjusts his weight, widening his stance.

'Gods, it hurts,' I cry, reaching out blindly, stumbling away from Grishen toward the suspicious slinger. He backs away, but I'm already close enough. My hand flashes out as his flashes down, but his leather coat hinders his draw while my dagger meets no resistance as it sinks into his throat. I tear it sideways in a torrent of blood and stab downwards into the other slinger's arm as he lifts a gun, and he drops it with a cry. Grishen's fist lands square on the man's jaw, poleaxing him backwards to crash into the ground, and I leap on top and slide the dagger into his heart.

'You need to know when to shut up sometimes,' I hiss angrily. 'Now, let's get your two friends between those chimneys.'

Together we drag the bodies through the pouring rain, and prop them against a wall. The blood on the street is already getting washed away, and hopefully anyone coming by will have their heads down and won't notice the corpses for a while.

Leaving the dead behind, it's not long before we reach another avenue, and despite the downpour, it's busy.

The further from the explosion, the more normality has returned to the city. People are hurrying about with a mission. Factories and warehouses are open, eating halls are distributing food.

'I'm hungry,' Grishen moans. 'I don't want to die on an empty stomach. Let's eat!'

'Why can't you just be serious?' I sigh, rubbing my temples.

'I've never been more serious,' Grishen says with a frown, turning toward a doorway where a queue of people wait beneath an awning.

'Don't you bloody dare,' I hiss.

'Now you've dared me, how can I resist. Just keep that hat pulled low and we'll be just fine,' Grishen laughs, adroitly avoiding my grasping hand.

To my utter disbelief, he walks straight up to the queue and it parts before him like meat under a butcher's knife. Then, he just stands and turns around, waiting.

My blood begins to boil, but he crosses his arms while everyone looks down, afraid to meet a deadly slinger's eyes.

'Damn you,' I mutter under my breath, then can't help but laugh as I join him and walk up to the counter.

'Choose a table,' he says, 'I'll sort the food. We'll be out of here in five minutes ... maybe ten.'

I walk toward the far corner. On the one hand, there will be no avenue of escape, but on the other, it will give sight of both entrances and the whole room.

Conversation dies away, and chairs scrape as people hurriedly get up and move. I can't help but applaud Grishen's audacity. We'll need that to get into the Palace, and after that, it's all down to me.

**

CHAPTER XIII

Somewhat refreshed with full stomachs, we're back in character again. I hunch over, sloshing through the puddles, one hand tucked inside my leather coat, while Grishen supports me, solid and dependable, willing to walk straight into the jaws of death at my side.

Would he have been this loyal and unshakeable if we hadn't paired? It's impossible to say, but a life of hardship can either break a man or forge him into something stronger. Grishen is definitely the latter, whereas Hargna is the former.

Hargna.

It's a coin toss if he delivers on our plan. I've seen the weakness in him, his flaws, and they concern me. But I've also witnessed a rebirth of sorts. I just hope he grows quickly into the man Valeria hoped he'd be, what I selfishly need him to be … a leader capable of seizing freedom for his people. His success will help keep the world gate closed for longer.

A long sigh escapes without me realising.

'Are you alright there?' Grishen asks softly.

'My back isn't happy,' I answer half truthfully, unwilling to share my doubts with him.

'Well, we're almost there,' he says calmly, 'but things aren't looking too good. There's a field hospital with tents for the wounded soldiers outside of the palace gates. As I guessed, none of them are allowed in. It looks a bloody mess, literally.'

'That doesn't sound bad,' I say, straightening a little, easing the ache in my back.

'Slingers are lining the perimeter fence as far as I can see, and there are more medical tents inside the gate. I don't think the All Father wants the inside of his palace covered in blood.'

'Well, this was never going to be easy.'

I glance up, taking a look for myself. No one will see the colour of my eyes or skin from any distance through the rain, especially as my face under the hat is as covered in filth and blood as is Grishen's ... but nor do I want to test my luck.

A squad of oilskin-clad soldiers hurries past, heading toward the city. How many of them were out on patrol when the barracks fell? A few hundred, maybe more. The storm will render their muskets useless, and the knowledge that ten thousand of their comrades were incinerated will drain whatever courage they have left, especially once Hargna rouses the mob to action.

Grishen whistles softly.

'This place looks impregnable. We're going to need the luck of the gods to get in.'

'Just follow through with the plan ...' I begin.

'I know the plan,' Grishen interrupts. 'It's mine after all. But I honestly thought a fey queen like yourself would have come up with something more devious and less likely to get us dead in the first few minutes.'

The sound of misery gets progressively louder as we slosh through the middle of the field hospital. Sobbing, cries for help, and desperate pleas for water all mix together, a symphony of torment.

'Please, don't take my leg,' a woman screams.

I wince as her agony rises to new heights. Perhaps I should feel sympathy, but the Astorians are only now beginning to reap what they've sown. Here, in Astgate, justice is coming.

'Twenty paces,' Grishen mutters. 'We've been noticed.'

A quick glance reveals a surgeon, his bloodstained apron soaked from the rain, red rings on his sleeves denoting rank, splashing toward the gate having seen my plight.

'Open the gate, quickly,' he shouts, and those impassable iron gates swing back, the slingers not even thinking to question us as we stagger through.

'What's wrong with her?' the surgeon demands.

'Stab wound to the gut,' Grishen answers for me as we slowly leave the gate behind us.

'Stab wound to the gut, Sir!' the surgeon growls.'

'Sorry, Sir,' Grishen says quickly, lowering his head in deference.

As the surgeon crouches, I close my eyes. He pulls my hand away from my stomach to reveal the bloodied bandages and a loop of intestine.

'That doesn't look good,' the surgeon says, standing, slipping his arm under my left armpit. 'I can take her from here.'

I'd rather stay with her, Sir,' Grishen says, not letting me go.

'Very touching,' the surgeon snaps. 'But no. Leave her to me.'

I let my knees buckle slightly, sagging against him.

'I need to see the All Father,' I croak, grabbing at the surgeon's apron.

'You'll see him soon enough. He'll be waiting for you in the next life,' the surgeon replies in a resigned voice.

'I know where Nogotha is.'

'What?'

'I know where Nogotha is,' I whisper again, my voice barely audible.

'I'll get a commander,' the surgeon gasps.

'NO!' I hiss desperately. 'I don't have much time left.'

Reaching inside my bandages, I pull some intestine free and let it fall to the ground.

'Oh gods,' the surgeon breathes, but he isn't horrified, just conflicted about what to do.

'Imagine being the one to bear such incredible news,' Grishen muses smoothly. 'The gratitude of our All Father would be limitless.'

I sag further, putting even more weight on the surgeon, and he gasps.

'Don't just stand there. Help me,' the surgeon orders Grishen. 'I have to get this slinger to the All Father before she dies.'

With Grishen supporting me on one side, and the surgeon on the other, we move unchallenged, weaving through the maze of tents.

'Out of the way,' the surgeon snaps at an orderly who is too slow to move, and with every step we get closer to the entrance.

'No badly wounded inside the palace, Sir,' a slinger standing guard at the entrance announces. 'You know the rules.'

'Of course I bloody know,' roars the surgeon. 'But this is a situation way above your station. Now either get out of my way or you'll find yourself holding a musket before the hour is out!'

I focus on the slinger's boots as what I can only assume is a stare off ensues. I just pray Grishen is keeping his head and eyes down.

'Sir!' says the slinger, and those boots move aside.

People rush around us in a torrent as if we're a rock in a river, but as we turn down a series of narrow passageways, tranquillity gradually replaces the chaos. A worn stone lintel marks our entry into a long chamber lined with wooden benches. Kneeling slingers flank us, their foreheads pressed reverently to the cold floor.

'All Father. Thou art our guiding light,' a priestly voice intones from my left.

'Show us the way in the darkness,' the slingers respond in unison.

'Shield us from the evil of the fey,' the priest continues.

'Let Thy truth be our armour,' the slingers reply.

I can't help but moan in despair. The slingers are religious zealots, loyal beyond reason. A man who fights for coin might surrender. A man who fights for vengeance might flee. But a man who fights for faith? He will die before he yields.

'Plant our feet on the path of righteousness,' the priest pleads.

'And steady our hands for the tasks Thou hast set,' comes the united response.

The prayers linger in the air behind us as we step through an archway, the flagstones giving way to polished wood, a rich red carpet running down the centre as we push further into the Palace. I memorise every turn, although the chances of getting out are minimal.

'Damnit,' the surgeon moans. 'Look at the mess we're making. There'll be hell to pay.'

I almost laugh, although it's true, our muddy footprints have left a terrible mess.

'You can blame it on me, Sir,' Grishen offers.

'Of course I'll bloody blame it on you,' the surgeon growls, 'and I don't need your blessing to do so either!'

A few more turns and we pause before two enamelled doors. From the boots, I can only assume two more slingers stand in our way.

'You aren't supposed to be here, Sir. Turn around.'

The voice is cold, unyielding.

'I know,' the surgeon says. 'But I wouldn't bloody be here if it wasn't important. I need to see the All Father, and I need to see him now!'

'You need to turn around before you get a bullet in your head, Sir.'

The slinger's response is assured, completely unfazed by the surgeon's rank, which means he reports directly to a higher power.

This is our destination. I squeeze Grishen's arm gently under my armpit, and receive a squeeze in return. He's ready, and it warms me to know that even if he isn't trained, that I can rely on him, even if it's to die by my side.

'You don't understand,' the surgeon pleads. 'She knows where Nogotha is.'

Silence. Whispered words. A door opens, a pair of boots disappear.

We wait.

I'm lowered to my knees. It's not where I want to be. I can hardly launch a lightning attack from such a position, but I need to maintain my deception. However, I'm worried about my short swords, if a scabbard pokes from beneath my coat ...

The surgeon kneels beside me.

'Hang on a little longer,' he says, a hint of desperation in his voice.

He's afraid. Afraid that if I die before the All Father gets the news, he'll likely die with me. He's right to be worried, his death is coming one way or another.

A lifetime seems to pass until the door opens.

No words are exchanged, but Grishen and the surgeon lift me up, and help me through the doors. They close silently behind us and the guards remain outside.

I allow myself a small, hidden smile.

My muddied boots sink into the plushest carpet I've ever felt as I'm led to a chair with red velvet cushions and tooled arms covered in gold leaf. Grishen helps me sit before he and the surgeon take their seats beside me.

'The All Father will be with you shortly. Stand when he enters the room. Do not speak unless spoken to first. Do not look him in the eyes.'

The voice is clipped, to the point.

A quick glimpse from beneath my hat brim reveals a young woman dressed in a plain white robe sitting behind a beautiful, ornate desk. She sits with a quill poised over a stack of papers, her eyes flickering back and forth, almost uncaring of our presence.

The whole room speaks of opulence, nothing like the austere presence the All Father likes to portray.

Suddenly she stands.

Grishen and the surgeon rise immediately.

I remain where I am, looking a few steps ahead at the floor, moaning softly as I rock backwards and forwards.

The white robes of the All Father and his sandaled feet give him away. The pairs of boots on either side are different to the usual slinger's boots. These are matte black and inlaid with intricate silver swirls, exquisite like everything else in this room.

The sandaled feet approach and stop before me.

Trembling with excitement as opposed to pain, I stand slowly, a hand under my leather coat, now gripping the handle of a gun, the other reaching out to the All Father for support.

'I hear you bring news of the Queen of Beasts. Tell me, where is she?'

'Right here,' I say, smiling up into that loathsome face, and pull the triggers.

***

The All Father staggers away, clutching at himself, but I haven't shot him.

Instead, his bodyguards are flung backwards off their feet by the blasts as I cast my gun aside and draw two more.

Grishen's guns thunder, firing through the chamber door as it starts to open, I fire both mine. My first shot kills the young woman as she pulls a gun from a desk drawer, and the second, the surgeon. My final two bullets I send after Grishen's just to make sure.

'The door!' I bark, tossing the weapons aside, pushing the All Father ahead of me as a shield while I draw another gun. He stumbles through the archway into an adjoining chamber, a lavishly decorated meeting room. A massive crystal chandelier spills warm light over a polished table ringed by thirty chairs. White marble busts on ornate pedestals stand between exquisitely detailed paintings depicting Astorian victories.

Two doors lead from the chamber. The one on my left bursts open, and a slinger rolls in, guns ready. I turn the All Father between me and the threat, but the slinger doesn't hesitate. The All Father's body jerks and crashes back against me as I return fire. My first shot goes wide, but the second takes my assailant in the chest, dropping him, just as another slinger steps through the door, both guns raised.

I twist frantically as he fires, the All Father's body shuddering under the impacts as I drop behind his falling body, frantically casting my empty gun aside. Without time to draw another, I whip my right arm forward, and the dagger from my vambrace flies across the room.

The slinger's gun roars and my dagger spins away.

Another roar, and I flinch in anticipation of the impact … just as the slinger's head explodes.

Grishen lowers his smoking gun, steps over the body, opens the door, and peeks around the frame.

'Clear,' he says, leaving it open, then dashes back to the entrance chamber.

I kneel and loot the headless slinger, taking his four unused guns to replace mine while I keep watch on the corridor the slingers had entered by and the unopened door on the other end.

A minute later, Grishen returns.

'The entrance chamber door is bolted and barricaded with the desk. It should hold a while.'

I nod to the remaining door on the other side of the chamber. He strides over, pulling it open to take a quick look inside, then glances back with a wry grin.

'Toilet,' he says. 'If you need to go, I can wait?'

'Idiot,' I mutter, smiling. 'Ready?'

Grishen's determined nod has me run light-footed down the corridor, a gun extended. It's become too easy to rely on these weapons, but there's no denying their ease of use and effectiveness at close range.

The thick carpet muffles my approach, and I pause, ready to open the door as Grishen joins me.

With a finger to his lips, he pushes down on my shoulder, and we both kneel as I turn the handle. The wood splinters above us as shots punch through the wood, and I fling the door open, firing at the slinger just as his next gun clears its leather holster.

Grishen's gun roars beside me, and the slinger jerks and twists with every impact, before crashing to the floor.

We're in a small, rectangular room, somewhere between a lounge and a library. Hundreds of books are stacked neatly in cabinets on two sides, whereas paintings adorn both the others.

I grab a chair, wedge it under the handle of a door to our right, then join Grishen as he opens a door opposite the one we'd entered through.

No gunfire greets him, nor when he darts a glance around the frame.

Beckoning me to follow, he slips inside, turning swiftly, before dropping to his knees and looking under the five evenly spaced beds in what is evidently the slinger's quarters.

A further doorway leads into an empty bathroom, and we quickly retrace our steps to the lounge.

'What's that?' Grishen asks, tilting his head.

I've heard it too, and it only takes me a moment to realise what it is.

'They're trying to break through your barricade,' I say, pushing the splintered door closed.

I move to one of the cabinets, and Grishen takes the other side. Between us, we drag it to support the door, then add the other for good measure.

'They won't get through that in a hurry,' Grishen mutters. 'But nor will we get out.'

I nod toward the only unopened door, and cross the room, easing the chair out from under the door handle.

'Your turn,' Grishen whispers.

The door swings open silently, revealing a sumptuous bedchamber with floor-to-ceiling panelled cupboards and an enormous four poster bed as centrepiece. Draped in heavy, dark velvet.

'Gods,' mutters Grishen as we step inside, guns trained on the robed figure who is sat on the bed reading a book under a flickering light.

He doesn't flinch. Doesn't scramble for a weapon. Instead, he calmly turns a page, then, without looking up, places the book onto a bedside table.

'I'm flattered you're here to kill me again, Nogotha,' he muses. 'But can it really be a beast like you is incapable of learning the simple fact that I'm immortal?'

My grip tightens around the gun, my knuckles white.

'Of course, I have to admit, dying is painful,' he continues, 'and rather inconvenient. Of all the hundreds of deaths I've endured, drowning in my own blood with your arrow in my throat was particularly unpleasant. I was quite grateful to your friend here for finishing the job.'

'I can assure you,' I say coldly, chilled by his power. 'There are plenty of other ways I can kill you that will be a lot, lot worse.'

The All Father laughs.

'I don't doubt it,' he chuckles. 'However, may I suggest you make the most of it this time, because it will truly be your last. After that, I can assure you, whatever you visit on me, I'll be returning tenfold. It won't be long before my loyal slingers follow your messy trail here, and however hard you fight, they won't kill you. No, they'll save you for me, whatever the cost.'

Grishen looks around, searching for another exit.

'There's no way out,' The All Father continues. 'Unless, of course, you take the coward's way. A bullet in your own head will be a mercy. However, I beg of you to stay alive for me, please!'

The All Father laughs, full of humour.

'You've been quite the adversary, Nogotha, but your reign ends here. The world gate will be open again in maybe four years, five at most, and this time, nothing will stand in my way. Part of me wishes I could keep you alive to see me conquer your world, but to your credit, I'm unwilling to take that risk.'

'Be quiet,' I hiss, my mind racing as I walk around the bed.

'Why? I'm enjoying this so much.' the All Father laughs. 'Come on. Kill me again. Shoot me, stab me, or something you haven't done before, but make it quick, time is ... AARG!'

I elbow the All Father in the face, slamming him back against the headboard, stunning him. Tearing his robe aside, I drive, twist, and slice my dagger into his groin, emasculating him.

His scream is raw, primal even.

It's an evil deed, but I garner some satisfaction from the sheer agony and horror on his face.

'What happens if I leave you like this?' I hiss, leaning close. 'What if I don't kill you? Maybe you can live on without your balls and whatever this is,' I say, chucking the putrid piece of flesh I've grabbed from under his robe onto his chest.

Grishen gags and holds the back of his hand to his mouth.

'He won't be siring any children, let alone taking a piss now,' he manages to say, looking horrified.

I look around the room, at the All Father, his feet drawn up into a foetal position, the tears of agony and hatred running down his cheeks as he looks at me through his bloodshot eyes.

'Let's take the coward's way out,' I say, pulling a gun and putting the barrel under my chin.

'Gods no!' Grishen cries, coming around the bed toward me.

I lift my hand.

'We have to, there's no escape. Kill him, then join me in the next life,' I say, my voice firm, unwavering. 'Promise me!'

Grishen's face is twisted with disbelief and shock.

'I. I, promise,' he whispers.

We stare at each other for what seems like an eternity, before Grishen pulls an axe from the back of his belt. He leans over the bed, lifts his arm and cuts down, and as he does so, I pull the trigger, and collapse a split second later.'

'What ...?'

I hold a finger to my lips and pull the second trigger causing debris to fall from the ceiling like snow.

Grishen squats beside me, his breathing ragged.

'What the hell is going on?' he whispers as I get up.

'You said he won't be siring any children or taking a piss now!' I breathe the words softly in Grishen's ear.

He shakes his head, blinking, unable to process as he's still in shock.

'Where's his toilet?' I ask.

'What?'

'Are you telling me he goes into the slingers' quarters to empty his bowels?'

Grishen frowns as he follows my gaze around the bedroom.

'Now look at his feet. They're absolutely filthy. There's another way in and out of this room, and I didn't want him to realise I knew.'

I open the doors of the cupboards one by one to find them all empty.

'This might be his room,' I whisper. 'But he doesn't sleep here.'

Reaching inside the cupboard nearest the bed, I run my hands over the wooden panelling at the back. It's polished to a deep lustre, absolutely perfect, not a scratch, no indication of it ever being used, but as I look to the floor, and the plush carpet ... something catches my eye.

I kneel and bring my eyes close to the floor, noting that the fibres are slightly worn and discoloured leading from the door to the cabinet on my right.

Grishen hasn't taken his eyes off me, and stands back as I step inside and push gently at the panelling, but to no avail.

'There must be a trigger mechanism or a hidden switch somewhere,' I whisper, stepping out to run my fingers under the bed.

Grishen takes my place at the panelling, desperately searching, knowing as do I that we have to find the way out of this room, or we'll die here, yet we find nothing. Banging comes from the lounge. How long the door and the cabinets will hold, it's impossible to say.

Grishen pulls an axe from his belt to attack the panelling, but I hold up a hand having heard something ...

Suddenly it comes again, the nearby sound of a cough, and I stand, looking to the All Father on the bed, horrified ... but it isn't him.

Again the cough, but louder.

Suddenly the section of panelling inside the cupboard Grishen is investigating swings inwards, and there before us, in a previously concealed chamber, stands the robed figure of the All Father.

'Surprise!' I hiss, pushing past Grishen.

The All Father stumbles backwards away from my advance, then before he can utter a word, I stab him in the neck.

'I haven't forgotten how much you hated drowning in your own blood,' I say, standing over his contorted body. I step back quickly, glancing into the bedchamber, and to my relief, the body of the other All Father is still there.

I turn to Grishen, gripping his arm.

'Close the door behind you,' I say, wondering about the source of magic that resurrects the All Father so quickly.

At least it's not the same body that regenerates and returns to life, but how that helps me, I don't know.

The chamber we're in has dozens of robes hanging on pegs, piles of sandals in a corner, and on the far side, a passageway, leading down below ground, and the smell rising up from it is like an abattoir.

This is the All Father's lair.

This is where I'll kill him once and for all.

***

The air is humid, pressing in on me like a damp shroud as I shrug off my leather coat, giving me better access to my weapons. Grishen follows suit, watching my every move.

I feel secure that there are no more slingers to face, just the All Father, but nonetheless I want to be ready for any eventuality. I reload my gun, my eyes closed, then simulate firing and repeat the action four times, committing the motion and feel to mind.

Next, I draw two guns at once, pretend to fire the first, re-holster, lift the second, then draw and aim the third while-holstering the second all the way to the sixth gun.

I'm ready.

'Not as fast as a slinger, but you definitely beat them with your killer looks,' Grishen chuckles as he practices his own draw.

'On the other hand, you're definitely the smoothest I've encountered,' I reply, flattered despite the timing of his comment.

'Ready,' Grishen says.

Stepping close, I wrap my arms around him, and he responds in kind.

'I owe you so much,' I murmur, keeping my eyes lowered. 'I can't express how much it means that you're here.'

Betraying Lotane again will never happen, but guilt washes over me nonetheless. However, the words needed to be said. I can sense Grishen's reluctance to release me as I step away from his embrace.

Drawing a gun, I enter the passage, beginning our descent, glad Grishen has my back, glad this will soon be over.

'Damn this darkness,' Grishen mutters unhappily behind me.

The lighting here is terrible, a flickering bulb every twenty steps or so. I have no problem, whereas he must be straining his eyes for all their worth.

'Do you want to wait back at the entrance?' I ask softly.

'No,' he whispers. 'I'm with you every step of the way. Just don't bloody leave me down here.'

With a foul stench thickening with every step, we edge cautiously down the passageway. The All Father knows we're coming, and whilst he's never put up a fight before, every animal becomes dangerous when cornered.

About fifty steps later, the passage ends and opens up to reveal a huge chamber. Stalactites and stalagmites restrict our view, with some joining to create huge, glistening columns. Pools of black water are everywhere, fed by the moisture dripping from the saturated rock.

No lights adorn the ceiling, but the walls are covered in an iridescent moss that sheds a putrescent light … and it seems strangely familiar.

We step carefully, keeping to the dry ground, avoiding the pools. I gesture at Grishen to move off to my right. If the All Father has a gun, separating will make us harder targets. But something tells me he won't rely on weapons.

A whispering fills the chamber, faint at first, then rising in volume, slithering through the cavern like the voices of the dead. My instincts scream at me to turn back, but fear is something I mastered long before I became Queen of the Fey.

As for Grishen, he's nervous, his footsteps hesitant, placed without certainty. I smile reassuringly across at him and he forces one in return.

The chamber is maybe twenty steps wide, but it's impossible to tell how long it is, and we're perhaps fifty steps in, when I see ... them.

Hideously deformed in their nakedness, men, women, and even children, step away from columns, rise up from behind stalagmites, and emerge dripping from pools. They stand there, gripping sharp stalactites as weapons, their red eyes gleaming, lips pulled back from sharpened teeth, their skin the translucent white of a corpse. Over a hundred stare their hatred at us, yet something holds them back from attacking, but it isn't fear.

'Why can't you just die, damn you!' hisses the All Father, stepping out from behind a pillar.

I raise my gun, sight along its barrel and squeeze the trigger.

The gun bucks in my hands, and as the smoke clears, the All Father is still standing. When I squeeze again, half his head explodes, and a hiss ripples through the hideous ranks that stand before us.

'Does this place look familiar, Nogotha?' the All Father says, stepping from behind another pillar as I shake the casings free from the gun, and reload. 'Even after all these years, we can't embrace the light. The caverns you imprisoned us in were the stuff of nightmares, and yet, we cannot forget, and nor can we let go.'

He steps out of sight before I can fire, so I look around, recognising the moss that those wretches I'd discovered below the temples had fed on, that and the flesh of the infirm.

A heartbeat later, he reappears off to the right.

'I think you dying here will have a certain poetic justice to it,' he calls. 'In fact, I think we'll eat you alive, just as your fey did to us. Now, for the love of all that's good, DIE!'

The stinking wave of foulness bounds, skitters, and crawls toward us.

My guns roar, Grishen's too, the sound deafening in the cavern's confines. With their ranks so tightly pressed, it's impossible to miss those skeletal white bodies. Blood sprays, inhuman shrieks pierce the air, but the carnage barely slows them. As I cast my last gun aside, I know we've killed maybe twenty of these things, but the rest don't seem to care.

I roar my defiance, draw two daggers, and leap forward to meet them.

A thousand hours of fighting are in my blood, a thousand shouted commands from Lystra are in my mind, and I know that whatever the odds, I mustn't stand still. Against overwhelming odds, I must dictate how and where the battle is fought. Grishen, on the other hand, only has the heart and soul of a warrior, and I fear it won't be enough, but his one hope is that the horde is converging on me.

A stalactite spins through the air, and I duck, ripping my right dagger across the belly of a three-armed youth, my left dagger blocking another stalactite used like a club. I lower my shoulder and barge straight into the pressing mass of bodies, my hands never slowing, daggers thrusting in and out of unprotected flesh with brutal efficiency.

With every step, a body falls, obstructing those behind. Every strike I deal opens stomachs, cuts throats, creating a slippery, bloody mess for those pressing forward or following me to slip in. The weight of bodies is almost overwhelming but also protects me, the long stalactites ineffective in such close combat, whereas my short weapons deliver horrifying wounds.

However, my arms are tired, and my breathing is already ragged.

I twist around a stalagmite, trip a man with a hideously distended belly so that he falls, impaling himself on the sharp tip, then twist my head sharply as fingers claw at my eyes from behind. I turn and thrust, my dagger blade opening up a woman's arm from wrist to shoulder, right to the bone.

Someone leaps on me from behind, and I throw myself backwards, stunning my attacker beneath me, using my momentum to roll to my feet, only to get knocked sideways.

My feet go from under me on the uneven surface and I lose my left dagger as I break my fall, sweeping my feet to knock the legs out from under two youths leaping forward. I twist away, stabbing as I do, get hit on the shoulder by a rock, then palm a spare dagger from my vambrace and fight on, bodies falling away, but always more taking their place.

My blows are becoming slower, a thrown stone glances off my head and I stagger straight into a thrust stalactite. I twist, but not fast enough, and it rips the skin above my hip before I bury my dagger in my assailant's eye.

Something heavy hits me across the shoulder blades and I stumble into a large pool. I catch a glimpse of Grishen still standing, fighting with his back against the cavern wall before the bottom of the pool disappears from beneath my feet, and I go under, the cavern ceiling vanishing in a rush of darkness as water closes over my head.

I kick desperately, driving away from the edge just in time as the horde leap in after me. Dropping my daggers, I swim desperately to the other side and drag myself out.

Heaving myself upright, I spit to clear my mouth of the foul tasting water, blinking frantically as twenty men, women, and a few youths, come around the pool toward my left. Those who'd jumped into the pool after me still thrash around desperately, unable to swim.

Breathing deeply, I reach behind my waist to find the comforting feel of my sword hilts. The musical sound of the steel as I draw them from their scabbards sends a thrill right through me, and as before, I don't wait.

I stride toward them, not allowing them to group, taking them in ones and twos as they launch themselves at me. Absent sufficient numbers, cohesion, weapons, or training, they die to my swords, or, as I cut their legs away, to the stalagmites as they fall and impale themselves.

The last one's head rolls to bounce into the pool and I walk around its perimeter, lancing my sword down to finish any who've made it to the edge and are trying to crawl out.

Grishen!

He's on his knees, head down, drenched in blood with a dozen pallid corpses surrounding him. I sprint to his side, gripping his face, forcing him to look up at me.

'Grishen?' I whisper, watching as tears run down those filthy cheeks.

'I'm not hurt,' he says, dragging in a deep breath. 'It's just that some of them were so young. I didn't want to, but ...'

'You had no choice,' I say, relieved he's uninjured. 'Have you the strength to continue?'

He smiles tiredly.

'I'll live and die by your side if you let me.'

'Forget the dying and living,' I say, touched by his words. 'Now's the time for killing.'

Grishen's eyes brighten as he picks up his axes, and with a grunt, stands, swaying slightly.

'Look at the bodies.' I kneel down, prodding at the corpses. 'Have you noticed how similar their features are? I think this is part of the secret behind the All Father's immortality.'

Grishen scratches his head, his brow furrowed.

'You could be right, and I had similar thoughts, but … if he's not the same man every time, then how can he remember his dying, and what's been said?'

'Let's keep moving and find out.'

Grishen hesitates.

'In a minute. You might be a legend with swords, but I'm better with guns,' he says, looking around.

'That pile of corpses says you're better than you give yourself credit for,' I say, but follow his lead.

A few minutes later, we're rearmed, our guns fully loaded, but as we work our way back through the bodies, it's my swords and Grishen's axes that finish off the wounded.

I turn frequently, but nothing has got past us, and there's no sign of other passages, so we keep pushing forward until the chamber narrows with no further sign of life, until …

Grishen taps his ear and points.

I've heard it too.

Ahead, a passageway looms, and a dozen steps in, an archway on the left breaks the rock formation, and without doubt, something awaits inside. I take the lead, my fey sight penetrating the gloom with ease, whereas Grishen is half-blind, the luminescent moss barely creating enough light for him to move independently.

I tap my chest, then point right, then at Grishen motioning left. He nods, intuitive to my command, and I know, given time, he could be deadly, a true comrade-in-arms, not just an enthusiastic one.

Warmth spreads through me as I visualise spending time with him, training him …

Not now, Malina!

A quick look around the archway leaves me reeling, my warm thoughts dispelled instantly.

I'd seen shades dismembering people like cattle, ogres feasting on the living, wolfen tearing flesh from bone. Yet something about this has me frantically swallowing down vomit.

It's the most horrifying thing I've ever seen.

**

CHAPTER XIV

Maybe three dozen naked, pallid men and women charge at us, stalactites gripped in skeletal hands, breasts sagging, rib cages visible, all veins, sharp teeth and filth.

We stand shoulder to shoulder, guns roaring in tandem, flinging them backwards, spinning them around. Over a dozen survive our hail of fire and reach us, but by then, my swords are already drawn, and I step in to meet them, Grishen with his axes behind.

My first opponent swings his weapon down to crush my skull, but I step aside, cutting upwards to sever his arm at the elbow while continuing my turn, my sword arcing around to cut through ribs and spine, exiting from his back in a crimson spray, before knocking aside a determined stalactite thrust, all in one movement.

A wild-eyed woman screeches in frustration at missing her chance, and I spin, my left sword whining through the air to completely sever her neck.

Then everything dissolves into a blur of motion as I parry, thrust, and cut. I sweep with my legs, tripping, use my elbows to smash faces, and with Grishen covering my back and finishing off the injured, the fight is over in seconds.

A dark part of me wishes none of our victims had died slowly. Their deaths were too quick, too painless, nothing compared to the suffering before us.

The chamber we're in resembles a grotesque cattle pen.

Maybe three dozen stone loungers carved from stalagmites are scattered throughout, each one contained by a sturdy barrier of bones and rocks to stop what's within, from getting out.

My desire to hunt for the All Father disappears as I wander forward, Grishen silent at my side, trying to make sense of what I'm seeing.

A woman is strapped to each lounger. Those closest are dead, some recently, others decomposing. From their skin, and whatever else is left, I can tell they're of Tarsian and Icelandian heritage.

The woman closest to us has been dead maybe a week, her stomach is open, a cavernous, bloody mess, and within this putrid, festering wound, sits a baby, the umbilical cord still attached as it gnaws at her ribs. Its red eyes fix on me as I walk slowly forward. There's knowledge in those eyes, an understanding of who I am.

It hisses, baring tiny, bloodied, pointed teeth.

The first few pens are the same, the women all dead, their faces a rictus of torment and horror, their flesh torn by teeth and nails. Some have been dead for days, others weeks, their decaying bodies bound in place.

But worse awaits, for those toward the rear are still alive.

One, barely clinging to life, stares downwards at her newborn biting savagely on her breast, sucking milk mixed with flesh and blood.

'Kill me!'

The desperate voice has me turn around.

The speaker's eyes are heavy lidded, she's drugged, but knows exactly what she's asking. Her stomach is huge, at least eight months pregnant, and her baby is pushing, trying to escape through her stomach. These spawn, undoubtedly those of the All Father, eat their way out.

'Kill me,' she whispers again, her voice raw. 'Kill me!'

'Kill me!'

The moan is taken up by the five other women, all of whom are in various stages of pregnancy.

'Gods,' Grishen chokes, his voice breaking. 'What do we do?'

Tears stream down my face. The beauty of childbirth, the bringing of new life into the world, has been twisted and infused with evil.

'Kill me!'

I nod, wiping my eyes with the back of my hand.

'Forgive me,' I say, as I draw a gun, and reload.

Grishen looks at me, shakes his head, and sinks to his knees. I leave him there without thinking the worse of him. If I hadn't endured the purges, I'm not sure I could do what needs to be done either.

I start at the front of the chamber and work my way to the back, my gun roaring, destroying the perverted creatures that hiss their hatred even as I shoot them. I step into the pen amongst the old bones, hair and excrement of those poor women still breathing, hold their hands, and tell them to close their eyes and think of their mothers before I put a bullet in their heads. After, I use my sword to cut out the unborn babies, ensuring they're truly dead before I move on. By the time I've finished, our ammunition is spent, so I cast my guns and harness aside, and Grishen follows suit.

I recall the chamber dedicated to me in the Great Hall of Victory, the model of me leaning over a crib, killing a child. How prophetic.

Grishen looks at me sorrowfully.

'You had no choice,' he says, repeating my words of earlier. 'I'm sorry I couldn't bring myself to help. Now let's find the All Father and put an end to his evil for good.'

I take one last look around. My soul is already so black, and now this deed feels like it's tarnished it even further. It shouldn't ... but it does.

Sighing, I take the lead. There's only one exit from this chamber, and I can only hope that nothing more like this awaits.

'Please don't tell me we have to go in there?' Grishen moans, covering his mouth with the back of his arm as we pause by a small archway.

The stench emanating from within is unbearable, the piles of human waste, covered in a living blanket of thriving luminescent moss, indicate some kind of repugnant method of farming.

I shake my head. There's no place for anyone to hide.

We pass six more similar chambers as we navigate the winding tunnels, sensitive to every drop of water, every scent, and every shift of stone beneath our feet.

The next two chambers I scout on my own, leaving Grishen to keep watch on the passageway. They're full of festering shelters, fashioned out of bones, hair, and flayed skin. Yet no one living remains. They'd all fought to defend their homes against the Queen of Beasts, save one exception.

We continue our search until the winding passage takes a sharp turn, and as we cautiously follow it round, a large cavern opens up before us.

There's almost no moss here, and Grishen clutches my shoulder.

'I can't see a damn thing,' he whispers softly, although his voice carries easily in the silence.

I put my lips close to his ear.

'Stay here. Leave this to me.'

'I don't know if this is where it ends, maybe further passageways and chambers await, but there's no doubt this chamber is something special, and I'm happy Grishen can't see it, for like everything else down here, it's horrific.

That there's a kind of perverse artistry at play is not in doubt. Huge, translucent columns formed from stalactites joining with stalagmites are everywhere, but there's no randomness about the placement and there's no doubt these have been somehow fashioned by the hands of man.

But it's what's within the glasslike columns that is truly gruesome … the mummified remains of previous All Fathers, many of whom are in advanced stages of decomposition, their fluids streaking the glassy tombs.

'Nogotha.'

My name is whispered, echoing around the chamber. I catch a glimpse of a white robe amongst the columns, yet by the time I've weaved my way through to where he should be, the All Father is no longer there.

'Killing women and children suits you, Queen of Beasts. Have you no shred of decency?'

I spin, my sword flashing out as I glimpse movement, only for my sword to clang off rock, the entombed body within staring back at me.

Another flicker of movement, but is it a reflection or the real thing, I can't tell.

'Nogotha.'

My name is spoken over and again from all around, but now I can detect three slightly different tones.

A scuff of a foot, and I twist, thrusting, but The All Father is already darting away, but it's a ruse, and I'm already aware of another coming at me from behind. This time, as I drop low and turn, my sword punches through the white robe, and even as those reaching hands drop away, I realise they've thrown something sparkling into my face.

I close my eyes, but it's too late, they're already burning, and tears begin to flood as everything turns blurry.

'How poetic,' the All Father laughs. 'The very moss my ancestors were forced to harvest, not only fed us, but helped us conquer this world, and will soon help us to conquer yours. When dried, refined and mixed with other elements, it's highly explosive, the main ingredient for gunpowder.'

'And in its raw form,' another voice says from behind, 'it also causes temporary blindness. Now you understand what it's like to be afraid of the dark. What it's like to be hunted when the monsters can see, and you can see nothing.'

Footsteps charge toward me, then as I spin and raise my sword, they veer away. Over and again this happens as I turn and swing blindly, then I gasp as my sword is bludgeoned from my hand and sent spinning away.

I draw my remaining weapon.

Again, those charging footsteps, but when they veer past, they keep running, and intuitively I know where they're heading.

'Grishen! Grishen!'

'You bastard!'

Grishen's yell of pain cuts through the darkness a moment before my second sword is sent flying from my hand.

'Are you alright, Grishen?' I keep my voice low, listening for any telltale heel scuff or change in the air.

'Better than the bastard who attacked me. I'm covered in his brains or something.'

I almost laugh with relief, but we're still in trouble. I'm unarmed, and unable to see, my eyes still stinging. If only …

Idiot.

If I could kick myself, I would.

It takes but a moment to open my spirit eye, and whilst the gloom remains, I can just about see. As with everywhere else, there are no clouds of elemental magic, and it's the black of uncreation that obscures everything. It's thicker here than anywhere else, as if it recognises the evil that has gathered in this place, and recognises the world's woes all originate here.

'You've been very quiet,' I taunt, my voice carrying in the darkness, my confidence rising. Even black has its shades, and I touch a stalagmite next to me, comfortable that I'm beginning to discern shapes.

'I think it's just me and you left. Everyone else is dead. Once you die, there will be no one to take your place.'

Yes. The columns are becoming clearer. I begin moving with certainty, confident that I'll be able to detect movement even if it is black on black.

'You still don't understand,' the All Father whispers. 'You're nothing but a beast, and beasts don't evolve, not like we have.'

Silently, I glide toward the voice, weaving through the columns. I don't need a sword to kill him.

I breathe deeply, his stench obvious. He's close, and I pause, taking note of the stalagmites, gauging their distance, positioning myself for his attack. He's emboldened, after all, he can see, and believes me blind and helpless.

A rattle of a stone off to my left, and I turn, only for a searing pain to rip through my side. I twist frantically, reaching out, trapping the All Father's wrist, not letting it go even as he pushes whatever it is, deeper into me.

I scream as my other hand blindly reaches out, finding the back of his neck, pulling him toward me, driving my forehead forward, feeling it connect, his cry of pain smothered by mine.

Pivoting to one side, I manage to hook my foot behind his ankle, and bring us crashing to the ground, trapping him beneath me.

'Die, you bitch. Die!' The All Father gasps as he writhes beneath me.

More searing pain follows as I lose my grip on his wrist, and I sob as he plunges whatever it is he's holding in a second and third time before I manage to trap his forearm again.

His arm is slick with my blood, and he twists it, and I struggle to restrain him. I smash my forehead down again, but he's fighting with a desperation now exceeding my fading strength.

'I knew it was my destiny to kill you, Nogotha,' he gasps. 'How does it feel knowing your long life is about to end?'

Everything is swimming, the pain, loss of blood, exhaustion … the longer this goes on, the less chance I have.

With no other recourse left, I push my head into his neck.

'You should know,' I hiss.

He resists, perhaps knowing what's coming, but my weight aids me, and suddenly the flesh of his neck is exposed.

I can taste his skin even before I close my mouth around it, and for a moment I hesitate. It's repellent, so foul and tainted, but I've no other choice.

His skin tears under my savagery. Just like a beast, I rip and rend, drinking his blood, knowing without it, I'll die from my wounds.

'You can't k-kill me. I-I'm immortal,' he gurgles, coughing up blood.

I fall alongside him, moaning, unable to continue.

'I killed you!' he whispers. 'I killed you.'

He lies there beside me, mumbling words I can't discern, then a final death rattle marks his passing. The All Father is dead.

Strangely, there's no sense of fulfilment, just a terrible sadness.

'Grishen!'

The word sounds so distant, so feeble, that I doubt he can hear me.

'Grishen.'

'Malina. Just keeping saying my name. I'll find you.'

I smile. He's always there for me.

'Grishen.' The words taste sweet, taking away the foulness and pain. I keep saying his name until his warm hands eventually cup my face.

'Don't leave me,' I whisper, just before the blackest of blacks pulls me under.

***

'Hello, Alina. What happened to you?'

'Brother.' I struggle to form the word. My throat feels thick, clogged, and it's difficult to breathe. I can't see, and rub my eyes. They're crusted, and I carefully scrape the flakes away.

Thunder rumbles in the background, deep and soulful.

'I won,' I say softly, my vision returning to reveal I'm lying in the All Father's four poster bed. The covers are still stained with his blood, but I don't care. My body is so heavy, I feel as though I could sleep for a month.

Karson sits at the foot of the bed, arms and legs crossed, watching me with his head tilted to one side.

'Victory and loss often go hand in hand,' he says.

'Is that my brother speaking, or someone else through him?'

Karson smiles, glancing up as the lamp in the ceiling shakes.

'It's just my observation, Sister. I mean, you don't appear victorious to me. Take a look at yourself.'

My laugh rasps in my throat, but it dies the moment I lower my gaze. The skin of my hands and arms are corpse white, translucent, and as I bring them toward my face, revulsion grips me. I don't have a nose.

Frantic, I thrust the sheets aside, uncovering my distended belly. I'm at least eight months pregnant …

'Oh gods,' I gasp, hands trembling over my stomach. 'Help me! Help me!' But my voice is drowned out by the thunder.

...

..

.

'Malina. I'm here. Don't worry, don't worry.'

Grishen's soothing voice pulls me from my nightmare, and I open my eyes to find him looking down at me as my head rests on his lap. 'You were having a bad dream.'

I blink up at him, my breathing shallow.

'How do I know I'm awake now?' My voice sounds hoarse, raw.

'Well,' Grishen says with a wry chuckle. 'The All Father is dead with his throat torn out a few steps that way, or so my hands discovered before they found you, and no dream could smell this bad.'

'Why are you half naked?' I ask, taking in his bare chest.

'Hah. I forgot you could see that. You were bleeding. The bastard stabbed you with a piece of stalactite. My shirt was the only thing I could use.' He pauses, eyes twinkling. 'Unless I should have used my trousers?'

I snort, then cry out as pain rips through my side.

'How bad is it?' I gasp.

'Bad, although it's hard for me to tell other than through touch.'

Rolling thunder echoes and the cavern shakes, sending dust and dirt cascading down from the ceiling.

'That's a nasty storm,' I mutter. 'I heard it in my dreams.'

'Was I in your dreams too?' Grishen asks.

'Don't make me laugh again,' I warn, smiling despite myself. 'But no, you weren't, although I'd rather you had been.'

Grishen smiles, but it's tinged with something, maybe pain.

'Are you alright?' I ask. 'I heard you cry out during the fight.'

'I'm fine,' he says, his hands gently stroking my hair. 'It's you we should worry about.'

The cavern shakes again.

'That's not a storm,' I murmur.

Grishen nods.

'You could be right. It's been going on for two days. It's probably cannon fire. Hargna must be laying siege to the Palace.'

'I've been lying here two days?'

'No,' he sighs. 'Four.'

'You must be dying of thirst.'

'The water running down the stalactites is pretty horrible, but it's kept me alive,' Grishen says. 'However, I suggest you never try it.'

'But I'm thirsty.'

'Then you need to drink,' Grishen says, untying some cloth from around his wrist.

As he exposes his skin, I see the puncture marks. There are so many.

My stomach knots.

'I-I mustn't. How many times have you …'

'Not enough,' Grishen says soothingly. 'You're far from healed and feverish.' He pushes his forearm to my lips. 'Now feed and sleep. When you wake again, hopefully you'll have enough strength to get us both to the surface.'

The urge to bite into Grishen's veins is overwhelming, but I resist briefly. Instead, I press my lips to his wrist, kissing him gently, my mouth finding its way to the crook of his elbow, and he sighs in pleasure.

Then, I can't hold back any longer, and his pleasure mixes with pain, the saltiness of his blood fills my mouth, and I drift away to sweeter dreams.

***

I awake shivering, and lie still for a moment, my eyes closed, the steady drip of water in the background. My clothes are damp from lying on the floor, and from fouling myself. I feel and smell disgusting, but as my thoughts sharpen, I realise I'm also stronger despite suffering from a thumping headache.

A smile parts my lips. Grishen has saved me again.

I open my eyes, the darkness giving away before my fey-sight to find Grishen slumped awkwardly against a stalactite, covered in dust and debris, his eyes closed, peacefully asleep.

'Grishen,' I whisper, sitting up, surprised and grateful that there's little more than the smallest twinge in my side.

Life blood. Did humans coin that phrase or the fey?

I owe him my life, twice over.

Would it be so wrong to wake him with a gentle kiss?

Lotane comes to mind, and love pushes back against desire. I kissed Grishen's arm in a moment of weakness, but it mustn't go beyond that, ever.

Instead, I turn and give him a playful nudge.

'Wake up sleepy,' I tease, expecting him to groan.

He doesn't. Instead, he slowly topples over.

I kneel there, biting my lip, realising for the first time that no blood pumps like liquid fire around his body and his heart is cold, grey, and still. A thin piece of stalactite protrudes from his lower back, a parting gift from the All Father he'd killed in our final fight. All the time Grishen had sat there, feeding me, keeping me alive, he knew he was slowly dying, and had said nothing.

Crawling around, I take his head in my lap as he'd done for me, and stroke his hair back, tracing the contours of his face, imprinting everything in my memory. My tears rain silently as I work hard to keep my anguish in check. I hadn't known him long, but we'd paired, and his loss cuts like a knife.

Time passes, an hour, maybe two, before I gently lay Grishen's head on the ground. His two beloved hand axes are leant up against a stalagmite, and I consider taking them, keeping a piece of him with me. Instead, I place them across his chest and fold his hands over them. I sit there a while before coming to a decision, and gently lean down to kiss his cold lips.

Lotane would understand.

'Goodbye, Grishen. In another time, another world, perhaps we …' I swallow hard, shaking my head. 'Well, I guess we'll never know. But what I do know is that you'll find Kralgen in whatever waits beyond, drink ale together, and tell each other the tallest of tales. Just don't forget to say hello to him for me.'

My heart aches terribly, an old and far too familiar wound.

Yet, however wounded my body and heart, I'm forged from steel, and whilst it might bend, it doesn't break. Centuries old conditioning takes over, not allowing me any more time to grieve, let alone rest, and I scour my surroundings, eventually finding my swords.

The cavern no longer shakes with the thunder of cannon fire, the debris scattered across the ground is already saturated, indicating it's lain there a while, as have I.

Swords in hand, I examine the chamber, and am relieved to discover this was the last one. The stain of the All Father has been removed from this world once and for all.

Stain ... I grimace at the foulness of my attire. Blood, brains, excrement, sludge, whatever it is, I'd almost rather be naked.

Sheathing my weapons, I make my way back through the passages, silent, aware, just in case, but there's no one left alive. The bodies lay where they'd fallen, twisted and broken, or float in the pools, their flesh fouling the water forever.

I recover two of my daggers and sheath them at my waist.

Occasionally my headache intensifies, forcing me to pause. I'm obviously still recovering, and it will fade in time.

But weakness offends me, and I'll not allow myself to be weak. Only through strength will I honour Grishen. Poor, loyal Grishen.

Eventually, I make my way back to the hidden entrance chamber. What will I find beyond the door? Hargna and the rebels slaughtered, and the Palace still under the slingers' control?

I breathe deeply, preparing myself mentally for more fighting as I locate the lever, and pull it down.

The inner door swings inward, and I slip into the cupboard, pressing close against the wooden frame, peering through a crack into the bedroom beyond.

It's empty.

As I step into the bedchamber, the first thing I notice is the absence of the All Father's body. The sheets have been replaced, but someone has slept in it, and left the covers strewn everywhere. It's hard to decide whether that's disturbing or not.

Pushing through into the lounge, it's a similar story. The cabinets look like an axe took them apart, although their splintered remains have been piled neatly in a corner. Of the door they barricaded, there's no sign. The carpet is filthy, the deep tread of countless boots ruining the fabric. There's no sign of the slinger Grishen and I killed here, but whoever tidied up the broken cabinets surely wouldn't have gone on to leave such a mess on the carpet.

I consider heading straight for the exit, but instead turn toward the slingers' quarters, my tread silent, edging cautiously to peer around the door.

The smell coming from within is all too familiar, and as I enter the room, it's to discover several bodies piled in a corner. The cleft chins and familiar clothing making it easy to discern these are slingers, and then amongst them, I spy the All Father's body. The room has been ransacked, the cabinet drawers lie strewn about, clothes are everywhere, the beds are upside down, and I breathe a sigh of relief.

If the slingers were in control of the Palace, they'd never leave their own quarters in such a fashion, let alone leave the bodies of their comrades and the All Father here. These have just been dumped here for convenience or out of laziness.

The Palace has changed hands.

Alert and still ready for anything, I peer into the bathroom to find it hasn't been vandalised like the sleeping quarters.

I know I should find out exactly what's happened, whether Hargna is still alive, but my headache is terrible, and my vision is narrowing. Despite being asleep for who knows how long, it's apparent it hasn't been enough.

Returning to the sleeping quarters, I close the door and jam it shut with a chair. It won't stop anyone for long, but I just need a warning.

Back in the bathroom, there's a water pipe in the ceiling behind a tattered curtain, and as I turn a handle on its side, cold water sprays out. Barely able to stand, the pain in my head is so bad, I remove my weapon belt, swords, and daggers, leaning them in the corner and kick off my boots. My clothes are stuck to me like glue, so I tear them apart in my haste to rid myself of them, and toss their torn, stinking remains aside.

There's a bar of soap, and I allow myself the luxury of a quick cleanse, ridding myself of the stench that I've brought with me and quenching my thirst at the same time.

Padding naked into the sleeping quarters, weapons in hand, I dry myself with a blanket, scavenge clean clothes from those thrown around the room, and pull a pair of boots off a corpse.

A bed leans on its side against a wall, creating a narrow hiding place, and I wriggle in amongst the twisted sheets and blankets and within seconds am asleep.

***

'Wake up, Alina,' I tell myself for the thousandth time, desperation, even pleading seeping into my voice.

My voice carries over the hiss of a thousand serpents writhing around my feet. They don't strike, choosing to ignore me, or perhaps, being a nightmare, they're not meant to notice me.

The background to this nightmare is forever changing, a frenetic kaleidoscope of images. One moment I'm overlooking a city akin to High Delnor, the next I'm standing in the All Father's lair, a blink of an eye later, I'm in Hastia, then Tars, then Midnor. On and on, familiar places, and then unrecognisable ones. Cities, towns, and great halls.

Famine, hunger, and disease are everywhere, the sickness pervading this world, the substance that binds everything together.

It feels as if I've been trying to wake for an eternity, but it could just as easily be a few heartbeats, yet my head feels like it's splitting apart as the images and hissing overwhelm my senses.

'Alina.'

'Karson!' I cry desperately, spinning around, searching for him.

But now I see only ghost-like figures, their lips move soundlessly. Some wear uniforms, others, tattered coveralls, then, naked ones appear, their faces absent noses.

'Come find me, Alina,' Karson's voice urges. 'Remember the tree you found me under where you planted the apple? Hold it in your thoughts. Visualise it, visualise me!'

Slowly, the ghosts and snakes fade away.

As I look down, grass forms thick beneath my bare feet, comforting, soft, and cool.

A fresh breeze ripples my loose, flowing robe. It shimmers, changing from white to black, and I recall how this garment perfectly reflects my inner turmoil.

To my left and right, familiar, distant snow-capped mountain ranges rise, straining to reach the sky, and alongside my meandering path, the crystal clear stream still tinkles merrily along, dancing over small rocks and pebbles.

Ahead, the old apple tree grows on the grassy bank, its branches laden with ripe fruit. Underneath, my brother sits, munching away, his twinkling eyes holding a hint of relief.

He stands and takes my hand, leading me to a sapling growing by the river.

'Is this the one I planted?' I ask, running my hands over the smooth trunk and vibrant, green leaves. It also bears apples, small, not yet ready to eat, but healthy and glowing, nonetheless.

Karson nods, smiling.

'Despite all the death you've dealt, it appears you have the ability to give life.'

'We should always meet here. It's beautiful,' I say, rubbing my temples, the throbbing headache receding in this tranquil place.

'As long as you don't look behind you,' Karson warns. 'Remember?'

I shudder.

'Only too well. Let's be honest, my dreams always have something unpleasant to overshadow the light, and I've no wish to see the mountains of dead.'

'Dreams are but a reflection of life, Alina.'

'I'm sure some people go through life without a care in the world, never facing adversity, never knowing sorrow,' I muse. 'I wish I could have been one of them. That I could look behind me to find nothing but beauty and happiness.'

'Maybe one day, Alina,' Karson says gently. 'But don't forget, despite the darkness, you've known happiness too, during your time in the fey world.'

'You're right. It's easy to forget the light when surrounded by darkness.'

'Especially when the darkness is of your own making,' Karson adds meaningfully.

'I know, little brother. I know,' I say, staring at my hands that have the blood of thousands upon them. 'I never understood when I killed Nogoth the responsibilities that had become mine. I embraced the fey world, and turned my back on this one. I should have been mother to both, as you once told me.'

'You've listened and learned, Alina,' Karson says, his voice carrying that strange blend of innocence and wisdom. 'There's still more to learn, but the voyage of self-discovery never moves as quickly as we'd like.'

I chuckle dryly.

'So, little and wise one. Having defeated the All Father, am I finally on the right path to set this cursed child of mine back on the right course?'

'Let's go and see, shall we?'

I nod, and he takes my hand.

In the distance, the valley we're standing in splits in two. The landscape blurs, flashing by, and we come to an abrupt halt where the path divides.

The path to the right had once been full of demonic creatures, winged, and violet-eyed, and, to a certain extent, it still is. However, where once they flew, now they are piled twisted on the ground, lifeless, hundreds upon hundreds, offering no clear route through.

'It seems you slew your inner daemons, Alina.'

'With Lotane's help,' I say, filled with warmth at his memory.

Then my gaze is drawn to the left-hand valley. It remains unchanged, exactly as I last saw it, choked with dead, both human and fey.

I swallow hard.

'Is this telling me what I think it is?' I ask, my heart heavy again.

'What do you think it means?' Karson prompts softly.

'That this is still my future, and always was. I only delayed it by taking the other path to get here.'

Karson nods, sorrow flickering across his face.

'I fear you're right. I didn't see it before, but I see it now.'

As I look around, I notice the snakes are back, hissing at my feet, and Karson begins to fade.

'Karson, what can I do about these snakes?' I ask as my headache begins to build. 'Their hissing drives me mad.'

'Perhaps they're trying to tell you something,' Karson smiles as his form starts to fade. 'Perhaps you should listen.'

The hissing rises to a frenzy, and my head is splitting. I collapse in agony, the hideous reptiles slithering over me. Yet strangely, despite being so close, their noise softens along with my pain, and their hissing reminds me of waves rolling over shingle, and suddenly I'm on a familiar shoreline, surrounded by a golden beach.

Then, in my dream within a dream, I fall asleep.

***

I awake, death's stench heavy in the air.

My small nook is warm, but I don't allow myself the luxury of staying there any longer. I crawl out, shake off the stiffness in my limbs, and ready myself.

A whisper, and I spin, my sword singing from its sheath, cutting through ... nothing.

I stand there for a moment scanning the chamber, only the dead for company, their lifeless forms exactly where I last saw them. Everything is still in place, undisturbed.

Shrugging, I lower the blade but keep it to hand. Who knows what I'll meet outside this room of death. Then I smile, grimly. Only more death.

The chair is still wedged beneath the door handle, and after removing it, I step quietly through into the lounge beyond. I've no sense of time, there are no windows, and suddenly it dawns on me that this was a purposeful design. The All Father, used to life underground, had hated the light.

As I walk down the corridor, the walls on either side are scarred. Whether from malice, out of boredom, or some other reason, it was purposeful, a further sign the Palace has fallen.

The waiting room is a ruin of splintered chairs and shattered wood. The once-polished table now bears deep, angry gashes, its edges chipped beyond repair.

A part of me finds it hard to justify such wanton destruction, but years of persecution must have created a reservoir of hatred that needed release far beyond when the killing stopped.

The blood and brains have been washed from the walls in the office, but the desk has been reduced to little more than firewood, the stone busts smashed to pieces. Hopefully, in the days since these acts were undertaken, any rage has settled, and cooler heads now reign.

Something sends a chill down my spine, a whisper, a half spoken word, and again, when I turn, sword ready, nothing but the ghosts of past slain keep me company.

It's not a pleasant thought. I'm on edge, and a legion of spirits following me around isn't the company I'm looking for.

I need to find Hargna.

As I wander down vaguely familiar passages, the red carpet the surgeon had worried about ruined beneath my feet, moans become clearer with every step, and as the chapel I'd passed through all those days before appears, I understand why.

The benches and pews that had once been used for worship now hold hundreds of wounded, all united in their misery. The floor is thick with congealed blood and human waste, and the air is heavy with the taste of festering wounds, while a few flickering candles give the scene a hellish appearance.

I sheath my sword. These are Tarsians and Icelandians, and beyond a shadow of a doubt, the All Father's troops wouldn't be keeping them alive if they were the victors.

Thankfully, they're almost all asleep, likely drugged.

'Water!' a man moans softly, and a woman staggers from the shadows, a jug in hand to ease his thirst.

Movement to my right has me turn, only to see another carer changing a bandage on the stump of a wrist.

This was the cost of victory, the cost of freedom.

I make my way silently between the aisles, surprised I must still have a conscience as every step tears at my heart. These people had fought for freedom, and will forever bear the price.

Even when I leave the chapel behind, more lightly wounded lay asleep across the corridors or sit propped against walls. All have bloodied bandages wrapped around wounds, but none look too serious.

Ahead, a pair of closed double doors bar my passage, but as I turn the handle and lean against the heavy wood, the right-hand door opens silently.

Lights flicker here like everywhere else, but the welcome taste of fresher air tells me I'm near the entrance, and sure enough, after a few short passages and turns, it yawns open wide before me. Of the gates that used to stand here, only a few splintered fragments remain. The stone lintel is shattered, and there are hundreds of pockmarks in the walls. Dried blood is everywhere, as are spent bullets, musket balls, and cartridge cases.

Two Tarsian sentries shelter just within the entranceway, fast asleep, legs outstretched, several empty bottles next to them. Dumbfounded at their lack of discipline, I walk past, stepping outside into the dawn's early embrace.

The evidence of a battle surrounding the Palace couldn't be clearer. Hundreds of graves are everywhere, the earth freshly turned over. The perimeter fencing to the south is riven in numerous places, and dozens of cannons, many twisted and broken, litter the landscape like broken toys on the scorched ground beyond.

Grishen's dream had certainly played out ... Hargna had used the devil's own weapons against the slingers.

'I only wish you could see this,' I say softly, closing my eyes and picturing Grishen's face. 'Your dream of an independent Icelandia has truly been born in the fall of Astgate. But the cost has been high, my friend. So high.'

The field hospitals that had stood both inside and out have mostly disappeared. Torn apart by canister and musket fire, only occasional pieces of white canvas remain bloodied and half buried in the mud.

The wind howls mournfully, carrying with it whispers, or perhaps hissing, like in my dream, and the insidious noise scratches at my nerves, and my head begins to ache.

Pushing aside the discomfort, I turn my attention to the horizon. Flames flicker to the southeast in the Astorian residential district, and the sky there is heavier with smoke than usual, although not from any factory chimneys. I'd expected a far more apocalyptic scene, and am surprised.

Turning around, I return to the Palace entrance and begin my search. Men and women sleep in bullet scarred and blood-stained corridors, and I frown upon seeing empty bottles everywhere.

I'm not sure where I'm going or if I'll find Hargna, but if he led this unruly bunch to victory, there's a good chance he's still here. The passageway opens into an eating hall, and I stand for a moment, staring at the destruction.

Tables have been turned on their sides to use as barricades, scorch marks blacken the walls where small fires had raged, and cartridge cases litter the floor. A huge pile of Astorian bodies, twisted, broken, and bloodied in death, are piled in one corner.

A desperate stand had been made here.

However, since that time, half-eaten food has been discarded on the floor, mixed with broken plates and bottles, alongside pools of vomit, old and new.

A tired looking Tarsian man stumbles around amongst the wreckage, going through the mounds of refuse, trying to find something to eat that hasn't begun to spoil.

'Where's Hargna?' I ask, turning away a little as he turns his befuddled gaze on me so he can't see my eyes. 'Where's Hargna?' I repeat.

'Hargna? Hargna? Perhaps I'll remember if you give me a kiss,' he grunts, lunging for me.

I grasp his reaching hand, pull him suddenly toward me, and stamp on the outside of his knee as he stumbles by. He collapses with a yelp as I twist his arm up behind his back, then kneel on the side of his neck.

'Tell me where he is or you'll never wake up again,' I hiss, removing some pressure.

'W-why?' the man cries, struggling. I bring my weight to bear again, counting silently as his struggles become weaker before easing the pressure a final time.

'Last chance.'

'D-down the hall, turn right at the fork and beyond the large chamber are the old slingers' sleeping chambers. He'll be there with the other leaders.'

Reapplying the pressure, I watch his eyes roll up, but relent. He'll have a headache to equal mine for his temerity when he awakens.

I rub my temples, even though I know it doesn't help, and follow the man's directions.

The corridors are again full of sleeping men and some women. The air is tainted by the scents of alcohol, body odour and sex, but I pass unaccosted, coming to a large chamber full of lounges and low tables.

Paintings hang askew on bullet riddled walls, their fabric shredded in a frenzy of destruction, statues are shattered, and broken bottles are everywhere. Even the lounges upon which dozens of people sleep are ripped.

This was no doubt where the slingers would relax, but this once beautiful room has been indelibly changed by the savagery of man.

Several passages lead off, but one has a closed door, and I step quietly to open it, not wanting to have a repeat of my earlier encounter.

A corridor awaits, lined with doors, and as I open the first one, I'm rewarded by the sight of naked bodies entwined on a series of beds. However, none are Hargna, and I press on, witnessing more naked flesh with every door I open. After a few more doors, it's apparent the quarters are becoming more lavish, indicating a rise in rank for those who used to occupy them. Armed with such knowledge, I approach a lone, embellished door at the end of the corridor.

It opens to reveal a much larger chamber than expected. Maps are interspersed with paintings and gold-framed mirrors on the walls, and its carved statues are still intact.

Like all the other rooms, this has five beds, but they're spread out, sumptuous with four posts and expensive linens, and there's no evidence of the wanton destruction visited on many of the others, but it also has something in common.

Empty bottles are everywhere, as are plates of half-eaten food

All the beds are occupied, but the one directly opposite has a longsword and leather armour propped against the wall beside it. As I approach, I recognise the gaunt face half buried amongst the pillows, and from the lifeblood pumping through his veins he's alive and well.

Hargna.

***

CHAPTER XV

Hargna is snoring like a pig as I take his shoulder and give him a shake. Frustrated after several unsuccessful attempts to wake him, I grab a jug of water from a cabinet and pour it over his face.

'What the hells!' he splutters, sitting up, blinking frantically. 'Malina?'

'Yes, it's me.' I reach out and flick a switch, turning on a bedside lamp.

'I thought you were dead,' he groans, looking utterly confused.

'Sorry to disappoint you.'

A naked woman stirs beside him, her hair dishevelled.

'I-I can explain,' Hargna stammers, looking flustered.

I shake my head, frowning. Who am I to judge? Valeria only just died, and he's already in bed with another woman, but everyone deals with loss in a different way.

'Shall I go get some food?' the woman asks, yawning.

'What? Yes. Go, go!' Hargna says, giving her a push.

The woman pulls on some clothes and stumbles tiredly from the room, leaving us in an uneasy silence.

'What's going on, Hargna?'

'What's going on?' Hargna mutters, getting flustered as he scrabbles around for his clothes. 'You've been gone over a week, and I thought you dead.'

He pauses, taking a breath to calm himself as he buckles his belt.

'But everything went according to plan. We took the warehouses, then killed any soldiers that were left in the city, and then we came here. We besieged the Palace at first, but when our kinfolk from the other cities arrived, we stormed it instead. It was a bloody, horrible battle, but we won, Malina. We won!'

'We won,' I repeat quietly, remembering my nightmare and Grishen's death.

'Where the hells have you been?' Hargna asks.

'Doing what I promised to do. The All Father is gone forever, but ... so is Grishen.' I choke on the final words, struggling to contain my grief.

Hargna shakes his head sadly, his sorrow mirroring my own.

'I'm sorry, Malina. He was a far bigger man than any I've known.'

'Thank you. He meant more to me than I realised, but the time for grieving isn't yet. So, tell me. How many men did you send to secure The Wall?'

Hargna looks at the palms of his hands, and then lifts his head.

'None.'

'None?' I echo in disbelief.

'Everything has changed, and we didn't need to.'

'Didn't need to.' I whisper, suddenly feeling sick.

'Three days ago, the day after we won,' Hargna continues, 'the Archbishop of the Church Eternal rode in with half a dozen slingers, calm as you like.'

'Did you kill him?'

Silence answers my question, except there's no such thing as silence anymore. The hisses have become whispers, loud, constant, scratching away at my mind like a rat. I briefly squeeze my eyes shut, focussing my thoughts, forcing myself to ignore them.

'Why the hells not?'

'He came under a flag of truce and ...' Hargna hesitates. 'It was him who told us you were dead.'

'Tell me, Hargna,' I ask, sitting on the edge of his bed, an invisible fist gripping my stomach. 'Just tell me why you didn't send a force like we all agreed, to secure The Wall.'

Again silence ... of a kind.

I want to shake Hargna till his eyes bleed but restrain myself.

He avoids meeting my eye as he gets dressed, pulling on clothes, armour and then donning his sword.

'We voted against it!'

'What?'

'Hargna. Have your woman keep her voice down, or you'll have to find someone else to keep you warm when we throw her out,' a gruff voice calls from across the room.

I don't bother to turn but reach toward a sword hilt.

Hargna raises his hands placatingly.

'Please listen,' he says softly. 'There was no need to send anyone. The Archbishop came seeking peace. He'd had an epiphany, a vision showing the fulfilment of an ancient prophecy. He said that you and the All Father dying together, locked in battle, has forever ended the fey threat, and with it, Astoria's plan to invade your world.'

Grishen looks at me expectantly.

'Don't you understand?' he continues. 'As long as no one knows you're still alive, then it will remain that way!'

I rub my forehead, the whispers making it hard to concentrate. What's wrong with me? Nothing that more rest won't resolve, I'm sure.

'There was never a fey threat to begin with,' I mutter.

Hargna takes my hand briefly, then removes it quickly when I frown.

'That wasn't all,' he says. 'He listened to our grievances, truly listened, and was moved by the depth of our suffering and the sacrifices we've made. As the leader of the Church Eternal, and now the highest-ranking official in Astoria, he offered reparations. Two years of medical aid and supplies if we agreed to end the bloodshed, leave the Astorian civilians alone, and resettle in Ast. We agreed!'

I squeeze my head between my hands. The whispers are intensifying, and they're like a thousand knives cutting into my brain.

'Are you alright?' Hargna asks, concerned.

'I'm fine,' I lie, awash with pain and despair. 'Why give up Astgate?'

'Because they want to ensure the world gate is secure. They intend to encase it in iron or something like that.'

Hargna looks so happy with himself, and on face value, it would seem we'd achieved all we'd hoped for. But I remember Grishen's words about the whole Astorian population being brainwashed into wanting the same thing … vengeance against the fey.

'I don't believe a word of it,' I whisper, struggling to focus. 'He's lying. You know this is all a lie. That's what they do so well.'

'He isn't lying. He begged us to choose what was best for both our peoples. Peace. How could we say no having won the war?'

I groan, shaking my head.

'You didn't win the war, you fool. You won a skirmish, a single battle. There's no peace, and you're all going to die as soon as the Astorian army comes, and they won't wait till the spring. The fact that the Archbishop somehow already knew what happened here means they're already on the move!'

'I'm no fool.' Hargna says evenly. 'He said we can remain armed, and take weapons, ammunition, and even the city coffers when we leave. This is a new beginning.'

'Hargna. You know the saying. If something's too good to be true...'

Hargna's jaw tightens.

'Forgive me for saying this, Malina. But, have you ever considered your unwillingness to accept peace is because your lust for killing is too strong?'

A long, aggrieved moan rises from the other side of the room.

'I think it's time we sent your woman on the way to fetch us all breakfast, Hargna. Now, allow me.'

I watch in a mirror as a tall Icelandian rises from bed. Three other men are now sitting up, half-drunk, befuddled, and annoyed, and each has a woman in bed.

'Sorry, Fasin. We'll go elsewhere,' Hargna says smoothly. 'Go back to sleep.'

'Too late,' Fasin laughs, picking up a bottle and taking a swig. 'This is a democracy now. Everyone here thinks she should get us breakfast. All in favour, say, aye.'

'Aye,' the others echo, chuckling.

'You should choose your friends more wisely, Hargna,' I say, loud enough for the man to hear. 'Not these drunk fools who should stay in bed and sober up if they know what's good for them.'

Fasin saunters up behind me, and I see him register my weapons before he meets my eyes in the mirror.

'Oh, shit!' he gasps, recognising who I am, and lifts the bottle.

As he does, I snap a vicious kick backwards to his groin, sending him tumbling to the ground, where he curls up, clutching himself.

'You bitch. You bloody devil bitch,' he whimpers.

'Ouch. That's got to hurt,' says one of the other men.

'Her balls are now bigger than yours,' another adds, laughing.

I ignore them, grab Hargna, and pull him to a map on the wall.

'Look. You still have a chance, albeit a small one. Even if the Astorian army has a couple of days march on you,' I say, pointing at the Delnorian plains. 'They still have further to travel. Rally your people and stick to our plan. If you get a large enough force marching on The Wall by tomorrow at the latest, you'll take it before the Astorian army gets there.'

The look Hargna gives me is one full of pity, and it takes me aback.

'I'm not doing it,' he says, gently pulling his arm free, looking deep into my eyes. 'You've been conditioned to always fight and kill, but I haven't. With the All Father dead, your people and mine are safe. Now, enough is enough, it's time to embrace peace!'

Fasin moans loudly. He's regained his feet and stumbles to his bed.

'She's the Queen of Beasts,' he cries, bending down.

The others turn toward me, sobering quickly as Fasin's words register and they realise who I am.

I give them a measuring stare while Fasin scrabbles on the floor.

'I'm not your enemy,' I say firmly. 'Hargna. Tell them.'

'It's true,' Hargna insists. 'It was her plan that helped us take Astgate. This victory is as much hers as it is ours. Let me explain ...'

'Explain, Hargna. What's there to explain?' Fasin shouts as he reaches under the bed. 'You're in league with the Queen of Beasts. While she's alive, there can never be peace. We don't need to know anything else.'

He straightens, a tangled slinger's gun harness in his hands.

'By the gods, don't do it,' Hargna pleads. 'You haven't seen what she can do!'

This isn't what I wanted, and I wait for longer than I should, hoping Hargna's desperate words hit home, but Fasin grips a gun handle, while the others suddenly throw back covers and leap out of bed.

My first dagger slices through the air even as Fasin's gun clears leather, burying itself hilt-deep, square in his chest.

'No!' Hargna cries.

His howl of despair doesn't give me pause as my second dagger takes a Tarsian in the throat as he pulls a gun from a bedside table. I leap at the remaining two, swiftly closing the distance.

Pulling a sword from its scabbard over my shoulder, I swing down in a brutal, two-handed arc. My blade cleaves through the first man from shoulder to hip before continuing into the second, sinking deep into his thigh even as his gun fires over my head. A heartbeat later, my sword tip punches up through his chin into his brain, and he collapses without a sound.

The women are whimpering, on the verge of hysteria.

'Say a word, call for help, or try to run, and I'll kill you all,' I hiss.

I quickly go to gather my daggers, concerned that the gunshot might have drawn attention. A familiar scrape of metal against leather has me whirl around to find Hargna levelling a gun at me across the room.

'I-I'm s-sorry,' he stammers. 'The killing h-has to stop.'

He fires both barrels.

Shocked, we both stand still, facing one another as the smoke clears.

I sink to my knees … never once taking my eyes from Hargna, who shakes like a storm-blown leaf, and yank my dagger from Fasin's chest.

'You always were an awful shot,' I snarl, then rise and stalk across the room, intent on cutting him in two.

The gun falls from his shaking hand, yet his shoulders are back, his chin high, and he looks at me defiantly.

'Those men you just killed, were leaders of the other cities,' he gasps. 'They came and fought for freedom, and having won it, they chose peace. Why would you do this? What's wrong with you? Are you so broken inside that death is your only answer to every problem?'

Hargna collapses heartbroken onto the bed and begins to cry.

'You were my friend,' he sobs. 'Why would you do this?'

I look over my shoulder at the women huddled in a corner, petrified, then back to Hargna, my ally, who I'd been about to kill. For him to shoot at me after all we'd been through …

A shuddering breath escapes my lips. His words have wounded me deeply, and I'm stunned by their simple truth.

I lower my sword, ashamed, and sit next to him.

'They were going to kill me.' I say softly. 'I had no choice.'

'There's always a choice,' Hargna whispers. 'You could have tried to subdue them.'

'That wouldn't have been easy …'

'And you think choosing peace was, after all we've suffered?' Hargna interrupts. 'Now, you can choose to accept peace, or go on fighting. But if you fight, the Astorians will know you're alive. What choices will they then make? What will that mean for your world and mine?'

I close my eyes and pinch the bridge of my nose, trying to concentrate. The whispering has risen to a fever pitch, clawing at my sanity, but I manage to push it aside. Is Hargna right? Am I so consumed by revenge and the lust for killing, that I can't accept a victory when it's offered, even if it's not the one I wanted?

And what of this world? Am I not responsible for it? How long before the magic of uncreation rises up to cleanse it? Or maybe, I shouldn't stand in its way and should just let it happen.

'We'll be leaving the city the day after tomorrow,' Hargna says into the silence, interrupting my thoughts. 'If peace is what you choose, then you mustn't be seen again. If anyone knows you're alive, it will jeopardise everything.'

I sit there, and for the first time in forever, I'm at a loss.

'Malina,' Hargna prompts, kneeling before me. He takes my hands in his, and this time, I don't pull away. 'Trust me, like I trusted you. Choose peace, choose life, and find a way to return home to Lotane.'

I close my eyes, conjuring images of Lotane holding me in his arms to help make up my mind.

'Peace it is,' I say.

Hargna sighs with relief, his shoulders sagging.

'I want to believe you're right,' I continue. 'But I can't fully accept it, not just yet. So, I'll hide myself far away where no one will find me, and watch from afar. If you're right, no one will ever see me again.'

I stand and look at the map on the wall near his bed.

'Tell me. Why is Astport on Astoria's east coast, not the north?'

'The old port became ice-locked. The Astorians blew a hole through the mountains to build the new one. Why?'

'None of your business, Hargna. Not anymore,' I say, smiling slightly to take the sting from my words. 'Now, do you have any gold?'

Hargna opens a bedside cabinet drawer and pulls out a heavy pouch.

'There's plenty more if it will help,' he says eagerly.

I shake my head and take the pouch, tying it to my belt.

'I won't see you again, Hargna. Unless … unless you're wrong.'

Hargna smiles sadly.

'You told me once you had Hastian blood in your veins. Embrace what it's like to be human, not fey. It's in our nature to choose love and peace over killing.'

I shake my head.

'I want to believe you, Hargna. But nor am I blind to reality. It's so rare that a good man like you rises to power, and the last one I knew who did so ...' My words die away, as long forgotten images of the High King screaming as he was consumed by elemental flames come to mind.

'What happened to him?' Hargna asks.

'He ... he trusted the wrong person,' I croak. 'Be careful who you trust, and remember, the strong will always prey on the weak ... and always be willing to make the hard decisions.'

'I'm strong now,' Hargna insists, his voice firm, 'and I'm not afraid to make those hard decisions. Trust me.'

I sigh, shaking my head sadly.

'So what about them?' I ask, jerking my head toward the three half-naked women huddled on the other side of the room.

'W-what about them?' Hargna gasps.

'They're a hard decision.'

Hargna begins to shake again, his pupils wide.

'I-I can't.'

'I know,' I say, studying him. 'You've yet to perfect your bluff. Now, farewell, Hargna, son of Harkonen, and forgive me a final time for what I'm about to do.'

I leave Hargna sitting on the bed, gather the women together, and then kill them before they even know what's going on.

'You truly are the Queen of Beasts,' Hargna calls as I close the door.

A half-dressed man stands in the doorway of the adjacent room, and his eyes widen as I approach.

'Nogotha' he breathes a split second before I smash his head into the doorframe and then kneel to stab him through the heart as he lays moaning on the floor.

I pick up my pace, eager to leave before anyone else awakens and the need to kill arises again. Hargna was right, killing comes far too easily to me. But what other choice did I have in this instance? No one can know I'm alive if peace is to have a chance ...

Yet inside, there's an ember of doubt that refuses to die and will keep me on this world for years to come.

The Astorians haven't changed in thousands of years. I find it hard to believe my supposed demise at the hands of The All Father has truly stilled the bloodlust in their veins, and that their dreams of conquest have faded overnight.

I just can't believe it has ... or perhaps that's just the darkness within me, hoping for more blood. Nonetheless, I'll stay vigilant, and if the need arises, and the Astorian dreams of conquest and vengeance rise from the ashes, I'll simply bury every leader who takes up the quest.

Even if I have to do this forever, I will.

But, for now, it's time to go somewhere far away, somewhere I can rest in safety. Somewhere that I'm loved.

Ssythla.

***

The streets of Astgate are already alive when I enter the city proper, and from the looks of things, sleep hasn't been a priority for a long time.

Tables line the pavements, pushed together and decorated with strips of colourful linen, their vibrant hues fluttering in the morning breeze. Despite the early hour, people are breaking fast and laughing with wild abandon, as though reborn. Children dart between the tables in a chaotic chase, shrieking in joy, while others lie curled up together, fast asleep, all under the watchful eyes of smiling parents.

I move openly amongst them, my head and face concealed by a loosely knitted shawl taken from a sleeping woman as I left the Palace. A jacket covers my swords, their hilts over my shoulder also disguised by the shawl.

The happiness is infectious, and I find myself smiling.

If only the wounded in the Palace could see what they'd bought with their suffering, for some, it might make it seem all worthwhile. This is what life should be without oppression.

The transformation is astonishing, one I never foresaw.

Not that these people have been idly celebrating the whole time. Wagons, once filled with gunpowder or other military sundries, now stand in the middle of the streets, packed with belongings, supplies, and notably muskets, all under stretched tarpaulins.

In fact, as I look around, I'm pleased to see more of these weapons near to hand, despite there being no immediate threat.

The whispering in my head rises again with a vengeance, and I stagger, disorientated, fighting back nausea as I bend over gripping a table.

'Too much wine, dear?' a woman asks, her hand light on my shoulder.

'No. No, I'm fine,' I say, shrugging her off, staggering away, gentle laughter following my every step.

As I head east, the city pulses with positive energy as people celebrate, pack belongings, or empty stores of supplies in preparation for their journey to Ast.

What's more surprising is the lack of destruction. There's no mindless looting, no reckless vandalism, and even where there are bloodstains on the cobblestones, the bodies have been removed.

So many people died in this rebellion, and yet, most of the fighting had been restricted to the barracks and the Palace. It's rare in a battle like this that there's so little collateral damage, but the city itself has so far mostly escaped unscathed.

To my right, the doors of a Church Eternal stand open. On impulse, I slip inside, expecting to see it desecrated and spoiled. Yet to my utter surprise, several sisters lead a service, while fifty or so Icelandians and Tarsians sit in silent prayer, hands clasped and heads bowed before the altar.

Whilst I'd passed through the chapel in the Palace, it's the first time I've stepped inside one of these churches, and I'm somewhat surprised.

Unlike within the Great Hall of Victory, there are no horrific depictions of my fey, instead the murals here are singular in their focus. Every wall, every image, every symbol is dedicated to one figure, the All Father.

He stands with his arms outstretched, sheltering families beneath each arm, standing as a protector, a guardian.

My breath catches in my throat as other images come to mind, those of Nogoth in the Mountain of Souls.

The similarity is undeniable. Had the All Father seen the temple murals of Nogoth and taken them as his own? Was this deliberate design, or some twisted coincidence? I wish I knew the answers, but talking to the dead is not one of my skills.

I linger a few more minutes, wandering around, admiring on a deeper level the powerful messaging contained within the images. The All Father, humble and disfigured, a shepherd dedicated to protecting his flock. His eyes are always lifted, his head slightly tilted as if listening to a divine message only he can hear.

At the altar, the service ends. Food is handed out, rewarding those loyal or foolish souls who believe this false narrative. Or, perhaps they don't believe it, but just want the extra food.

I leave swiftly before the congregation notices me, and return to the streets.

The wind is picking up, the air heavy with the promise of rain. People are gathering up belongings, laughing and shouting as items tumble down the street before every gust, and it's not long before I have the streets mostly to myself.

I keep close to the buildings, taking what shelter I can as I press on, an outsider, unwelcome in this city that I helped save. If I'm seen, the news will spread like wildfire, and what then?

Nonetheless, I hum a tune, my footsteps light. True, the city remains oppressive, the buildings, blocked monstrosities without any thought to pleasing lines or architecture, but it has changed, because the people have changed.

Laughter and voices occasionally lift above the wind, and suddenly I laugh with them, because if Hargna is right, then I've won. My beloved fey and Lotane are safe.

A whisper from behind has me turn, but there's no one there, a flicker of movement off to my right, the same. What the hells is going on?

This isn't tiredness.

I'm disorientated and completely out of sorts. My senses are confused, and I'm positive it's not through lack of sleep nor recovering from injury.

My happiness evaporates as a darker realisation takes hold.

I was trained to heed my instincts, and I'd baulked at drinking the All Father's life blood until I'd had no other choice. Am I infected with whatever disease caused his hideous appearance? Are my symptoms the result of my body trying to fight off the virus?

I guess I'll soon find out. I just hope my nose doesn't fall off.

Even as my mood changes with the realisation that I'm not well, the city begins to change too, almost as if mirroring my unease as I enter the main Astorian sector in the east of Astgate.

At first, it's subtle, the streets absent people and celebration, a ghost town, where the ghosts peer between drawn curtains, and disappear when you look in their direction. Then, it's because the streets aren't empty, far from it.

Bodies lie strewn across the pavements, some Astorian musketeers, others clearly civilians. Shops and warehouses are smashed, vandalised, and looted, their doors torn from their hinges, while others are burnt out husks.

There was always going to be collateral damage and casualties, but as I crouch beside the corpse of a young woman, the congealing blood pooling beneath her tells me she didn't die in the initial uprising, nor in the immediate aftermath.

She was killed hours ago.

I don't doubt Hargna set patrols to maintain order, but either they, or others, are now working outside of their remit. Who knows whether they're taking advantage of the shift in power to right historic wrongs, or, more simply, to just act out their base desires, but these streets are no longer safe.

A whisper comes from behind, and I roll, palming a dagger as I do so, come to my feet, and … nothing, so I sheathe the blade. Why do these whispers come and go at random? Whispers aren't the symptoms of a virus, at least not any I know. Headaches, yes, whispers, no.

Unless the All Father was driven mad by whatever he suffered from. I'd often seen him talking to himself. Could that be possible? I shake my head. Such speculation is useless unless there's something I can do about it, and right now, there isn't.

My mission is to reach Ssythla, and anything else is a distraction, and I can't afford to be distracted.

The deeper I push into the Astorian sector, the worse things become.

Bodies are scattered along my route, and now, having been left to rot, so are rats. Everywhere they're gorging in plain sight, no fear evident as they pause briefly to watch me walk by.

I round a corner and nearly trip over a body sprawled across the cobblestones. The musketeer, his face contorted in a final grimace of pain, has his chest caved in as though crushed by some massive weight.

Beyond him, the small plaza is a slaughterhouse, with maybe a dozen civilian bodies scattered around, each one a testament to the breakdown of order that's engulfing this part of the city. None of them appear to be Astorian. Is this the result of one mob establishing loot rights over another?

As I pick my way through the bodies aiming for the next street, a shadowy group of men emerge from a nearby alley, and judging by the bulging packs and muskets, they're looters. Then, when I catch sight of three battered and bruised women manacled in their midst, I realise they're much worse.

The men are laughing, jostling one another, their attention fixed on a shuttered shop's reinforced door, the last untouched building on the street.

They haven't noticed me yet.

But they will.

I hiss in frustration and turn away, keeping my head down, picking up my pace, determined to reach the next street and continue my journey unaccosted.

'What's this?' a man calls, his voice carrying an edge of drunken bravado.

Carry on walking, Malina. Just ignore them. Get out of this city. There's nothing you can do.

I keep my stride steady, my head down.

'Where do you think you're going?' he continues loudly. 'Stop where you are.'

I could easily outrun them, but the darkness inside urges me otherwise. Was I not trained to reap the souls of the wicked? But no, I'll try to walk the path of peace that Hargna has chosen.

'Please, just take your loot and go!' I call.

'Hold up, there. I said STOP!'

My footsteps slow, and the resulting laughter is dark.

'The time for fighting is over,' I say, turning to face the group of eight men. 'I'm not your enemy.'

'Then you can show how much you love us then,' one says, leering with obvious intent. 'All of us.'

'Run!' cries one of the women, then collapses under a flurry of blows.

'Shut up, you mouthy bitch,' yells her assailant, much to the amusement of the group.

'You should have taken her advice,' I hiss.

Laughter greets my words, but it dies away as I draw my swords.

The men exchange uncertain glances, backing away, unaware it's already too late, and raise their muskets threateningly. On the battlefield, these weapons are deadly at range, but in a surprise, close encounter, without their matches lit, they're just an unwieldy, big club.

The scattered debris makes the ground awful to walk on, let alone fight on, but moving forward, I can at least see where I'm placing my feet.

I advance swiftly, closing the distance, and don't feel any resistance as my right sword point shatters the man's teeth closest to me, and exits the back of his neck. My left sword is already punching through another's ribs as I duck under a swung musket, and take my assailant's leg off at the knee before the blade continues its arc, cutting open a man from groin to neck. I sway back away from a punch, cut the hand off, and then stumble badly as a piece of debris turns under my foot.

A bearded Icelandian launches himself at me, and even as my sword buries itself in his gut, brings me to the ground, smothering me with his weight. His hands go around my neck, and I just have the sense to cut my left sword into the ankle of a Tarsian who is about to kick me in the head.

The Icelandian is crying and screaming in my face as he digs his fingers deep. I drop my sword, reach around his back, swiftly pull a dagger from my vambrace, and stab him repeatedly in the side.

With a heave, I shove him off, then roll to my feet.

Only one looter, a young Tarsian, remains standing, clutching one of my swords in his trembling hands. Three others are still alive, sobbing on the ground, bleeding out.

'I-I just w-want to t-take the loot,' the Tarsian stammers, shaking the sword at me, his face streaked with tears and snot.

'It's too late for that,' I say flatly. 'Far too late. Fight for your life. Make it mean something.'

I sway away from two wild slashes, the blade hissing past my face, twist aside from a clumsy lunge, grab his wrist, and pull him toward me as I thrust my dagger up into his throat.

'You should have taken the loot,' I murmur, taking my sword from his fading grip while he sinks to his knees, gurgling.

I retrieve my other sword, and despite their pleas, kill the wounded, and then swiftly go through the packs, picking one that's stuffed with food and water flasks.

'What about us?' one of the women asks, her voice hesitant, afraid.

'Search the bodies,' I say, keeping my back to them. 'You'll find the key to the manacles. Then gather as much food as you can carry, and either hide away or leave the city.'

'My whole life was here,' another cries. 'Everything's gone to shit.'

I nod sadly, heaving the pack over my shoulder.

Time to follow my own advice. If I stay, I'll end up killing my way to the city limits. Better to find a rooftop, wait for nightfall. I wasn't thinking clearly, choosing to leave during the day. At night, I can move faster, remain unseen, unchallenged. I own the night, whereas the day belongs to others.

Even as the thought crosses my mind, the whispering starts again, and my head pounds. I groan, unable to drown it out.

'It was your fault, wasn't it? All of this?'

The voice is familiar, the woman who'd urged me to run.

'Find the key,' I say, starting to walk away. 'You have your lives. Be grateful for that.'

'Grateful?' she spits. 'Grateful to the Queen of Beasts? I don't think so. Yes, I saw your damned eyes. Don't even try to deny it.'

The clouds are boiling as I arch my back, seeking an answer to my quandary. I want to walk a peaceful path, to give it a chance, but these women could reveal the secret of my continued existence.

Thunder rumbles, low and menacing. A storm gathers in another attempt to cleanse this filthy city of the humanity that contaminates it. Given time, it will wash away everything, including the blood of the many fallen, including the blood of the innocent.

It seems I have my answer, and I turn back, my heart heavy, sword in hand. Time is the greatest healer. I know this to be true, because the faces of the thousands I've slain have faded into oblivion, and this terrible deed will fade in time like all the others.

Or so I hope.

***

CHAPTER XVI

The open countryside.

Fields of swaying grasses under a perfectly clear sky, so wide and endless it aches. The chorus of a thousand birds, the scent of endless blooms carried on the wind ... nature's heartbeat in tune with my own.

What greater medicine is there for a tortured soul?

Such thoughts of the distant fey world keep my spirits out of the mud as I trudge east through the mire of reality toward Astport, that and the growing hope that my fight might finally be over.

It's been seven days since I left Astgate, seven days since I've had to kill, yet despite not drawing my swords since, every step is still a battle, and death surrounds me.

Astoria is withering. Entire forests rot, fallen trees sinking into the sodden, hungry earth that sucks at my boots with every step as I steer clear of the busy roads that snake their way toward Astport. Wildlife has abandoned this place. There are no deer, no birds, no wild boar or even the skitter of squirrels. Only the skeletal remains of livestock grazing on yellowed grass, waiting for a death as inevitable as this land's decay.

And yet, there's something cleansing about the hardship of this journey, something raw and honest about waking beneath the sky, even if it's dark and troubled. I accept it as penance for the blood on my hands, for the sins that refuse to fade with time.

Killing has never burdened my conscience. It was always justified, necessary, even righteous ... the conditioning of my youth saw to that. I told myself that taking the lives of those with evil intent always made the world a better place.

Yet, taking the lives of the men and women in Hargna's bedchamber, and then the captive women as I fled Astgate, has plagued my every step, their death following me like shadows. They did not deserve to die, and yet I silenced them as if they had ... to ensure no one knew that I lived.

In this world, I am death. I walk and people die. Friends, enemies, and strangers. Only in the fey world have I known peace. Only there have I lived without the need to kill.

I ache for Lotane, for his arms, for the beauty of the land that quieted the storm within me. Yes, I'm responsible for ensuring peace exists between the different races, but so much is down to what the Saer Tel have crafted over the millennia. When you live in paradise, anger and hate have very little place to take root.

I pause, my fingers running over the trunk of a silverwood.

The bark, once smooth and shining, is dulled and soft with decay. The tree rots from within, still standing only because it leans on its stricken neighbours.

Boreholes from insects mar every trunk in sight, and where there should be birdsong, there's silence. This is a graveyard, not a sanctuary.

A few steps away, a brackish stream foams with yellow scum, undrinkable.

Anyone who looks upon such sorrow will know nothing but despair themselves. What good can come from the Astorian people when surrounded by such decay?

I know the answer to that question only too well, or at least I once thought I did. Now, I hope that under the leadership of the church, they will put aside their quest for violence and revenge, with redressing the balance with the Tarsians and Icelandians, just the start.

My stomach growls.

It's been two days since I last ate. Water is no issue; it rains often enough, though even the rain is tainted and bitter on the tongue. But food is another matter. There are no edible roots, no wild berries, no fruit trees...

Fruit.

My dream of Karson comes to mind. The old apple tree, the sapling I'd planted and the river, clear and bright. It was such a beautiful place, like this place probably once was ... If only it could be again.

I stop in my tracks as an idea magically coalesces.

Is this what it means to be both Saer Tel and the mother of two worlds? Has the solution fallen into my lap like an apple from a tree? Or was that always the message I was supposed to take away, and I was just too blind to see it?

My breath is shallow as I grasp the enormity of my epiphany.

If I make this world a beautiful place, will the hatred and anger evaporate like a puddle on a hot, summer's day? If the land heals, will the people heal with it?

I look through my spirit eye, unsurprised to find myself surrounded by boiling black clouds of uncreation, thick and suffocating. There's no sign of the gold, not even a flicker.

Not yet.

But is there anything to lose by trying?

The Saer Tel often dance naked, or wear the lightest of garments, so they can join with nature, and feel its pulse. Yet I can't afford to leave my clothes, weapons or backpack behind, not here.

The song of creation comes to mind, that haunting, beautiful melody flowing through me as if it's my own blood.

I forget the sodden earth, the steady drip of water. I forget the blustery wind and the overcast sky. I forget my hunger and discomfort, and give myself over to the dance.

Almost immediately the discordant song of uncreation rises, tries to take hold of me, to use me as its vessel for vengeance.

But this time I'm ready.

I close my mind to the howling rage of its defilement, focussing on beauty, on growth, on life, and continue, coaxing, luring, seducing, my steps sensual and hypnotic, a dance of defiance against the darkness.

A sudden flash of gold, brilliant against the darkness inspires me, and despite my cumbersome gear, the stiffness in my limbs, I spin and twist, dancing with wild, desperate passion, unchained.

And the gold shines again.

I reach out, fingertips trembling, hesitant, uncertain, and the gold pulses toward me, reassuring, and willing.

I gasp in expectation as it flares brightly, and then ...

The whispers return.

They scratch at my mind, nails against raw flesh, and the song dies, the gold disappears in a flash, and the darkness thunders as if scorned and betrayed. The wind howls, battering me, sending me to my knees in the mud, drained, spent, defeated.

Movement behind me has me spin around, grasping for a dagger, but there's nothing, just the mocking sway of the trees in the gale, as I twist again and stab at half seen people.

Keep calm, Malina. It will pass. It always passes.

I crawl and sit with my back to a trunk, uncaring as water seeps through my clothes. Evening fades into darkness, and still I sit, cradling my aching head, lost in the whispers.

Madness.

I have no fever, no sickness I can name. I'm not dehydrated, and despite being hungry, I'm not weak. Can madness be spread by a virus? Was this the All Father's way to kill me, by having me take my own life?

Yet I'm beginning to realise there's a predictability about the intensity. Early mornings and late evening is the worse. Yes, the whispers come and go during the day, but they're not as loud, invasive, or painful.

I push myself up from the ground, angry with myself.

What would Lystra think if she saw me cowering in the dirt? What would Lotane say if I let pain and exhaustion keep me from my path?

I exhale, steadying myself, and begin to dance again, the song of creation not just in my mind, but also upon my lips.

Were these words ever meant to be spoken aloud? They mean nothing to me, and yet they mean everything. Each syllable falls like a mountain, heavy, undeniable, eternal.

Casting exhaustion aside, I dance as if it's the last thing I'll ever do, as if my lifeblood spills to the ground with every step. I give everything, my voice rising above the howling wind, uttering words that weave into the gusts, so that they're carried swirling around the trees, through the yellowed grass, and into the boiling clouds of uncreation.

The song of uncreation rises, tries to drown out my own, but I lift above it, laughing, embracing it as if a petulant child, and tame its rage with unconditional, unyielding love.

Then, from one step to the next, gold erupts around me, blinding in its brilliance. Unfettered, unrestrained, a force of pure renewal. Like within the underground, my every step, my every touch, heals a thousand years of corruption instantly, renewing and re-energising.

In this moment, I'm not just alive, I am life itself.

I dance through the ruined forest, weaving restoration into every breath, every flicker of movement, aware on a subliminal level, that there's a finite amount of time. Sure enough, the black of uncreation begins to return. It isn't with anger, nor malice, but more so, with regret.

Does it fear betrayal, to be abandoned again?

My elemental magic had been sentient, had feelings. So why not this?

Slowly the radiance dims, flickers, and then the black slowly closes, leaving me in darkness once again, which for a fey like me, is just a lighter shade of grey.

I look around and smile, satisfied. Like the land, I'm fully replenished, and Karson's words again echo in my mind.

'Despite all the death you've dealt, it appears you have the ability to give life.'

'I hope you can see this, little brother,' I whisper into the night air.

The temperature drops, my breath misting in the cold. Snowflakes drift down, unnatural in this season and I'm concerned.

The land might be strong, and so am I, but without elemental magic, I'm as vulnerable as any mortal. I can't afford to be brought low, not when my mission has just grown beyond what I ever imagined.

Despite my excitement at what I've achieved here, I need to reach Ssythla, and have their mages help me recover from whatever ails me.

After ... I'll return and watch over Astoria and while I wait for the truth to reveal itself, I will heal the land and its people too.

With my mind set, and a renewed sense of purpose, I press eastward, the darkness granting me safe passage along the cobbled roads, where I can spot danger long before it spots me.

This far from Astgate, it's like I've stepped back in time into the world I once knew. Fields are neatly enclosed by slate and stone walls. No factories, looming warehouses, or paved roads scar the land.

Yet there's nothing to block the wind, no warm chimneys to lean against, or allies with whom to shelter. As the snow fall strengthens, the wind pierces my clothes and I turn toward a light just to the south, shining like a beacon through the darkness.

A farmhouse emerges, nestled alongside two barns, a handful of chickens running wild in the yard. Several fields behind hold dying crops, drenched and rotting. The animals scatter as I approach the front door.

I consider my options.

I cast aside the simplest ... killing another innocent now the war is over. Nor will I steal. I have enough gold to buy his farm a thousand times over.

I knock hard, then step back a dozen paces, knowing that a visitor at this hour will only be met with hostility, and I'm not going to give my conditioning any excuse to take control.

A curtain twitches, and a few moments later, the door creaks open, revealing a thin, wiry man, his face hollowed by a lifetime of hard labour. Behind him, a woman rests her hand on a boy's head as he peeks from behind her skirt.

'Get on yer way!' the man yells above the wind, raising a wooden stick as if it were a musket. 'I'll shoot you if you don't get off my land!'

I almost laugh at his bluff. His grip is unsteady, his voice quivering. He's terrified. But I'm not here to threaten, I'm here as a stranger in need, absent the desire to kill.

I spread my arms wide.

'If I were to ask for supplies for a week, hot food for the night, and a dry place in your barn till morning, how much would you ask?'

The farmer tightens his hold on the stick, shaking it at me.

'There's nothing a vagrant like you could own that I'd want. Now get off my land!'

Irritation flares. I've asked politely, and I'm not used to pleading.

'I'm no vagrant. Now, I suggest you set a price!' I snap.

'I said, get off ...'

My dagger thunks into the doorframe by his head, closer than I'd intended, but with wet hands, it was as good a throw as could be hoped for.

'And I asked, how much?'

'N-n-nothing!' the man stammers, looking at the quivering blade as his wife and child run crying into the back. 'Just take what you want!'

I shake my head.

'What's wrong with you? I don't want it for free. I asked you to set a price. An honest price.'

'I-I d-don't know what you want me to s-say,' the man stammers, so frightened he can barely talk.

I sigh and approach the farmhouse, tugging my shawl around my face.

'I'm sorry,' I say softly. 'Truly I am. Now, drop the stick and close your eyes.'

The man shakes uncontrollably as he stands there, tears forcing their way out from under his clenched eyelids. Guilt weighs heavily on my shoulders. Am I such a monster that I must frighten everyone?

I yank my dagger free of the soft wood, and look into the farmhouse. A fire glows merrily in a hearth, casting golden light over rough wooden walls, tables, chairs and cabinets. The woman and child huddle in a corner. A pot simmers over the flames, its rich aroma setting my mouth to watering.

'Open your hands,' I say softly, but firmly.

A sob escapes him as he reaches out, opening his hands, palms up.

'Now, listen carefully,' I murmur. 'I didn't mean to frighten you or your family. We just got off on the wrong foot.'

I hang my empty pack off his left hand, pull out a gold coin and place it in his right.

'You'll fill my pack with meats, bread, cheese, and whatever else you have, and fill the flask with drinking water. Your wife will bring me a warm meal, dry clothes, and the filled pack to the nearest barn. I'll sleep there tonight.'

I pause to ensure my words settle before I continue.

'You'll do this immediately, and then lock yourself in your farmhouse and stay inside till midday tomorrow. Now, keep your eyes down, and look at what's in your right hand.'

I place my hand on the top of his head, ensuring he complies. I've no wish to have the blood of this family on my conscience.

His fingers tighten around the coin, his breath coming in short, excited gasps.

'I-is this real gold?'

'Yes.' I keep my voice soft, but slightly menacing. 'And if you just do as I ask, you'll live to spend it wisely. Do you understand my meaning?'

'I do, Mistress. I do.'

'Good. Because then we'll both be the richer,' I say, turning away.

Behind me, the farmer exhales shakily, his voice breaking.

'Kara. Fetch the bread, the jams, the cheese ...'

His voice dies away as I approach the barn. The snow isn't settling, for which I'm grateful. I still have a week's hard travel ahead of me to reach Astport, but at least I'll do so with a full stomach and the rare satisfaction of leaving behind a family, happy and unscathed.

The barn door groans as I push it open and a wave of warmth greets me, the sweet scent of hay, the low bleating of goats, the sharp squeals of pigs shifting in their pens. The goats, unconfined, bounce about wildly, eager for a new distraction, while I keep a close watch on the farmhouse.

I'm relieved when a short time later the wife hurries across the yard, laden with what I'd requested, the farmer standing stiffly in the doorway, urging her on.

'You can leave the things just there, thank you,' I say.

She jumps at the sound of my voice, nearly dropping the bowl of steaming broth, but steadies herself before setting it carefully on the ground. My pack follows, a neatly bundled pile of clothes resting on top. Without a word, she turns on her heel, hastening back across the yard.

I bring everything into the barn, change into the dry clothes, and then watch the farmhouse while I eat the thin, yet tasty broth. I stay awake for a further hour, watching the lights go out in the farmhouse. The front door remains closed, the farmer thankfully doing nothing reckless.

With a sigh of contentment, I lay on the straw.

The goats, bold little creatures, nestle against me as if sensing I'm no threat. One nudges at my shoulder before settling with a satisfied bleat. Another curls against my hip. Their small, warm bodies press in around me, a comfort I did not expect, and as I drift toward sleep, a rare smile tugs at my lips.

Truly, I am the Queen of Beasts.

***

'Tars? Why in all the hells would you want to go to Tars?' growls the captain of the sleek, armed ship *Seasprite,* docked alongside the pier. 'The bloody Tarsians hate Tars. It's too damn hot, even for them.'

I've learned that this type of ship is called a *schooner.* Gone are the biremes and triremes and square sailed ships of my time. Everything has changed.

The captain is clearly disgruntled at being pulled from his cabin. A lump of meat caught in his beard confirms I've interrupted his early dinner, and from the sour expression on his face, he's not inclined to be accommodating. He'd be even less so if he knew my true destination.

I keep my head down, the cowl of the brown robe pulled low, arms crossed, and hands hidden within my sleeves. Whispers scratch in my mind, muffling the splash of waves and the rhythmic creak of the ship's timbers.

'The missions of the Church Eternal are not for you or me to question,' I say softly. 'And, in this instance, knowing your livelihood will suffer, you'll be generously compensated.'

Orghast grunts.

'That's two weeks there, and the same back. We were planning on fishing this month. That's a lot of missed catches.' He frowns. 'I'm not so sure. Go find another ship.'

'What's your name, Captain?' I ask softly.

'Orghast.'

'Well, Captain Orghast. Let's stop this charade. You'll take me to Tars because the church wills it, and you'll take me because you have no choice. Now, if you insist on wasting my time, the next most experienced crew member will be promoted to captain, whereas you'll find yourself incarcerated at the Archbishop's pleasure.'

Orghast's face darkens.

'Y-you can't do that!' he blusters. 'I have friends in high places!'

'Are you sure you want to walk this path?' I ask, pushing aside thoughts of gutting him. The conversation isn't going as smoothly as I'd hoped, but I won't resort to violence, not now. Instead, I turn on my heel and walk back along the pier, shaking my head.

'Where are you going?'

'To fetch a slinger,' I say, not looking back.

'Why a slinger?' Orghast calls after me.

I pause, and half turn back toward him.

'If you have friends in high places,' I say, raising my voice. 'There's no point having you incarcerated. You'll be shot instead.' I take another step. 'You have an hour to get your affairs in order!'

'Wait!'

His boots thump against the wooden planks as he rushes to stand in front of me.

'Forgive me, Sister,' he gasps, breathless. 'I'm tired, and had a little too much wine. I meant no offense. We can leave for Tars tomorrow morning, as the Church wills it.'

'Why not tonight?'

'We need supplies for the journey,' he says hurriedly, sweat beading his brow. 'We usually only go out for the day before our nets are full.'

I shake my head, tutting.

'But,' he adds hastily, 'if I have my crew bring in a few favours, we can be ready to go at first light, when the tide and winds are with us!'

I nod slowly, relieved I'd managed to bluff my way on board. There were other ships, but Orghast's was small and sleek. A larger vessel would have meant a higher-ranking captain, one who might not have been so easily coerced.

Uncrossing my arms, I reach beneath my robe, fingers dipping into the heavy pouch at my waist. I pull free three gold coins, holding them out between my fingers.

'The church requires my journey to be fast and discreet. Deliver on your promise without incident, and you'll receive three more before we set sail, and another three at journey's end!'

Orghast's eyes gleam at the sight of the gold. His entire demeanour shifts, shoulders squaring as if he's suddenly proud to serve.

'Sister, you have my word,' he says with a toothy grin. 'Be here at first light.'

Perhaps I should have led by offering the gold, but I'd worried that doing so would raise suspicions. As I turn away, the captain rushes back to his ship, calling for his crew as I head into the streets of Astport.

It's more a large town than a true city, and the scent of salt and fish is the same as any other port I've known. Taverns, brothels, and eateries line the roads, their raucous patrons spilling into the streets. Laughter and arguments rise into the night air, punctuated by drunken shouts and the occasional clatter of a toppled chair.

I walk unaccosted, the stolen brown robes of the Church Eternal shielding me from the interest of drunkards, pickpockets and cutthroats alike.

Theft seemed a guiltless crime compared to killing its previous owner, that I'd felt no qualms whatsoever slipping into a Church Eternal and helping myself to the garment from a small antechamber off the main chapel. It's a simple disguise, but an effective one.

Figures drift toward me, then right through me.

The first time it happened, I'd drawn my sword and tried to cut them down. Now, I know better. Now, I can distinguish between the real and the imagined.

The ghosts are frequent companions. Everywhere I go, they haunt me. Their ethereal figures flicker at the edges of my vision. Sometimes they materialise in full, lips moving soundlessly, their whispered voices drive me to the edge of insanity at times.

Most appear to be Astorian, although others might be Surian or Rolantrian, and some are without noses, like the All Father's brood beneath the Palace.

The Palace.

It appears every city had one, a seat of power for when the All Father deigned to visit. Astport is no exception, and it sits nestled into the mountainside, a grotesque shrine to his pestilent memory, overlooking the harbour below like a vulture perched over carrion.

What will happen when the people of Astgate hear of his death?

Will they mourn, or will they celebrate?

I expect it's down to their nationality. The Astorians will grieve him as a martyr, whereas the Icelandians and Tarsians I've seen will be quietly jubilant. But these are the ones who stayed behind, who didn't heed Hargna's call to arms. Perhaps they're simply content with their lot.

Shaking my head to banish the thought, I retrace my steps back into town toward an eatery I'd passed earlier in the evening.

I'm surprised by the levity of everyone as I walk. Astport is as far from Astgate geographically as it is in terms of atmosphere … or was, I correct myself, remembering the celebrations before my departure.

Laughter spills from taverns, children race between carts and barrels, families gather at food stalls, their faces lit by the glow of lanterns. Unlike Astgate, there's no tension in the air, no simmering resentment, and whilst the sea breeze can't do much about the overwhelming odour of fish and industry, it still manages to blow the smoke from a thousand chimneys inland.

I pause, looking up, and for the first time I've been here, the stars and moons are visible and I take a moment to study them.

They're the ultimate celestial puzzle, and I ponder for the thousandth time how their presence and alignment was ever mechanised to unlock the moon gates. I shrug. If Nogoth, in all his millennia of life, never unravelled the secret, then what chance for me?

Two Icelandians lumber past, familiar in their gaunt, underfed look, backs bowed under the weight of fish crates. It seems ridiculous that with such a plentiful supply of fish, they should be malnourished, but then it's just the Astorian way of keeping them weak physically, mentally, and subservient to boot.

'What can I get you, Sister?'

Without realising it, I've arrived at my destination, and curse myself for being off guard, even for a moment.

'A quiet seat, and your best dish,' I reply, keeping my head low. 'A hot drink wouldn't go amiss either.'

The waitress nods and beckons, smiling.

I follow her inside, and she ushers me to a quiet corner where I sit, massaging my temples.

'Fish of the day and a mulled wine coming up,' she says cheerfully, then hurries off to the kitchens.

Despite the fact that all the other patrons are outside, I'm not alone, and it's certainly not quiet. Ghosts pass through the walls, their silent figures pacing the floor, watching, waiting. The eatery flickers and shifts before my eyes, one moment a grand dining hall, the next a church, then a dark cave. They bow before and whisper, keeping me constant company, torturing me, even if they don't appear malignant.

I don't know how long I sit there, head lowered, my mind battling against exhaustion and madness before the clink of ceramic rouses me as the waitress places a plate and a steaming goblet before me.

'You're unwell,' she says, kneeling to see my face. 'You've been moaning when I've served the other people.'

I flinch, turning away before she can get a better look.

'Forgive my shyness,' I murmur. 'I fell into a fire as a child, and bear terrible scars. I've no wish for my face to be seen.'

'Of course, Sister. Hopefully, the food will help,' she replies, and leaves me be.

Her kindness is touching, but I know it would wither the moment she saw beneath my hood. If she knew I wasn't a true sister of the Church Eternal, if she glimpsed the truth of me, she'd scream, rouse a mob, and I'd be burned at the stake before the sun set.

I shake the thought away, irritated by my own cynicism, pick up a fork and stab it into my food. I must stop being so disenchanted with humanity and assuming the worse of everyone.

To my surprise, the food is tasty, seasoned well, the wine spiced and warming. As I savour each mouthful, something remarkable happens, the voices fade. Not completely, but to a murmur, something distant, like a conversation heard through thick walls. Pleasure has dulled the torment.

When the last bite is gone, I push the empty plate aside, leaning back, enjoying the warmth spreading through my body.

'That will be a copper,' the waitress says, her tone light and full of good humour, and well it might be. The eatery is thriving, chairs full outside, the air thick with laughter and conversation.

I know without looking that I only have gold in my pouch. However, it holds no real value to me and I have more than I could ever spend.

I place a gold piece on the table.

The waitress gasps.

'Please, just take it,' I say. 'The quality of your food is only matched by your kindness.'

The waitress stands there, uncertain, but then scoops up the coin.

'I won't complain if you stay for a small piece of my best warm apple cake,' she offers. 'People say it's priceless, but I'll let you have it for a gold piece.'

I can't help but chuckle.

Then I'd better try it,' I say, sinking back into my seat, the buzz of conversation strangely soothing as it merges with the whispering.

Then I remember my dream and Karson's advice.

'Perhaps they're trying to tell you something,' he'd said. *'Perhaps you should listen.'*

My brother's advice rarely makes sense, but this … so, instead of resisting, I embrace the whispers. I don't fight them. I let them wash over me, visualising waves lapping gently at a shore instead of the writhing mass of serpents that usually accompany them.

The pain increases, my eyes water, but I persevere, desperate to try anything and everything.

Then, to my amazement, for the first time, I hear … them.

Fragments of conversations that aren't from the living outside begin to filter through.

'Grain … diverted, Tars …'

'Demonstration … Midnor … down …'

'Army … River …'

I breathe slowly, staying calm, as a ghost of a man materialises before me, his lips moving. He wears a slinger's coat and wide-brimmed hat, but there are too many voices at once, layered over one another, making it impossible to focus. But at least they're voices …

The waitress returns, placing a plate before me, on which a piece of sugar-frosted apple cake sits invitingly.

'And another mug of wine,' she says, setting it down beside the plate before flouncing off.

I almost cry with relief as my headache recedes, leaving just the residual ache of tiredness. The whispering fades too, barely there, present, but on the fringes of my consciousness, no longer an irritant.

Taking a bite of the cake, I sigh at the warmth, the cinnamon and apple melting on my tongue. Karson was right. The ghosts are trying to tell me something. But what?

As I sip my wine, I let my thoughts drift with the whispers, while viewing the accompanying images with growing interest.

'Here. A final one on the house,' the waitress says.

I haven't felt this warm and comfortable in as long as I can remember. A full stomach, the gentle buzz of alcohol, and now absent my headache.

I wonder if they have a room here that I can rent for the night. It might seem strange when my church lodgings would be in town, but I can just continue to play on feeling unwell.

Several more images come, and go, but then another comes to mind … the ghostly figure of a hunched Sister of The Church Eternal sitting alone in the corner of an eatery.

It takes me a moment to grasp the significance.

There are no ghosts, I'm not going mad. I'm seeing myself through someone else's eyes.

The realisation sends a jolt down my spine, and I barely manage to set my mug down without spilling it.

Someone is watching me.

I cross my arms, sliding my hands up my sleeves just as two pairs of booted feet approach my table.

'When I heard a Sister was unwell, I was worried. But, when I heard she'd paid for her meal with gold … well, then I became very concerned. No sister can amass such wealth unless through nefarious means. Men, keep the sister company.'

Two slingers sit, one on either side of me, their legs pressing close, hemming me in.

I keep my head down as a chair scrapes across the floor, dragged from another table, and my stomach knots as a pair of sandaled feet and a white robe appear. I don't need to look up to know who it is.

The All Father.

How he lives I have no idea, yet he does, and has found me. But, if he knew it was me beneath this cowl, I'd already be dead.

Suddenly, all my hopes and dreams evaporate. There was never going to be peace, it was all a lie. Hargna had been deceived, and I'd let myself be taken in too. My shoulders sag, and I sigh.

'So,' the All Father, begins, his voice firm. 'Let's start with the pleasantries. What's your name, Sister?'

I whip the daggers from my sleeves, slamming them back into the slinger's chests either side as I kick the table, sending the All Father tumbling back out of his chair in horror.

'Do you really need to ask?' I hiss, standing over him.

'Nogotha is ALIVE. She's here ... eatery ... guards dead ... Send more, brothers!'

The All Father's lips haven't moved, yet I've heard his voice as clearly as if he'd spoken aloud. He scrambles away from me as I advance.

'They're on ... way. Accept ... fate ... honour, Brother. You cannot die ... will live ... our minds forever!'

The All Father has backed up against a wall, and snarls his defiance, hatred plain on his face.

'You just don't get it,' he rasps. 'There are hundreds of me, and just one of you. You can't kill us all. One day, you'll make a mistake, and will die, whereas I will always live and ...'

I kneel and slam the dagger into his chest.

A scream has me spin around, and there stands the waitress, her fist pressed against her mouth, eyes wide with horror. Two women rush inside, drawn by the commotion, and their screams join hers.

I'm up and inside the kitchen, away from the crowd outside, pushing a cook viciously from my path before the screams die away. He barely has time to react before I grab hold of the heavy oil vat perched on the counter. With a savage heave, I tip it toward the open flame of the grill.

A wave of heat follows me out through the back door as it ignites with a whoosh. Hitching up my robes, I sprint past some confused families who can hear the screams but have no idea what I've done.

After a minute of taking random turns through the labyrinth of darkened streets, I find a quiet corner.

Breathe, Malina. Calm down.

I pause, pressing myself against a damp wall, secrete my daggers within their vambraces, adjust my hood so it settles low over my face, then set off at a determined pace. I stride fast but resist the lure to run. A running sister would draw attention and people would remember my passing.

The shouts behind me swell, echoing through the street as I head toward the harbour. I glance over my shoulder, the flicker of orange flames bright against the night sky.

'Why did you have to alert the slingers?' I whisper silently, my anger laced with regret.

The clamour of a siren pierces the night, and people spill into the streets to see what the alarm is about, and I have to weave my way through a wall of humanity until finally, the docks come into view.

Resisting the urge to quicken my steps, I walk calmly across the pier toward the schooner.

Orghast stands ahead of me, arms crossed, his face bathed a bright orange, whilst around him several crew members lug crates of livestock and water barrels up a gangplank and onto the deck of the *Seasprite.*

Casually, I stand beside him and turn, only to gasp in amazement.

Fanned by the stiff breeze, the fire I'd started has become an inferno, leaping from building to building like elemental magic.

'Will you just look at that?' Orghast murmurs, transfixed.

'If that wind shifts, will we be safe here?' I ask, knowing the answer.

His eyes widen as my meaning sinks in.

'To your stations!' he bellows, ushering me up the gangplank. 'To your bloody stations!'

Other crew members appear, climbing out the hatches, some half asleep, others slightly drunk, but the captain's loud voice and the sight of the roaring flames sobers them in an instant.

'We cast off in five!' Orghast roars. 'Get those supplies on board. Now!'

I stand by the ship's wheel, an illusion of calm, while inside, I'm screaming at the delay as crowds pour from taverns and brothels to gather on the docks.

Any minute now, a horde of slingers is going to erupt onto the pier, and if they do … only the freezing water will offer me an escape route.

'You six, lower the rowing boat!' Orghast bellows, pointing at some men, his voice rising above the chaos. 'Petty officer, Sams. Cast us off once that last crate is on board, and get eight men on the long oars.'

The crew leaps into action.

Orghast joins me, taking hold of the ship's wheel. Every second lasts a minute before the mooring lines are thrown on board. Then, after what seems an age, the schooner edges away from the pier, the rowing boat tugging the prow toward the open sea, the long oars sweeping slowly.

Gradually, the distance increases, and I breathe a sigh of relief.

'Once we're clear of the harbour mouth, we'll lower the sails,' Orghast says aloud, half to me, half to himself as he peers out to sea. 'There's a gentle swell, but nothing to be worried about.'

I nod absently, but my mind is elsewhere, distracted, trying to discern a dozen conversations at once, fragments of sentences interspersed with whispers coming and going.

'Killed ... brother.'

'Find ... Beasts.'

'Secure ... city ... fire.'

I shouldn't be surprised by what's just been revealed. The Saer Tel have conversed through thought for millennia. I just never considered that human minds might one day develop a similar gift.

The All Father isn't physically immortal, but it appears his mind, his thoughts, his memories are, and as long as even one of his ilk live, this war will never end.

'Sams. Winch the rowing boat on board, then ready the sails.'

Orghast's barked commands bring me back to the present.

The crew are hard at work, and my eyes sweep over them with quiet approval. I chose well. Orghast is a true captain, sharp and decisive. His men are trained, efficient, their movements practiced.

The rowing boat is hauled back onto the ship, and the crew scurries up the rigging, their silhouettes spider-like against the mast.

Sams grins every time Orghast glances his way, eager to please, and I detect a family resemblance.

As we near the harbour mouth, a dozen slingers push through the crowds to sprint along the pier. They wave frantically, their figures illuminated by the burning city behind them.

They reach the end, their shouts lost to the wind and the flapping of the lowered sails, and thankfully Orghast's attention is out to sea. Gunfire flashes, but even their sound doesn't reach us, and nor do their bullets.

I turn my back on them, and stand at Orghast's shoulder, gazing at a horizon as dark as my mood. There's no sense of victory at my escape. I'd foolishly hoped this war might be over, whereas it's only just begun.

My best efforts, Grishen's sacrifice, and Hargna's dreams hadn't been enough … the immortal All Father still lives, and he's right … I'll die, trying to find and kill them all.

There's a Palace of the Ancients in every city,

They don't need to travel. They're rooted, they rule, and they breed.

Even now, at this very moment, another All Father is already taking the place of the one I just killed, plotting, scheming, and waiting.

My plans need to change again.

There's no rest for the wicked, and as the city burns behind me, I know one thing for certain …

There's no one as wicked as I.

***

CHAPTER XVII

With little more than a hammock, slop bucket, desk, and chair, some might consider my cabin no better than a prison cell.

Yet it suits me perfectly.

The narrow walls offer a sense of security, the creaking timbers sing me to sleep, and the unrelenting scent of salt and tar reminds me that, for now, I'm untethered from the world's troubles.

I pick at a plate of diced fruit to finish off my evening meal, then, having put the plate on a recess in the table, swing out of the hammock to stand steady despite the heavy swell. It's over nine days into a so far unpleasant journey and I have my sea legs back.

Opening the tiny closet, I strip off my robe, belt my short swords around my waist, then throw the robe on again, ensuring the hood is pulled low. I remain dressed all the time, but it's a relief to remove my weapon belt when at rest. However, I daren't leave it or my gold unattended in case someone tidies my cabin or even searches it.

Satisfied all is in order, I unlatch my door, and step into the narrow corridor beyond. The ship sways, the wooden planks groaning underfoot, but I make my way up the steps to the deck with practiced ease.

A howling wind greets me, tugging at my robe. The sails are taut, and the schooner skims over the waves as if it understands my urgency.

Four seamen are keeping themselves busy, checking knots, ensuring the cannons and row boat are secure, adjusting the sails, always under the watchful eye of Orghast. When Orghast sleeps, Petty Officer Sams, his nephew, takes command, and the routine never falters.

In addition to a cook, the ship carries sixteen regular seamen and as everyone takes shifts of four hours while under sail, we've been making steady progress despite the angry seas.

'Good evening, Sister,' Orghast shouts, beckoning for me to join him on the raised quarterdeck. 'Can you feel the change in temperature?'

His initial reluctance to take me on board has long faded, replaced by professionalism and mutual respect. He is, without doubt, a fine captain.

'Yes,' I reply. 'It's definitely slightly warmer.'

He nods once, eyes scanning the horizon. Orghast is not a man prone to idle conversation, which suits me just fine.

'We'll pass Rolantria in the morning,' he booms. 'Then we'll turn west, hugging the shore, keeping as far from the Isles of Sin as possible. If the wind holds true, we might even make Tars a day or two early.

My neck aches as I nod in gratitude. I've kept my head lowered for so long that I wonder if I'll ever be able to walk straight again.

I drift toward the stern, planting my feet wide, gripping the timbers with one hand, my hood with the other, fighting the wind that's determined to unmask me. I enjoy my time on deck. It's dark enough, so I don't feel exposed to prying eyes, and I've always felt safe in the dark.

Focusing inwards, I summon the distant whispers to the fore.

What I can hear is still incomplete, fragments of conversations, but I know, without doubt, I'll soon be able to hear every word that's being said whenever I choose.

Despite the vileness of the All Father's blood, it had not only saved my life, but given me this new, unexpected power to spy on my enemy.

'The reb ... force ... ambushed. Our army ... vic ... Any sur ... crucified. Astgate ... ours. We must ... factories ... priority ... world gate. Invasion ... years.

I push the whispers to the back of my mind and shake my head.

Hargna is dead, the rebels slaughtered, crucified. The Astorians had simply played for time, and manoeuvred them into the open.

How many times had Lystra told us to listen to our instincts? For once, I truly wish mine had been wrong. Hargna had been an optimist, a dreamer, and I'd been blinded by his goodness, wanting to live in the light.

I glance at Orghast over my shoulder, legs braced against the roll of the sea, his grip steady on the wheel as he fights the elements with the kind of determination that only seasoned sailors possess. He's a good man, polite, fair to his crew, and decent to me.

And yet after what's just happened … I know better.

All that goodwill would dissolve instantly and turn to disdain, or worse, hatred, if he thought me anything other than an Astorian Sister.

There is so much hate in this world, an unbroken, ever-churning cycle of vengeance, passed from one generation to the next. Will it ever end, and if so, how?

Karson called me the mother of both worlds, and if so, I have truly failed this child. Yet, like twins, this world and the fey realm are forever joined, and if I don't stop the All Father, his thirst for vengeance will lead to not just the death of the fey, but both worlds as the magic of uncreation eventually wreaks vengeance.

I open my spirit eye, peering into the elemental fabric of existence. Even here, far from Astoria's industry, black clouds of uncreation dominate the slivers of blue.

Of the nine days we've sailed so far, only two have been relatively calm. The rest have been tumultuous, ranging from heavy swells to storm-tossed waves, the winds testing every knot of the Seasprite's rigging.

'It gets calmer the further south we travel,' Orghast shouts, almost as if he's read my mind. 'Once we turn west along Rolantria's coast this'll start to die away.'

I wonder if it's because we're further away from Astoria's industry.

'But then,' Orghast continues, 'we'll have to deal with fog banks instead. It's the warm air meeting the cold water, so someone once told me.'

A flicker of light catches my attention on the horizon, northward. I stare hard, waiting, and just when I'm beginning to think it was a figment of my imagination, I see it again. Definitely a ship's lantern.

'How many ships travel this route, Captain?' I ask.

'Enough. Everything from fishing vessels to slavers to pirates.'

'Pirates?'

'Of course. The Isle of Sin's bloody pirate fleet often preys on ships along this route. Why else do you think we lug those cannons around?'

I drum my fingers on the railing, fixated by the single lantern on the horizon only for it to be joined by a second a little distance off to the right, and then, a short time later, another.

'Captain. We have three ships astern.'

'What?' he says, glancing over his shoulder. 'Are you sure?'

'Positive.'

With a curse, Orghast hammers on the ship's bell with a wooden mallet and within minutes, the entire crew is on deck.

'Sams, the helm!' Orghast bellows.

His nephew takes the wheel, and Orghast comes to stand beside me.

He's silent as the ship lifts and drops, staring, waiting.

'There isn't three, there's bloody five!' he growls. 'Damn it. They ain't going to be fishing vessels nor traders. They can only be bloody pirates.'

My fingers tighten around the railing.

'Can we outrun them?'

'My Seasprite is a fast girl, so it depends what ships they are. If we hug the coast come daylight, they might steer clear or find easier prey. But if they persist and get close enough to use their cannon ...' he shrugs.

'Let's see if we can outrun them first.'

Orghast nods grimly.

'By the All Father's will, let's hope so!' he says, kissing his knuckles.

'By the All Father's will,' I echo, copying Orghast's gesture.

Orghast claps me gently on the shoulder.

'Right. I'm going to get some sleep. Sams, the Seasprite is yours. Unless something untoward happens, wake me and the crew just before dawn.'

I watch Orghast round up his crew, issuing quiet instructions. Within minutes, lanterns are extinguished, plunging the ship into near darkness, leaving just the small lantern at the helm and the moon and stars for illumination. I can only approve. If those ships are following us, he just made it a little harder. With a final wave, he and all but two of the crew disappears into the warm glow below deck. I know I should follow and rest, but I'm not tired, and I want to listen to the whispers.

However, maybe because it's the dead of night, there are none to be heard. It would seem the All Father, or Fathers, sleep like most other mortals.

I go and stand next to Sams, interested in the large map housed behind a large glass pane on the wheel pulley housing. It shows coastal routes, currents, ports, and islands, all carefully inked in fine, precise strokes.

'You must have incredible eyesight to see any of that,' Sams chuckles as I trace our route. 'I can barely make out the compass.'

'Years of studying religious texts under candlelight,' I reply smoothly, my fingers tracing the intricate web of sea routes. 'Tell me. Why don't we continue due south past Rolantria, give a wide birth to the east coast of the Isle of Sins, and then cut west again toward Tars?'

Sams flashes me a quick smile.

'It looks easy enough on the map, but in reality?' He shakes his head. 'We'd likely never make it. The pirate fleet's main harbour is on that side, and they have coastal batteries to defend it. If we were spotted, we'd either be blown to pieces or get chased down for sure.'

So we hug the coast and hope for the best?' I ask.

'Don't worry, Sister,' Sams grins. 'I'm sure those bastards following us will give up. The Astorian navy patrols between Tars and up the Rolantrian coast during daylight. The pirates won't risk a battle without the chance of easy loot.'

'Let's hope you're right,' I say.

With a nod, I leave Sams to his duty and make my way back to the stern, drawn once more to the darkness stretching endlessly behind us.

Except the ships' lights to our north are more visible now, flickering in and out of sight as the swells rise and fall. They're not gaining, but they're not falling away either. I doubt they can see us, not when we only have a compass lantern lit, but unless we or they change course, they have no reason to lose us.

With several hours to daylight, I finally give in to reason and head below decks, the absence of the whispers in my mind, for once strangely disquieting.

***

The ship's bell jolts me awake, and I roll out of my hammock, already fully dressed. Stepping out into the corridor outside of my cabin, I'm swept along by the other crew members as they pound up the wooden stairs to the deck. Orghast follows at a more sedate pace, his movements almost regal. He's been through this before and it shows.

The eastern horizon glows with the first blush of dawn, painting the clouds in deep purples and streaks of amber as the crew buzz around like bees, checking the rigging.

To our north, the five ships are much closer, their ominous shapes rising above the angry waves.

'Sams,' Orghast says, his voice calm but firm. 'Have the cannon made ready. If those pirate bastards think we might fight, they might just go on their merry way.'

'Prepare for battle!' Sams yells, relinquishing the helm as Orghast joins me on the slightly raised quarterdeck and takes his place at the wheel.

'Don't worry, it's unlikely we'll fight,' Orghast says quietly to me as I stand next to him. 'I just like to see Sams excited and it's good practice for the crew.'

He gazes fondly at his nephew as he bounds around the deck barking orders.

The crew leap to obey, run below decks and then work in relay to pass up cannon balls, chain shot, powder bags, spikes, water buckets, ramrods, wadding, swabs, and torches.

For the next few minutes, I watch, impressed, as the gun rails are greased, pulleys are tested, and the cannons are run smoothly in and out.

Sams looks toward us.

'Load!' Orghast bellows.

I'm impressed. For a merchant ship, the crew are highly trained. In just over half a minute, the eight cannons are loaded, and torches lit.

'If the pirates close and engage, we won't return fire,' he says, watching the looming silhouettes behind us. 'We'll drop the sails and let them board. It's happened to me twice in the last five years. They'll search the ship, take our supplies, threaten us a bit, and then leave.'

'But why not fight?' I ask. 'You have cannons.'

'To fire them, we'd have to turn side on,' Orghast explains. 'We'd get off one broadside, maybe two before they passed our bow and stern, and their shots would carry through the length of our hull. We'd all die within a minute.'

I fold my arms, considering his words.

'So why all this?' I nod toward the ready crew, the loaded cannons, and the torches burning like small embers.

'If they see us armed and ready to fight, they might let us go.'

'And you're confident they'll let us go even if they board?' I press.

'Gah. As near as can be. If we were laden with goods or slaves, they'd possibly put a crew aboard and take the whole ship and us too. But no, we're carrying nothing of value and mostly worthless to them.'

He looks over his shoulder at the lights.

'They've really closed on us during the night,' he says. 'Well, dawn is but a few minutes away. We'll know their intentions shortly.'

He loops a rope around the wheel to keep the ship steady, then walks to the stern. The Seasprite passes through a bank of fog, and for a while it's like we're in an ethereal realm where sound is swallowed whole.

When we break clear, Orghast begins counting slowly under his breath. The water is definitely calmer, although the sails are still full, and we're making good speed.

'Nine hundred,' Orghast mutters as the ships break clear of the fog bank. 'Look at those beauties. Cutters, all five of them.'

I watch as flags are run up the masts.

'Thank the gods,' Orghast says, laughing. 'It's our navy.'

Flashes and billowing smoke erupt from their bows.

'And they probably just want us to drop sails for inspection or to join us for breakfast,' he adds, winking. 'What a relief!'

He turns around, drawing breath.

'Don't give the order, Captain,' I say, pressing the tip of a dagger to his lower back hard enough for him to flinch in pain.

'What the hells, Sister,' Orghast hisses, spinning around, trying to trap my hand, but he's too slow.

I grab the back of his neck with one hand, and press the dagger's edge to his throat with the other, shielding my action with his body, and for the first time, raise my head and look directly into his shocked eyes.

'Do you know who I am?' I whisper, baring my teeth.

His ruddy cheeks pale, and he trembles violently.

'Tell me!' I demand when he says nothing. 'You're taught about me from the moment you're old enough to listen, so you should know.'

'The Queen of B-beasts,' he stammers.

'That's right. Now, do you believe me when I say that I can kill you, your nephew, and every one of your crew and you couldn't do a thing about it?'

He manages to nod.

'Good. Because if you do as I ask, I won't need to, and it will stop me from devouring your nephew's soul, and condemning him to the hells for all eternity!'

I pause briefly, letting my words sink in.

'Now,' I continue, my voice low. 'Can we outrun them?'

'No.' The word barely escapes Orghast's lips. 'They'll be on us within the half hour.'

'Let's return to the helm, Captain. Your crew will be awaiting your orders. Make sure they stay at their posts.'

I steer him toward the helm.

'As you are!' Orghast bellows, as I keep my dagger against his kidneys.

'Keep heading due south,' I say, spotting the next fog bank rapidly approach.

Whispers scratch at the fringes of my mind, catching my attention.

'I've found her. Not long... my ... not long!'

'Do you have a long glass?'

Orghast says nothing, just reaches into a leather bag, and then passes one to me.

'Think of how much you love your nephew before you do anything stupid,' I say, taking it, and returning to the aft rail.

As I train the long glass across the Astorian navy vessels, it takes but a second to see a white-robed figure with a long glass of his own standing on the forecastle of the centre boat.

'Bastard,' I hiss, returning to Orghast's side, placing the long glass on the map.

'Forgive me for saying so,' Orghast says, his voice lowered. 'But we can't outrun those cutters, and we'll be sunk if we fight them.'

We pass through another thick bank of fog.

'Captain!' Sams' voice cuts through the silence. 'What are your orders? Shall we stand down?'

'What shall I say?' Orghast whispers. 'It's highly unusual to stay at action stations if we're not facing an enemy.'

I say nothing as I look at the map, my dagger briefly going to Orghast's groin, a silent warning.

'Stay at your stations!' Orghast bellows. 'I'll tell you when to stand down, Master Sams!'

'Whereabouts are we now?' I ask.

'About here.' Orghast says, tapping on the map off the south-eastern corner of Rolantria. 'We need to turn west now, or we'll be in pirate waters before we know it.'

I trace my finger along the map, calculating silently.

'How much do you earn in a year, Captain?''

'What?'

'Simple question. How much do you earn in a year?'

He huffs, shifting uncomfortably.

'After expenses, paying the crew, maintaining the Seasprite, not much. Enough to get by.'

I growl, making him flinch.

'Somewhere between two and three gold pieces,' he adds hastily.

I reach inside my robe, yank the gold pouch free, and thump it down on the map.

'There's a good chance we're going to die, but there's about seventy gold pieces in there. If we survive, you'll be rich, so I suggest you do everything you can to make that happen when the time comes.'

Orghast swallows hard, his eyes flicking between the pouch and me.

'When the time comes,' Orghast mutters, half to himself.

The fog bank parts like a curtain, and for the first time in weeks, the sun makes a rare appearance, and gulls appear, hovering, looking for scraps.

'Turn a few degrees to starboard.'

Orghast stiffens.

'That will take us too close to the Isle of Sins!' he moans. 'We can't just sail into their harbour. They'll blow us out of the water if we approach unescorted.'

'Question me again, Captain, and your guts will be round your ankles,' I hiss, looking back at our wake.

This time when the navy cutters appear, I don't need a long glass to see the All Father standing amongst some uniformed officers on the prow of his ship.

Flames and smoke blossom, and this time, a few seconds later, water spouts appear a hundred paces from the stern.

'Uncle?' Sams' voice wavers with uncertainty.

'It's *Captain* to you, Master Sams,' Orghast bellows. 'Another word out of turn and you'll be sent below decks!'

More fog envelops us, thicker than before. Orghast reaches out to the ship's bell, but I stay his hand.

'I should ring it, or we might run into someone,' he says.

'No.'

Again, we're through into a patch of sunlight, and off to the southeast, a distant shoreline briefly appears. Even in that snatched moment, I catch sight of walls and dark grey buildings. Two small fishing boats are just off our port side, and I can see the crew's surprise and panic as they catch sight of us and our Astorian flag.

Another rumble of cannon, and this time the splashes are just off our stern.

'Closer to the coast,' I demand, gripping Orghast's shoulder.

'They won't run aground,' he says, his knuckles white as he grips the wheel.

I ignore him, praying for us to reach the next fogbank,

More roars, and this time, the shots bracket us. Water showers the decks before we're swallowed up again by the damp fog.

I have her. I have her!' the All Father in the following ship crows.

'Kill her. Kill her. Don't let her escape!'

I mentally push the distracting whispers away.

The crew are shouting in concern.

'Quiet,' yells Sams, his voice breaking slightly. 'Maintain your stations. Trust in the captain!'

Orghast turns to me, his eyes imploring, but I shake my head.

'When we leave this fog bank, Captain, we will fight. Do you understand?'

Orghast bites his lip.

'Do you understand?' I repeat, my voice low, a menacing hiss.

I receive a determined, abrupt nod.

Then suddenly we're out in the open sea, the fog behind us, into the bright morning sunshine and we're amongst over two dozen anchored pirate ships, the fortified walls of the harbour and citadel looming over us.

'Order your crew to open fire, and find us a way through!' I command.

Orghast looks at me in disbelief, but only until I lift my dagger.

'Open fire, and keep firing!' he shouts.

'On what?' Sams retorts.

'Anything,' bellows Orghast. 'Bloody target anything!'

'Open fire!' Sams' shouts, echoing his uncle's order.

The Seasprite's guns thunder, sliding back on their runners, and the wooden sides of the two vessels we're slipping in between erupt in a shower of splinters.

Shouts and screams carry across the water, and a siren goes off from the harbour walls as men and women stream onto the decks of the surrounding ships.

The crew are already readying the guns again, swabbing the barrels, ramming down the powder charges, wadding, and balls, before spiking the charge through the touchhole.

'FIRE!' Sams' screams, and the guns roar a second time, and at such close range, it's impossible to miss.

Then we're past the first two ships, leaving them wrecked in our wake, their hulls a broken mess.

Ahead, the decks of the next two pirate vessels are already swarming with sailors, and they're frantically preparing their guns for a broadside for when we pass between them.

Orghast spins the wheel, bringing us around the stern of the next pirate ship and along their port side instead of their starboard.

The frantic screams of the pirate crew rise to fever pitch as they realise they've been outmanoeuvred, and our cannon roar. At such close range, the cannonballs punch through the wooden hull and across the deck, tearing planking and men apart.

Ahead, ships are lowering their sails, preparing to give chase.

Then splinters begin to fly, and two of Orghast's men drop screaming to the deck as our ship is raked by intermittent musket fire.

Suddenly, gouts of flame from the island, followed by a roll of thunder, announce the harbour gun batteries opening fire, and I find myself gripping Orghast's shoulder tightly.

'We're done for,' he cries, biting his lip so hard that blood runs down his chin.

Yet not a shot lands near us, and I turn back to see the five Astorian navy cutters frantically trying to manoeuvre amongst the pirate ships, spouts of water all round them, rigging and masts falling.

Broadsides begin to go off between the powerful navy ships and the pirate vessels as we skim through, mostly unmolested, Orghast spinning the wheel left and right, throwing the schooner around like a small skiff.

Cannons roar on a nearby pirate vessel and I watch as one of our starboard cannon gets spun onto its side, the top half of a seaman behind it disappearing in a bloody spray.

'Reload!' Sams yells, running up and down the deck, stepping in to help the crews. Suddenly he staggers back against the mainmast and slides down.

'SAMS!' Orghast cries.

'GO!' I command, taking the wheel, and Orghast almost flies from the quarterdeck to help his nephew.

A deck rail explodes in a deadly rain of splinters and a port cannon and crew are out of action. Our starboard cannon keeps firing, their crewmembers blackened by powder smoke.

'The sails!' Orghast yells, looking up from Sams. 'Target the sails!'

The cannon crews scramble to obey, loading chain shot instead of cannonballs.

The Seasprite shudders, once, twice, but keeps moving, responsive to the helm.

Then a deafening crack, and the base of the mizzenmast below the quarterdeck shatters. There's a terrible groan, and it falls over the port side, the sail and rigging fouling the ship, slowing it dramatically.

A man goes overboard, snared by a trailing rope, but his screams for help go unanswered, as six of the port-side gunners go to work, hacking away in a frenzy with belt hatchets.

Splinters from musket balls tear up the planking, but no one is hit, and within a minute, we're free, and picking up speed again.

Musket fire continues to harass us, the map glass shatters, and one of the ship's wheel spokes just disappears as I'm picked out as a target, but for once I'm charmed, and except for some splinter wounds, I'm not hit.

The three starboard cannons continue to roar, sending chain shot ripping through enemy sails on the closest pirate ships whose anchors were raised to give chase.

And then, bar some fishing boats, there's nothing but open sea ahead, while behind us the battle continues to rage.

Three pirate ships list helplessly, two are aflame, their masts and sails burning ferociously, and as I watch, the navy cutter with the All Father on board erupts in a violent explosion as fire or a heated cannon ball ignites its powder magazine.

With four powerful, albeit heavily damaged Astorian ships amongst them, the pirates turn their full fury on the enemy in their midst, their hatred of the Astorian navy outweighing any thought of pursuit.

A few minutes later, we slip into a fog bank, and away.

With a sigh of relief, I take a moment to focus on the whispers at the edge of my consciousness, bringing them to the forefront of my thoughts. Now the voices are clear as if spoken right next to me.

'What happened?'

'Is he dead?'

'Our brother died nobly!' a firm voice says, quieting the clamour.

I can't resist myself.

'His body was blown to pieces,' I say silently. *'He'll be food for the fish and seagulls, if they can stomach the taste of his putrid flesh!'*

Shocked silence follows my mental declaration.

'I know you can hear me,' I continue, cold and assured. *'I can sense you now, and I know you're afraid, and you should be. I know your secrets, I know where you are, and there's something else I want you to know.'*

I pause, letting them wait, enjoying the moment.

'I'm coming for you. All of you!'

Silence, a void, nothingness …

'We'll be waiting!'

***

There's no celebration aboard the Seasprite. No cheers, no laughter, just a silent, dazed disbelief among the crew. They stand motionless, barely able to process the fact that they're still alive.

With a following wind ensuring our progress, I tie the ship's wheel in place, and go down to the deck where the stench of gunpowder, sweat, and blood hangs thick in the air.

I grab the first two sailors I come across.

'Get the cook boiling water,' I snap, shoving them toward the deck hatch, 'and come straight back with a bottle of spirit, bandages, and a needle and thread. NOW!'

Their surprise at my rough gesture and commanding tone snaps them from their daze, and they thump down the stairs, shouting.

I kneel by Orghast. Sams' eyes are closed, but he's alive, and cursing.

'Sorry, Uncle,' he cries. 'I tried my best.'

'You did fine, lad,' Orghast sniffs. 'I'm proud of you,'

Blood soaks Sams' shirt from the waist up, and yet Orghast just holds his hand, as if sheer willpower alone can keep the boy from slipping away.

'Move,' I say, pushing him aside. Lifting the shirt, the familiar hole of a gunshot wound glistens. With dagger in hand, I turn to Orghast, who moans in fear, yet before he can even move, I cut one of his sleeves away, screw it up in a ball, then press it hard against the wound.

'Sams. Hold this tight against here,' I say, taking his hand and putting it over the cloth. 'You understand?'

The lad nods, gritting his teeth against the pain as I cut away his shirt so it doesn't get in the way.

Turning him roughly to look at his back causes him to cry out.

'Don't hurt him anymore!' Orghast cries, distraught.

'I'm trying to save his life,' I retort. 'Now, attend to your crew. Any badly injured, send them to me. After that, check your ship and don't you dare change course. Now, GO!'

Orghast glares at me, but his will doesn't match mine, and he stumbles off. He's a good, professional captain, but shock can unhinge even the most able.

Leaning forward, I take a closer look at my patient. The skin on Sams' back is unbroken, but heavily bruised and swollen.

'Be brave, Sams,' I say. 'You're going to be alright.'

I run my fingertips gently over his skin, locating the solid bulge of a musket ball beneath the skin.

My dagger slices across the taut flesh, and in a small eruption, the ball and a stream of blood drop to the decking. Credit to Sams, he only whimpers, although his body is shaking badly.

The two sailors I'd sent below reappear, placing everything I'd asked for beside me.

'More hot water,' I demand, without looking up, threading the needle with steady fingers. It's thicker than I'd like, but this is a ship, not a dressmakers, and it will do.

Orghast bellows at his crew, his voice bringing order to the chaos, and I allow myself a moment's relief. While he keeps them occupied, there's no time for mischief.

I pour spirit over the needle, then push the bottle into Sams' hand.

'Drink!'

He swallows several times before I pull the spirit away.

'Now, count backwards from a hundred, and I'll be done. Ready?'

The lad nods, and I smile at his bravery. He barely flinches as I sew up the small cut in his back before rolling him over and doing the same to the entry wound. I wipe the blood away with some spirit soaked bandages, pleased with my handiwork.

'Now I understand,' Sams moans.

From where he lies, he can see right into my hood and he's studying me intently.

'Then I suggest you keep quiet and don't do anything foolish that will make me regret saving your life,' I say softly. 'Now, sit up so I can bandage you.'

Sams hesitates, his expression unreadable.

'Why?' he mutters. 'Why help me?'

I shake my head as I bind the bandages tightly around his waist.

'Maybe I'm not as bad as everyone thinks I am,' I say with a gentle smile.

Sams looks around at the carnage, at the bloodied deck, the wreckage of battle, and the bodies of the crew he'll never laugh with again. Then he looks back at me, eyes filled with something I can't quite place.

'I think you probably are,' he whispers, trembling.

Two other sailors stand nearby, waiting, but their wounds are minor, and only require cleaning and binding. I keep my head down, angry at myself for being unmasked again.

Orghast comes over to check on Sams, but I intercept him.

'One moment,' I say, gripping his forearm tightly as he tries to pull away.

'Take Sams to his cabin. He needs rest and if he pulls those stitches, he'll risk infection. Otherwise, he'll be fine … as long as he doesn't say anything to anyone.'

Orghast stiffens.

'He knows?'

'He does. Now, make sure he understands the gravity of the situation while you put him in his bunk. Then I want you to join me at the helm soonest.'

I release Orghast's arm and head to the quarterdeck. From the crew's demeanour, I'm aware they're uncomfortable that I'm taking the helm, but their discipline stops them from interfering. Checking the compass, I release the ship's wheel, and bring the Seasprite around a few degrees toward the southwest. She responds more sluggishly than usual, and as we settle on our new bearing, it's obvious she hasn't returned to an even keel.

Securing the wheel, I dart to the starboard side and lean over the rail. A hole, jagged and dark, mars the smooth planking, but I know the Seasprite had definitely been hit by cannon fire twice.

'Get the captain!' I yell, pointing at a sailor as he turns toward the sound of my voice.

'I don't take orders from a sister,' he shouts back angrily. 'Not when I'm aboard my captain's ship. Not when you being on board had something to do with us almost getting killed.'

I point to the side.

'We're holed below the waterline,' I yell. 'Do you want to sink or pick an argument?'

The rest of the crew looks on. They're already distraught at losing their crewmates, and this outburst could turn ugly.

'You don't sound like no sister to me!' he shouts, but nonetheless leaps through the hatch, calling for the captain.

Orghast comes bounding up moments later, the sailor in tow.

He doesn't even look at me as his sharp gaze sweeps across the ship.

'We've got four pumps, and you lazy bastards are standing around,' he bellows. 'Two to each pump and the rest of you, lower those sails now.' He steps in to shove the slowest. 'Pump for your lives unless you enjoy swimming with the sharks!'

He disappears below decks and emerges again a minute later carrying tarred sailcloth and a wooden cone, and comes to join me at the helm.

'Don't suppose you fancy a swim?' he asks, without a hint of humour. 'My poor ship and crew. They'll never be the same again, thanks to you.'

Dropping the items at his feet, he strips off, his darkly weathered face and hands utterly at odds with his pale body. Yet he's tough, all sinew and no fat. Gathering the items, he runs to the main deck, tosses them at a member of his crew while another ties a rope around his waist.

Without hesitation, he leaps over the side.

I tie off the helm and lean over the rail. He's down for a count of maybe twenty before he surfaces, lifting his hands. A moment later, the wooden cone and sailcloth join him in the water.

This time he's down for longer, but when he finally appears, he's empty handed.

He's hauled on board, the crew slapping him on the back. There's no joy or celebration, just relief. Nonetheless, his face is dour as he tiredly climbs the steps to join me on the quarterdeck.

'Well, don't just stand there, even if Master Sams is taking a nap!' he shouts back at the crew. 'Take shifts on the pumps, and get the sails hoisted.'

He stands unashamed, allowing the wind to dry his body before he begins to clothe himself. His movements are slow and tired.

'It's not looking too good,' he says, pulling his boots on. 'I've plugged the hole best I can, but the planking is badly splintered. The pumps will have to be manned from here to port or we will go under. So, tell me, Nogotha. Where exactly will we be docking? Ssythla, by any chance?'

'Yes. The southernmost tip. However, let me assure you, Captain, that I'll keep my word. I want you, your nephew, and your crew, to live. Your ship will be repaired without harm coming to you or them.'

'Hah. If only I could believe that.'

'You have to, because the alternative will end up with you dead. Now, no more questions. Look to your ship, keep your crew in line, and leave me be.'

'Yes, Captain,' Orghast growls, and stamps off, his displeasure plain to see, yet nor does he disobey.

As the day draws on, we continue on our voyage south while the Seasprite receives some loving care. Timber and tools are brought from below, and the crew work in shifts, manning the pumps and shaping timber to repair the railings. Between rests, they often glance my way, and I know trouble is brewing. I don't want there to be as the only way it will end is with blood.

Day turns to night, and still Orghast and the crew toil away, and whilst their work is physical, they also get to rest, while I don't dare.

'Captain,' I call.

I note several of his crew speak to Orghast while gesturing angrily in my direction, before he waves them to silence and comes up to join me.

'What?' he asks, stifling a yawn.

'I'm going to pass you the helm. You'll keep on this heading throughout the night, passing the helm to a crew member if you have to rest. I intend to keep your nephew company while I sleep. If I'm aware of the ship changing course, or if there's any attempt by you to break our agreement, he'll be the first to die.'

'Is death the only currency you bargain with?' he snaps.

'If I thought the gold was enough, I'd leave it at that,' I say, not rising to his comment. 'Just keep that crew of yours from doing something foolish.'

I look him in the eyes, until he nods, then take my leave, keeping my head down, ignoring the soft curses and mutterings the crew direct my way. I smile to myself. Perhaps my behaviour is undermining their belief in the All Father and the church.

I walk down the steps to Sams' cabin, then pause at the door. A gentle lantern's glow emanates from underneath. Sams should definitely be sleeping, Orghast must know he needs rest … just like he knew I'd also need rest, somewhere safe.

Moving silently, I pull my robe over my head, draw a sword, then hold the robe on its point behind the door as I knock lightly on the wood.

'Sams. It's Malina, the Sister from the Church Eternal,' I say, loud enough to ensure he hears.

Pressing the latch, I throw the door open, the bang as it crashes against the wall matched by musket fire that has my robe twitch as the ball smacks into the passage wall behind me.

Stepping inside the small room, I quickly sheath my sword and don my robe, before easing the musket from Sams' shaking hands, placing it on the floor and sitting on the small bed next to him.

I wrap one arm casually around his neck, a dagger in hand, as Orghast pounds down the stairs, and along the corridor. He comes to stand in the doorway, and his body sags as he sees us sitting there.

'Did that sound like a one-off roll of thunder to you, Captain? I hope so,' I say. 'Because if there's any more, I'm going to cut your nephew's throat like lightning. What do you think, Captain?'

'No. No more. I swear!'

'Swear on your nephew's life,' I say, caressing his neck with the dagger's edge.

'I swear on Sams' life,' Orghast rasps.

'Close the door, Captain. This is the first and last time you'll disobey me and live.'

Sam's cabin is modest but comfortable. A small bed instead of a hammock, and a cushioned chair in the opposite corner. I help myself to some unfinished food on a plate, wash it down with some water, blow out the lamp, bolt the door, and then take my place in the chair.

'Goodnight, Sams. Sleep well, and you'll see your uncle again on the morrow,' I say, then close my eyes.

***

I wake, rested and refreshed, grateful for an uninterrupted night's sleep absent dreams. Sams is fast asleep, and I move quietly to his side and gently touch his brow.

His temperature is good, and I smile. Despite him trying to shoot me, I hold no ill will toward him. Picking up the old musket, I break off the hammer mechanism, rendering it useless, and then slide it quietly beneath his bed.

The wooden door fits well, but there are a few thin cracks, and I take my time, peering into the corridor beyond, watching, listening, ensuring it's empty.

Beyond the gently creaking hull, there's nothing. No strange shadows, no shallow breathing, nothing but the sound of a ship at sea. Still, I wait a little longer before I unbolt and cautiously open the door.

Still nothing.

Dagger ready, I slip quietly along the corridor toward the deck hatch.

As I reach the bottom step, snatched conversation filters down, as does the creak of hand pumps, the flapping of sails.

I conceal the dagger back up my sleeve as I ascend the stairs, feeling vulnerable with my hood up. My peripheral vision is compromised as is my hearing, but I don't want to risk the bloodshed that being identified would bring about.

I breathe a sigh of relief upon reaching the deck, yet at the same time, despite a breeze, the air is warm and humid.

Orghast is at the helm, his face shadowed from exhaustion. The crew are scattered about, some sleeping, sprawled out on sheets of folded sail cloth, while others tiredly man the pumps, their movements sluggish, shirts clinging to sweat-slicked skin.

Other than the heat, everything is as it should be, and I'm relieved. This crew has suffered enough.

'Thank you,' I say to Orghast, trying to soften the tension between us. 'Sams is doing well. He's asleep, no fever, and his colour is good.'

A shuddering breath escapes Orghast, his eyes misting, and he brusquely wipes his tears away before they can form.

'Please don't get angry,' he says, trembling with fear. 'But we won't be able to make it to Ssythla. We've repaired the hull as much as possible below decks, and the water ingress has slowed, but the pumps are wearing out, and we're slowly taking on more water. I give us four or maybe five days before we founder.'

To see him in such a way fills me with regret. In his eyes, I'm the very monster he's been raised to fear his whole life.

'Show me where we are,' I ask.

Orghast brushes broken glass from the map. There's a hole in the middle of Astoria from a musket shot, and I can't help but hope it's an omen.

'We're about here,' he says, pointing to the map. 'If we turn due west now, we can make Tars.'

I stare at the map, considering my options. There's a possibility he's lying about the ship's condition, but the squeaking pumps tell me they're not working as well as they should, and with the exhausted crew flagging, there's more chance he's telling the truth, especially considering how scared he is.

'We continue southeast for another couple of hours until we reach here,' I say, pointing to the map. 'Then you can head to Tars.'

Orghast grits his teeth.

'Listen. I've never sailed these waters before,' he mutters. 'But I've heard it gets near impossible to navigate further south. Why not turn west now?'

I glare at him till he looks down.

'You have your orders, Captain,' I say, and move to the stern.

There are no whispered conversations to listen in on, and as the sun has still yet to crest the horizon, I can only imagine it's because the All Fathers aren't early risers.

The gulls are, though. They hover and dive, their wings outstretched, rising and falling like the waves, utterly unconcerned by the shifting tides of power and war. But they should be, because the cancer of industrialisation will affect every living being before long.

A gust of wind sweeps past, attempting to whip my hood back, and for a moment, I let myself breathe it in, the scent of salt, the bite of brine. The sea calls to me, something ancient, something deep.

Absent magic, I can still sense its power, and by comparison, my own insignificance. Does this world really need my help when these seas could rise up and wash away every trace of humanity? Probably not. But nor do I want to risk my world suffering the same fate if I'm wrong.

Not forgetting that I'm to blame.

If Nogoth still lived, Astoria would never have risen, no factories would now belch their poison into the sky. Yes, the fey would have invaded, and hundreds of thousands would have perished, but is that not the case anyway ... and absent the Saer Tel's healing hands, the world has just sickened.

I'm surprised how much time has passed when I'm broken from my thoughts by wildly flapping sails. The sun has passed its zenith, and the steady wind has turned blustery, creating small white-capped waves.

'Sister!' Orghast calls, his voice rising above the snapping canvas. 'We have to turn!'

I go stand by his side as he points ahead, and now I understand his fears. Towering waves, the water twisting and breaking, await. Beyond it, vaguely visible through the mist and spray, an island looms, but between the tropical sanctuary and us, is the maelstrom.

'The Seasprite will come apart if we attempt to pass through that,' he shouts, fighting to hold the wheel steady. Below, the crew frantically pumps away, but they're casting concerned glances in our direction.

'There's no need, Captain,' I say, unhooking the waterproof bag holding the long-glass. Removing the heavy instrument, I place it on the broken map case. 'Do you have a lighter?'

He reaches into a pocket, and as I open the bag, he drops one in.

'Listen carefully,' I say. 'When you make Tars, leave your ship behind. You, or Sams, might be tempted to talk to someone in authority about me being on board. Just don't, because if you do, you'll be executed.'

I pause, letting my words sink in.

'You were complicit in my escape,' I continue. 'Because of you, five navy ships were sunk. Pay off your crew, disappear with the gold, and live a good life.'

The sun is off to the west, the island directly to my south as I step away from Orghast to the rear rail, casting aside my robe. Orghast glances over his shoulder in disbelief as I unhook my scabbards, letting my swords fall to the deck. My shirt, trousers, and boots go into the bag and I pull the drawstring tight, fold over the top, and tie it again, pressing it as flat as possible to remove any air before securing it to my belt. My two daggers are secure, sheathed within my leather vambraces.

Orghast gapes as I step onto the rail, balanced, poised, staring down at the water below.

'Remember what I said, Captain. Say nothing.'

Sketching a brief salute, I dive over the portside into the hungry sea.

'Help me.'

The silent plea escapes me unbidden, a habit of a lifetime spent wielding magic so hard to lose, but this battle will be won by skill and muscle alone. I swim under the heavy swells, long, slow strokes, not fighting, but gently easing myself through the sea, enjoying its cool embrace.

Learn to love something, and you'll never need fear it.

Lystra's words echo in my mind, a lesson drilled into me in countless battles, in endless nights of training beneath a starlit sky. She was right. Immerse yourself, and the body will forget exhaustion. Lose yourself, and fear will never take hold.

Sunlight filters through the waves, turning the world below into a turquoise wonderland. Schools of iridescent fish dart around me, inquisitive to my lumbering form, humbling me with their speed, turning left and right in perfect synchronicity.

They surround me, inquisitive, bold, their shining scales reflecting the world around them in fractured, shimmering light. For a moment, I am one of them, part of this pristine, unspoiled realm, where the troubles of the land do not exist.

Reluctantly, I silently bid them farewell, and rise to the surface, drawing breath while checking the sun's position above the towering waves to my right. Having got my bearings, I joyfully immerse myself again, eager for the next spectacle.

Deeper I swim, finding calmer waters. Below, an octopus, its tentacles ribboning outward, slips off into the dark abyss in search of prey. This is a different world down here, and I'm but a visitor, and as much as I find these underwater denizens strange, I'm the stranger.

Over and again, I break the surface, breathing deeply as I tread water, locating the sun and the island before returning to the depths.

A dolphin comes to investigate. It circles, watching, assessing, before coming closer, eyes intelligent and warm. I reach out, and as my fingers brush the smooth curve of its beak, it clicks in greeting.

I hold its fin, and off it goes, spearing through the water. Had I been able to open my mouth and yell with excitement, I'd have done so. It reminds me of riding my nightmare, that thrill of raw power, the speed and exhilaration unmatched.

Releasing the friendly creature, I rise to the surface to find the sea becalmed, and a golden beach within easy distance. The tides assists as I increase the power of my strokes, keen to reach land. Before long, the sea bed rises gently under my feet and I wade through the surf while it pushes me with friendly enthusiasm toward the shore.

The sea breeze and sun feel incredible on my skin as I walk onto the damp sand. For a long moment, I simply stand there, the breeze tangling through my hair, exhilarated by an unexpected sense of rebirth.

Drawing breath, invigorated, I head south, naked, enjoying a sense of freedom long forgotten.

The vegetation bordering the beach is lush, a thousand beautiful shades of green, red, yellow, and orange. After the grey bleakness of Astoria, the rainbow of colours leaves me breathless.

Leaving the sun behind, I walk into the undergrowth, the calls of a thousand birds joining together in welcoming song.

This is what the world was meant to be without the spread of humanity.

Pure. Unspoiled. Free.

Within half a dozen paces, I'm rewarded with bunches of plump berries. I gorge myself, enjoying their sweet taste, feeling both thirst and hunger satiated before I return to the beach and the surf line.

Despite there being no need for urgency, my body hums with renewed energy, and I begin to run. Not for survival, not for battle, but for the sheer joy of it.

The sand shifts beneath my feet, the waves lap eagerly at my heels, and not long after I reach the small island's southern shore.

The sun is dropping toward the horizon, but there are at least two hours of daylight remaining, and the next island isn't far, so I run into the waves, welcoming the cool water as much as I'd embraced the warmth of the sun's rays.

Powerful strokes have me cross the small channel into another paradise, then a half hour later, yet another.

A shiver runs through me, a pleasurable jolt, a sense of awe, as I find myself on familiar ground.

After hundreds of years, or indeed, if my age is gauged by this world's standards, thousands, my footsteps have brought me full circle, for there to the south, rising majestically into the sky, is the Mountain of Souls.

***

CHAPTER XVIII

Birdsong, the whispering swish of the surf, and the rustle of a million leaves stir me from sleep, ushering in the beginning of a new day.

My perch in the tree, though hardly luxurious, ensured I rested safely, and I wake with a lightness of heart I haven't enjoyed since I was enfolded by Lotane's arms.

Lotane.

It's been too long since circumstances allowed me the indulgence to think of my love, and I allow myself a few minutes to remember the soft curve of his ready smile, the music of his laughter, and the sense of oneness as we lie, limbs entwined, in the quiet aftermath of our joining.

How is he? Has he healed? What's he doing? Does he dream of me?

I have a thousand questions with no answers, only the faint, fragile hope that one day soon, I'll have them.

A short leap to the ground and I stretch my muscles while taking stock of my surroundings. Once, the north of the island was scarred by a ssythlan town and docks. Yet there's no residual sign of any habitation.

The power of nature has erased everything, and my spirit eye confirms what my heart already knows, this island is awash with elemental magic and the gold of creation.

There's a strange sense of wrongness as I pull on my shirt and trousers, an affront to this place that has thrown off anything manmade, but, while flimsy, they will still offer me some protection from scratches and bites. However, there's something about being barefoot that allows me to connect with my environment, so I hang my boots around my neck.

Tucking Orghast's lighter into a trouser pocket, I step lightly into the undergrowth, gathering fruits from bushes and trees, filling the waterproof bag. I'll need something more substantial to eat, but with the island teeming with wildlife, that shouldn't prove a problem.

A tall sapling soon becomes a rudimentary, but serviceable wooden spear, and I'm as ready as I'll be with what I have to hand.

Despite the hundreds of years, it seems like only yesterday I walked this land. The flora is so familiar, the scent and sounds a thread of memory woven into my very essence.

I know my initial stay here was traumatic, a ritual of fear, blood and death, and as for my departure, it was even more so, but if truth be told, in between, the best times of my life were had here.

However perverse, I've come to realise that for me to truly savour life, the threat of death must be at my shoulder. To feel the most exquisite pleasure, it has to be mixed with an element of pain.

To eat when famished, to drink when parched, to truly enjoy one, the opposite must always be present.

Even this paradise, with its bright abundance of flora and fauna, intuitively lives to this rule.

From one moment to the next, the bird eats the fat, lazy insect, the snake eats the satisfied bird, or the red wolf eats the swollen snake. Then, however lucky, or powerful, the survivors, time, and then nature, consumes them all.

Slipping back into those years of training takes but a moment, the rhythm of the forest as familiar as my heartbeat. Cries of greeting and happiness blend with cries of alarm, and death, each part of a timeless melody, the song of creation itself.

Animal trails allow me swift but silent passage as I head toward my old home, alert but at peace.

But as the hours stretch, unease creeps into my thoughts.

There's no sign of any life other than animal, and whilst the island is better for it, I'd hoped to find ssythlans here, and I experience a tinge of regret and doubt over my decision.

Had I continued to Tars, I could have slipped into the crowds and made my way to Ssythla with ease, of that I have no doubt.

No, Malina, I admonish myself. *No doubts, no regrets. Just solutions.*

Soft, squeaks, squeals, and grunting, has me slow, placing each foot carefully, testing the ground, ensuring no dry twigs betray my presence.

My spear arm is drawn and ready. A wooden spear is a good thrusting weapon, but inaccurate for throwing, yet the piglet I hear will not let me get close and I'll not risk losing a thrown dagger to the undergrowth.

Then, through leafy fronds, I spot the creature, its snout buried in the damp earth, rooting around, digging up roots and worms with wild enthusiasm.

Its head is toward me, but patience will have it turn away and then ...

A blur, a squeal, and a red wolf snaps the creature up in its jaws and, with two savage crunches, swallows it down.

I freeze, watching as the wolf's powerful muscles bunch and shift, its scaled hide gleaming like burnished metal beneath the filtered sunlight.

Slowly, it looks up and its dark green eyes stare into mine.

The shivers that run down my back are anything but pleasurable as a primal growl rumbles, low and menacing.

RUN.

No! Despite the instinct to flee being almost overwhelming, that would lead to my death, and I wasn't trained to run.

The wolf lowers its head, the rolling power of its shoulders obvious, and moves toward me.

I widen my stance, planting bare feet into the earth. My wooden spear suddenly feels so inadequate, and might not even penetrate its scaled hide, but using my daggers will have me in reach of its fangs.

I twist my feet, lower my body, and turn my hips.

My first thrust must be perfect, right down the wolf's gaping maw, a death blow before it can tear me apart.

The wolf stops just out of reach, like me, a perfect killer waiting for the right moment to strike. We stand there, frozen in time, neither of us moving a muscle, until ... it makes its move.

Not to attack, but to crawl forward on its belly, whining like a puppy until it reaches my feet.

A giant tongue slurps over my bare toes, warm and wet, before the beast lays its head on my foot and lets out a series of soft yaps.

'You can't be serious!' I whisper, suddenly conflicted over whether to kill this creature or not.

A whine meets my disbelief and those red eyes soften.

'You're supposed to be a bloodthirsty, merciless killer,' I murmur, half in disbelief, half in amusement. 'And so am I.'

Laughing softly, I kneel and place my spear carefully to one side, watching the wolf.

'I won't tell anyone about this if you don't.'

I offer the beast the back of my hand, and after a sniff he licks my knuckles.

'You better not see me as dessert.' I mutter.

Never having expected to fuss a red wolf, I wonder how best to approach the task, but when I lean over to fuss its back, it growls and rubs its head against my leg.

'Ouch! That's like getting scraped by tree bark,' I say, lifting its head carefully away.

As I do so, a gentle whine comes from those ferocious jaws.

'Ah. Is this where you like it?' I ask, scratching its ears where the scales are smaller like shells on a beach.

A whine, and a twist of its massive head, and I start rubbing around its jawline, kneading at the firm muscle beneath the scales. The wolf exhales deeply, pressing into my touch, but then ...

'What's this?' I say, feeling a scale standing proud.

A series of whines meets my probing, yet the beast doesn't pull away.

Twisting that giant head allows me to see behind the scale, and there, embedded underneath, is what looks to be a broken tooth.

'Hah. Now I see your purpose. You aren't friendly, just desperate. Let's see what we can do, eh boy?'

The wolf snuffles and shakes as I pluck at the broken end of what is probably a rival wolf's fang, but I can't get enough of a grip.

I pull a dagger from my vambrace and lift that giant head, resting it against my thighs.

'Don't forget it was you who came to me for help,' I say, looking into its eyes. 'Just remember that, when this hurts.'

The wolf is utterly at my mercy, its life in my hands.

I could kill it now, press the blade deep, end the beast's existence before it has the chance to turn on me. It's the sensible thing to do, but I just can't.

Instead, I go about gently worrying the point of my dagger between the scales. It isn't easy, but eventually the weapon is in position.

I tense my thighs, holding its head firmly, add pressure with my forearm, and begin gently twisting it to both open the scales, and to bore a small hole into the side of the broken fang.

The wolf shudders, whining, but I don't relent, and then, as I apply some upward force, the fang reluctantly slides free of the wound.

Within a heartbeat, the wolf is on its feet, its gums pulled back, fangs gleaming. It's so close, I can smell its breath, and I won't even be able to react before it bites my face off, but, almost as if just remembering what I've done, it quietens. With a soft whine, it licks my face before turning and darting off into the undergrowth, the foliage barely moved by its passing.

Shaking my head in wonder and relief, I retrieve my dagger, wiping the wolf's blood from the blade before securing it back into my vambrace.

As I continue my journey, my every sense is alert for danger. The red wolves had never used to come this far north, always preferring the jagged volcanic terrain to the south, or perhaps, on reflection, that was because they were driven there.

Now they've reclaimed their kingdom, and the whole island is theirs again.

I pause every so often to eat fruit and berries, having plucked them from the bushes and trees. It seems gathering supplies was unnecessary considering the abundance of food around, yet I leave my pouch full, as where I'm going, there won't be any food, unless there's an edible rock I'm unaware of.

Memories of Lotane surface, and I can remember the wild joy in his eyes as we raced through these same trees, the heat of his body against mine when we collapsed together in laughter, tangled in the humid embrace of the jungle.

A slow, shuddering breath escapes me, my skin tingling with the memory of his hands, the way he discovered my body. They were such heady days. We were so strong, so vigorous, so in love, and it endured even when the blood magic that bound us was severed. A love to last a lifetime ... with a few painful falling outs along the way.

Another hour slips by, then another, by which time I have a dead snake hanging from my belt, and some edible roots stuffed in my already bulging pouch, and now the terrain begins to slope upwards.

But instead of ascending, I work my way east, keeping to lower ground

As I look up at the Mountain of Souls, rising majestically above the treetops, its mist-wreathed peak barely visible through the foliage, it seems like only yesterday I was here.

Nothing has changed … except the one thing I'd needed to stay the same. Where once there had been a gaping entrance, a cave mouth wide enough to swallow a dozen men, now there's only rock face, as if it never was.

With a frustrated grunt, I push on, and it's just past midday when I reach a large, familiar rock formation marking the entrance to a narrow gully.

How many times did I pass this way, excited at the day's beginning, exhausted and triumphant at the day's end?

Despite there being no sign of life or passage beyond that of animals, I approach quietly, although after so long, I doubt I could move any other way.

Ahead, a massive boulder looms, obstructing the gully, touching both sides, an impassable object, yet I know differently and as I draw closer, I note with satisfaction that the hidden narrow gap still remains.

I've rarely felt such anticipation as I slip past, one of several hidden tunnel entrances to the Mountain of Souls just beyond.

Except … nothing but a solid wall of rock awaits.

I rest my head against the cool surface, willing my non-existent magic to come to my aid, but … nothing.

Like the eastern cave entrance, no rock fall has blocked this passage, no seismic upheaval either. This was sealed magically, and there's no doubt the others will have been too.

I sigh, look up to the heavens, then with a shrug, pull on my boots, cast my wooden spear to one side, and begin to climb.

The gradient isn't punishing to start, although the loose scree makes every step treacherous. Despite the vast bulk of the Mountain obscuring the sun, it's still hot, and I take my time, working my way around to the west.

My final hope for entry is that the ssythlans only sealed the lower entrances when they departed, and that the balconies high up still remain.

I push myself faster, driven by the realisation that if my gamble of coming here doesn't pay off, my chances of leaving this island aren't favourable.

Reckless, I clamber up over sharp, volcanic rock, scree, up sheer faces, hanging on by my fingertips at times. Hours pass, yet I push my fatigue aside, my body a slave to my will.

As I gaze west at the setting sun, the view has me catch my breath, and not just because of its beauty, but because I've stood here and watched this before from almost this exact spot.

Yet, however carefully I look, there's no sign of a balcony anywhere.

Higher I push, confident in my location, excitement building. The Soul Gate, like the world gates, isn't of ssythlan origin, but an ancient artefact. Like them, it must be indestructible, and the long outcropping above is unmistakable, shaped like a huge balcony, and I know I've finally made it.

I climb around, taking my time, draw level with the outcrop, then stop and smile. There's no balcony, no Soul Gate, nothing but mountainside. The ssythlans have closed all the entrances.

I stand there, my chest rising and falling, the wind whispering through the crags, whispering to me.

'Only the strong survive.'

Lystra's voice is as clear as if she were standing at my shoulder.

I lift my head to the sky and howl, then continue my climb.

***

I awake, aching and uncomfortable, my body protesting the night spent curled against unforgiving stone, although thankfully I'm not cold.

Never have I climbed so high.

Above me, wispy clouds swirl, tantalisingly close, their delicate strands decorating an otherwise perfectly clear sky. Below, the whole island is stretched out like a living map at my feet.

From up here, I feel like a god, overseeing the world I've created.

Emptying my pouch, I finish the fruit, the sweet taste utterly divine.

This place had held such horror and pain, where every day was a battle to survive. Yet it was here that I had learned to savour the simplest joys, the taste of fresh food, while enjoying the quiet beauty of a sunrise.

With the lower entrances and balconies sealed, there's only one other option for me to enter the Mountain of Souls.

For a moment, I'm reluctant to ascend the last few steps, and it was the same reluctance that had me stop short of the crater rim the night before. However, with daylight, and feeling fully refreshed, there can be no more delay.

The final ascent is easier than the treacherous climb below. The rock face smooth, the gradient less severe, and within minutes, I crest the rim of the crater and into a forest of dense undergrowth.

I recall my first time in the training circle, looking up at nature's beauty, tantalisingly just out of reach, and whereas then, I'd have done anything to escape, now, I'm trying to find my way in.

Pushing through the dense foliage, I cut and loop long vines over my shoulder, preparing for the descent ahead, squawking birds voicing their protest at my daring invasion of their realm.

Yet this was my home long before it was theirs ... mine, Lotane's, Kralgen's, Nestor's, Fianna's ...

Names and faces come to mind, some of which I haven't thought about in centuries. Seeing what the world had become, would they have been happy with my defeating Nogoth, or mourned what came after?

Would they make the same choices again?

Would I?

What would have been the lesser of the evils ... the systematic conquest of this world by the fey every millennium, or its ongoing subjugation and destruction by the Astorians?

'Focus on the here and now, Malina.'

Gradually the foliage clears, my progress becomes easier, the terrain clearing, and suddenly the bottom of the crater is revealed.

A flash of memory seizes me, so vivid, so real, it steals my breath.

Images of screaming children, running, fighting, striving, desperately trying to take one final breath.

I don't know how long I stand there, unable to move, but thankfully, the images fade, but not the cause of them ... for there, far below, is the training circle.

The vines I've gathered are sturdy, but I weave them carefully together, tying, then checking each knot, knowing that if this is the only way in, this is the only way out. If the rope breaks, this will become my personal tomb.

Tying off the woven vines around the trunk of a sturdy tree, I step backwards and test my handiwork, pulling hard. Satisfied, I step over the crater's edge, and lower myself down the magically smoothed walls into the training circle below.

The last step is akin to leaping off a cliff, exhilaration mixed with trepidation, but as I release the vine, and my feet touch stone, I can't help but kneel, and press my forehead to the ground, eyes closed.

Home.

How is it possible that this place, once a crucible of pain, blood, and death, still feels like home? I'd already found a home on the fey world, wrapped in Lotane's arms, yet this too feels right, as if I'd never truly left.

Visions of training here, sparring with Lotane, being schooled by Kralgen, and all the while Lystra's voice exhorting us, demanding perfection, flash through my mind.

Without conscious thought, I rise and begin stretching, going through what's now an ancient morning routine, the ghosts of Chosen past by my side. I follow up with shadow fighting, snapping punches and kicks, high and low, leaping and spinning, landing perfectly balanced, always moving, a flickering flame.

An hour passes before I stop, suddenly aware of something my rush of nostalgia had me overlook. The training circle is absent any debris, not even a leaf mars its perfection, and the entrances into the mountain remain open.

Instinct has me turn and gaze up at the balcony from which past ssythlan elders had overseen the training, and discover ... nothing has changed. There they stand, five of them, robed, observing, and as they stare into my upturned face, they bow deeply before turning away and disappearing into the darkness beyond.

I don't believe in any gods, although I've cursed them often enough, but in this moment, it's as if for once in my life, they've smiled on me.

A whisper of movement announces twenty ssythlan warriors as they enter the training circle, and whilst the rest of the world might have moved on, they haven't changed at all. They move like water over stone, their double-bladed staffs gleaming in the dim light.

They encircle me, silent and precise, a perfect ring, yet there's no threat, for they kneel, and raise their arms, holding out their weapons at arm's length as if a gift.

Only the gods know if there is any kind of protocol for a moment like this, but I couldn't care less. Around the circle I walk, placing my hands over theirs, pulling them to their feet.

'Nogotha.'

As they stand, each one says my name, their sibilant tongue as refreshing as a summer's rain as it washes over me, full of love and reverence.

What does it say about the human race, that the fey can remain loyal, and hold love for their leader and respect their orders for millennia, whether bound by magic or not, whereas humans can forget so quickly.

By the time I finish my circuit, their hisses are like waves on a shingle beach as they chant my name in unison, only falling silent as the five ssythlan elders approach.

Despite the dark circumstances surrounding my leaving, there's no awkwardness over this return.

The five elder mages drop to their knees and touch their foreheads to the ground, before rising to their feet. Their serpentine features always have perpetually upturned lips, like a snake's smile, and yet, even had I never seen their kind before, their happiness shines like the sun.

After everything I've endured since my return, I allow tears of joy to run unashamedly down my cheeks.

'I am Syantra.' The central elder steps forward, speaking in the Ssythlan tongue. 'We have waited for your return for thousands of years, and now the circle of life has completed a full turn. Welcome home, Nogotha. Here your story began, but as for where it will end ...' His eyes gleam with reverence. 'Only the gods know.'

He bows deeply and extends an arm in a very formal, human-like gesture and I place my hand on his forearm.

With a swish of robes, he leads me from the circle while the other elders remain behind with the warriors.

As Syantra leads me into the mountain, my fingertips trace the undulating pattern of the tunnel walls.

'*I'm back.*'

My greeting is barely a whisper, not just to the mountain, but to the spirits of my long-lost friends.

'Everything is just as I remember it,' I murmur.

'Everything is. It's only you who has changed,' Syantra muses, turning to look at me closely, his forked tongue flickering as if he can taste the difference. 'What has befallen you, and what brought you back to your forgotten children when the moons are unaligned?'

He resumes walking, respectfully turned toward me in interest.

'Forgive me, Syantra, that you felt forgotten,' I begin, full of remorse. 'Your loyalty humbles me, and I ask for your forgiveness. I tried walking a different path to Nogoth, one that fostered peace between the two worlds.' I shake my head. 'Yet peace has only led to war.'

Syantra listens in silence, his gaze steady, absorbing every word.

'The Astorians, under the All Father's rule, found a way to open the world gate,' I continue. 'They briefly invaded the fey world before I managed to close it. Yet their intent to destroy the fey remains, and their science is powerful enough to achieve this. Even worse, the magic of uncreation is rising, and I must do everything I can to stop both these forces.'

Syantra places his hand on the passage wall, and a pang of jealousy mixed with loss runs through me as the wall folds back, revealing a gently ascending passage.

'Some of what you said, we knew,' Syantra says as he leads the way. 'Ssythla still maintains links to a few in Tars, yet our influence beyond their lands is non-existent. News reaches us slowly as our kind can no longer travel freely. To be seen is to be hunted, tortured and experimented upon.'

I nod thoughtfully, then half smile as we enter the observation chamber. Nothing has changed, from the exquisitely carved round table to the hooded sin hawks sitting patiently on their perches, it's as though time has stopped here, holding its breath, waiting for my return, except for one thing. My figure now graces one wall instead of Nogoth.

'So tell me, Nogotha,' Syantra says, gesturing toward a stone-carved chair, before turning to a jug and goblets set upon the table. 'What is your will?'

I lower myself slowly into the chair, considering my response.

'The All Father is not one man, but hundreds, and must be stopped, the Astorian stranglehold on the other nations broken, and the balance humanity has with nature, restored, all before the Astorians can reopen the world gate again.'

'And how long might that be?'

'Four or five years, maybe less, if left undisturbed.'

Syantra shakes as he hisses with mirth, the wine sloshing in the goblet I take from his scaled hand.

'Three very simple tasks for someone as powerful as you, Nogotha!'

'Powerful? I lost my magic.'

Syantra's tongue flickers, his nostrils flare, all trace of mirth gone.

'We all lamented the severance of the blood magic that bounds us, but believed this was a further ... purposeful distancing ...'

Syantra pauses, and I'm astonished to recognise the elder is struggling to control its emotions. Those vertical eyelids are blinking back tears, and I'm suddenly overwhelmed with guilt. Syantra had already called the ssythlans, my forgotten children. What mother deserts her children for four thousand years?

'No,' I say. 'It wasn't purposeful. The Astorians captured and tortured me, and now my magic is lost. But that won't stop me from fighting them till my last breath.'

The scaled skin around those black eyes crease, the slightest glimmer of humour returning.

'That which is lost can be found. That which was gifted, can be gifted again,' Syantra intones, almost like a mantra.

'Really?' I gasp. 'Is that possible?'

The elder laughs.

'Is that not the reason you came here, Nogotha?'

'I fear I've yet to accrue the wisdom you credit me with,' I say, smiling. 'I came here for two other reasons. The first was to see if the Soul Gate still stands. Using it will help me not only hinder the opening of the world gate, but to kill as many of the All Fathers as I can.'

Syantra nods, a quick jerky motion.

'It still stands where it has always stood. We sealed the Mountain to preserve it, nothing more.'

He tilts his head, regarding me with curiosity.

'So, what was your second reason?'

The flush that spreads over my skin is one of undiluted excitement. Whilst a selfish reason, it's also an important strategic one.

'I need to talk to my consort, Lotane, in the fey world.'

A few irritated clicks, and Syantra shakes his head.

'The mirror between worlds still stands, but it has long been dark. Neither you, nor our brethren in the fey world have entered the Chamber of Thrones for centuries. Now, absent your blood magic connecting you to anyone, it will be impossible for you to summon anyone there.'

I sip on the wine, refusing to let this drawback unsettle me. It's another problem of my own making, but I'm used to that now.

Lotane.

To see his smile, to hear his voice, even if only through the mirror's cold glass, would have meant everything. Coordinating for the inevitable Astorian invasion would have been pivotal too. I have no false illusions, that however hard I try, I can only delay, not stop it from happening.

However, having elemental magic will help me immensely. I hadn't considered that possibility at all, and if I become impervious to weapons again? Surely that's too much of a stretch … but I have to know.

Syantra was right, I've come full circle. It's time to start at the beginning, and once I have my magic back … the All Fathers will feel my wrath.

***

'What's your name?' I ask, suppressing my revulsion as the slinger's face shifts, a grotesque distortion from something beautiful, with deep, soulful eyes and smooth skin, to a nightmarish visage. A rabid wolf's snarl twists her mouth, her muzzle wrinkling, fangs curving downward, gums oozing blood.

'Serenta,' she replies calmly.

'Hello, Serenta. Do you know who I am?'

'The Queen of Beasts,' she says conversationally. 'Nogotha.'

Even in the early morning gloom of a grey, cobbled alleyway, her smile shines.

'Indeed I am. What would you do to make me happy, Serenta?' I ask, concealing my face with my hood. It's raining, and such attire is not uncommon, although the wealthy use umbrellas.

'Anything,' Serenta says, her eyes searching mine. 'Making you happy will make me happy. Ask me to do anything, absolutely anything, and I'll do it!'

I look toward the Palace of the Ancients framed against the towering mountains, wondering whether a warren of tunnels lies beneath.

'The All Father is making an address to the public today, isn't he?'

Serenta nods, her lips peeling back from her gums, saliva stringing between her fangs.

'Yes. At noon from the Palace grounds.'

'Would you be able to kill him?' I ask, watching her carefully. 'The moment he begins his speech?'

Serenta tilts her head.

'I will try my very best. He's always surrounded by his bodyguard, and they're on high alert because of you. It won't be easy, but you can count on me!'

'All I ask is that you try, Serenta,' I say, adjusting my hood. 'Obviously keep this to yourself and don't do, or say anything that I wouldn't be happy about, and a final thing.'

Serenta looks at me expectantly.

'Make sure you aren't captured alive. Now, off you go, and good luck. I'll be watching!'

Serenta kisses my hand, and I try not to flinch as her huge wolf-like tongue slurps over it. Then, with a quick nod, she dons her wide-brimmed hat, strides to the end of the alleyway, and joins the hideously deformed morning throng going about their business.

I linger in the shadows, then move slowly, bent over, holding a wooden staff ... an old woman tottering along with an obvious limp.

Age always makes someone invisible.

A youthful face invites attention, admiration, or jealousy. But no one looks twice at the elderly. There's nothing to see but an unwelcome reminder of the future that lies so far ahead, that it will never catch you, until one day it does.

However, there's one exception to that rule. To those who prey on the vulnerable, I'm a dream come true, right up until I become a nightmare.

Twice I've been followed into quiet alleyways by ne'er-do-wells and twice I've left alone, my soul blade glowing brightly beneath my robes.

People walk around me as I limp slowly into the next street, my head low. My right leg twinges with every step, compliments of a slinger's bullet in my outer thigh following my assassination of an All Father in High Delnor four days earlier.

Having drained the life from a musketeer, it's close to fully healed. Yet it's a rude reminder, that despite the ssythlans infusing me with magic again, I'm not immune to injury. Sadly, that ability, just like Nogoth's power of the quickening, is lost forever.

Nonetheless, my magic is back.

I'm like a mother carrying her first baby that kicks to make itself felt. It squirms with pleasure, eager for attention, for love. Never again do I want to feel barren, stripped of the life that grows inside. I would rather die than have my baby torn from me again.

A bell tolls eleven times, and I turn uphill, joining the flow of people.

It's almost midday as I near the Palace of the Ancients. The throng before the wrought-iron gates is deep, and I don't even attempt to push my way through. The enemy is learning. Within that crowd will be Astorian agents alert for me.

Instead, I work my way around, trying to find somewhere discrete that still gives me an unobstructed view to watch from. Until now I'd made every kill up close and personal, my mocking smile the last thing every All Father saw before their death. However, recently I've only just evaded capture twice, and now with my injury, I've decided to use another tactic.

Serenta.

A church dedicated to the Astorian's immortal leader looms nearby, smoking with a rare malignance, drawing me like a magnet through the chattering throng, my head down, listening, constantly alert.

The street outside is empty, and I slowly make my way up the worn steps. Two elderly people sit together on a pew in the front row, but otherwise, it's empty, the clergy probably gathered to listen to the All Father's address.

A quick glance around reveals a wooden door that looks like it will lead to the clock tower. It's locked, but that's no problem. A simple thought, a gentle touch, and the stone wall beside it folds back to allow me entrance before sealing itself without a trace behind me.

I stifle a yawn, drained despite the insignificant use. In time, my power will be able to raise oceans and mountains, but for now, shaping stone is about as much as I'm able to achieve.

A circular stone stairway beckons. Leaning my staff against the wall, my silent steps take me up, shade-like, the dust barely stirred by my passing. Yet someone hasn't been quite so stealthy.

Scuff marks indicate someone has very recently come up these stairs, and in itself, that wouldn't cause my instincts to prickle, I'm sure the clock needs occasional maintenance or setting, but there's no sign of someone coming back down.

My soul blade gleams as I pull it from inside my robes. The sound of soft, regular breathing reaches me, and my magic squirms in happiness at my silent praise.

Up I go, until with a final turn, the boot soles of a slinger come into view, toes down as he lies on his stomach. Another step shows him holding a long rifle, butt against his shoulder, eye pressed intently to a long-glass attached above the barrel which pokes through a small, open, maintenance hatch.

He's so absorbed in his task, that he's completely unaware of my approach, and is bound by blood magic before he has a chance to react.

'Stay silent, leave your rifle, and sit there,' I say, pointing to the corner of the tower, and the slinger obeys without question.

The slinger's firing position is incredibly comfortable. He's created a gentle slope of cushions to lie on, and another pile to rest the rifle on.

As I settle myself down, I look through the long glass.

'Tell me, quietly, everything that you believe might be of interest to me,' I murmur.

'There are six other firing positions like,' the slinger gushes, eager to please. 'Each one covers a different segment of the crowd providing security for the All Father's address.'

My fingers tighten on the rifle stock.

'What else?'

'There are a further fifty soldiers dressed as civilians in the crowd, and ...'

'Would you be able to shoot the All Father from here if it made me happy?' I ask.

The slinger hesitates.

'It would be unlikely,' he admits. 'There's a stiff sea breeze, the range is a challenge, and he'll be surrounded by his personal guard. But I'd be delighted to try.'

I sweep the scope back and forth, scanning the shifting tide of the gathered masses. The throng is restless, with maybe a thousand people milling about the gates, shifting between the hideous and the mundane. I focus on a woman, who shifts into a dog, yapping at those closest whenever she's jostled. Another man leers with undisguised lust at two women nearby, a half dozen eyes popping out on stalks to get a better view.

Then, with a gentle adjustment, I focus on the palace grounds. A ring of snarling, ferocious slingers stands guard at the railings. Others are lined up outside the palace gate.

A raised podium awaits the All Father, before which, four slingers stand shoulder to shoulder.

But where is Serenta?

I continue my search, but identifying her proves more difficult than I'd realised. The slingers rarely shift from the form dictated by their inner darkness. I don't doubt she's there ... but where?

The All Father steps out from the Palace in his signature white robes. How people can fawn over this creature initially baffled me, but now I understand a little more. Unlike many leaders, no one could possibly envy him or covet his throne. They truly believe he suffers for them, and seeks to prevent his fate from becoming theirs, a divine shield standing between them and the monstrous fey.

He's escorted by a tight circle of personal slinger guards, their garb subtly distinct from the others, a mark of prestige.

They pass through the first line of slingers, and I tense in anticipation, awaiting the moment Serenta steps from the line, guns blazing, but ... nothing.

Where the hells is she?

Blood Magic is impossible to overcome, so the only answer is that she's been captured. But how would she have given herself away?

Then I realise impatience is getting the better of me. I'd asked Serenta to kill the All Father once he began his address, and now I realise how foolish that was.

She isn't part of his bodyguard, and the podium is too far from the slingers at the perimeter, or those just outside the Palace for her to be able to reach him before she's cut down.

I'm too far to hear the words coming from that putrid mouth. Whether the All Father shifts, or is in human form, he's just as repulsive, and I'm not interested in him, other than to see him die in front of everyone.

'Do you know Serenta?' I ask of my silent companion.

'Yes,' the slinger beside me answers immediately. 'She's an exceptionally talented, ferociously loyal slinger who's been selected to join the All Father's personal guard next year. She reported in ill this morning.'

Ill.

I hadn't considered there might be a way to circumvent my order, but if she's genuinely ill ...

'I might have you attempt a shot at the All Father after all,' I murmur, considering options. Would it be better to make an attempt that fails over none at all? Over the last two months, twenty-three All Fathers have died at my hands. Not a single one I set my sights on escaped.

Think, Malina. Don't let pride get in the way of solid strategic decisions.

I start to put the rifle down, and as I lower the butt to the cushions, the scope elevates, and I catch a glimpse of ... something.

Making myself comfortable, I bring the long-glass to focus on the Palace rooftop, something I hadn't even considered. It's fortified, crenulated, and way too far from the All Father for a successful gunshot.

But Serenta is up there, just beyond the lip, out of sight of everyone.

Even for me, she's only just visible, and now I understand why the other snipers haven't spotted her. I'm in the most elevated position outside of the Palace, and they're as blind as the crowd below.

But what she's doing, I don't know. She's moving around, working frantically, then disappears.

My hopes sink, but then I can barely believe my eyes as over the parapet a cannon barrel edges forward. Its muzzle is already lowered and roughly angled toward the podium.

For a fleeting moment, Serenta appears, peeking over the edge, her face radiant, just before a shift takes place, replacing it with a slavering wolf.

Two heartbeats later, a gout of fire and smoke billows forth and the cannon recoils out of sight.

Bringing the long-glass back to the podium, there's no All Father, no guards, just a massive swathe of blood and chunks of meat where hundreds of canister balls had torn them into tiny pieces.

Bringing my scope back to the rooftop, Serenta appears, nods in satisfaction, then puts a gun under her chin.

I don't stop to watch.

Screaming replaces the cannon shot's echo, and it's not just because of the All Father and his guards' death. The canister had swept away many of the perimeter guards, leaving dozens more writhing on the ground injured, and even the crowd hasn't escaped unscathed.

I've dealt a bigger, public blow to the All Father today than in any of the last two months, and I haven't even got blood directly on my hands.

'You will go about your daily business from hereon,' I whisper to the slinger beside me. 'You will do and say nothing that might upset me or bring suspicion on you. Then, once the All Father reappears, resurrected, once you have a chance to kill him, you will do so, then take your own life. It will make you the happiest you've ever been. Do you understand?'

I receive an enthusiastic nod as I pass the rifle back to the slinger.

'Wait a minute more before you leave your post,' I say, heading down the stairs, gripping my soul blade.

'Twenty four and counting,' I whisper into the corner of my mind. *'Where will I strike next? Which one of you shall I choose?'*

It's been a while since an All Father has responded. They still communicate in this fashion on occasion, but nothing they say is of strategic value.

'You kill us in one's or two's, but we number in the hundreds. In time, we will turn your world to ashes. Your paltry efforts to stop us will never be enough.'

I almost laugh.

'For once I'm in agreement with you,' I reply, *'and it's good to know your plans haven't changed. But there's one thing you should know … most of mine have. I'll let you find out in time what those changes are, but let me assure you of the one thing that hasn't changed … I will kill you all!'*

I close that part of my mind off, uncaring of any response as I smile to myself.

It's time to return home.

The Mountain of Souls awaits.

***

I'm surrounded by nearly sixty burnt out candles, their wax decorating the floor, slightly reminiscent of the stalagmites below the Palace at Astgate.

At the break of day and every night I'm able to, I sit here, my back against the pulsing Heart Stone, staring into the glass and the empty chamber of thrones beyond. It's a time for contemplation, a ritual of silence in which I sift through a thousand possible plans.

Where to strike next is always foremost in my mind, but killing the All Father alone won't stop the gate from opening. Several times I've revisited Astgate, reaping the souls of those associated with the reconstruction of the giant factories powering the world gate.

Musketeers can be easily replaced, slingers, almost as easily, and even the All Fathers feel limitless in their number. Yet scientists and craftsmen practice their whole lives to become masters of their crafts, and they're not so easily replaced.

A ssythlan warrior glides into the chamber bearing a tray of meat, fruits, and water. Having left it on the ground next to me, he leaves as quietly as he arrived.

I love all the fey. They're my people, my family, my children, but there's one who I need to see more than any other. It isn't just the fey world I'm fighting for, I'm fighting to be reunited with my love, and whilst that moment draws closer every day, it's still so very far off. However, in the interim, just to see him … would ease my soul.

'Where are you, my love?' I whisper.

'Malina.'

The voice is his, velvet and familiar, rich with the weight of longing, but it's just my imagination, a cruel whisper conjured by my own desperate mind.

Tears threaten to spill. I'm surrounded by those who adore me, yet the absence of the one I'm in love with is like a knife through my heart … I've never felt so lonely.

'Lotane,' my voice catches. 'Where are you?'

I pick up the tray, barely tasting the exquisite food, not because I have any appetite, but because I must. Every day I'm not out reaping souls, I'm training with my ssythlans. I'm now stronger, faster, and deadlier than ever before.

Yet alone, I'm not enough. I'll never be enough, and whilst my new plans have been put in motion for over a month now, Lotane and my fey back home are a pivotal part of them. I have to connect with them, and the mirror is my only hope.

Having finished my breakfast, I rise, and leave the candle burning. I can't afford more time here. My morning training awaits, and after that, something I've been dreading for over a month.

Tray in hand, I turn, my footsteps heavy, my heart heavier, and head toward the chamber exit.

I look around, recalling how we were bound to the Heart Stone. How this room was used to teach us while asleep. Mantra upon mantra inserted, plans a thousand years in the making insidiously implanted, languages and customs taught. A process refined over millennia by Nogoth and the ever loyal ssythlans.

'Alina.'

How often do I hear him speak my name? If I close my eyes, I can picture a thousand dawns I'd wake to him saying my name, and it still wouldn't be enough.

'Alina.'

I freeze in my tracks, afraid to turn, unwilling to experience the heart-breaking disappointment.

'Alina!'

I spin around, the tray falling from my hands, as framed within the mirror between worlds, stands my eternal love, a lantern at his feet.

If I thought for a moment that I could run and leap through to hold him, I'd have done so. Instead, I tread nervously, afraid he's but a figment of my tortured imagination and will disappear any second.

In perfect synchronicity, we approach the mirror.

His face is burnished gold from the lantern light, highlighting the strength of his jaw, the curve of his lips. Calf-length, leather boots, black trousers, and a white shirt, which looks painted on his body, enhance his already natural beauty.

Suddenly, as if freed from a restraint, I walk swiftly to the mirror, my hands and forehead touching one side, as his touch the other, despite being millions of leagues apart.

'You came. I knew you would!' My words croak, caught in a throat constricted by barely restrained emotion.

'I never would have thought to, but the elixir of life began flowing again,' Lotane whispers, his own voice husky. 'I can't believe you're at the Mountain of Souls. It's been almost two weeks since you left, and I've missed you every day like my heart was torn from my chest.'

'Almost two weeks.' I laugh, although it's half mixed with sobs. 'I've missed you every day for nearly five months. I've lost count of how many tears I've cried.'

We sit by unspoken consent, our fingertips still touching the mirror.

'I feared the worst but hoped for the best ever since Izetha came to me,' Lotane says softly. 'I never gave up hoping. After all, we promised to die together, and I knew you wouldn't break that promise to me.'

'Never,' I say, my eyes shining.

'When can I hold you again?' Lotane asks, biting his lip, swallowing hard.

Tears run unchecked down my cheeks, a blend of happiness and sadness behind the torrent. Pleasure and pain ... so often a perfect combination, but not in this moment.

'It will be a long time, my love,' I say, my voice breaking. 'But our reunion will be all the sweeter for when it happens.'

Lotane's smile wavers.

'How long?'

I hesitate.

'Fifty of your years,' I say at last. 'I need to prevent the world gate from being opened by the Astorians until the moons align.'

'Fifty years ...'

Lotane's head bows, and whilst his hair hangs like a curtain, obscuring his face, tears fall like silver rain onto his lap, disappearing into the fabric like they never existed.

'Fifty years,' he repeats, lifting his head, brushing his hair back and the tears away. 'If you can wait five hundred, I can hardly complain about fifty.' He chuckles, but it's forced. 'The question is ... would you prefer me old and wrinkled when we meet again? Or should I start drinking the elixir?'

My laughter banishes the bittersweet feeling, and I smile, absent any sadness.

'We will grow old together one day, my love. But for now, we stay young, we stay healthy, we stay alive!'

Lotane nods, but a frown appears to mar his youthful brow.

'Easy for you to say,' he murmurs. 'But Izetha told me you lost your magic and immunity to injury. Not forgetting there's a million strong Astorian army waiting to invade. So, how can we possibly do any of that?'

'With faith!'

Lotane huffs, and shakes his head.

'Faith? I have faith in you. But what happened to us at the gate was horrifying. Not forgetting that in the interim, however skilled you are, against those weapons, one mistake is all it will take now you're vulnerable, and, and ...'

It breaks my heart to see Lotane distraught. He's so strong, but his heart is so big, and love can defeat any warrior.

'I know, my love. I know. Don't worry. I've been shot more than once, but I understand the risks, and I've changed my methods. There's also the plan.'

'You're trying to change the subject,' Lotane says, a hint of frustration in his voice. 'But I'll humour you. What's the amazing plan you've devised that will save us all?'

Now the time has come to tell him, I hesitate. I know what Lotane will think, and I'm almost too afraid to share it.

A ssythlan elder comes to stand at my shoulder, waiting respectfully.

'Nogotha. It's almost time.'

'I'll be with you shortly,' I say, keeping my attention on Lotane.

'Your plan,' he prompts.

I swallow hard, unable to recall the last time I was so frightened.

'It's not even my plan, not really.'

Lotane frowns.

'Go on.'

'There's so much I need to share for you to completely understand,' I continue. 'But this world is rotten, diseased to the core. All the people have been corrupted, the land poisoned, and the magic of uncreation is rising. This is a battle of survival that affects both worlds, not just ours.'

I pause, steeling myself.

'If there was another way with even the smallest chance of success, I'd take it, but there isn't. Balance has to be restored, whatever the price.'

Lotane leans forward, suspicion evident.

'Stop being so guarded. Even if I don't like the plan, just tell me.'

I nod, wishing there was more time, but there isn't, I have to be somewhere important, and I can't miss it.

'You'll continue to raise the mightiest army the fey world has ever fielded,' I say. 'If a fey is old enough to crawl or fly, I want them ready to fight. You have fifty years, after which, you'll lead them through the world gate into Ssythla.'

Lotane shakes his head, confused.

'What? Surely we have to defend the world gate from Astoria?'

I smile sadly.

'It will be defended, in a fashion. But, you'll lead the main fey army through the world gate at Ssythla, and then together, we'll go on to destroy the Astorians, and conquer the world.'

I hold his gaze, willing him to understand, even if I haven't explained everything.

'Nogotha!' the elder hisses.

'I know,' I snap, looking over my shoulder.

Lotane is shaking his head in disbelief.

'We need to talk more about this!' he exclaims.

'We'll talk every one of your days,' I reply, rising to my feet. 'I'll heed everything you have to say. I promise.'

Lotane inhales sharply, the softness gone from his face.

'There has to be another way, Malina. There has to be! How can you possibly contemplate doing this after all we went through to stop it from happening again? We'll be as bad as Nogoth if we succeed!'

'Enough, my love,' I say gently, yet firmly. 'Enough.' I touch my fingers to the mirror. 'You'll understand more when we talk tomorrow.'

'Don't go!' Lotane pleads, rising to touch the mirror. 'Not yet.'

'I have to,' I whisper. 'We have so much to talk about, you and I, but even here, I cannot ignore my duties.'

It breaks my heart as I turn away, for even without looking, I know Lotane is still standing there, touching the mirror, staring forlornly after me, conflicted and confused.

Strange, we were stronger before this moment, now I feel weak, and for what comes next, I can't be.

Despite the ssythlan elder leading me, I could have found my way blindfolded to our destination.

My mind is awash with what needs to happen and Lotane's verdict.

We'll be as bad as Nogoth.

Every night I've sought alternatives to no avail. I am the mother of two worlds. One is dying, and seeks to bring the other one with it. Humans as a race cannot be trusted to live peaceful lives, nor simple ones. How can I let them be when they'll destroy the very world which supports them, and the fey world thereafter? They're a cancer, and the only way to treat a cancer, is to cut it out.

Without a doubt, Nogoth had tried to find different ways, until, after millennia, he'd honed the only one that had worked.

Now I'm Nogotha. Queen of the Fey, and his successor in more ways than one.

I'd fought my inner daemons with Lotane's help and thought I'd prevailed, but I should have known better. Life is about balance.

Sharks exist to kill the bigger fish, to stop them from decimating the smaller fish, and so on. They aren't evil, nor are their actions. They keep the seas and oceans in harmony through death. It's a simple cull, just like a farmer culls his herd, ensuring the land can sustain what remains.

That is why the likes of farmers were spared by Nogoth, not only to ensure the human race thrived again, but because they understood balance.

Every day I learn something more from what I'd considered Nogoth's evil, but which in fact, had been nothing of the kind.

As our footsteps slow, I realise we've arrived at our destination.

The ssythlan elder unlocks a door with an ornate key, and bowing deeply, steps aside and ushers me through.

I pull my hood low and walk into the gloomy room lit by a solitary moon globe.

Fear already thickens the air, and I look around, my spirits soaring, for in the course of life, there's no greater thing than birth. Birth is the beginning of everything, and I've truly arrived back at the beginning.

I draw a deep breath and say the words I heard on the day I was born.

'Hold on, and don't let go.'

***

THE END

Dear Reader and fellow fantasy lover.
PLEASE REVIEW THIS BOOK
If you enjoyed this tale, then please take a moment to rate or review it on Amazon. It would mean SO much to me.
Thank you.
Marcus Lee

***

This is not the end of Malina's and Lotane's tale. A final book will follow ... in time.

BOOKS BY MARCUS LEE

THE GIFTED & THE CURSED

'What the gods give with one hand, they take away with the other, for if you are gifted, you shall also be cursed.'

In the Ember Kingdom, a dying land riven by famine and disease, Daleth, the Witch-King, plots his conquest of the neighbouring Freestates. Gifted with eternal youth, his power is responsible for the decay afflicting his realm, and now other kingdoms must fall to quench his insatiable thirst for life.

However, on the cusp of the invasion, Maya, a huntress, is arrested, Daleth's soldiers kill an old farmer's wife, and a young outcast is enlisted into the Witch-King's army. Three minor events that nonetheless have the potential to alter the destiny of generations.

For Maya is gifted with the ability to heal and can influence the hearts and minds of men if she but finds the strength to do so. The young recruit carries a gift of reading thoughts and has no love for the king he serves. As for the vengeful farmer ... he's an ancient warrior gifted in reaping souls who now seeks to fulfil a long-forgotten oath against unbeatable odds.

The world will soon be soaked by the blood of war, but with these three individuals' fates inescapably entwined, the faint light of hope begins to shine. Alliances will have to be forged, enemies convinced to become friends, and a flicker of love given a chance to become a flame for there to be a chance to fight the encroaching darkness of the Witch-King's evil.

Book 1 - KINGS AND DAEMONS

Book 2 - TRISTAN'S FOLLY

Book 3 - THE END OF DREAMS

Book 4 – THE CIRCLE OF FATE

***

BOOKS BY MARCUS LEE

POEMS INSPIRED BY TRUE LOVE

'The perfect gift for yourself or the one you love.'

Poems Inspired by True Love welcomes the reader into true love's warm embrace, taking them through a soul-gripping journey of laughter, lust, and undeniably romantic moments.

Through emotive storytelling and sultry lines, poet Marcus Lee lovingly awakens one's psyche to the innermost amorous stirrings of the heart. In equal measure, these poetic outpourings serve as a vital reminder that one is not alone in their ocean of feelings.

Above all, this poignant collection of over 100 poems invites you to "behold a radiance that burns and sustains you', a radiance that goes by the name of True Love.

***

Printed in Great Britain
by Amazon .

61087809R00201